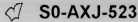
"What's so special about these arrows that you have to keep stealing them back?" he asked, keeping his voice idle as he retrieved the last one from the closet shelf.

"What's so special?" she retorted. "Do you have any idea how hard it is to make them?"

Quent gave her a look that clearly said he didn't care, but that he had other things on his mind, and was rewarded when he saw her swallow. Hard. He submerged a grin, and a flare of hope. "Right, then. You make them yourself?"

He tipped the arrow from end to end, and inside, the small metal weight rolled from one end of the hollow shaft to the other. It was a bloody brilliant design, and he could well understand how difficult it would be to create one, let alone multiple bolts like this. When the arrow slammed into its target, the little weight barreled into the tip. It lodged into a mechanism that shot a starburst of metal spikes from the sides of the point.

Perfect for scrambling *ganga* brains. A bloody fine way to kill them, if a chap didn't have a small explosive like the bottle bombs he and his friends used.

"Yeah, I make them myself, genius. And it takes a long damned time. So I'd appreciate it if you'd give it back to me." She held out her hand as if she actually expected him to put the bolt there.

"Come and get it."

Romances by **Joss Ware**

ABANDON THE NIGHT
EMBRACE THE NIGHT ETERNAL
BEYOND THE NIGHT

Abandon the Night

JOSS WARE

AVON
An Imprint of HarperCollins*Publishers*

AVON BOOKS
An Imprint of HarperCollins*Publishers*
10 East 53rd Street
New York, New York 10022-5299

Copyright © 2010 by Joss Ware
ISBN 978-0-06-173403-8
www.avonromance.com

First Avon Books paperback printing: March 2010

Avon Trademark Reg. U.S. Pat. Off. and in Other Countries, Marca Registrada, Hecho en U.S.A.
HarperCollins® is a registered trademark of HarperCollins Publishers.

Printed in the U.S.A.

10 9 8 7 6 5 4 3 2 1

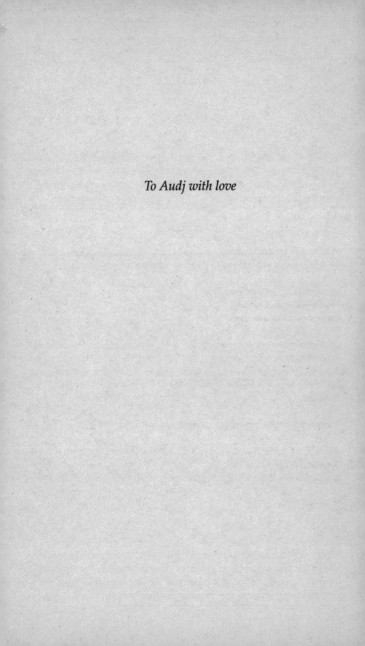

To Audj with love

ACKNOWLEDGMENTS

Once again, I find there are many people to thank for their support for this book and for the series as a whole.

As always, thanks to my agent, Marcy Posner, and my editor, Erika Tsang, for believing in this series and helping me to get it off the ground. Also, much appreciation to everyone at Avon and HarperCollins, especially Amanda and Christine, for everything you do on behalf of these books. You make a great team!

My deepest gratitude to Gaylene and everyone at NBPR for their support and creativity in promoting this series.

Thanks to Dennis Cruz for introducing me to canela tea, and to Dennis Galloway and Scott Turner for continuing to brainstorm with me. And also to Lara Adrian, for taking the time to read Quent's story, and for her great endorsement.

Hugs to Tammy and Holli for being my stalwart critique partners, and to Jana DeLeon for being an early reader as well. Also to Kristina Cook for doing an early read and helping to spread the word. As always, big thanks to my mom, and also to my mentor, Robyn Carr, for their unfailing support and advice on all fronts.

Lots of hugs and kisses to Kelly Young, for always listening and being the wise woman when I need you.

And, of course, much love to my husband and children—thank you for understanding when the deadlines loom, and for ignoring the piles of laundry and neglected housework when things get down to the wire. I couldn't do it without you!

Abandon the Night

PROLOGUE

Brummell-Marcombe Manor
Wiltshire, England
April 1997

The nape of Quent's neck prickled and he turned to see his father standing in the doorway, holding a riding crop in his left hand. He slapped it against his trousered thigh, and the sound settled in the room, ominous and full of promise.

"You thought it would be amusing," Parris Fielding said, stepping over the threshold into Quent's spacious bedroom. *Slap.* "Trying to show me up."

Though his palms dampened, Quent remained still. Seventeen years old, he was taller than his father, broader, stronger . . . but Fielding held the crop.

The backs of his thighs still bore the welts from last time.

Quent knew better than to defend himself from—or even comprehend—whatever sin his father attributed to him today. There was nothing he could say. He curled his fingers into his palms and wondered if it would be this time. If Fielding would finally kill him.

Slap.

He'd come close three years ago. Close enough that Quent had been in the hospital for a week from a "ski accident."

It had indeed been a ski pole that had inflicted the injuries. But Quent hadn't been holding it.

Quent's mother, Starla Tamrit-Brummell Fielding, had deigned to visit once, flying in from Venice where she was filming on location. And then back the same day.

Parris Fielding, however, had been there every day. For hours. Updating the media with bloodshot eyes, reluctantly allowing photo ops of his disheveled self arriving and leaving the hospital. Shielding his face as if to keep the press from seeing his grief and worry.

He'd even, famously, postponed an important Brummell Industries board meeting so that he could remain at his only son's bedside.

Slap.

Quent lifted his chin, allowing the hatred he felt for the man who'd given him life to show in his eyes. Three more months and he'd be eighteen . . . and free.

Would he live that long?

Fielding stepped closer and, in spite of himself, Quent's heart rate picked up.

"Maybe this time I'll mark up your pretty face," he said. His eyes danced with dark fury, and Quent saw the dull sheen on his high forehead. Other than that, he looked as if he'd just stepped out of the boardroom— every hair in place, his slacks creased and his shirt tucked in.

No, his father didn't drink to excess. Didn't use. His vice was the liberal employment of his hands and fists . . . and, as his son had grown taller and stronger, he'd supplemented them with riding crops, belts, and ski poles. And, once, a nine iron.

Someday, Quent feared, he'd resort to his hunting rifle. Or the pistol in his office. But then, Fielding's amusement would be over much too quickly.

Slap.

Fielding strolled casually to the French doors that opened onto a vast balcony, flung wide to the fresh spring breeze. He closed them with a quiet click before turning back to his son. He wasn't breathing hard, and every hair was still in place. Even in the midst of his most furious of attacks, he remained well pressed and neat.

Slap.

Quent swallowed and thought about running. His muscles bunched beneath his skin, his stomach tightened and began to churn. But in the end, he didn't. He knew it would only be worse if he did.

And that, as vast as the Brummell-Fielding estate was, there would be no escape from his father.

Not until he was eighteen.

Three more bloody months.

The crop sliced through the air, whipping past his ear and onto Quent's shoulder. He felt the sting through the T-shirt he wore, and before he could gather a breath, it came again as Fielding pivoted, this time, cutting across his back. And then again. And again.

He staggered, felt the burning in his back, the warm drip of blood. He raised his hand to ward off the next blow. But instead, Quent felt the sting down along his right arm and onto his belly and couldn't hold back a groan of pain. Fielding's face was drawn and dark, furious. His eyes, flat and cold and intense.

"Pledging money to UNICEF, " he spat. *Whip.* "Half a *million* pounds!"

Half a million pounds from Quent's own trust fund . . . twice as much as his father had offered the same charity . . . and barely a drop in the bucket of the Brummell-Fielding trillions.

Quent swiped a bleeding hand over his face just as the crop slashed his thigh, and then his hip. He twisted and turned, trying to avoid the pummeling that only became worse as Fielding became more incensed.

Sweat and pain blinded him, fear and anger drove him, and he stumbled toward the bag of golf clubs in the corner. Quent knocked into it as he dodged another blow, this time the crop slicing along his left arm. Tumbling against the bag, he collapsed onto the rug in a dull clatter of metal clubs. He rolled away as Fielding came after him, faster and harder, and Quent's fingers closed around a slender metal handle.

Cool and heavy in his grip.

He tightened his fingers, pulling it out, and tried to drag himself to his feet . . . but the crop came more quickly, and his father's biting words, raving about being upstaged, followed.

The club, solid in his hands. Quent knew he could swing out, smash it into the monster who came at him . . . he could kill him.

He could stop him.

CHAPTER 1

Sixty-three years later
City of Envy

Over the years, there were many times Quent regretted not taking that golf club to his father and putting an end to the fear and torture . . . but never had he felt the regret as strongly as he did now.

Quentin Brummell Fielding looked down at the object on the table in front of him: a clear crystal, perhaps the size of a large man's thumb. Its clarity was so pure, the stone was tinged with pristine blue and faint gray . . . yet when it was held to the light, it allowed the beam to shine through unencumbered, untainted. Faintly ice blue.

Delicate tentacles trailed out from the sides and behind, stylized rays from a sun. Or, in this case, a full moon. Like slender fiber optic threads, the tentacles resembled veins erupting from a heartlike crystal—perhaps a millimeter or two thick where they sprouted from the stone, and becoming as slender as hair or fine thread as they branched out.

"So this is what does it. What gives them immortality?" Quent prodded the crystal with a small pair of forceps. His fingers shook. "*This* is why they destroyed the world." He looked up at his friend Elliott, who, in a battle for his life, had hacked the crystal from of one of the immortal humans known as the Strangers.

Removing the crystal was the only way to kill them.

"Yeah," said Elliott, who was also known to his friends as Dred. "Once the crystal is introduced surgically, embedded in the soft tissue, it sort of roots itself into the body."

Quent poked the stone a little more sharply. A tip of one of the tentacles broke off and glinted like a minute shard of glass. If he'd used the golf club that day, sixty-some years ago, his father would be dead. And perhaps the world would still be the same, instead of the overgrown wasteland it had become.

But he had not. Quent had rolled under the bed, clutching the five wood—out of reach of the vicious attack, throbbing, broken, bleeding, half fainting from the pain—and remained innocent of murder yet another day.

And then, thirteen years later, Quent's father had helped to destroy the world. All for a little crystal that allowed Fielding to live forever.

If Quent had known then what his restraint had cost mankind . . .

"Are you certain you want to try and read it?" Elliott asked. He'd been a physician, a trauma surgeon, back in Chicago before everything had changed . . . before Elliott and Quent and three other men had entered a cave in Sedona, Arizona. They'd been on an adventure, using a map that Quent had acquired that supposedly led to a lost Anasazi treasure.

Sedona was a place known for its mystical properties and concentration of energy, but none of them had any idea how mystical and powerful it would turn out to be.

They had emerged fifty years later to find the human race nearly extinct and twenty-first century civilization annihilated. Somehow, they'd resurfaced unaged and unscathed from the destruction that had occurred half a century before. And now, after seven months of trying to find a way to rebuild their lives, the five of them still had no explanation for how or why.

How had they been suspended in time for fifty years?

Why the hell them?

And what the hell was there for them in a world that offered nothing of their previous lives but grief and bad memories?

Quent looked at the crystal, trying to submerge the rise of hatred it invoked. And the deep, nauseating pull in his belly.

This particular stone didn't belong to his father, but somewhere in this strange new environment that could only be described as post-apocalyptic, Parris Fielding had one of these crystals embedded in his body. It had kept him alive and preserved for the fifty years that had elapsed since the Change.

"Yes," he replied. "I'll try."

Under Elliott's watchful eye, Quent stripped off the gloves he'd taken to wearing when he was in unknown places. They protected him from the barrage of memories, images, and sights that assaulted him when he touched something unfamiliar. If he wasn't protected, the psychometric ability to read inanimate objects could paralyze him, sucking him into whatever horrors or violence the item had experienced. Not long ago, Elliott had found Quent collapsed in an alley, barely conscious, lost in a vortex of memories that weren't even his.

Since then, Quent had become much more careful about what and how he touched things . . . but with this eerie arachnidlike crystal in front of him, he wasn't ashamed to admit he was grateful for Elliott's steady-ing presence.

Just in case.

He glanced up at Elliott, met his calm blue eyes, and nodded . . . then looked back down and gently touched the center of the crystal with the pad of his left index finger.

Immediately, he felt a rush of . . . water. The sensa-tion of being under water, submerged, surrounded by heavy, fluid weight pressing on him . . . The sea? It rippled and surged against and around him, powerful and relentless, dark and unforgiving. And cold. The crystal had been in the sea.

Quent steadied himself, pulled back from the tug that would pull him into unconsciousness, and focused half his mind on the room around him, the table beneath his other fingers, his friend watching, the chair beneath his arse . . . and went a little deeper into the crystal's memories, touching the stone with a second finger.

White light stunned him, shocking and bold, cutting through the dark sea . . . and then darkness. Pulsing, pumping, throbbing darkness . . . he shifted in his seat, adjusting his feet on the floor, grounding himself . . . but opened his mind a bit further, tried to separate the faces that blurred in a whirlwind around him . . .

And then he felt a strong tug gripping his arm, and the room slammed back into his consciousness. The crystal was gone, his fingers curled empty into the table top, and Elliott leaned over him.

"You all right?"

Quent nodded, vaguely aware that he needed to catch his breath. "I'm all right. Why did you take it away?"

Elliott settled back in his seat, a face that was con-sidered handsome by most, drawn and tight. "You were gone for more than thirty minutes. Your breathing and pulse increased, your color faded. It was time to come back."

"Thirty minutes?" Quent tried to shake off the wave of unease. Lost for a half hour and it had felt like mere seconds. This fucking ability of his scared the rot out of him sometimes.

Most of the time.

"Was it worth it? Did you get anything important?"

Quent shrugged. "I'm not sure. I saw a lot of faces . . . some of them seemed bloody familiar—members of the cult, right . . . but they flew by so quickly. But one thing I'm damned certain of." He glanced down at the crystal, then back up at Elliott. "It comes from the ocean. Deep in the ocean."

Just then, a soft knock interrupted them. Elliott rose quickly and went to open the door, exposing three newcomers on the threshold: Wyatt, Theo, and Lou. Beyond them was a spare, windowless room lined with computers, monitors, printers, and an old license plate hanging on the wall.

A coppery-haired woman sat at one of the desks, five monitors arrayed in front of her, fingers typing madly, earbud cords dangling from beneath her hair. He knew from experience that anything short of another apocalypse wouldn't interrupt Sage from her work.

In fact, if he didn't know any better, Quent might think he was looking into a control center for NASA or even a computer call center . . . but outside of this hidden subterranean computer lab, working electronics and those who knew how to operate them were nonexistent.

"We didn't wait," Elliott said as the newcomers filed in. "Quent's already done his thing."

"How'd it go?" asked Wyatt. He was one of the five men who'd been in the Sedona cave with Elliott and Quent. He looked from the crystal to Quent, as if to assess any damage. His rugged face was flat and sober.

The other two men, Lou and Theo Waxnicki, had been living here in the city of Envy since the Change. It was they—self-proclaimed "fucking computer geniuses"—who'd collated and built the clandestine computer lab in the decades following the mass destruction. Twin brothers, the two had been working in tandem to construct an underground Resistance against the Strangers by building a secret computer network that could be used for communication as well as research. The driving force behind the Resistance was that the more they knew about the immortal humans who had brought about the Change, the better prepared they would be to combat and eventually destroy them.

Quent, Elliott, Wyatt, and the two other men who'd been in the cave with them—Simon and Fence—had become key members of the Resistance in the last month, partly due to the paranormal abilities at least some of them had acquired. And partly because they had unique knowledge of twenty-first century civilization before the Change, which was from where the Strangers had come.

Because, of course, they'd lived there.

"The experiment was a little rough," Elliott said before Quent could brush it off.

"Well?" asked Lou. Although his eyes gleamed with intelligence and spirit, the lines in his face and the subtle stoop to his shoulders belied his nearly eighty years of age. Despite his experience living through the horrors of the Change and the difficult reconstruction that followed, he still bore a youthful air and wore his long silvery hair in a low ponytail. Glasses that had been at the height of geek trend in 2010 perched on a slender nose, and today, he wore a bright yellow T-shirt with "Forget about the bollocks, here come the Sex Pistols" on it in hot pink.

Quent wasn't certain if it was a shirt Lou had worn in his youth, or one that he'd found more recently. Either way, it wasn't something he'd ever expected to see a seventy-seven-year-old man wearing.

Lou's twin, Theo, was a different story all together, and he was the reason the Waxnicki brothers had been willing to trust the five men from Sedona who, like Theo, possessed superhuman skills, with the secrets of the Resistance. Theo had been caught in a subterranean computer safe-room during the Change. Something had happened to put him into a sort of sleep mode—perhaps similar to what occurred with Quent and his friends. Lou had found him a few days after the devastation and had been able to awaken Theo.

Yet, over the next fifty years, Theo had hardly aged at all, only recently beginning to sprout gray hairs and stubble that needed to be shaved. So he looked no more than thirty years old, although, like Lou, he'd lived through the months and years following the annihilation of the world. And, like Quent, Elliott, and Simon, he had acquired his own superhuman ability.

"From what I was able to tell," Quent explained again, "the crystal comes from the ocean. Deep in the ocean."

"Not a surprise, given what we've been able to find," Theo said. He wore his jet black hair cropped short around the ears and neck, almost militarily so, but longer and spiky on top. "Between all the damn crystals and the new landmass that seems to have erupted in the Pacific, plus the fact that, thanks to you, we know that the Strangers were all members of the Cult of Atlantis before the Change, the clues continue to point in one direction."

Quent nodded. *Atlantis.* Indeed, he'd been the one to recognize the symbol used by the Strangers as one identifying a group to which Fielding had belonged. He'd had no idea that the Cult of Atlantis was anything more than an exclusive club of powerful and wealthy world players until a few weeks ago. His knowledge had collided with the information Lou and Theo had collected over the last half-century, and the results were nightmarishly disturbing.

"Fifty *million* American dollars to even join the fucking cult," Lou said, shaking his head, eyes sober. "According to what Simon was able to find out from that female Stranger." Who was, now, also dead—despite her unnatural crystal.

"What a fucking bargain for immortality," Quent said. His head had begun to pound, and everything felt tight and stretched. He always felt this way whenever he thought about his father and the hand he'd most certainly played in causing the Change.

No one was certain exactly how it had happened, of course, but the curious Lou and Theo had hacked into satellites about a year after all hell broke loose and saw that the rest of the world was just as damaged as what had become known as the city of Envy. And they'd recognized a new continent in the Pacific Ocean that may have caused the great earthquakes, tsunamis, and violent weather that followed for almost two weeks.

Quent realized his jaw hurt from clenching it so hard, and that his shoulders seemed unable to move.

I'm going to kill him. I'm going to find him and, this time, I'm going to fucking kill him.

I should have done it years ago.

That had been his first thought on seeing a picture of his father, of Fielding, standing with two others who, with Fielding were known as the Triumvirate of the Strangers. One of them was now dead. That left two more, and countless other members of the cult. He stood, suddenly needing to get out of this room.

"I'm going now," he explained, knowing that his decision was abrupt. But he also read the understanding in Elliott's eyes. "Up. See you in the morning."

If Fence, the big, bald guy who always had to make a joke—whether appropriate or not—were there, he would surely make a comment about whether Quent was going up alone or not. Admittedly, Quent was relieved the guy wasn't there to do so.

Because he'd be hitting too fucking close to home.

"It's raining," Wyatt said.

Quent shrugged. But his friend was looking at him knowingly and that made him feel like even more of a wank. "Later," he replied, gathering up his gloves and leaving the room.

He passed behind Sage, who actually glanced up as he swished by, but neither of them paused to exchange pleasantries. She offered a vague smile, then returned to her five computer screens, keys clicking noisily, aqua blue eyes focused on the monitor.

On the spiral staircase that snaked up inside an old elevator shaft, Quent met Simon, who was likely coming down to see if he could drag Sage away from her work and up into his bed, since it was nearly midnight.

Power fucking to ya, old chap.

Gloves back on, Quent knew it was safe to jab angrily at the numbered buttons that would, at one time, have selected the floor and opened the door to the elevator, but now acted as a passcode to enter and exit the secret stairs to the computer room.

Great buggering sense of humor the Waxnickis had. Too damn many spy movies. They thought they were fucking James Bond.

Yet, Quent accepted the fact that the computer network and the information they were collecting had to be kept secret, not only from the Strangers, but from everyone else in Envy. Very few people believed or even knew of the horrors their fellow man had suffered at the hands of the Strangers—both during the Change, and in the fifty years since. And since the few who had tried to make their knowledge public had disappeared or otherwise been destroyed, the Waxnickis stuck with their plan of stealth and secrecy.

The elevator shaft opened, and Quent stepped into the dark, ruined hallway of what had once been a casino resort in Las Vegas. At this far side of the building, in an area that hadn't been maintained after the Change, the corridor seemed deserted and abandoned—a state the Waxnickis carefully preserved, despite their daily visits to the lab.

He could make his way along the halls back to the occupied area of the hotel, and up onto the fifteenth floor, where he had been given a hotel room for his own residence. But when it came time to make the turn that would take him in that direction, he kept straight on.

Outside, rain poured. Heavy, steady, but straight so that it looked like a gray and black shower curtain obstructing the night.

If Quent had hoped Wyatt was wrong, or that it might be little more than a soft drizzle, he was bloody disappointed.

Still, not because he expected anything—he wasn't that cocked up—but because he needed to *feel*, he stepped out of the building and into the downpour.

Since the Change, the climate in Vegas had shifted from that of a dry desert to an almost tropical one. Rain was plentiful, the temperature mild or hot, and the air humid and too close at times.

Having lived in England until he was eighteen—when he moved an ocean away from Fielding and his riding crop—Quent was used to the damp. And now, as the heavy rain pounded on him, he walked, letting it soak through his stretchy silk shirt, suede jeans, and leather sandals. Good, practical clothing wasn't always easy to find, but he'd been lucky and had come across an old suitcase filled with duds from a guy about his size. And the guy had had decent taste, which helped.

The city known as New Vegas, N.V., or, more commonly, Envy, was the largest settlement of people in hundreds of miles—and as far as anyone could tell with the limited communication and transportation, it was the largest in the world. The irony that the formerly hedonistic city, with its superficiality and flashiness, should now be the cradle of humanity was lost on no one who'd ever visited the Strip—including Quent.

Now, with the massive shift in landmass and tectonic plates, what had been the North Strip was under water—covered by the Pacific Ocean, which, unbelievably but irrefutably, now covered California and part of Nevada and Washington. Only a cluster of high-rise casino resorts remained standing, and of those, many of them were in disrepair.

The Strip's neon lights still glowed red, blue, yellow, and green, but much more feebly and in less abundance than they'd done a half century earlier. And the part of the Strip that remained visible was empty of people—a condition that would have been inconceivable back then.

Quent couldn't help himself. He looked up, trying to peer at the jagged rooftops and glassless windows above him, searching for a lanky shadow, slender and sure and sleek.

But all he got for his trouble was a face battered with sharp raindrops and another wave of anger.

At himself of course. For his foolishness. For wasting his time.

For not fucking swinging that damned five wood sixty-some years ago.

Hell. Could his one decision have made a difference? Kept the Change from happening? He might have spent the rest of his life in jail back then, but at least he'd have had a life.

Quent drew in a deep breath of clean, damp air, then exhaled. Turned his thoughts from the rage that never seemed to completely leave him.

Zoë wouldn't be out in this weather, lurking in the shadows as she was wont to do. She wouldn't be slipping down, all warm and slender and bold, to join him in a dark corner, hot and urgent and sassy.

A combination of lust and fury tightened his jaw, hitched his steps.

What the bloody hell was he doing out here in the buggering rain?

All he wanted to do was find Fielding and kill him. Quent's life, his purpose for being, had funneled down to nothing but that.

Everything else was just a fucking way to pass the time.

Even walking uselessly in the rain. Even rolling in the sheets with Zoë.

He wasn't cold, though he was as soaked as if he'd been swimming, and he kept inhaling random droplets of rain. Wet grass and bushes brushed his bare toes as he trudged away from the inhabited area of the city. The clean smell of fresh rain mingled with the underlying must of decay and mold, here in this narrow walkway. Two buildings rose, half destroyed, jagged, and overgrown, the one on the left taller and more forbidding than on the right. If he straightened his arms to the sides, his fingertips would brush the brick. Soggy leaves and the gentle give of wet dirt softened the cracked and uneven concrete beneath his feet.

The first time he'd met Zoë, she'd saved his life, appearing from nowhere to skewer the *ganga* that had attacked him. She'd shot an arrow that lodged in the skull of the zombie-like monster, which scrambled its brains and dropped it dead.

No sooner had the creature collapsed than she demanded that Quent return her arrow.

He hadn't even been certain she was a woman or a slender young man . . . until she came close enough to touch his face.

And that first time she touched him, just a faint brush of fingertips over his cheek, as if she wasn't used to doing such a thing, it had seeped into his skin, warm and gentle. Hesitant, and yet . . . solid.

Now Quent leaned against the ivy-covered wall, sending an additional shower of droplets scattering from the leaves. And he looked up again into the unrelieved darkness. Still fucking searching.

Rain blinded him once more, and he turned away, frustrated.

After their first meeting, she'd disappeared, slipping into the shadows, *without* her precious arrow. He'd taken it with him here to Envy, but before he turned to go, he called after her, into the dark, and invited her to come and retrieve it any time.

A few days later, she had found him in Envy, walking beneath a clear moon, and once again demanded her arrow to be returned. Despite her belligerence and god-awful haircut, Quent was compelled to kiss her.

And that had been all either of them needed. It felt as if something had been released, unleashed . . . snapped.

The sex that night, and the few other times they'd gotten busy since, had been hot and fast and urgent. It had left him with curled toes, breathless—and, despite its ferocity . . . comfortable. Settled. Until she sneaked off into the night without a word. Taking her precious arrows with her.

After that first night, it had become sort of a game. From up on a rooftop, or a high window, she'd shoot an arrow where he'd be sure to find it, then disappear into the night. A day or so later, Zoë would show up, all self-righteous and annoyed and demanding it back, as if he'd stolen it right from her quiver . . . and then they'd get to it. On the bed. In the stairwell. Against the backside of the hotel. Wherever they managed to tear each other's clothes off. This had been going on for two weeks, but he was unable to keep her out of his mind for long.

He spun suddenly, his foot squishing into mud and then jolting against a wedge of sidewalk, nearly tripping himself. *Bloody buggering hell.*

What the fuck was he doing wandering in the rain looking for a rude female Robin Hood when there were plenty of other willing partners inside?

Galvanized, he started back.

But once he got inside, rain dripping audibly from his hair and shirt and rolling off the hems of his jeans, Quent knew he had too much of a bag on to go to the Pub. Though the pints were plenty and the waitresses friendly, and Elliott's lover, Jade, often sang onstage in a definite foreplay sort of way, Quent walked past. His leather sandals squished softly.

Maybe after he changed into dry clothing—the suede jeans were already shrinking from the rain—and did something with his hair, he'd change his mind. But unlikely.

What he really should do . . . what he suddenly wanted to do . . . was to go back to the computer lab and touch that crystal again.

If Elliott hadn't interrupted him earlier and pulled the stone away, Quent might have been able to get more from the gem. The blur of faces might have eased from the fast-forward of a video to a slower parade, and he might have learned something. Identified someone. Seen his father.

He might be able to discover where the Strangers lived or came from. And then he could do what he had to do.

After that . . . Quent had no thought. He'd probably die in the process, for surely he couldn't simply kill a leader of the Strangers and walk away unscathed.

Inside his room, Quent moved directly to the closet and felt up behind the lip of its shelf. Force of habit, first thing he always did when he came back into his space. And when he realized he'd been checking to see if the latest of Zoë's precious arrows was still there—it was—he felt yet another blast of fury that he was still playing this game.

That he still cared to play it.

"So that's where you're hiding them now."

Quent froze. A rush of heat and anger, a sudden weakness in his knees, and the tug of a smile, conflicting and paralyzing, caught him for a moment. He collected himself, emptied his expression, and turned.

"What the hell were you doing out in the rain for so long?" Zoë said in her low, rusty voice. She looked like a Bollywood actress with a rubbish haircut—exotic features, cinnamon-skinned, and her ink black hair cropped and falling every which way around her high cheekbones and jaw. A wide mouth, pointed chin, high, plum-sized breasts, and long, lanky limbs completed the package.

She leaned nonchalantly against the wall across the room, behind the door through which he'd just come. The quiver and bow she normally wore over her shoulder rested on the floor. Her entire being shouted condescension and belligerence—but for her dark almond-shaped eyes. Even in the dim room, lit only by a small lamp in the corner, Quent felt the weight of their gaze. Hot.

Blood surged through his body. "Were you waiting for me?" he asked, his arrogance matching his haughty gaze. "Or was it just that you hadn't discovered my latest hiding place?"

She stepped away from the wall, graceful and lean in her tight black tank top and baggy, hip-riding cargo pants, and moved farther from the door. Just into the room. Watching him. His mouth dried. The blood rushed through him faster, his heart pounded.

"You've gotten a hell of a lot more creative since the first time you stuck them under the bed," she said.

Damn straight. Quent still remembered the impotent fury he'd felt when he discovered that Zoë had come into his room and taken back another arrow he'd retrieved . . . without seeing him. Without playing the game.

Without the wild, hot tumble on the bed or against the wall bang he'd come to expect.

His body felt alive, awake, ready, but he maintained the blank expression and a casual stance . . . although he had a feeling his bedraggled state might take the edge off his insouciance. "What's so special about these arrows that you have to keep stealing them back?" he asked, keeping his voice idle as he retrieved the last one from the closet shelf. He'd touched it so many times that it didn't bother him to do so anymore; same as the other parts of his room.

"What's so special?" she retorted. "Do you have any idea how fucking hard it is to make them?"

Quent gave her a look that clearly said he didn't care, but that he had other things on his mind, and was rewarded when he saw her swallow. Hard. He submerged a grin . . . and a flare of hope. "Right, then. You make them yourself?"

He tipped the arrow from end to end, and inside, the small metal weight rolled from one end of the hollow shaft to the other. It was a bloody brilliant design, and he could well understand how difficult it would be to create one, let alone multiple bolts like this. When the arrow slammed into its target, the little weight barreled into the tip. It lodged into a mechanism that shot a starburst of metal spikes from the sides of the point.

Perfect for scrambling *ganga* brains. A bloody fine

way to kill them, if a chap didn't have a small explosive like the bottle bombs he and his friends used.

"Yeah, I make them myself, genius. And it takes a long damned time. So I'd appreciate it if you'd give it back to me." She held out her hand as if she actually expected him to put the bolt there.

"Come and get it," Quent said. His voice dipped way low and he met her eyes.

She met his right back. Hot. "My clothes will get wet."

He smiled. Not with joy or mirth, but with promise.

Her lips moved, parted just a bit, softened, in blatant promise.

Fuck. He had a hard-on the size of a cricket bat and she hadn't even bloody touched him.

"Right, then," he said, marshalling his control, keeping his voice nonchalant. "You can always take off your clothes. And then they won't get wet."

She turned away suddenly, and for a moment, for a catch of his breath, he thought she would reach for the door. Turn the knob, *leave.* But then, her back to him, with one swift, smooth movement, she whipped off her skinny little tank top. And sent it flying in a soft arc.

Quent smiled, this time with relief and delight. But he didn't move. Not yet.

Her bare back was smooth and taut, and her cargo pants rode low on the gentle flare of her hips. He'd never found that look sexy until now. Ragged, dark hair brushed the nape of her neck, but that long, sleek expanse of mahogany skin from shoulder to bum made her look like a slender Shiva.

She kicked off her shoes, some nondescript dark ones

that tumbled against the wall, and then he heard the quiet snap—*un*snap—of a fastener. Zoë turned back to face him then, and in spite of himself, he caught his breath.

Her hands at her waist, obviously ready to draw down her trousers, her slender, muscular arms alongside those high, palm-sized breasts with tight dark pink nipples . . . the dark hollow of her throat and the shadows near delicate collarbones . . . her long, slender neck. And the arrogant lift of her chin. Challenging him yet again.

Bloody buggering hell, did she know how to play him.

"What," she said, drawing her gaze slowly, heavily, over him, "the hell"—she unzipped her cargos—"are you waiting for? Get out of those wet clothes." The trousers fell, exposing lean legs and a little white swatch of panties that sagged a bit.

"Come here," Quent said, in a desperate attempt to regain some control over the situation.

"You're dripping wet . . . I don't want to get cold." Her challenging look swept over him and he knew he wasn't going to be cold himself any time soon.

"If there's one thing I can promise you, it's that you're not going to be cold," he promised, tossing the arrow aside. She didn't seem to notice.

"Is that right?" she challenged, her voice rough.

"What do you think?"

The next thing he knew, their bodies were smashed together. Somehow, her warm, sleek skin became plastered against his soaking clothes. Her hands shoving into the dripping mess of his hair, his palms cupping her panty-covered bum, their mouths ferocious and demanding.

Oh God. Yes. Thank you.

And then, it became all about Zoë. There was nothing but her—spicy, warm, sleek and strong. Her mouth soft and full, fitting to his, teasing away then coming back for more . . . her breasts pushing into his wet shirt, one of her legs wrapping insistently around him. Her hips lifting and grinding into his.

The bed bumped into his thigh and he cracked his knee on the edge of the table next to it, but he hardly noticed as they tumbled onto the brocade coverlet. He couldn't get enough of her—the essence of her skin, somehow hinting of the same cinnamon flavor as its dusky color, the strength of her legs, twining, shoving between his, just as urgent to get it on as he was.

Her fingers pulled at the buttons of his jeans, difficult because the buttonholes had shrunk from the dampness, and Quent found himself almost laughing as she swore and yanked and bitched between kissing the hell out of him.

Good God, she can kiss. Her tongue swiped deep and strong, teased and thrust as she sucked and licked and nibbled, then pulled away and breathed a sharp, furious curse. Then went back for more with full, sleek lips matching his, fitting, slipping and sliding as their breaths mingled and her fingers fumbled.

"Let me," he said finally, removing his hands reluctantly from her smooth skin, where they'd been relearning that long, curving spine, down beneath the warm cotton of her panties. Zoë arched against him, her breath warm and labored against his neck as she tipped to the side, sagging next to him on the bed.

For a heartbeat, they lay there, breaths rough and unsteady, and their eyes met. Caught. Quent felt as though something sharp and sudden pierced him, something uncomfortable, and saw Zoë catch her breath, then her eyes shutter. He thrust the moment away by yanking violently at the stubborn fly of his increasingly tightening jeans. Fucking last damned time he wore suede. The buttons exploded, popping and dropping as if he'd just undone a row of snaps, and then she was there, sliding her calloused hands down into his warm package.

He groaned aloud as she covered him, deft fingers closing around him, freeing the pounding center of his universe. And then the little sigh-groan Zoë gave when he slipped free nearly sent him over.

Jeans still around his hips, damp and heavy and awkward, he pressed her back onto the bed, half covering her and sliding his hand down past the stretched-out elastic of her panties, to her slick warmth. Oh God, she was full and wet and ready, and she shifted and sighed, shoving herself against his palm.

"You sure you came here for that arrow?" he asked, watching her face as he fingered her.

Her almond eyes, half shadowed by the dim light, closed and her lips parted for a soft puff of breath. "Damn right . . . It's mine."

He shifted his fingers, teasing them against her, coaxing and stroking, watching her breathing change, her eyelids flutter. "Then why don't you go get it," he suggested. "Don't let me keep you."

He settled his mouth over the closest of her hard, gathered-up nipples, sucking it suddenly and firmly as she tightened and arched next to him . . . then a blaze of pleasure barreled through him as she gasped and shuddered her orgasm beneath his fingers and lips.

Oh yeah, luv, that's it. Let me show you how good it is.

He coaxed everything he could from her, waiting, teasing softly till she settled, then did it again. This time, leaving her clawing for breath, even writhing a bit . . . and reaching for him.

"Guess I'll be going now," she said in a raspy voice. Her full lips twitched up at one side. "Now that you mention it." Her fingers closed around him and gave two—count 'em, two—quick, long strokes . . . then she was over him, and up and off the other side of the bed.

Quent's breath exploded in a great gust and he flipped over toward her. But instead of being halfway across the room, as he'd feared, there she stood, right by the bed, a wicked, wicked smile on her well-kissed lips. Naked.

"Zoë," he said, not caring if he sounded desperate. He was. Oh, bloody fucking hell, he was desperate . . . so desperate he thought about begging. Bloody Quent Brummell Fielding, begging for a woman.

"Well, shit, if you'd take off your damned clothes, I might be convinced to stick around," she said. "They're cold as hell and sticky too."

Quent let out his breath in a gust of humor as he realized that, indeed, he was still fully clothed except for the raging hard-on thrusting from his open fly. He tore off his shirt and peeled the bloody jeans off, and when he'd slapped them to the floor in a damp pile, he looked up.

She moved toward him, pushing him back onto the bed, none too gently. The next thing he knew, Zoë had settled over his hips, her hands flat and warm over his chest, and lowered herself down. *Oh God . . . God . . .*

He squeezed his eyes shut, clamped his hands on her to keep the bloody damned minx from moving before he could regain control. Her deep, low laugh teased him like a smoky whip and he opened his eyes to meet hers, to read the same lust blazing there.

She tightened around him, he groaned as the pounding surged harder, almost lost it, and brought himself back.

And . . . *no*. In this way, he would be in control. With a swift move, he flipped her onto her back. Zoë half laughed, half gasped in surprise and delight as he took over, as he wasted no time before he brought them into the long, sleek rhythm.

The ride turned frantic, and Quent lost all sense of details but for the soft gasps and sighs, the slide of leg, the scrape of nails, soft lips, the rising, gathering pleasure, and everything became slick and hot and pounded through him, barreling to the edge . . . and over.

At the last second, he remembered, somehow, and twisted away with a deep grunt of release and effort . . . blinding pleasure trammeling through him as he reached what he needed. And held on as he slipped into the hard-won ease of sleep.

10 June 2010
6:00 A.M.

Devi is up and making coffee while I log in to check email so that he doesn't notice. He'll scold me if he knows, for we are on holiday. Three more days, and I'm back at the office to revise another design for the die shop. But for now, Dev and I have our first holiday since our honeymoon, and we are enjoying every moment of it. Even though we haven't left home and there is much work to do, it's nice to have a break from the rigors of the office.

10:00 A.M.

Something odd is happening. There are reports of very strong earthquakes in Phoenix, LA, Dallas and Vegas, Denver, St. Louis . . . everywhere. And at the same time, dark gray clouds are rolling in here. Looks like a nasty storm coming. I find it very disconcerting and a little bit creepy that it should come on the heels of massive earthquakes. Devi and I are surfing the Net on our laptops, looking for updates.

Noon

The ground is trembling here, in southern Nevada. Are we having an earthquake here? The Internet is down. Cell phones are dead. TV too.

Something very frightening is happening.

—from the diary of Mangala Kapoor

CHAPTER 2

"You did it again."

Quent opened his eyes. He had no idea how long it had been . . . had he slept for hours or minutes? . . . but he didn't care. Zoë's voice, husky from disuse, and, he hoped, pleasure, was always welcome.

Because that meant she hadn't slipped off into the night.

The room was dark but for the glow of the small lamp he always left burning when he exited the place. The curtains were drawn tightly enough that he couldn't tell if a seam of daylight might play around the edges or not.

She lay next to him, propped up on one elbow, her breasts shifted slightly down toward the bed, tempting him with their perky nipples and smooth, feminine curves. Zoë and Quent weren't touching, but he could feel the warmth of her body, and the slightest dip in the mattress from her insubstantial weight.

"Right," he replied and half sat up, dragging a hand through his still-damp hair. It tended to curl up when it became wet and then dried on its own, leaving him resembling a messy teen needing a haircut.

This wasn't the first time Zoë had mentioned the fact that he pulled out just before—or, hell, in this case, right as—he came. *Bugger it.* Quent wasn't sure how to explain to a woman who lived in a time when the human race had been so destroyed that it was considered almost criminal not to procreate as much as possible, that *he* came from a time when a responsible man didn't have unprotected sex with a woman he wasn't married to . . . and even then, it was fodder for discussion.

And, quite frankly, it wasn't something he wanted to talk about now.

"Are you going to keep doing that?" she persisted.

Quent felt a strange discomfort trickle through him, leeching away the remnants of his pleasure and satiation. "Probably." He really fucking didn't want to talk about this.

But then the memory of their previous conversation about this very subject, and how he was trying to keep her from getting pregnant, flooded his mind. She'd said something along the lines of, *Oh, I never thought about that the other times.*

The other times.

What fucking other times? Before she started making these night-time visits . . . or since?

Angry all over again, he added, "At least if you get pregnant, you'd know it wasn't me." *Probably, anyway.*

"Yeah," she said after a moment, as if she'd had to think about it.

Quent's belly tightened. Time to change the bloody subject. Back to something he could handle.

But before he could, she beat him to it. "You never thanked me for helping you find your friend who was kidnapped. The Corrigan woman." She looked at him sidewise, eyes slanted meaningfully.

Quent released a short laugh on a gust of breath. "Right, then, what the hell do you think *that* was?"

he said, spreading his hand to encompass the twisted sheets and clothes strewn over the floor.

She smiled back at him, sending another pang of lust twining down past his belly. "I thought you were just hot-damn happy to see me."

That too. But he was damned if he'd say it.

I never thought about that the other times.

The other times.

Right. He was a nice little shag when she was in Envy, and that was just fine with him. A little cork pop, keeping the tubes lubed, and he was fine with that. Keep it simple and easy. And when she left to go wherever the hell it was she went when she disappeared, he could care less what she did.

"Shame on me for not thanking you properly," he told her with a sly smile, "for helping us to find Sage."

If Zoë hadn't seen Sage being abducted from Envy a week ago by a bounty hunter who worked for the Strangers, they might not have found her as quickly and easily. That was, in fact, how Quent had come to be in possession of Zoë's latest arrow. The one that now lay on the floor, hopefully forgotten.

He reached over and stroked the pad of his thumb over her nipple. It hardened and the dark rose areola gathered up prettily beneath his touch, tempting him to taste her again. She arched slightly toward him, and he leaned forward to kiss the side of her neck. How could she taste like cinnamon all the time? Spicy and sweet and a little salty . . .

She moaned softly, and he felt the lift of her pulse beneath his lips. *Yes, indeed.* Then, reluctantly, he pulled away. His mouth anyway; he kept his hand in place, gently cupping the weight of her breast. There were other things to talk about.

"We did find Sage," he told her, wondering if they would actually have a bloody conversation. "In Redlow."

"Yeah, I saw that she was back. She's getting some from the smokin' guy with the ponytail, isn't she?"

The smokin' guy with the ponytail was Simon, of course. Even Quent could admit that Simon resembled a Hollywood actor, with his sculpted features and the long hair that some women seemed to find attractive. "I could grow my hair longer," he offered, gently tweaking Zoë's nipple. "Wear it in a queue."

She snorted and, to his surprise, reached to brush her fingers over the unruly mess of his hair. He realized with a start that he couldn't remember her ever touching him except with demand, when they were going at it.

Except for that very first time, when she caressed his cheek.

"You'd be a lot damn safer if you cut this shit off. Or at least shorter."

"Safer? You mean so you won't be able to pull on it when we're fucking?" He resisted the urge to close his eyes; her fingers, gentle on his scalp, felt so good.

She looked at him in exasperation. "You're blond, genius. The *gangas* go after blondes. Didn't I fucking tell you to wear a bandanna to cover it, so I wouldn't have to save your ass again?" Quent laughed and she narrowed her eyes, realizing he'd been teasing her. "Dumb blonde," she added. And gave a sharp little tug on a curl.

Then he sobered. "When we found Sage, we also found Remington Truth too. Sort of."

Only recently had Lou and Theo Waxnicki and their Resistance learned that Remington Truth, a former leader of the U.S. government's National Security Administration, had also been a member of the Cult of Atlantis. A variety of clues had helped them put the pieces together that the *gangas*, who came out only at night and called for *"Ruuuth . . . ru-uthhh . . ."* were really calling for Remington Truth, searching for him by order of the Strangers. The fifty-some-year-old Truth had had blond or silvery hair, which explained why the *gangas* abducted anyone with light hair.

As for brunettes and redheads . . . they were simply mauled and torn apart if caught by a *ganga*.

Quent, with his honey-colored hair was apparently blond enough that the simple monsters thought him a candidate to be Remington Truth . . . and that was how Zoë had come to rescue him.

A fact that she continually reminded him.

Zoë eased back and sat up, all remnants of teasing or flirtation gone. Her velvety eyes grew serious. "Holy hot damn. And you just now fucking decided to tell me?" Then she crossed her arms under those delicious breasts. "You sort of found him? What the hell does that mean?"

"Right. Well, apparently, the Remington Truth that the Strangers—and the *gangas*—have been searching for since the Change is dead."

"So they've been looking for a dead man for fifty damn years?" Zoë gave a little rusty laugh. He saw a flash of dark humor in her eyes. "Fucking boulder-heads."

He couldn't have said it better himself. *Gangas* were not only brainless, but so awkward they couldn't climb anything but low stairs.

"We're *told* Truth's dead, though we don't know how long that's been the case. This is according to his granddaughter . . . whose name, interestingly enough, is also Remington Truth. Same really blue eyes, but she's got long dark hair—no wonder the *gangas* were confused."

That bit of information was just as interesting to Zoë as it had been to Quent and his friends, if the way she straightened up was any indication . . . although he wasn't exactly sure why. Did she realize how badly the Strangers wanted to find Truth? Did she know that the Strangers had feared the man for some reason? That was why the Resistance was so intent on trying to find him—whatever the Strangers feared could only be a benefit to the Resistance. If they found it first.

"His granddaughter," she said, eyes narrowing in thought. Or suspicion.

"Or so she claimed, before pulling a gun on us and disappearing. I'm not certain how much credence we ought to give her statement." Quent felt a wry, humorless smile tug his mouth. "You might also find it interesting that, after she slipped away, she forced your friend Ian Marck to drive her off at gunpoint."

He watched her reaction closely. Aside from being a bounty hunter who worked for the Strangers, Ian Marck could also quite possibly be one of Zoë's "other times." The big Slavic-looking blonde and Raul, his father, had kidnapped Jade to fulfill a bounty for one of the Strangers, so he was already on the Resistance's shit list—and when Quent learned that Zoë was acquainted with Ian, that had just bumped him up a few notches.

"My friend, huh?" she repeated. The expression on her face gave him nothing, of course. She was just as practiced as he was at hiding his thoughts. That was probably how he'd managed to live eighteen years with Parris Fielding without being killed.

So, he pressed, "Wasn't he the guy you went to talk

to at the festival last week?" After she'd been making eyes at Quent from across the room. Very promising eyes, full of blatant invitation.

"You mean while you had your hands all over that blond chick's ass?" Zoë returned coolly. "You looked pretty busy, plastered against her on the dance floor. Wonder how she felt about you eye-fucking someone else over her shoulder, genius."

"It was you I was looking for," Quent said before he could think. *Fuck. Knobhead.* Then, to try to salvage the moment, he gave her a burning smile. "I figured you'd be hot to retrieve your arrow again."

Zoë looked at him and for a moment, he couldn't read her expression. Then she smiled in a way that set his blood to boiling and surging, and reached down between them . . . to where he was already tightening and lifting in response. "Damn straight."

And the next thing he knew, the low light blotted out as she moved toward him, pushing him back onto the bed, her slender, calloused hands very busy.

When he woke, she was gone.

And so was the arrow.

"I want to go back to Redlow," Quent said, looking around at his companions: Wyatt, Elliott, Jade, Fence, Lou, Simon, and Sage—the usual suspects. The only person missing from their cartel was Theo Waxnicki, who'd declined to join them because he was in the throes of a computer project . . . and most likely because he didn't particularly like to see Simon and Sage together. "Remington Truth might be gone, but she left in a hurry. We might be able to find something helpful she left behind."

Half-filled cups of coffee and tea littered the table,

along with empty breakfast plates. The group sat in Lou's favorite quiet corner of one of Envy's communal restaurants—which was more like a cafeteria with one or two entrees each meal—that served most of the population. Since most of the living spaces or homes taken over by Envyites were simply hotel rooms, none of them had access to full kitchens. So through community service and coordinated scheduling, meals were provided in the restaurants to any resident of the city who regularly contributed to the community.

Despite the fact that Quent's body felt loose and sated from a very busy night, something ugly and heavy had settled in the pit of his belly along with the omelet he'd just eaten. He didn't know what it was, and he had no intention of spending time trying to sort it out. There were other things to attend to.

Like finding Remington Truth, and, more importantly, Fielding.

Maybe after he hacked the crystal from his father's body Quent would feel normal again. Although what the fuck *normal* would be for him now was a mystery.

He'd been raised with limitless resources and the ability to fall back on anything from his name to his billions of inheritance. Now he was simply Quent. No skills, no resources, nothing to offer this stark, simple world where money and celebrity status meant nothing.

Wyatt was nodding in agreement with Quent's conclusion. He set his coffee cup down with a little clink. "I'm with you. I need something to do besides sit around here. We can take Dantès back with us. Maybe he'll lead us to her."

Dantès was Remington Truth's ferocious-looking dog, who had become attached to Wyatt when he figured out how to release him from the guard position she'd left him in.

Lou was also nodding in agreement. "Excellent idea. You can search the things she left behind—see if there's anything there that might help us."

"And Quent'll be able to tell if any of it belonged to Truth—the old mofo, not the hot piece of ass who pulled the gun on you," Fence said. He was, of course, trying to hold back a chuckle, his impossibly straight and white teeth wide in his face and dark eyes dancing. "Wish't I'd been there to see you all walking into that frying pan," he added, his suppressed chuckle squeaking a little bit.

"Yeah, it was a real party. Crazy woman fucking took a shot at me," Wyatt said flatly.

"You sayin' she was a little quick on the trigger?" Fence replied jovially. "Better her than you, eh, brother?"

Wyatt snorted, and probably would have responded if they hadn't been interrupted.

"Good morning," said the tall, rangy man who approached the table.

Quent put him in his late thirties, with a handsome, rugged face that looked like it would belong on a cowboy. However, instead of a buckskin shirt and ten gallon hat covering his messy, sun-streaked hair, he wore something more along the lines of Quent's personal assistant: a pale blue button-down shirt and worn chinos. The guy needed a haircut like mad, and could use a shave, but his eyes were sharp and intelligent and his demeanor professional.

"Hey, Vaughn," Jade said with a smile. "Want to join us?"

Quent glanced at Elliott, but his friend had risen from his chair to offer Vaughn Rogan, mayor of Envy, his hand in greeting. "Have a seat," he offered. "We're just about finished, but could stick around for a bit so you don't have to eat alone."

"A chick magnet like Marlboro Man never eats alone," Fence muttered in Quent's ear.

Although Rogan had once had an eye for Jade, whatever that had been seemed to have passed and settled into pure friendship and sincere regard. Elliott had saved the mayor's life a few weeks ago at the risk of his own, and since Jade and Elliott had gotten together, the two men had moved beyond any undercurrent of competition to become more than simple acquaintances.

"I'm obliged," Rogan said, and snagged a nearby chair, dragging it to the end of theirs. "It's good to see all of you here, because I had a few things I wanted to talk to you about."

He did a brief glance behind him, as if to ensure that no other table was within hearing distance. A woman lingered nearby, and he waved her over for a moment to answer a question regarding a broken wind turbine— "send Jackson out there"—then turned back to the rest of them. "Coffee would be good," he said, sounding weary.

But Jade had already poured him a cup and settled it in front of him. "What's wrong?"

Rogan took a slurping sip and closed his eyes as if savoring the taste. Then he set the cup down. "Nothing's really *wrong*," he said. "I just have a lot of things that need to be attended to. Which is why I wanted to talk to you."

"Aren't you worried about your chances for reelection if you're seen hanging out with crazy Lou Waxnicki?" asked the old man with a wry smile. "You know most of the town thinks I lost my mind during the Change."

Rogan nodded, his lips in a grim smile. "Their loss," he said. Then the corners of his eyes crinkled with real humor. "Though I think you do your fair share of promoting that fallacy by talking about your nonexistent granddaughter all the time."

Lou laughed, his eyes gleaming behind their glasses. "Can't be too careful." Then he sobered. "If the Strangers knew we were on to them, we'd be fucked before we even had a chance to do anything. And since most people haven't experienced the horrors Jade has seen and lived through, they simply can't and won't believe that the Strangers are interested only in controlling and suppressing us. Among other things."

It still threw Quent when he heard a man of seventy-seven use the f-word, even though he knew that he'd actually been born *before* Lou and Theo Waxnicki. He guessed he'd be using the word when he was that old himself.

Rogan had taken another loud sip of coffee, and was nodding. "You don't have to tell me. And that's part of why I wanted to talk to you." He spanned his gaze around the table. "Here's the deal," he said, leaning forward, his voice low and rumbling. "I don't really know where you men came from or what makes you so . . . different . . . but I know that Envy needs you.

"I've been mayor here for four years. But the people of Envy have spent the last fifty trying to survive and to build a civilization that resembles, as much as it can, the one that existed before the Change. But there are areas that we've neglected. Lou, Theo, and I have talked long and hard about what can be done to protect and grow our race now that we've reestablished the— what do you call it?" He looked at Lou.

"Infrastructure." Lou removed his glasses and wiped off one of the frames. "We're doing pretty well here—electricity, food, clothing, shelter—using things we've scavenged or grown or made. But beyond the walls of the city, it's pretty much every man for himself. It's the fucking Wild West out there sometimes. And we've lost a lot of medical and pharmaceutical knowledge, and of course, there's no communication to speak of. I told Vaughn that you'd probably be willing to help, considering your familiarity with twenty-ten and the years before."

Quent slid a look at the older man. Had he really told Rogan everything about them? Obviously the mayor knew of Elliott's healing powers, for he'd been a recipient of that ability himself.

Lou gave him a slow, deliberate nod as if to say that the mayor could be trusted to know the truth about them. But Quent wondered if that also included telling Rogan that Fielding was Quent's father.

Rogan set his coffee cup down. "It comes down to this. Elliott, we need your medical skills, and Jade tells me you've been planning on doing house calls when she goes on her missions to the other settlements. That's good, but I'm here to ask you if you'll make Envy your home base and work with us to better develop our infirmary."

"Already been planning on it," Elliott interrupted. "But I didn't want to step on any toes."

"No worries there. Your expertise will be welcomed."

Elliott nodded. "I've been talking to Flo Gradinski, and she wants to help too. Nursing and other stuff."

"When she's not making up hair dyes and cosmetics," Jade added with a smile.

"Flo? That's good," Rogan nodded. "She'll be an asset. And there are others who want to learn what you can teach them." Then he looked at Simon. "I understand that you have some experience in security and law enforcement?"

Quent smothered a smile at Simon's expression—it went dead blank. From what he knew about the guy, his experience wasn't precisely *in* law enforcement . . . but quite the opposite. Which would explain his reticence.

"Not sure where you got that impression," Simon responded. But then Sage shifted beneath the table and Simon jolted slightly, a pained expression flitting across his face. "But . . . eh . . . why do you ask?"

"We need to organize a more extensive—security, I guess—system here. I understand that there was an incident with Sage recently. She was assaulted and you—er—took care of the attacker."

"He won't be a problem again," Simon assured him.

Rogan gave a wry smile. "I got that impression."

"He didn't kill him or anything," Sage interrupted earnestly.

"I know," Rogan said. "But that just indicates how much we need to establish a better way to deal with this sort of thing. For the most part, crime is minimal here in Envy. But outside the city, and even sometimes within, there are problems."

"And as the society continues to develop, it'll only grow," Lou added. "We don't have formal jails or even a real legal system. It's very simple: if someone does something wrong, he's exiled from the city walls on the decision of a sort of jury."

Rogan nodded once more. "So I want Simon to advise our minimal security and law enforcement team. I have a feeling you'd have some suggestions."

"Uh. Sure," Simon responded, but only after another kick from Sage, who beamed a smile that lit up her beautiful face.

Quent listened as Rogan went on to discuss other projects he had in mind, asking for advice from Wyatt because of his experience as a firefighter, paramedic, and former Marine. And Fence, who volunteered to work with a group of men to teach them survival and navigational skills in the wilderness. Fence had been their guide through the caves in Sedona, and even he had something to offer in this new environment.

Perhaps it wasn't as clear to anyone as it was to Quent that the mayor had no specific request to make of him. That simply drove home the point that he had little to recommend himself—except for the fact that he was going to find Fielding, and was going to rid the world of another Stranger.

And if he survived that, maybe he'd go on and simply hunt Strangers. For the rest of his life.

Because no one was going to find useful a man who knew how to pick an excellent bottle of cabernet.

Or to fill out an Italian suit, or invest in real estate.

Or to headline a charity event.

Especially a bloke who fell into a coma of black dreams whenever he touched something.

Ruuuth . . . ruuuth . . .

Zoë woke to the low moans of *gangas*. Distant, but coming closer. The moon beamed through a hole in the roof above her, right in her face. *Crap.* She'd overslept.

Her own damn fault, though, for wasting time in Envy all night last night. And then hanging out much too long in the town, observing from high on the rooftops instead of resting. It had been near evening, still rainy and dark, when she finally sneaked out of Envy.

Normally, she slept during the day when it was safe—relatively safe—and hunted when the moon and the *gangas* were out. And so that when she dragged herself out of the nightmares, it was into sunlight.

Not darkness.

But last night she'd given in to her base urges, to her curiosity—and that curious *need*—and slipped into Envy.

And she'd waited for Quent . . . and waited for him . . . and waited. She'd nearly given up when he finally came to his room, dripping wet.

What the hell had he been doing walking around in the rain?

And why the fuck had she waited for him?

The little shiver deep in her belly told her the answer, and she didn't like it one damned bit. Zoë flung off her light blanket and glared at the three filthy windows. The moon tried valiantly to shine through, but it was fighting a losing battle with the years of soil encrusted there.

It really nuked her that she kept thinking about the guy. The first time she'd seen him, up close, after she'd drilled an arrow into the skull of the *ganga* who was carrying him off . . . she'd been . . . well, *hell*. Attracted.

But not in an amorous way. More like a night fly to a candle or lamp. With curiosity. Desirous of warmth. Even companionship?

His cheek had been warm, and smooth. And there was something about his reaction when she laid her hand on his face. He stilled, arrested as if touched in some deep way, instead of simply finger pads to skin. It was ass-crap weird the connection she felt.

Even though it had been three weeks since that first time, she still remembered the feel of his cheek under her fingers. The first time, in how long, that she'd felt real, warm, solid human flesh? . . . And damn if the sensation didn't still resonate, even though they'd gone at it many ways since.

And now here she was, oversleeping because she'd been crazy stalking him.

This guy. This Quent, who talked like the guy in those old DVD movies about the spy. There was something unusual about him.

She was curious. That was all.

She could be curious.

But, really. She was too damn busy to be wasting her time hanging around Envy for a little nookie from the man with honey-colored hair. He didn't cover it with his bandanna during the day, but wore the cloth tied around his forehead. When the sun burned down on him, his skin glowed mellow and golden next to a blinding white shirt. He appeared as warm in the daylight as his cheek had felt that first time.

Yeah, well. Fuck. She'd watched him—and his friends, but mostly him—during the day, after she'd sneaked out of his room. She'd had to pull away from the fingers that had closed around her wrist even in sleep.

Now . . . the dull grating of *ganga* moans dragged the last vestiges of sleep from her eyes and mind. As she sat up, something scuttled in the corner—probably the mouse family she'd disturbed earlier. They'd dug their way into what had once been an upholstered sofa and turned it into little more than a pile of dirty stuffing, nibbled brocade, and a gnawed wooden frame.

Zoë listened, crawling carefully through the remnants of someone's abandoned living room to a grimy window. She was safe up here, on the fourth floor of an old apartment building—for the boulderheaded *gangas* couldn't climb unless they had easily accessible, shallow stairs, and the only stairwell was buried beneath half a wall and a pile of rubbish.

She rubbed a peephole in the dirty glass, taking care not to press too hard in case it was ready to shatter or fall away. Mold and mildew contributed to its opacity, and as the spores were disturbed, the dull, earthy scent became stronger. Some sort of trailing vine or other tenacious growth sprawled from the edge of the window's frame, clustering over the glass. But she could see through the hole down to the overgrown street and rusted-out automobiles below.

There they were—*gangas* clustered on the ground, milling about aimlessly, calling for *"Ru-uuthhhh"*—which was apparently a nuked-up version of "Remington Truth." She couldn't tell for certain how many there were through the trees and jagged walls that obstructed her view. At least five or six, she judged. Too far away, and too many trees to get a good enough shot with her bow.

But that was only a momentary setback. Get her closer and there'd be mashed *ganga* brains galore. She reached for her hunting shirt.

The shirt reeked, but Zoë had long become accustomed to the rank smell. Regularly dredging her hunting clothes through boggy, mucky water and allowing the dirt, algae, and whatever else rotted in the swamp to dry on it had created a shield of sorts. The *gangas* couldn't scent her human flesh when she wore it.

Probably because she smelled just like them. Maybe even worse.

But that was what had saved her before.

Climbing down on her knotted rope, a small pack on her back and the quiver of arrows over her shoulder, Zoë grimaced. She wondered if Quent would have let her get near him if she'd been wearing this shirt that first night they met.

It probably would have been better if she had been. Then she wouldn't be wasting so damned much time looking for him, waiting for him, rolling around in the sheets with him.

But hot damn and whoa, it was fantastic sheet-rolling.

And why the fuck was she reliving those moments, over and over?

She had work to do. For Naanaa and the others. She had to find the man responsible for taking them away from her.

The rope ended just as Zoë's feet touched the ground, and with a practiced flip of her wrist, she unloosened it from its anchor. It slithered down silently, landing with a quiet thump at her feet. Just as she began her stealthy movements into what had been the front vestibule of the apartment building, a new sound caught her attention.

A low rumble, a mechanical purr.

Zoë's fingers tightened around the grip of her bow.

A vehicle. A rare sound . . . one that she'd only heard a few times in her life. But a sound that she'd never forget. Which meant that *he* could be coming.

Her heart slamming in her chest, stomach tight, she stepped over a buckle of heaved-up tile and inched along the side of the room covered by old mailboxes set flush into the wall. She knew their numbers had long rusted out as tenacious moss filled the cracks, but the metal still felt cold when her bare arm brushed against it. Tendrils of ivy coiled down like Rapunzel hair, sifting gently as she moved past them.

Slowly.

The rumbling sound grew louder, and Zoë found herself pressed into a dark corner of the room, suddenly paralyzed, brought back to that horrible night. She was safe here, in the dark corner. She struggled to focus on the moment, the burning anger and determination that had driven her for a decade . . . not the immobilizing fear.

She would damn well beat this.

Memories couldn't hurt her. They held no threat.

The rumbling sound, the smell of her shirt, the feel of damp, dank wall beneath her fingers, against her cheek . . .

Zoë squeezed her eyes shut, hard, and found other memories to cling to. Smooth, golden skin . . . firm, skillful lips . . . thick waves of honey hair and the warmth, the stroking, the proximity of him. The comfort.

Her eyes opened again, and despite the trickle of perspiration down her spine and the nauseating swirl in her gut, she eased out of her protective corner as a beam of light cut through the darkness. Then the rumbling sound of its engine stopped.

Zoë swallowed and made herself examine the scene beyond shattered glass doors that somehow still stood intact. *Gangas* staggered about, clustering around the big, boxy vehicle.

Moonlight gleamed on the black metal, and even from her distant view, she could see that dings and scratches and even patches of rust marred the rumbling box on wheels. Its roof was as tall as the *gangas*,

and the large black tires lifted it high off the ground.
A rider would have to climb up to get into the fierce
monstrosity.

Doors on either side opened, and three people
emerged. Two men and a woman. Her heart pounded.
If it was him, she'd have to get closer for a decent shot.

At first Zoë couldn't see much detail, for the much
taller *gangas* clustered around the newcomers as if
drawn by a magnet. Then one of the men raised his
hand and lifted something like a lantern that gave off
an odd greenish light. The *gangas* stumbled backward,
arms knocking clumsily into each other. Their groans
turned louder, then quieted.

Damn. I could use one of those.

Then the man turned in her direction, and the green-
yellow light clearly illuminated him.

When she saw his face, her first reaction was to jolt
back into safety. Her belly dropped like a stone and her
heart paused, then started up again, faster and harder.
But Zoë resisted the urge to hide. He couldn't see her.
And she wasn't fifteen anymore, and terrified out of her
fucking mind.

Well, she was terrified out of her fucking mind.

But it was him. Finally. *Finally.*

She was terrified, but prepared. The whip-thin
willow bow felt solid in her grip, and the weight of the
quiver over her shoulder comforting.

The filthy wall beneath her fingers, Zoë watched as
he seemed to speak to the *gangas*. The man looked
around fifty years old. The light plastered over his
white-blond hair, making his sharp cheekbones appear
gaunt and shadowed. She remembered that about him,
the way the light made his face skeletal.

He looked no different than he had ten years ago.

Raul Marck. The man who'd taken everything from her: her home, her family and friends . . . security, comfort, love. The man she'd been hunting for a decade, and only one time since that horrible night had she seen him.

Zoë shifted her bow, and reached stealthily over her shoulder for an arrow. Her pulse stormed through her body, filling her ears with its dull thudding. Dampness grew on her palms, but her fingers were steady.

The *gangas* were listening to Raul, just as they had done before. They had to take their orders from someone; God knew they weren't intelligent enough to know what to do on their own. That was why, even though she hunted *gangas* every night, she knew the whole ass-load of blame fell on Raul Marck's shoulders. He'd given the orders. He'd picked her settlement.

He'd killed her family.

She looked at the other man, who stood near the woman, and wasn't surprised to recognize Ian, Raul's son. He bore a resemblance to his father, with the same Slavic features of high cheekbones, square chin and broad forehead. Ian's hair was darker blond, and with his dark, slashing brows and wide mouth, he could be considered handsome—if a girl could get beyond the fact that he was a bloodthirsty bounty hunter.

He was a ruthless son of a bitch, but he wasn't the target of her hatred. So she might allow Ian Marck to live another day.

Zoë turned her attention to the woman standing next to Ian. She'd never seen a female bounty hunter before. The woman stood close in front of Ian, about as tall as his jaw and maybe half as wide as his shoulders. She looked about Zoë's age, and had dark hair. Even from the distance, Zoë sensed stiffness, perhaps anger or annoyance from her.

Then, as they shifted and the *gangas* moved away, she realized why. Ian was holding her arms behind her. She wasn't a bounty hunter, but a prisoner.

Or, more likely, she was going to be *ganga* dinner.

Well, didn't that just suck.

CHAPTER 3

Zoë contemplated her options as she moved toward the other end of the building, where she hoped to find an opening that was nearer her target.

More than anything, she wanted to drill a nice metal bolt into the skull of the man who'd set *gangas* onto her family. But once she killed Raul Marck, she figured the *gangas* would no longer be under his control, and would likely attack the woman and Ian. Zoë didn't give a rat's ass about Ian, but she supposed she'd better not let the defenseless woman get torn to shreds.

And if she rescued the woman, she'd have to get them the hell out of there immediately, and there might or might not be a chance to get off the shot.

Damn. Damn. Damn.

For almost ten years, she'd been waiting for a chance like this. The last time she'd been too far away, and not as good of a shot. But now . . . she was perfect in her aim. And she could get closer, pick off a damned fine shot. But some stupid woman had to mess it up.

She nearly tripped over something large and bulky in the middle of the room, but caught herself and kept going when she saw faint gray around a jutting corner. By the time she got around the corner and found another window, the scene outside had changed.

Now she was much closer to the gleaming black vehicle, which still seemed to loom like a horrible dark monster, ready to reanimate on its own . . . but the *ganga* party was farther away. The zombies seemed more agitated, their grating cries more urgent. Raul had stepped onto something that made him taller than the creatures, and once again he held up that green-yellow light as he spoke. She wondered where she could get something like that.

Zoë strained to listen, holding off on her aim to see what was going on. Filtering through the moans and cries, she heard something that sounded like "barley the main" and "leet." And then, more distinctly and powerfully, she heard *"bring to me."* He held up a paper and seemed to be showing the *gangas* something. A picture?

Zoë snorted. No fucking chance. Hadn't *gangas* been abducting anyone with light hair for the last fifty years as they searched for a silver-headed Remington Truth?

Then Ian moved, shoving the dark-haired woman in front of him as they made their way closer to Raul. Ian stepped up on whatever dais had raised his father, and pulled the woman up with him.

Holy crap. Were they going to toss her down to them right now?

Zoë gripped her arrow. She could probably get two or three of the *gangas* before anyone realized where she was, if she was fast. Two for sure . . .

Settling it into its comfortable groove on her bow, she raised it and shifted so that she aimed through the window. If someone turned to look, they'd see her . . . but it was too late to worry about that now, if she was going to have a chance to save the brunette.

Ian gripped the woman's arm, but instead of looking frightened or shocked, the prisoner seemed more . . . annoyed. Pissed off, in fact, if Zoë read the expression on her face correctly. The woman didn't like being man-handled around, that was certain.

Damn. *Wish I could get closer.*

Raul had moved next to Ian, and he was still talking about *barley the main* or *hardly do pain* or something like that, but now he was touching the woman's hair. The woman's head jerked and she twisted away, glaring up at him as she said something sharp to Ian. He laughed, looking down almost affectionately . . . and she responded with something just as furious that wiped the smile off his face. He gave her arm a little jerk as if to remind her he still had control, and she stilled. A play of moonlight over her features showed a mutinous expression on her face.

During this little altercation, Raul had gathered up her now loose hair and pulled the dark tresses forward. It was damned creepy the way he spread it over the front of her shoulders, as if demonstrating something to the *gangas.*

Her hair? He was showing them her long hair?

Her long dark hair.

So now the *gangas* were supposed to change what they'd been doing for fifty years and suddenly start looking for someone with long dark hair?

Fat fucking chance, Marck.

Zoë nearly laughed aloud. And then she noticed awkward movement nearby, appearing suddenly from behind a cluster of bushes between her building and the crowd around the Marcks. Very close, moving toward the window near which she perched.

She raised her bow again. The zombie's orange eyes glowed like two round flames and its broad shoulders—wider and higher than any man's—blocked out much of the view behind him. The telltale shuffle and the whistle of breath became more audible as the *ganga* staggered closer. It seemed to have become separated from the pack.

Probably too much information overload on its brainless skull and it was trying to escape.

Zoë was pretty certain the zombie couldn't scent her—not only was she wearing her hunting shirt but she was downwind, and the smell of the Marcks and their captive would already be in the air. She waited until the *ganga*'s eyes were close enough that she could see the black iris in their centers, and she let the arrow go.

Whissst. Silent and deadly, it slammed into the monster's skull, dead above those glowing orbs. The monster fell to the ground next to the bushes.

Buh-*bye, you rotting creep.*

A quick glance toward the *ganga* training meeting told her that they were either too far away or the noise was too loud, or both, for either of the Marcks to have seen what happened. They might find the dead *ganga* later, but he'd fallen close to the bushes and she'd be well-hidden or long gone by then. Hopefully, after having retrieved her arrow. She couldn't slip out to grab it now, but—

Suddenly, Zoë noticed that the woman seemed to be staring in her direction.

Just fucking great. Had she seen what happened?

Look away, you idiot.

When she finally did, it was because Ian was pulling her off the stage or whatever they were on. At least he wasn't about to feed her to the *gangas*. Yet.

Now what?

Zoë looked from Ian and the prisoner to Raul, who'd lowered his green-yellow lantern, and was sending the *gangas* off into the dark now that they'd received their instructions. The shuffling, awkward creatures faded into the night as Ian tugged the woman off in a different direction. Zoë was torn as Raul turned and started toward the vehicle.

Which one? Which one?

She slipped another arrow from her quiver. *She doesn't seem to be in any danger at the moment.*

Raul Marck, you bastard . . . prepare to die.

The arrow slipped into its notch almost of its own volition and she raised the bow, fingers curling around the back end of the bolt. Was she close enough?

Raul stood near the vehicle. The *gangas* had scattered, shuffling off into the night in a cluster. As their moans dissipated, silence settled over the area. The soft clatter of a dead tree's branches and the rustle of some foliage filtered through the quiet. Zoë could hear her own breathing, steady and accelerated, but audible only to her ears.

Ian and the woman were standing in the shadows near a tree. Zoë glanced over at them and her eyes widened. Well, that was interesting. Kissing? Definitely. The woman's arms were up around his shoulders, and his had slid down around her ass. She definitely seemed to be a willing participant.

Great time to be playing suckface. Why don't you really get down to business so I can finish mine?

She grinned, drawing back on the bowstring, her hand steady, her eyes narrowed, focused on her target. His white-blond hair gleamed in the moonlight and the moans of the *gangas* had begun to fade into the distance. The very stance of his slender body bespoke annoyance and impatience as he flipped through the pages of a small book.

Zoë pulled the bowstring past her ear and shoulder, gave a quick glance over at the two who were going at it, and settled her sights one more time on the man who'd killed her family.

Three . . . two . . . one.

A split second before she let the arrow fly, a loud howl of pain struck through the quiet, and it was too late for her to stop. The bolt released just as Zoë swore under her breath, the bolt flying true and straight toward its target. Raul shouted and fell as, pissed the hell off, Zoë turned to see the woman sprinting away from Ian, who was on the ground. Writhing.

Damn.

But that was all she had time to think, for the woman was running straight toward her hiding place.

Fuck. She knows I'm here.

Zoë slipped the bow back over her shoulder and eased into the shadows. What the hell was she going to do now?

As the woman scrambled through a half-open window of jagged glass, Zoë saw Ian staggering to his feet under the tree. And over by the vehicle, Raul was using the door's handle to pull himself upright. She'd fucking *missed.*

Damn.

Now that she was inside the building, the woman had the sense to stop blundering about, and shifted into the shadows. With any luck, Ian hadn't noticed where she'd run—but Zoë didn't believe in luck.

"Over here," she hissed. "For fuck's sake."

"Do you know a way out of here?" the woman replied, moving toward the shadow in which Zoë was hiding.

"I dunno. I thought you were in charge," Zoë replied snarkily. "You fucked up my shot."

"Sorry," the escapee replied, just as snarkily. "Next time I won't skip rehearsal."

In spite of herself, Zoë cracked a smile. "Come on." She started off toward the back of the building, away from Raul and Ian.

Shouts and angry voices followed them into the depths of the structure and Zoë wished for a light so that neither of them tripped or ran into anything. Especially her unwanted burden.

Then suddenly, a small pinpoint of illumination glowed and Zoë's belly dropped again. But then she realized it was her companion, and for a moment, she was torn between annoyance and delight. She decided on annoyed delight, knowing that they were far into the corridor that led to the opposite side of the building from their pursuers, and that a small beam of light wouldn't be noticeable.

But annoyance that the woman seemed to be reading her damned mind.

"Careful," her companion said, and Zoë looked down in the nick of time and avoided tripping over a large object with hard edges that would have hurt—and been loud—if she'd landed on them. A big metal trash can.

"This way," Zoë said when they came to an intersection, and veered to the right. The elevator doors she'd been searching for gleamed dully in the low light, and she yanked out an arrow, kneeling before her bossy companion could say a word.

She'd done it so many times before—slipping the tip of the arrow into the crack of old elevator doors—and levering them open. There was always the danger of loud creaks or other noise, but this time, they opened, rolling apart heavily but silently.

Huh. Mistress Luck. First time in a long time the bitch had shown her softer side.

"Come on," Zoë said, peering into the dark shaft. The doors were barely wide enough for her to slip through—good thing the other woman was skinny too. She reached back and grabbed her companion's hand and angled it so that the light shone into the dark— something she wouldn't have bothered doing if she were alone.

"Hot damn." The elevator was down, instead of up, on the basement level . . . which left the top of the big box only a few feet down. Releasing the light, Zoë reached for the metal cable nearest and tested it with her weight . . . not that she was going far, but she didn't want the noise if it collapsed.

Just as she was ready to slip in, she heard a crash. The large trash can. She jumped into the shaft, grab- bing onto the cable. "Get your ass in here," she ordered in a fierce whisper.

The other woman didn't need to be told twice. "Close the doors," she said urgently, for the first time fear sounding in her voice. She'd grabbed a different cable and they dangled next to each other in the dark.

"You grab one, pull it toward the center. They won't close all the way . . ." Zoë began, but her tag-along was a quick study and she'd already begun to tug on the heavy doors. The backs of their hands bumped as the doors closed nearly all the way, leaving a crack only as thick as a set of fingers.

She turned off the light without being told. "I don't know how far up I'll be able to climb."

"No, we're going down." Zoë slid about four meters and her feet touched the elevator roof. Moments later she had the top of it open—a trick she'd learned from watching a few spy movies, and one that had come in handy for escaping *gangas* more than once. The little trap door gave a deep groan when she pried it open, but it was so low that she had hope if their pursuers heard it, they'd think it was just normal building sounds.

"What the hell is that horrible smell?"

"What—oh." Zoë realized that in the close area of the elevator shaft and their proximity, her hunting shirt was doing its job. Stinking. "It keeps the *gangas* away."

"Crap. I would say." Her voice sounded plugged up all of a sudden, and Zoë smiled. The woman continued, "Are you going to give me a name? In case, you know, I have to get your attention? Or at least thank you for helping me? You were going to help me, right? I saw you shoot that zombie."

Yeah. Whatever. "Zoë."

She dropped silently into the inside of the elevator and had the pleasure of landing on something soft and musty. And then part of it moved, and she stepped away, disgusted. Snakes were so fucking annoying.

The nameless woman hung by her fingers from the top of the elevator for a long moment before finally letting herself drop. "Don't like heights," she said breathlessly, pulling to her feet.

"Watch out for the snake," Zoë said helpfully.

But instead of a frightened or at least surprised reaction, her still-nameless companion said nothing but "What's the plan?"

"We hang out in here for a bit. They'll have to give up sooner or later, and they'll never find us in here." Zoë grinned in the dark. Surely the woman wouldn't want to stay in the small space with her stinky shirt and a snake for very long.

If she didn't, she could go on her fucking merry way and maybe Zoë would have another shot at Raul Marck. Rage blasted through her again at the realization that she'd lost her damned chance. All because of this woman.

But once again the bitch surprised her and said nothing about being stuck in the small dark place. Zoë felt her move and figured she was leaning against the wall. In the small windowless cube, the darkness was fully complete. Even with the door at the top open, the area was black and blacker.

"So do you want me to just say 'hey you' when I want to talk to you?" Zoë said after a long moment of silence. Silence, that is, except for the faint slithering sound as Mr. Snake tried to find a safe place to sleep again.

The low light came on again and Zoë found herself looking down at a long green snake tail. Clear of any markings but a long black stripe, the scales were a nauseating puke color.

"Nope, not poisonous." She looked up at Zoë with a gleam of humor—and a bit of malice—in her dark blue eyes. "Figured I'd better check if we were going to be in here awhile." Then the light went out. "And you can call me Remy."

And that was when it all clicked into place.

She was hiding out with none other than Ms. Remington Truth.

Remy could hardly stand to breathe. The smell emanating from this woman—or her shirt, as she claimed—was so incredibly rank, it was like being in a room with *gangas*. Or rotting potatoes. Or something even worse.

But she supposed it was better than being in the company of Raul Marck and his much too-good-looking son. Who happened to kiss really well.

If she'd known the man she'd kidnapped at gunpoint three days ago was Ian Marck, she'd have figured out another way to escape the people who'd found her in the quiet little home she'd made for herself in Redlow. She still didn't know what had possessed her to tell them her real name, but what was done was done.

And since she didn't know how to drive those truck-like vehicles known as humvees, she'd had no choice but to seize the opportunity when she'd seen Ian climbing into one. Employing her handgun had seemed like the best way to induce him to take her on as a passenger. Since no one but the Elite and a few bounty hunters had mechanized vehicles, she figured it was the most expedient way to escape, since no one would be able to chase them.

Of course, she hadn't realized what a horrible, bumpy trip it was going to be, over heaved-up concrete roads or the rough, uneven ground. Next time, she was going to walk or ride one of the wild mustangs that roamed throughout the area.

She shifted against the wall, still breathing through her mouth, and winced as pain radiated through her leg.

Damn.

The blood seeped through her jeans and she felt some of it trickling down into her sock and shoe. Now that she'd stopped moving, now that the adrenaline rush had ebbed, she realized how damn much it hurt. *Holy crap.* Pounding heat and spiraling pain.

Going through that window, ragged with glass, hadn't been the best way to get inside the building. But it had been the fastest, and it wasn't as if Remy hadn't been injured in the past. But this . . . this was agonizing.

"So'd you knee him in the balls?" Zoë's voice sounded faintly accusing. It rasped low and husky, as if it weren't often used. "While you were fucking lip-locked? That's damn nuked up."

"No I didn't knee him in the balls," Remy told her from between tight teeth. Which was a mistake, because that meant that she drew in a breath through her nose. For a moment—a brief one—the stench overshadowed the flaming pain in her leg. "Although I would have if I'd had to." She closed her eyes and continued. "I jabbed him in the gut, then kicked him in the shin."

And then, surprised that she'd managed to get him to release her, she'd run toward the building where she'd seen the arrow come flying, hoping she wasn't making a mistake.

She still wasn't quite sure.

"Ah. Girly fighting."

Bite me, she wanted to say, but then she remembered the sure, strong arc of the arrow and how it had lodged into the *ganga*'s skull. This babe didn't mess around.

Except, possibly, with scissors, because no one could consider the hacked-up job of her hair any sort of style. She was pretty enough—a man would probably think she was beautiful, with super smooth skin the color of light mahogany, high, elegant cheekbones, and an exotic shape to her eyes and mouth. But her hair was a disaster, and the boxy shirt she was wearing . . . ugh. It was not only caked with dirt, but seemed as if it were stiff enough to crack if she bent at the waist.

"So what were the Marcks doing with the *gangas*? Looked to me like they were trying to send them on a new mission. Looking for someone with dark hair? Who might be related to Remington Truth, maybe?"

Remy's mouth dried and her stomach did a little flip. Could this woman know? *How?* Instinctively, she reached for the crystal and found its comforting round shape beneath her fingertips, hanging there safely at her belly. Warm, even through the shirt.

You'll know when to use it. When the time is right. Until then . . . guard it with your life.

Her grandfather's last words to her. On a deathbed of confessions, grief, and guilt.

"Is that a yes?"

"It's a bounty they're looking for," Remy replied, trying to ignore the pain shooting up her leg. That was the truth, thank God. "You know that's what they do."

"Yeah, when they're not fucking feeding villages and families to *gangas*. Your little stunt back there, by the way, blew my best chance to take out your boyfriend's father." Her words came out tight and full of loathing, but Remy heard the pain deep in her voice and resisted the urge to touch Zoë's hand.

Probably not a good idea with this prickly one. "Sounds like you have a history with him."

"So what bounty are they after?"

Okay, then. Apparently I'm the only one allowed to share. But that was okay. Best to divert her from her earlier questions. "A member of the Elite has run away and they're looking for her. There are a few *gangas* that have the capacity to understand differences in appearance."

"Coulda fooled me. I've never seen one with any more brain power than it takes to stagger around. What's the Elite?"

"You know . . . the ones who . . . well, the ones who

wear the crystals." Remy caught herself before she said too much. And it was taking more and more effort to keep her voice steady in light of the pain gyrating around her leg.

"That's what they call themselves? The Elite? And one of them ran away. Can't imagine why the fuck she'd do that."

How much did this woman *know*? Remy frowned, once again glad for the darkness. "Yeah. Her name is Huvane. Uh, Laurie or Mallory, or . . . something like that. She was . . . with them from the beginning." She closed her eyes, counting to ten, breathing to alleviate the pain. It wasn't freaking working.

"Are you all right?" Zoë asked.

Remy curled her lips inward, then relaxed them. No sense in playing the martyr. "I cut my leg pretty badly when I dove through the window. It's bleeding and it hurts like a bitch in heat."

"That's not good. I knew a guy once who died from a cut."

"Thanks." Too damn bad the crystal Grandpa had given her wasn't the healing kind. It would come in handy about fricking *now*.

"Put that light on and let me take a look. I know a guy who's a doctor."

"A doctor? There aren't anymore doctors," Remy said, but she pulled out the light. "Any who survived the Evolution would probably be dead, or old and dotty by now."

"Not this one," Zoë told her. And then she sucked in her breath. "Holy nuking crap."

Remy had a moment of triumph that she'd shocked this rude, abrasive woman, but then she looked down at her wound and realized how serious it was. *Good God.*

That wasn't *bone* showing through there, was it? She felt a little faint.

"You've got to get to someone who can help you," Zoë said, her dark eyes serious and—*Whoa! Was that compassion there?* "We can leave just before dawn. Three hours at the most, if I can catch a horse. Will you trust me?"

An interesting question. Hadn't she already done so? But, yes, she would. She had to.

Because if something happened to her, all would be lost.

She nodded.

Zoë looked up and down the corridor.

Empty. Silent.

She slipped her keycard into the slot of Quent's door, listened for the soft click, and then withdrew it just as silently. Breaking into the room where they programmed the keycards and making her own had been one of the smartest things she'd ever done. He'd never asked how she'd gotten into his room—she wondered if he even wanted to know.

The slender knob went down without a sound, and she pushed the door open. Her heart was pounding and her mouth had gone dry . . . just as it always did.

But this time, it was for a different reason.

It was daylight. *Exposure.*

She didn't think he was inside . . . but what if he was? Her belly flipped.

But the room was empty and she slipped in. The space smelled like him and she closed her eyes for a moment, leaning against the door. And just breathed.

Then she shook it off and walked briskly over to the window. She meant to yank the curtains closed, but she paused for a moment to look down onto the ravages of 2010 Las Vegas, awash in a blaze of sunlight. Those same rooftops and high window ledges, balconies, and even wall-less rooms that she frequented under cover of night and shadow appeared fragile and forlorn in the day.

Overgrown with whatever tenacious greenery could find root and spread up, down, or across, the buildings looked as if they needed to be trimmed. Irregular holes dotted the walls where windows or doors had been. The city's silhouette was one of jagged walls and rooflines, where the force of earthquakes, torrential storms, and battering tornados had torn away all but the skeleton of the buildings. And even then . . . steel beams curled and rusted and were eaten away by Mother Nature.

Zoë pulled the curtains closed, leaving only a three-finger-wide strip of sunlight to play over the bed.

The bed. A wave of anticipation and warmth shot through her. The covers were straight and unwrinkled, the pillows neat against the headboard. She reached across the sunbeam and brought a pillow to her nose, breathed in, and smelled him.

And then, as if realizing what she was doing—how ridiculous she must look—she shoved it back into place.

The rest of the space was just as neat as it had been the other times. Shadowy and darker now that the curtains were closed, but clear of clutter. Very impersonal. Much more impersonal than her own home—the one she always returned to after a hunting trip.

Or a visit to Envy.

Zoë tightened her lips. She was wasting too damn much time here. *I should get the hell out of this place.*

If it weren't for Remy, by now Zoë would have

tracked down Raul Marck and shoved an arrow into his cold stone heart. Then she would have been back at her own little home, a cozy space where she made her arrows and still cooked some of Naanaa's recipes. And where she kept the few things she'd salvaged from her family's belongings.

But, despite her annoyance with the whole damn situation, she couldn't leave Remy, especially if she was somehow really connected to the infamous Remington Truth.

So Zoë had caught a mustang—rather easily today, perhaps because it was just after dawn, and the horses were still sleepy. She'd ridden as hard as possible with a feverish and injured woman clinging to her. By midday, they'd approached Envy. The city was enclosed by massive walls of old vehicles, debris, and even things called billboards that protected it from *gangas* and other predators—wolves, lions, tigers, and so on.

Entering the city through its gates was never a problem for her—the gates and walls were meant to protect those within, not to keep people out. Although she was usually asked for her name and plans (whether she was planning to stay on or travel through), this time the sight of Remy's gray face and the bandage made from Zoë's blanket precluded any delay.

So Zoë'd attended to her . . . well, *friend* was too damn strong of a word for the bitch who'd nuked up her chance to skewer Raul. Whatever. Zoë'd gotten Remy through the gates of Envy and, with the help of the guards, to a place called Flo's.

Once the man who was Quent's friend, the doctor named Elliott, had arrived to attend to Remy, Zoë slipped away. She sure as hell saw no reason to stay, and she didn't want to draw any attention to herself.

She'd check back later and figure out what to do then.

Last night, Zoë had removed her hunting shirt and tied it up in an old plastic bag so that the stench wouldn't dissipate . . . and so that Remy's precious nose didn't have to smell it.

But if she had to be honest with herself, Zoë figured some of the stink still clung to her. She eyed the door to Quent's bathroom.

It had been a long time since she'd had a hot shower.

ca. 11 June 2010
Time uncertain

I write "circa" because I am not certain if a full 24 hours have passed or if it is still the same day of the events. Everything has become a very dark and ugly blur. I am paralyzed and terrified and I cannot sort it out.

For the first time, I realize why I write in longhand in a paper journal. So that when all of Nature has taken over, and the machinations of man—the very ones which I have helped to create and improve and that now seem so inconsequential—have been destroyed, there is still this, my private diary.

Perhaps I sound calm in my written words, but I am not. Perhaps writing is the only way in which I can keep from screaming in terror and disbelief. At times, I can barely keep my hand steady to write.

Devi is here with me, thank God.

I cannot describe what is happening. It's simply too terrifying. But I believe the world has ended.

Or if it has not, it has knocked upon the door of its demise.

—from the diary of Mangala Kapoor

CHAPTER 4

Quent opened the door to his room and rushed in. *Where the hell did I pu—*

He stilled, and, the hair lifting on the back of his arms, his belly tightening . . . he closed the door deliberately.

But, no. She'd only just left yesterday morning, and her presence simply lingered. Wishful thinking.

But now he recognized the soft *shhhhh* of spraying water from beyond the bathroom door. And filtering through, along with the faint warmth of shower humidity, he smelled . . . orange. And spice. Female spice. Cardamom, cinnamon, whatever it was . . .

When he saw the bow and quiver, her shoes, and a small pack settled on the floor, his belly pitched and dropped with a heavy thud. And then he let that smile come. And the heat blossomed through him.

Thank God I hadn't left for Redlow.

He owed Theo Waxnicki a big, bloody thank you, too, for insisting they wait one more day to leave, so he could prepare a device for them to take and expand the communications network they were building.

Quent started for the door of the bathroom, kicking off his sandals and already starting to unbutton his shirt. A nice burst of heat and steam got him in the face, and he stepped in quickly and shut the door. Orange and spice filled the air, not cloying, but subtle.

He caught a glimpse of her behind the translucent shower door—long, curvy, shadowy—and he swallowed hard. His heart was simply pounding, and he couldn't move.

At that moment, one of the double shower doors opened a crack, and she poked her head out. Ink-black hair slicked back from her breathtaking features, droplets of water glistening on her skin, her mouth curved in a very welcoming smile.

"Well, what the fuck are you waiting for?" she said, her eyes hot. She stepped one long leg out, putting a slender foot on a thin white towel and grabbed him by the arm. And tugged.

He went.

The next thing he knew, Quent was in the steamy shower, his hands full of warm, sleek woman, his clothes plastered to him in places—and stone dry in others—as the shower beat on them. She was tall and warm and strong, pulling him up against her, twining a leg between his, and he let himself go.

Hot, wet mouths, tongues dancing and tangling—there was nothing of the coy here, nothing of the restrained. They starved, they wanted and took from each other, hands battling to have the right of way, hers tearing at the buttons of his shirt then sliding under it, over his chest . . . his filling with her breasts, her ass, her hips and the low, sweet curve of her back, all so hot and sleek against him.

Zoë felt the cool tile against her skin, the strength of Quent as he pushed her up against it, his mouth taking . . . and taking . . . from hers. She settled her hands over the smooth, muscular plains of his chest, her fingers dipping into the spread of hair that grew there, golden and brown, and tight, and she tipped her head back against the wall as he moved to maul sensuously the strong cord of her neck, the sensitive skin beneath her ear and along her throat.

She shivered beneath his hands and mouth, and felt her body gather up tighter, her nipples hard and ready, the warm rush of pleasure superseding the blast of water in her face and over her shoulders. He groaned something into her neck, and the low, guttural sound almost like desperation sent a sharp pleasure-pain shooting down low, deep and hard and promising.

"Oh, yes," she whispered against his hair, thick and dripping and warm against her face.

"Zoë," he muttered. "I . . ."

"Don't talk," she ordered, busy at his waist, pulling at the soaking denim taut around the top button.

He laughed against her shoulder, husky and warm, then surged forward to capture her mouth with a long, deep, probing kiss that had her hands dropping away and clutching his shoulders to keep herself upright. *Oh God.* She couldn't breathe, she didn't *want* to breathe . . . she wanted this to never stop. Never end.

His broad, square shoulders, strong and solid, moved fluidly under her fingers as he fumbled with the fly of his jeans down between them. Muscles shifted, flexing beneath her fingers, and at last Zoë had to pull her mouth away to gasp in a breath. Then she went back to taste him, his jaw and cheek, wet and lightly stubbled, then his full, hungry lips again.

He shifted against her, and suddenly he was there, hands on her hips, lifting her, mouth crushed to hers, breaths mingling with the steady beat of rain . . . he settled her against the tile wall, spine flat and stable, and then . . . *oh.*

Zoë cried out against his mouth just as he groaned. *Yes, yes, oh, Quent.* He filled her, perfectly, fully, and then, hands on her hips, her legs around his shower-slicked body, he moved. He didn't wait, he went on. Hard, fast, desperately.

One hand curled into his thick hair, her head tipped back again so she could breathe, could cry out and pant with the coming, Zoë closed her eyes for the gathering of pleasure. Her body tightened around him, she felt his heart pounding beneath her other palm, she levered her body, shifting crazily against him, *with* him, battling in that timeless rhythm . . . reaching for what she needed. She felt him readying, tensing . . . and her own peak just . . . there. Just . . . *there.*

She might have screamed his name as she caught it, she might have cried out, but she didn't care because the world burst, hot and strong, and she was with him, against that warm, solid body, shuddering and groaning against hers. Sagging with her, bracing them both up with one powerful hand and the opposite knee against the slick wall.

After a moment of pounding satiation deep within, and water over and around, she dragged open her eyes to find his staring down at her. The first time she'd really seen them, in full light. Blue-flecked brown, glazed with heat, laced with what could only be called chagrin. His lashes spiked together from the water, and his jaw shifted as if he struggled with speech.

"Ah, Quent," she managed to breathe. *Oh God. Oh my God.* They were still joined, and she looked up and gave him the smile . . . the smile that told him how she felt, how deep and lovely and *finished* she felt.

"Zoë," he whispered, the water pounding down over the back of his shoulders and neck. "My God . . . I'm . . . sorry." He looked stricken.

"Sorry?" she repeated, although she suspected she knew what he meant. "How could you be sorry for *that*?"

His lips moved in what might have become a smile—a very satisfied one, she suspected—if he hadn't caught himself first. "Zoë, I lost it. I—"

"You lost what? Your mind? That's a fucking compliment, in case you didn't know," she said tartly, but she tried a slanted look along with it as he helped her disengage and her feet slide to the floor. "Don't apologize, or you're going to piss me off."

"Zoë," he said, his voice stronger. "We can't just igno—"

She stood away from him, her hand once again flat against his chest, but this time, the heat had ebbed. "Just forget about it, all right? Now you're just damned ruining the moment."

His face tightened. "Right, then, you think I'm just going to blow this off? The chance that you might get pregnant? Are you out of your bloody fucking mind?"

Zoë drew in a deep breath, fear trammeling through her. How had such a lush, lovely feeling changed into panic so quickly? She gathered her composure, stepping back, fighting to appear cool and removed instead of terrified that she was going to . . . lose . . . *this*.

This *too*.

Hot tears gathered at the corners of her eyes. She hoped like hell he thought it was remnants of the shower. For a moment, they were at a stalemate. The water blasted around them, and she reached over to whip the knob off, her movement sharp and jerky.

He did the same with the other valve, and suddenly, there was silence in the steamy space except for the last bit of water dripping off. The rasp of their breaths as they dragged in hot, watery air. Zoë stepped out of the shower, reaching for a towel as her heartbeat filled her ears.

Wrapping the terrycloth around her, she turned to look at Quent. He still stood, braced against the wall with one arm flexed, head bent, face turned sidewise to look at her.

"I know you don't like to talk," he said, his words clipped and precise. Very accented. Then, they got sharper. "You don't like to do much of anything but f—" He snapped off the words before he completed the sentence, but she knew where it was going.

A wave of hot anger rushed over her . . . then subsided. Sure. What the hell else was he going to think?

If nothing else, Zoë was brutally honest with herself. She knew nothing about being with people. Interacting with them. And it didn't matter, because she had a mission. A lifelong mission, and she wasn't about to abandon it for anything. Or anyone. Even . . . *this*.

"Yeah," she said. "You nailed it. Or should I say, *me*?" Her laugh was rustier than she would have liked, and she lifted her chin to make sure she looked him in the eye. So he could see that she thought it was rude and funny. "And you're right. I don't like to talk. So can't we just roll around in the sheets a bit, then get back to whatever else we need to do? It seems to work out just fine."

He moved then, pushing himself away from the tile and coming toward her. Tall, graceful, tawny-skinned and sleek . . . more than a little pissed off. His large hands settled on her shoulders, and though she was a tall woman, she felt small and delicate beneath them.

"Right, Zoë. I'm all for the rolling in the sheets, or the quick bang in the shower," he said. His words slapped. "But if something else comes of this, I'm not going to be so bloody blasé about it. I don't know about your fucking 'other times' or your other lovers, but this isn't a bloody joke to me."

"All right," she said more calmly, resisting the need to bite her lip, to keep back the horrible sting at the corner of her eyes. *What the hell is wrong with me?* "That's . . . fair, I guess."

"And if you're fucking around with Ian Marck, or anyone else, how're you going to know whose it is?"

"Ian Marck?" Zoë could hardly control her shock. Is that what he thought? "I wouldn't go near that bastard with anything but a good, sharp arrow, for fuck's sake, Quent. His father—" She stopped, swallowing. "I don't know where you got that ridiculous, boulderheaded idea, but there's not a chance in hell I'd let him come close enough to breathe on me."

"No?" he asked, his voice suddenly quiet. "Right. I confess, I'm relieved to hear that, at least. And how about . . . the others? Zoë."

"How the hell do you think I can sustain *this* and still . . . do the other things I need to do . . . *and* be getting busy with someone else? You *have* lost your fucking mind. Don't you think you keep me busy enough?" There. That was all she was going to give him. All she dared. And even that borderline confession cut deep, left her feeling ill and pasty-mouthed.

He looked at her for a moment, searching. "Right. There's that, then." His mouth, full in just the right places, not so pretty as to be feminine, relaxed a bit. Then his eyes caught at hers, bluer than brown now—or maybe it was just the light—and suddenly she couldn't breathe.

Zoë broke away and bent to gather up her clothes. As she turned to leave the bathroom, her knees felt weak—but she wasn't sure if it was lingering pleasure or apprehension.

"Zoë," he said behind her.

She was back in the cooler bedroom, her clothing gathered against her towel-wrapped, damp body. "Yeah?" she said without turning. Her hair dripped crazily over her shoulders, trickling down in every direction.

"Are you . . . leaving?"

She sat on the bed and the towel tucked under her arms came loose. *Yes. No. I don't want to. I need to get the hell out of here. What the fuck with all the talk? Can't we just let things* be?

Zoë tucked the terrycloth corner back in place, noting absently that it was much thicker than the ones she had. He'd come from the bathroom, wrapped in a low-slung towel of his own. And now he stood there, his long, bare feet settling on the floor in front of her.

She looked up slowly, along his muscular calves, covered with golden brown hair, to the towel, clean but dingy with age, over the flat belly that curved in at the sides into masculine hipbones that set her mouth to watering. She admired the broad expanse of his chest and the smooth bulk of his arms, not too ripped, but more than solid and capable.

"Are you finished?" he asked, his voice low and rough. "Because I think I've sorted out the answer."

A glance down told her that he'd already begun to fill out under the towel again, and that familiar stab of pleasure-pain bolted down through her middle. She looked up, her heart thudding . . . yet emptiness curled inside her.

Just then, a loud knock at the door broke into the tension, startling her so that she jolted.

"Quent!" came a male voice. "You in there?"

"Bugger," Quent muttered, glancing at the door. He hurried over to the dresser, opening drawers rapidly. "Where the hell did I stow it?" he said under his breath.

"Quent! What the fuck? You all right in there?"

"Yeah," Quent called back, still pulling drawers open, rummaging through them, occasionally pausing to shove a hand through his unruly hair.

"Well, hell, you had us worried something had happened. What's taking so long? We've been waiting. You gonna open the fucking door?" This last sounded more than a little annoyed.

"Not a chance," he muttered. Then, with a triumphant noise, he went to the closet and moments later retrieved a thick book. Zoë saw part of the title— something about *Monte Cristo*—briefly before he went to the door.

He pulled it just wide enough to stand in, holding the door so as to block any view of Zoë or the bed. "Found it," he said, giving the book to whoever was there.

"You sure you're all right?"

"Yeah, Wyatt. I'm fine. Just got a little distracted."

Zoë heard Wyatt's snort from behind the door, and she pictured the hard-faced man rolling his eyes. She'd seen all of Quent's friends at one time or another, although she'd never met any of them.

"Yeah, I see that. We're all fucking waiting for you downstairs, and you decide to take a damned shower? For all we knew, you'd fallen into the dark pit again, for chrissake."

"Right, sorry 'bout that," Quent said—but even Zoë could hear that he wasn't. "Look, I'll be down later." He shut the door and turned back to look at her.

"What the hell was that all about?" she asked. "The dark pit?"

"So now you want to bloody talk," he muttered, re-adjusting his towel.

"Well, we could find something else to do," she said, allowing her lips to curve into a naughty smile.

Quent came over and took the bundle of clothes from her arms, setting it on the table. Then he sat next to her, the mattress shifting with his weight. But, to her surprise, he didn't reach for her. "What did Raul Marck do to you?"

Whoa. Nothing like being blindsided. She moistened her lips, retucked her towel "He's a bounty hunter."

Quent nodded. "I know. *What* did he do to you?" His eyes were so close, serious. Determined. The glaze of lust was gone, the heat and desire . . . replaced by something else. Compassion?

Zoë's throat burned. "He . . . they're after a new bounty now. Someone overheard them, talking."

"Someone overheard them?"

Shit. She hadn't planned to tell him about her connection with Remy. *But why? Why does it matter? They've been looking for Truth. You could help him.*

But she's beautiful. So beautiful. And smart. And brave.

She'd *be able to stay. Here.*

Zoë swallowed and realized her belly felt ugly and heavy. *Why do you care if she stayed?* She couldn't burn away the image of Quent, his hands all over that blond woman on the dance floor.

"Zoë," he persisted.

"They were talking about another bounty. A woman, someone who left the Elite. She ran away. That's what they called them—the Elite."

"The Elite?" Quent said, as if turning the word over in his mind. "Fuck. I never knew what he meant." He looked stricken, his face suddenly drawn and serious. "The bastard."

Zoë frowned. "Who?"

When Quent looked back at her again, she was struck by the loathing in his eyes. Not directed at her; she recognized that immediately. Loathing, despair . . . and pain.

Something she'd seen in the mirror, once or twice.

"My father," he said, his voice grim. Dull and grim. "He's one of the Strangers, or, apparently, in their nomenclature . . . the Elite. He'd used that word to talk about some of his friends and colleagues." Then he seemed to shake it off, his mouth quirking in annoyance, and the expression in his eyes became determined. "Tell me what Raul Marck did to you."

Zoë opened her mouth to evade, but before she realized it, the words came tumbling out. "He set the *gangas* on my family. Everyone. Killed them all, destroyed everything." *Damn.* She blinked hard, *harder*, the tears burning and shaming her. "It was more than ten years ago," she added in defiance of the tears and grief. "I was almost sixteen."

"I'm so sorry," he said, his voice rough. "Ah, Zoë,

I'm so sorry." He moved then, gathering her, towel and all, against his warm chest. His arms curled around her, holding her so that her face, now damp with tears, buried in his shoulder.

She closed her eyes, feeling her lashes brush briefly against his skin like the butterfly kisses her mother used to give her. But she kept her arms curled in front of her, cuddled between them. Distance was good.

Yet . . . at that moment, she couldn't keep the distance. She'd never told anyone what happened—even that simple sentence.

There'd been no one to tell.

"I was the only survivor," she heard herself say. When was the last time she'd been held? Simply held?

Simply curled up next to a living, breathing person, with no other demands. It was much nicer than curling up next to Fang, her sometimes pet. A wolflike dog that came and went as he pleased, just as she did, from the little abode she'd created. She gave a short little laugh, more damp than was polite, into his shoulder. *Wipe your nose*, she could hear Naanaa say.

"Something funny?" he asked, gently lifting her face.

She nodded, looking at him through eyes glassy with tears. "This is much nicer than curling up next to my dog."

His mouth moved, but compassion still showed in his blue-brown eyes. "I think so too. Their long noses tend to get in the way." He thumbed away a trickle of her tears, his fingerpad gentle beneath her eye. "Will you tell me more of what happened?"

"That evening, I'd sneaked away to meet someone. A guy. We weren't supposed to be out at night, but we were close to home. Close enough to see the lights, and besides, no one had seen zombies around for years. There were trees to climb, if we had to escape anyway. It wasn't like we were stupid," she added. "There was an awful swampy bog, and I slipped and fell into it. All the mud and everything—it was mucky and it reeked like a bitch, and I didn't just stumble, I fell all the way in." Even now, she couldn't laugh, couldn't even find the humor in the image of her dripping in swamp mess.

With the telling, she'd pulled away from Quent's moist skin and now she rested her forehead against his shoulder, talking down into the space between their bodies. Her fingers still curled up between them like a child's, the wiry hair on his chest brushing against the back of her hand.

He breathed easily, regularly, and seemed in no hurry to urge her on, so she took a moment to swallow and smooth out her voice, which had become frighteningly unsteady. "Rick pulled me out, but I was such a nuked mess that I didn't have the balls to go back looking— and smelling—like I did. Even though everyone should be asleep, I knew I couldn't take the chance because we weren't supposed to go by the bog. Which is of course why we did . . . because it was private. So Rick went back to get me something to change into, and some water to clean me up with."

Now her voice broke and the next few words were hardly audible. "I never saw him again. Or anyone." She pushed on in harsher tones. "He didn't return and he didn't return, and I just knew the idiot'd gotten caught, so I finally sneaked back. When I got close enough, I heard them. The moans. The grunts. And the cries. The horrible cries."

Quent tightened his arms around her, making a sort of shushing sound she vaguely remembered from childhood. From Naanaa.

"I'm so sorry, Zoë. So sorry." He rocked her a little, and she sniffled, aware that her nose was dripping something ugly down into the cavity between them. She swiped at it, swallowed hard and angrily, and tried to get control.

It was ten years ago.

"Raul Marck was there. I didn't know who he was at the time, but I'll never forget him. Or that big black thing he drives. He or the *gangas* set fire to the five houses in our little settlement, which must have driven everyone out of them. Down into the waiting arms of the *gangas*. By the time I got back, there was hardly anything left." She shook her head. "I still don't know why."

"And if you hadn't fallen in the bog, you'd have been one of them," Quent said, holding her close. So tightly she could hardly breathe. His hand settled warm and flat over her skin, and began to smooth up and down her spine, bumping onto the terrycloth towel, and up again.

"I figured that's what saved me in the end. The zombies couldn't smell me, you know, with the ass-crap mess I was wearing. I smelled as bad as they did."

"I'm glad you fell in the bog, Zoë," he said after a while. "I'm sorry about what happened to your family, but I'm glad you fell in the bog."

That makes one of us. "There are times when I wish I'd been home when it happened." Most of the time.

She half expected recriminations, but he just hugged her closer. "If you had, we wouldn't be here now."

She began to feel the deep, low-down stirring in her belly, the sweet warmth funneling through her as she became re-aware of him. The scent of him, more real than what lingered on the pillow, the solidness of his body, the very masculine curve of his arms and shoulders . . . the strong pulse in his throat.

Zoë kissed him, lightly, gently. Just brushed her lips over that tender curve above his collarbone. So soft. He shuddered and she felt his chest expand against hers, then settle. Closing her eyes, inhaling him and the gentle orange-cinnamon from her *naanaa*'s soap recipe, she parted her lips and brushed them over him again. A soft groan came from deep in his chest and this time, his arms tightened reflexively around her. Her tongue slipped out, gentle, yet probing down against his skin, teasing and tasting.

"Zoë," he whispered. "What are you doing to me?"

She knew the answer to that. Smiling against him, suddenly flooded with something light and real, she kissed him just beneath his earlobe . . . then gently sucked it into her mouth, all the while feeling him lift and grow down against her. He shuddered and arched closer when she probed her tongue deep into his ear, his fingers curling into her back.

Then he pulled away, looked down at her with those blue-flecked eyes, and covered her mouth with his. She lifted against him, her arms around his neck, and they shifted together, sliding prone onto the bed, towels loose and falling away.

His hand moved, whipping away the terrycloth and then reaching for her. The next thing she knew, he was holding himself over her, kissing gently along the curve of her own collarbone, his mouth light and gentle . . . so different. Sweet along the sensitive skin of her neck, sending blasts of shivers down and over her, tightening her nipples so that they almost hurt, shooting down to her core, where she felt heat and damp and throbbing.

"Quent," she murmured, reaching for him, closing her fingers around his cock, lifting her hips. "Please . . ."

She hardly knew where she was, what she was doing, just that this was Quent, and that he made her forget it all. He made her slide into something so hot and warm and familiar that she never wanted to leave.

"Zoë," he said, and she felt the tremor in his mouth as he bent to brush hers, "stay with me."

She closed her eyes against the temptation, kissing him fiercely, smothering whatever he was about to say, and guiding him into her.

They both sighed and groaned when he slid deep. She arched up against his belly, rough with hair . . . and then they moved together, knowing each other's rhythm, skin sliding against skin, soft sighs and gasps and rasping breathing.

Zoë looked at him once, saw the deep pleasure, something compelling and desperate there, so intense that she felt that stab in her belly . . . and then she closed her eyes.

For she dared not let him read what was in hers.

Some time later, Quent felt Zoë shift away from him. The sheet tugged gently. He tensed, keeping his eyes closed. His heart began to beat harder when she eased away, slowly and stealthily.

Then the sheet collapsed next to him, and the mattress released.

Quent watched from between slitted lids as she walked toward the bathroom. The stripe of daylight that emerged from between the curtains had dulled to little more than a late-afternoon glow. How long had they been up here? Three, four hours.

Not nearly long enough.

She came back out, her hair falling in wild spears around her face, her naked body smooth and graceful, that orangey, spicy scent back in the air. She looked over at the bed. He felt her eyes settle on him, her hesitation and the hitch in her step.

But it was just that—a hitch. She kept on going, toward her clothes on the table next to the bed. He had a moment of temptation, to reach out and grab her arm, pull her back down next to him . . . but he'd done that before. And she'd still left.

The knowledge filled him with emptiness.

As he watched, she stuffed the clothes in her small pack and pulled out new ones. Silently, swiftly, she tugged on a dark red tank, as snug around her tight breasts as a bra. Then the rest of her clothes—panties of boring white cotton, and the same dark cargo pants loaded with pockets. All with no sound but the soft swish of fabric, and the faint click of a snap connecting.

Quent spied as she gripped the arrows to keep them from clunking together when she lifted the quiver and her bow, slung her pack over her back. Then she stopped and looked toward the bed.

He opened his eyes then, and, Zoë froze.

"I guess if I offered to go get us something to eat, it wouldn't change your mind," he said. "Pizza?" Once before, she'd mentioned a fondness for pizza, and he'd brought one up from the Pub.

She shook her head.

"Where do you go when you leave? What do you do?"

Zoë spread her hands, one of them awkward, laden with her weaponry. "I hunt."

"*Gangas.* And Raul Marck."

She nodded, reaching for the leverlike knob. "I have to go."

"I'll go with you."

"*No.*" The word cracked like a whip.

He hadn't expected anything different, but neither had he expected such a vehement response. Bruised a guy's ego a bit, it did. More than a bit. He opened his mouth, then closed it. *Not going to beg or plead. Not becoming to a Fielding.*

"Be safe," he said instead. Though it cost him to keep the words steady.

Zoë's stance eased, as if she'd been expecting more of an argument. "Quent," she said, pushing down the lever, then hesitated. She drew in her breath and continued, "Thank you for listening to me—my story."

Don't leave. "I'm glad you told me."

"I never told anyone about it."

"Ever?"

She shook her head. "Ever." The door lever clunked as it opened.

"What would you have done if I hadn't been here? When you came?" He sat up, feeling like a wank, desperation written all over him.

She shrugged and pulled on the door. "Been fucking disappointed."

Then she walked through. The door closed heavily behind her, the metal latch clunking loud and final.

Quent snatched up the closest movable object— a pillow—and whipped it through the air. It spun, knocked into a lamp and sent it crashing to the ground.

Fuck. *Fuck.*

A loud knock came at the door, setting his heart racing and his body shooting up from the bed. Then he mentally shook sense into himself. She wouldn't knock. She'd fucking swagger right in.

"Quent?"

He recognized Elliott's voice. *For chrissakes, can't they just fucking leave me alone?*

Knowing that it was futile to ignore his friend—nor would it be kind, because there was the very real chance that he could slip into that dark coma of memories at any given moment, if he touched the wrong thing—he stalked to the door and flung it open.

"Well," Elliott said, eyebrows high as he swept his gaze over Quent—who had forgotten that he was stark naked. "I guess you're okay."

Without waiting for an invitation, he pushed his way into the room. Quent swore under his breath and shut the door with a dull metallic clunk and turned just as Elliott noticed the broken lamp.

"Everything all right?"

"Yeah, doc, can't you see? Everything's fucking fine—I was just taking a nap."

"I see." Elliott spoke in that physician's voice he had: calm, easygoing, without a hint of condescension . . . yet anyone with a brain could sense the underlying skepticism. And compassion. *Bugger him.*

"So, uh . . . are you sure everything's all right?"

"What, did Wyatt send you up here to psychoanalyze me?"

"You look upset."

"Congratulations on your diagnosis, Dred. I am upset. Wouldn't you be a little fucked up if your father had destroyed the goddamned world?"

Elliott sighed, but compassion still warmed his eyes. "I saw her, Quent."

Quent shrugged noncommittally and bent to pick up the shattered lamp. His balls swayed back beneath his arse, reminding him that he really should put on some shorts.

"I was coming up to talk to you about a patient that showed up today, not to check on you," Elliott said. But when Quent shot him a skeptical look, he smiled. "Well, and to see what you were up to. You sort of disappeared, and the last time you did that, Jade and I found you passed out in an overgrown alley."

"Tell me about the patient."

"She had a bad laceration, through tendons and muscle. If she was lucky enough not to bleed to death, the wound would probably have gotten infected and she wouldn't have made it. Someone was smart enough to bring her here—she seemed to know about me."

"Your reputation is rampant," Quent said dryly, dumping the remnants of the lamp into a rusty garbage can. He dug in his drawer and pulled out a pair of briefs—tighty-whities, but one couldn't be picky in a post-apocalyptic world. You took what you could find that was uneaten or unmildewed after fifty years. "Could you help her?"

"Don't tell Jade," Elliott said with a funny smile, "but I healed her." He shrugged. "She doesn't like it when I do too much of that, because . . . well, you know . . . it's not just a simple matter of healing."

The expression on Elliott's face provoked another wave of bitterness. Quent recognized a bit of chagrin there, but laced with affection. And beneath it, comfort and assurance that, no matter what, someone would be there. Someone cared.

Someone wouldn't go running off as soon as the afterglow ebbed.

Quent turned away as he grabbed a pair of cargo shorts. Then, before he could catch himself, the words tumbled out. "Her name is Zoë. She's the archer with the special arrows—remember?"

Elliott nodded, but didn't speak.

"She visits me . . . occasionally. A booty call sort of thing. It's mutual," he added, trying to make it sound casual and even a little base. "Her parents were killed by *gangas*, courtesy of Raul Marck."

Because Raul Marck had abducted Jade and turned her over to the Strangers—the Elite—Elliott's mouth tightened into a white line. But, again, he remained silent. Which left Quent with nothing but the compulsion to continue talking.

"She comes and goes. Sometimes she leaves while I'm sleeping. Most of the time."

Elliott had settled himself against the door, arms folded over his middle. "I can see how that might bother you."

Normally, that sort of generic shrink talk would set Quent's hackles to rising, but not today. Not now. "That's the pisser of it all. It bothers the hell out of me that she can't be arsed to say good-bye. That she won't stay for more than a few hours."

"You want her to stay."

"I'm usually the one who leaves. Or who makes light of it, keep it cazh, you know."

"Or who arrives at a function with one woman, and sneaks off with another during the course of the evening. Then takes the first one home after."

Quent chuckled uncomfortably. Put like that . . . "So you heard about that? With Marley Huvane?"

"I think that you . . . uh . . . mentioned it once."

"Right." Quent shook his head. Great. That was discreet. "I must have been pissed drunk."

"That would be correct. You've had occasion to mention your other conquests . . . Bonia Telluscrede, Lissa Mackley, and the others. No details, though."

Elliott didn't need to say anything further; Quent was already starkly aware of the trail of women— celebrities, models, socialites—that littered his past. Not that he'd trampled on their hearts, led them on and left them hanging. No, he simply didn't get close enough for that to happen. You had to be with a woman for more than a night or two for her to get ideas about permanency.

Fuck.

Here he was, panting after a woman he'd been with occasionally over a couple weeks? Yet his mouth didn't want to stop. "There's something about her."

"It's not because you're not in control? That you're not calling the shots?" Elliott asked. It was an obvious question and one that Quent had to turn over in his mind. "An ego thing?"

"I don't know," he replied honestly. "Could be. Doesn't feel like it." Then he refocused, shifted his thoughts. "This patient . . . what did you want to tell me about her?"

Elliott seemed to accept that it was time to change the subject. "I scanned her."

Quent nodded. While he'd acquired a psychometric ability that seemed to turn around and bite him in the ass every time he used it, Elliott had come out of the Sedona cave with a more practical skill: not only the capability to heal, but also of scanning his hands over a body and being able to see inside. Like a human MRI, in 600 resolution color.

"Let me guess," Quent said, "she's wearing a crystal. She's a Stranger?" That would be the first time they had a Stranger—or an Elite—in a situation where they might have the opportunity to learn more about them, or Remington Truth.

"No. Well, she's got a crystal, but she's not wearing it like the Strangers. It's not embedded in her skin."

Elliott's face had a look of distaste on it, and Quent imagined it had to do with a recent event in which Ian Marck had forced Elliott to attend to a very sick Elite member, whose embedded crystal had become infected.

His friend continued. "It's a different kind of crystal. This one is smaller. About the size of a dime, and it's faceted. And it's brilliant orange."

"Does it glow? And how did you find it?"

"It doesn't glow that I can tell, and it's not set into her skin like the immortalizing crystals. She wears it like a belly button ring." He shook his head. "It's as big as her navel and from what I can tell, it's in a setting so it dangles—it's not set in her navel like a belly dancer. I didn't get a really good look, though."

"Right, then. You're thinking it's not just a piece of jewelry."

Elliott shook his head. "I scanned her through her clothes; she wouldn't take them off or let me do anything but roll up her pant leg. So she doesn't know that I know, but that's what I saw during the scan. I felt a real snap of energy when I got near the crystal, so I'm thinking it's definitely more than just a gaudy piece of jewelry."

"You want me to touch the crystal and see what I can tell?"

"Well, I don't think she's going to let anyone close enough to do that. She was pretty annoyed that I even had my hands over her, let alone *on* her. But I was thinking . . . if you came down with me to the infirmary, I might be able to get something of hers for you to touch. A shoe even. Maybe you could get some information . . . because she's not a Stranger, but she's definitely something. Or some*one*."

"You didn't get a name?"

Elliott shook his head. "Your pal Zoë—is that her name?—actually brought her here to Envy, but she left as soon as I arrived." He flashed a quick grin. "And now I know why she was in a hurry to get out of there."

"Bugger you."

"And the patient. She wasn't saying anything. Pretended not to understand when I asked her name or where she came from."

"She was pretending?"

"Definitely pretending."

"So if she's on to you, and you healed her, she might already have gotten the hell out of there."

Elliott grinned again. "I thought of that. She's all bandaged up right now, and I told her she had to stay still for two hours or the healing process would stall. We've got another ninety minutes."

"Well, I'm all for something to do other than sit here with my bag on," Quent said, gesturing to leave. "I'll go down with you."

Elliott turned to the door and wrapped his fingers around the knob. "I've known you for ten years—not counting the fifty we were sleeping—and I've not seen you this worked up about a woman. So it's either an ego thing, or she's the one."

Quent gave a sharp, short chuckle. "Kind of a leap from ego to soul mate, don't you think? Can't it just be that she's awesome in bed?"

But Elliott was shaking his head. "Nope, I don't think so. Not the way you're looking."

CHAPTER 5

Remy looked around the small room yet again. Apparently, she was in what they called the infirmary—an area of one of the hotel resorts where sick people were lodged.

The space was clean, if not worn, with a comfortable bed, two chairs, and a window that looked down from the second floor. It was covered with curtains that, at the moment, were wide open. The window vented but it would not swing fully wide, so there was no chance of escape from that angle. Aside from the fact that Remy wasn't fond of dangling off the ground more than a foot or two.

One of the three doors led to a bathroom with running water, apparently, for a busy, motherly woman named Flo had been in and out with warm water. Two other doors offered potential exits—one that seemed to lead to a corridor and another that probably led to the room next door.

Remy's leg didn't hurt any longer, though it was wrapped in a rather bulky bandage beneath her loose pants. Still fully dressed in the buttoned shirt she'd been wearing yesterday, she'd washed up in the small bathroom and brushed the tangles out of her long hair, thanks to Flo. The woman had brought her some shampoo that smelled like roses and a thick, creamy conditioner to use afterward. Now she wore it in a thick braid down her back.

Yet Remy felt like a prisoner. She wasn't certain why, but something about this place made her uncomfortable.

Zoë had certainly made herself scarce. Not that Remy needed her any longer—and yeah, the woman had probably saved her life, she had to give her that credit—but the way she disappeared as soon as the man who called himself a doctor came in was almost creepy.

And the self-proclaimed doctor was much too young to be a real one. Unless he was a member of the Elite, which she was certain he wasn't. Although there was something . . . different about him.

The quasi-doctor had told her not to move around for at least two hours, but she'd sensed that for the load of bullshit it was. Either he was overly cautious about the healing process or he didn't want her to get any ideas about leaving, which of course she had had even before arriving. She figured she'd play it easy and have a good meal, get some rest, and then sneak out in the night. Hide somewhere in Envy until it was safe to leave in the morning, and then be on her way.

Noise from below drifted up through the vented window, and Remy heard voices and the normal sounds of people interacting. And then the sound of a dog barking.

The deep bark reminded her of Dantès. It sounded just like him, and for a moment, sorrow swept over her. She and Dantès had been through a lot together in the last seven years, and she missed him. She'd expected him to have found her by now too.

Only six days had elapsed since she'd escaped from Redlow and those four men and one woman who'd caught her by surprise when they said they were looking for Remington Truth. That had been a narrow escape, simply because she hadn't expected anyone to ever find her in Redlow. Did she regret pulling a gun on her visitors and setting Dantès to guard them? It might have been a little impulsive, but, no, she didn't. She'd learned never to be too careful. Of course, if she hadn't slipped and told them her real name, she wouldn't have this problem anyway.

Anyone seeking Remington Truth was an automatic adversary. Elites, bounty hunters, *gangas* . . . even these people, because only the Elites and those close to them knew about her grandfather and how important he was. And how detrimental he could be.

Could have been.

Now it was up to Remy. She reached for the small crystal beneath her shirt, allowing its inherent warmth to filter through the thin cotton. She'd have bled to death before taking off her clothes and letting that doctor— or whoever he was—see this.

Restless and nervous, Remy looked around the room again. She thought Dantès would have tracked her down by now. He had such an uncanny ability to do so, and the little fragment of crystal she'd embedded inside his leather collar had never failed them before.

Outside, the dog was barking louder now, and its bark had shifted into a desperate pitch. Right near her window.

A strange sense of foreboding . . . and wonder . . . flushed over her, and she bolted up from the bed. Screw the doctor and his orders, *that* was Dantès. She was sure of it.

Remy looked down from the window. It was him, and he was down there, whining and prancing in small circles below the window as he looked up and bark-whined. He'd found her. Tears stung the corner of her eyes. Her warm, stalwart friend. The only one she could trust in this whole world.

And then Remy recognized the man who walked up to stand next to Dantès and her belly dropped to her knees. *No freaking way.*

It was the man from Redlow—one of the four who'd found her. The one over whose shoulder she'd fired her gun and shattered a vase, in order to make a point. *What the hell is he doing with Dantès?*

And the dark-haired man was looking right up at her. She dodged back from the window, but it was too late. He'd seen and recognized her and was already rushing into the building.

Shit. Shit.

She had to get out of here.

Heart pounding, she scrabbled for her bag, grabbed up her shoes and yanked on the door—not the one that led to the corridor, but the one that led to the adjoining room. Fortunately, it opened, and she found herself in another infirmary room. A woman sat in bed and gaped at her as Remy dashed in, and then to the next adjoining door. It opened and she found herself in yet another occupied room.

Damn. Why couldn't they be empty?

Her bag banging against her back, Remy slipped into a third room, also occupied, but when she got to the adjoining door, she found it locked.

"*What* are you—?"

She ignored the outraged demand of the man who struggled to sit up in bed, and went for the door to the corridor. So much for escaping unnoticed. Now everyone could tell where she'd gone.

Remy stepped into the hall, just as she saw the dark-haired man reaching for the door of her room. Stifling a gasp, she turned away and began to walk as casually as she could *away* from him. Surely he wouldn't recognize her from behind.

Holding her breath, heart pounding, she found a door leading to stairs and realized, belatedly, that her leg seemed to be working just fine—no pain, no blood seeping through the bandage or her cargo pants—she started down the stairs.

Bump, bump, bump . . . down she went, listening for the sounds of pursuit as she went down not one, but two flights. Taking a lesson from Zoë, instead of going to the ground floor as her opponent would expect, she continued down until she was two levels below, into what was labeled *B2* in faded, peeling red paint. Then: *No Ex t Th s F oor.*

Crap.

Out of the stairwell, she found herself in a dimly lit corridor that clearly wasn't often used. Bare lightbulbs burned and she wondered fleetingly how often they had to be replaced, and if they were rewired when they burned out or whether new ones had to be found to replace them. She had her own source of light, thanks to Grandpa, whenever she needed it, but most everyone else had more limited options.

The hallway had once been painted white—floor, ceiling, walls—but now was dingy with age and grime. It was also cooler down here, almost chill with the damp and subterranean location.

Remy rushed through the corridor, avoiding random piles of debris and hanging cobwebs, splashing through an occasional puddle. The usual rodents skittered out of her way, and she even saw the wide eyes of some other, larger nocturnal animal—*a possum?*—staring at her from one dark corner. The rough walls and uneven floor sprouted occasional black spots of mildew and trickles of water or shallow pools, but nothing green grew down here. She saw rooms that appeared to once have been storage or laundry rooms as she hurried along, and guessed they might still be used to wash. Remy picked up her pace, now looking for another stairwell that might take her up.

Then she heard a familiar sound that filled her with both delight and dismay. Dantès!

He barked as he ran, and she could hear the clicking of nails on the concrete floor.

She turned to meet him, and the large black-and-tan animal barreled down the hall toward her. Crouching, she opened her arms, and the next thing she knew, she was on her butt on the damp floor, and he was mauling her with his long pink tongue, whining with delight and wriggling with pleasure as she hugged and kissed him back.

Dantès looked more wolf than dog, which she assumed was from the inbreeding over the last half-century of domesticated canines and the wolves and coyotes who roamed. A motley collection of brown, copper, black and white fur, he had intelligent, compassionate eyes, tall triangular ears, a long, sweeping tail—and absolutely terrifying canine teeth. He probably weighed almost as much as she did and his shoulders were as high as her hips, his ears brushing her breasts. He was a huge dog, a formidable protector, and her best friend.

"Good boy," she said, murmuring into his face, petting the softest part of his skin—the backs of his ears. "I've missed you, Danty-boy. Good boy to find me."

When she sensed another presence, Remy looked up with a combination of annoyance and acquiescence.

The dark-haired man stood there watching, hands on his hips as if he had somewhere else he'd rather be and she was making him late. She recognized the same impatient, arrogant air that had caused her to fire—albeit impulsively—at him back in Redlow. The man had a chip on his shoulder a mile wide, and although he might be considered handsome if he ever smiled, at this moment, he simply looked annoyed as hell.

It made her want to pull out a gun and do it again. Unfortunately, she no longer had her firearm, thanks to Ian Marck.

"You've been taking care of Dantès?" she asked, pulling to her feet, a loose strand of braid swinging into her face, her bare arm brushing against the damp, rough wall. No sense in making a move until she fully assessed the situation. He might be arrogant and rude, but he wasn't dumb. Nor was he mean and vicious—for she'd noticed the way her dog glanced at the man, as if he were comfortable with him and not a threat.

Which he was, dammit—at least to her.

"He's a great dog." The man's features softened a bit, but he still looked as though he had a stick very far up his butt. "Very smart." Somehow the tone of his words implied that the canine was much smarter than his mistress.

As if knowing he was being talked about, Dantès looked back at the man and then up at Remy. She saw curiosity and uncertainty in those amber-brown eyes, and wished there was a way to explain. Instead, she petted his head and made the gesture for him to sit next to her. He did so.

"Thank you for taking care of him," she said, watching the man closely. "I'm Remy."

"I know that," he said impatiently. "Are you going to admit defeat and stop running away now?"

"Sure," she said with as much authenticity as she could muster. *Over my dead body, you arrogant ass.* "Though, it sure would be nice to know the name of the guy who outsmarted me."

He scanned her with cold, dark eyes. "Yeah, I believe you."

Remy shrugged. "If you don't want to tell me your name, I'll have to make one up."

"Let's go."

"Okay . . . Dick." She gave him a very cold, tight smile. "Where are you going to take me, Mr. Head?"

A flash of something—appreciation? annoyance?—lit his eyes, but was gone in an instant. "No one's going to hurt you. We just want to talk to you."

Remy snorted and Dantès looked up at her, then back at Dick, then back at her. He whined briefly, as if sensing the tumult in the air, but kept his attention focused on his mistress. She patted the side of her thigh and Dantès fell into step with her as they walked along the hall, continuing in the direction she'd been going.

She walked with a limp, grimacing in pain as she looked away, to make herself look weak and slow. He'd be less likely to expect her to take off if he thought she was injured.

She needed a distraction; something that would take him by surprise so she could run. But so far, there was nothing. Just piles of debris that made homes for the rats, snakes, and other creatures that made their living in the dark and cool.

At last, they came to the stairwell. This one was dirtier and danker than the one down which she'd come, although it was still lit with grimy yellowish lights.

Up the first flight of stairs, slowly, heavily, she groaned softly as she stepped with her right leg, playing up her injury. Dantès, as was his habit when she allowed him, edged just a bit ahead of her—three or four stairs—then eased back to meet up with her. When they were approaching the landing of *B1*, the first level below the ground, the dog got there first and began to bark furiously. A sharp, high-pitched yip that echoed in the stairwell.

Remy knew that bark and what its nuance meant, and suddenly she smiled.

She called Dantès back and he obeyed, changing from a bark to a brief whine of reluctance. But he obeyed. He always did.

Dick didn't ask what had bothered the dog, and Remy wasn't about to offer. She reached the landing first, and just as she got there, she managed to "dump" her bag off her shoulder as she lurched to the side, as if losing her balance. The bag opened, and something— she hoped it wasn't anything important, but, oh, well—fell a few steps down behind Dick, and, as she'd expected, he turned back to retrieve it. At least the guy had manners.

This gave her time to get to the landing and find the source of Dantès's annoyance. She ordered the wary dog up past the landing, and quickly kicked up the pile of leaves and debris in the corner. The bright green reptile with its black markings tried to slink away, but she was too fast.

Remy picked up the snake—it was at least three meters long, as thick as her wrist, and quite harmless— and, holding it behind its head and one end of the tail, kept her back to the stairwell as she heard Dick approaching. Huddling the snake against her, she waited till he was almost there

Just as she heard his shoe grind softly on the nearest stair, she turned and flung the snake into his chest. Dick reacted just as she'd expected—he shouted, flailed, and then fell back as he lost his balance.

But by the time she heard his furious swearing echoing up from the stairwell, she had bolted through an external door and out in to the sunlight.

Quent and Elliott were walking across what had once been the divided six-lane Las Vegas Boulevard toward the infirmary when a shout drew their attention.

Wyatt had come dashing around the corner of the building and obviously seen them. "She's gone," he called, coming toward them. Even from a distance, Quent could see that Wyatt looked bloody pissed off. "She got away."

"Who?" Elliott asked as their friend drew near.

"The woman. Remington Truth," Wyatt told them when he was close enough not to have to shout.

"Remington Truth was here?" Quent repeated. "And she got away?"

Elliott was shaking his head, his eyes full of reluctant comprehension. "Shit. Don't tell me she was the patient with the leg injury."

"I don't know what injury she had, but she came from the infirmary. She was limping a bit . . . I saw her—Dantès found her, tracked her somehow. When she recognized me, she took the hell off."

"Didn't you go after her?" Quent asked, then realized what a rubbish question. And that was before Wyatt slammed him with a dagger look. "Right. But she got away anyway." He was careful to keep any hint of disbelief from his voice. "What'd she do? Sic the dog on you again?"

"She threw a fucking *snake* at me. On the stairs. Damn lucky I didn't break my fucking neck, falling down."

"A snake? Bloody hell. What'd you do to her?" he said with a grin.

"Fuck you."

Always lots of brotherly love between the three of them.

"So that was Remington Truth," Elliott said, looking at the building ahead of them as if searching for Remington's room window. It had been one of the smaller casino resorts, and now part of it had been turned into the infirmary. "Damn. I shouldn't have left her alone, but I didn't know." For Wyatt's benefit, he described the crystal he'd seen during his scan. "I knew there was something unusual about her."

"Did you check with the guards to see if she got through the gates?" Quent asked.

"Was just on my way there when I saw you," Wyatt said. "She had Dantès with her, so she'll be easy to spot."

"You go check the gates," Quent said. "I'll go look around, see if she's hiding somewhere up that way." He gestured toward the southwest end of the enclosed city that remained mostly uninhabited and where Lou and Theo Waxnicki had created a secret entrance. Not that there was any chance Zoë would know about it if the rest of the Envy population didn't, but there was still a chance.

Remington. He reminded himself. Not Zoë. He was looking for Remington.

Right.

Of course, if he found Zoë, he could try and talk some sense back into her. Or at least lure her back upstairs. He didn't have his gloves with him, but he'd be careful and quick. And if the worst happened, they'd know where to look for him.

Quent walked behind New York–New York, away from the neat and landscaped Strip, toward those older buildings that were still safely inside the enclosure, but hadn't been maintained as residences. The protective walls had been made early on, after the Change. Instead of stone or brick, the enclosure had been cobbled of whatever large masses the survivors could find—billboards, cars, semi-truck trailers, airplane wings, and filled in with smaller debris from the ruined buildings. They stretched more than fifty feet high, and were impossible to climb—for *gangas*, animals, and humans.

As he moved along, Quent couldn't hold back a snicker at the image of Wyatt having a snake thrown at him. It was lucky he hadn't been hurt badly in his stumble down the stairs, although Wyatt was well used to having to defend himself in a variety of unexpected situations. A former Marine who'd seen action in the First Gulf War, and who'd come home and made his way up to fire chief in a suburb of Denver, Wyatt had gone on the same humanitarian mission to Haiti in 2004 that Quent and Elliott had.

All three of them had met there for the first time, helping to rebuild a hospital after Hurricane Jeanne. Quent had gone because he knew it would wank off his father if he actually got his hands dirty as well as donated a six-figure stipend, and also because his celebrity status would give the mission more media attention. Elliott had finished med school at Michigan, and Wyatt was just returning from the Middle East.

The three men had bonded as only people can do when working together on a life-and-death mission, and from what Quent had seen, there was much more death than life in the poverty-stricken country.

A noise caught his attention, pulling him from his thoughts. He paused, listening and looking. He wasn't alarmed, for there was nothing more threatening behind the walls of Envy than a few rodents or, apparently, reptiles and other members of the human race. Quent had no qualms about handling any of the above.

Although he waited, he heard nothing unusual, and after a moment, continued his walk. This time, he edged closer to the building along which he walked, noticing that the sun was lowering enough that shadows from the tall, close buildings had grown long. The area was growing darker, making it more difficult to see anything on the ground or through the glassless windows and doors.

As he avoided puddles from the previous day's rain and chunks of concrete or hunks of rusting metal, Quent realized he was wasting time. He should be hunting his father, not looking for Remington—or, to be honest,

Zoë. Hanging out in Envy and doing buggering nothing, bringing nothing to the table or offering anything as compensation for what he thought of as his room and board here in the city. The arrangement was one of a commune, and though he and the other chaps from Sedona had been afforded heroes' accommodations because they'd helped to save the lives of some teenagers a few weeks ago, Quent just didn't see himself fitting in here much longer.

Just as he hadn't gone to work or had a career back in 2010, other than to manage his billions of investments, he saw no place for himself here. His life had consisted of shagging lots of gorgeous women, attending charity functions, giving media interviews occasionally, and planning and taking his friends on Indiana Jones-like adventures that, while often exciting and dangerous, really had little benefit to offer to the world.

Sure, he'd visited places like Kuala Lumpur and Cambodia, and that had prompted him to help bring attention to those in need there—call him a male Angelina Jolie, but with smaller lips and definitely no urge to adopt a dozen children, but that was about—

The next thing Quent knew, he was flying through the air. He landed with an *oomph* on something hard and unforgiving, and realized he'd tripped on something he'd missed in the shadows. *For chrissakes*. He hoped no one had seen him, and he supposed it served him right for laughing at Wyatt and his snake.

Quent pulled himself up, his fingers closing around something that . . . *too late* . . . he realized was an old car door. With a door handle, rough and rusting, but nevertheless filled with memories that captured him.

He opened his hand, pulled away, but at the same

time his other palm rested on a different area of the car. Because he had no other way to drag himself to his feet, before he knew it, he was slipping into a maelstrom of speeding images and squealing tires, a dizzying blur of memories that sucked him right in.

"Quent! Open your fucking eyes!"

Deep in a swirl of whizzing pavement and loud, rushing noises, Quent felt himself being shaken and shifted, and he filtered back to awareness. Zoë was there, sounding more than a little panicked, and just before he opened his eyes, he felt her hand crack against his cheek.

The slap brought his lids wide and he looked up to find her bent closely over him. "What the hell is wrong with you?" she demanded, sitting back on her haunches. "Are you playing some kind of game?"

The sun had sunk much lower, and the shadows grown long and dark. He could hardly see her face. But from the tone of her voice, he got that she was more terrified than angry. *Not a bad thing. As long as she doesn't slap me again.*

"Thanks," he said, keeping his voice mild. "It wasn't a joke. I didn't mean to scare you."

"You didn't scare me, you pissed me the hell off." She'd backed away. "Dammit, I knew I should have left when I had the chance," she added in a mutter.

And at that moment, the plan crystallized in his mind like a bunch of glass shards coming back together to form a very clear window. *Yes. Kill two birds with one stone.*

Quent pressed a hand to his forehead. "Ugh," he said, and made a show of struggling to his feet. "Sorry, mate. Didn't mean to keep you."

"*Mate?* What the fuck does that mean?" She stood next to him and Quent found himself having to hold back from touching her warm skin.

"Just . . . it means friend," he explained.

"Oh." She paused, looking at him with mistrust in her very stance. "What the hell was wrong with you?"

"Remember today when you asked me about the deep dark pit that Wyatt was talking about? Well, you saw me fall into it."

"You seem fine now."

He nodded. "I am. I'm usually more careful."

"Whatever." She turned to go, which was exactly what he was waiting for.

"So if you're going to disappear off into the dark again, I should probably warn you."

Zoë snorted and turned back. "About what? The *gangas*? The lions? The wolves? I can take care of myself."

Quent smiled, knowing that his teeth probably gleamed mockingly at her. "I know that. I was talking about me."

"What do you mean?" she said suspiciously. And she took a step back.

"I mean that I'm going with you this time, Zoë."

"No fucking way." Her voice was adamant, and filled with affront. "I don't want or need you or anyone with me."

He kept smiling because he knew he bloody well had her. "That wasn't what you were saying earlier today, when you were begging for more." His voice dipped low and he sought her eyes in the dim light.

"I can get that anywhere." She tried to sound blasé, but he could hear the unsteadiness in her voice. As if she, too, were remembering. Oh, so reluctantly.

And don't you even fucking think about getting it anywhere else. "All right, then. No sex, if that's the way you want it. Purely platonic. Neither of us needs the distraction anyway, so I'm on board with that. But I'm coming with you, like it or not."

"Definitely fucking *not*."

"Look," Quent said. "I know you're looking for Raul Marck—"

"Yeah, and I finally found him. I would have scrambled his fucking brains to bits if that damn woman hadn't messed everything up by getting herself cut up. Now I have to find the bastard again, and I don't need anyone getting in my way. Especially you."

"Right, then. But it'll be a lot easier if you just let me go with you."

"Why is that?"

"Because I'm going to follow you if you don't. And then you'll waste even more time rescuing my incompetent arse. I'm blond, remember?"

"For fuck's sake. I should have just let you lie here."

And the fact that you didn't speaks volumes, Zoë, luv.

"Why do you want to go with me?" she demanded.

"It's certainly not because of your charming personality," he said with a soft edge to his voice. "Although there are some parts about you that I find more than a little delightful. It's because I want to talk to Raul Marck before you kill the guy."

"What for?"

Quent opened his mouth, then decided to wait. "I'll tell you all about my mission on the road. It's not so different from yours. Deal?"

Zoë stared at him for a minute, and he could feel the annoyance coursing off her in waves. Her hair sprung out in tufts all over and the high curve of her cheekbone caught the last bit of sunlight just right and gleamed sharply. She'd settled her hands on her hips, and she looked as if she were about to launch into some long tirade or lecture and tear him a brand-new arsehole.

But after a moment, she released her tension, sighing in defeat. "All right. I'll let you come with me, but *only* because I don't want to be wasting my time saving your ass. And you have to do exactly what I tell you at all times. No questions, no arguing."

Quent grinned. "You have my word."

Zoë snorted. "Not sure how much that means." She looked him over. "Well, let's get the fuck out of here."

"Uh, one more thing," Quent said easily.

"What?"

"I need to get a few things."

"You've got to be fucking kidding me. You black-mail me into taking you with me, and now you want me to wait while you pack a damned suitcase?"

Quent stepped closer to her, and reached to skim a hand down her bare arm. "I'll make it worth your while, Zoë. I have a feeling it'll be the last soft bed and hot shower either of us see for a while."

"Well, if you put it that way . . . I might as well get *something* out of the damned deal." She leaned into him, cinnamon, curves, warmth, and all. He suddenly felt light-headed, and wondered if this was good idea after all.

She was right about the distraction.

But it was too late. He was lost. "Whatever you want, luv," he managed to say as she plastered herself to him and his world sunk into hot, sleek, strong kisses and Zoë.

Always, only, Zoë.

It's over. Whatever it was, it has ended. By my calcula-tion, it has been more than a month since that day it all began. This is the first time I've desired to sit and put my thoughts on paper. There were days of paralysis and terror, and then numbness. Now, we are bent on sur-vival.

There is now only one other survivor besides Devi and myself. A young man named James.

After the first earthquakes and terrible storms, many of us gathered together at the elementary school. We thought it was merely something we could wait out. But then three days, maybe four, after the events began, people began to die.

Devi tried, and I helped, and so did others, but they fell as well. Devi could find nothing wrong with the people who died, and my beloved doctor was worn ragged and weary by his inability to save any of them.

Now, weeks later when the grief is not so raw, he theorizes that it was some sort of poisoned gas or bio-chemical event caused by the physical upheaval of the earth and its storms.

It appears that for some reason, Devi, James and I were immune to whatever it was.

A miracle, perhaps. Or perhaps it is not a miracle to have been left to live when so many have died.

But I cannot deny that still having Devi with me is a miracle of grand proportion.

We have no access to the Internet, to cell phones. Even a radio, running on electricity from a small generator, gives nothing but static or silence.

—from the diary of Mangala Kapoor

CHAPTER 6

What the fuck was I thinking?

Zoë had been asking herself that question, in various ways and laced with an assortment of expletives, since she and Quent had left Envy.

Barely had the sun's glow begun to lighten the sky—for they'd returned to Quent's room just as twilight settled over the city and the rest of the night had been spent in a variety of pleasurable activities—when she'd eased from the bed. He was snoring the sleep of a man well sated; his sleek, golden body sprawled amid the tangled sheets.

The image was temptation enough for her to slide back in next to him, but Zoë knew better. Then it would be noon before they left, and she had work to do.

Work that had gone terribly by the wayside in the last few days. The thought made her itchy inside—a different itch than the one Quent seemed well able to scratch—and even a little nauseated. Zoë knew that every night she spent doing something other than hunting the zombies, somewhere, one of them was attacking and tearing someone apart. On the orders of Raul Marck.

Someone's grandmother, father, sister, friend, lover . . . As long as he was alive, he was demolishing people and families with his rotting-fleshed monsters.

The very thought fairly destroyed her, made her crumble inside and turned her world dark and empty. There was no other purpose, no other reason she'd been left alive other than revenge—to rid the world of Marck, and as many *gangas* as she could, one at a time.

Zoë had no time for the sort of distraction Quent provided, as satisfying as it was. It would be even worse if he was with her all the time. *What the hell is wrong with me? I work alone. I live alone. I am alone.*

So she crept around the room as she'd done several times before, gathering up her things, hardly daring to breathe. He'd be furious, but she owed him nothing.

She'd already saved his damned life. What more did he expect? He should be the one doing *her* a favor—and leaving her the *hell* alone.

Zoë didn't allow herself to glance toward the bed a last time, though her heart was heavy. She silently turned the doorknob, careful not to let it clunk, and slipped out into the hall. Pulse pounding, palms slick, she eased the door shut and started off, slinging the quiver over her shoulder.

She made it to the ground, jogging down the flights of stairs without delay—of course, his room had to be on the fifteenth floor, which was a pain in the ass for a variety of reasons—before she slowed her pace.

Guilt had no place in her morning, so she pushed away the image of Quent waking to find her gone. He'd forced her into the agreement, and he'd had no business doing so. The only blame she allowed herself to acknowledge was that she'd done nothing to save her family, and that she hadn't killed any *gangas* in the last three days. That was the longest she'd ever gone without scrambling zombie brains since she'd begun hunting them.

And it pissed her off. And it was because of Quent.

She came around the corner, heading for the exterior door, and *holy ass-load of shit,* there he was. Standing there, tall and imposing, fully dressed, vibrating with anger.

She lost her breath for a moment, then frantically regrouped.

"How the fucking *hell* did you get here?" she blurted out, hands going to her hips as she tried on a persona of annoyance. It was bullshit, because her knees had nearly given way and her belly dumped to her ankles when she saw him. *Fuck. Fuck. Fuck!*

"I'm faster than you," he said tightly. His eyes—oh, his eyes were no longer hot and smooth, sliding over her like a promise. Now they burned with fury, and stared at her, flat and sharp like brown glass shards. "And, apparently, smarter. Since I anticipated just this sort of event."

Zoë shifted her stance. "Well, now that you're here, let's get the hell going." What else could she do? *Dammit.*

She strode past him, but his hand whipped out and closed over her arm, yanking her back so hard she stumbled. Zoë caught her balance and pivoted around, her own fury slicing through her. "Take your fucking hand off me."

"Again," he said, just as icily, but with an underlying calm, "that was not what you were saying last night."

"Last night is over. This is serious."

"Yes," he said, very softly. So softly, the back of her neck prickled as if a ghost had settled over it. Her belly felt leaden and solid. "And we had a goddamned deal."

"So, all right. Let's get going." She tugged and he

released her arm. She still felt the imprint of his fingertips, and a glance told her that the impressions were still white on her dark skin. "Don't touch me again."

His response was a mocking snort-laugh. Then, with a peremptory gesture, he indicated for her to lead on.

So she did. They walked through the gates of Envy just as the top of the sun broke the horizon. And then he really pissed her off.

"Right, then. What's the plan?" he asked, pausing beside a decrepit building that once was a house. A large square of cracked concrete sported irregular rows of grass and a rainbow of wildflowers far enough away that it might once have been the footprint of another home.

They were beyond the view of the guards, and the landscape stretched before them, hilly, green, punctuated with pre-Change buildings and signs. Farmland sat to the east, the fronds of cornstalks waving gently in the morning breeze. And beyond, mountains stretched high in nearly every direction, as if embracing Envy and its environs.

"I go where the *gangas* are," she told him. And she rarely traveled during the day, and wouldn't be doing so now if he hadn't been so fucking persuasive back in the room, with the comfortable bed and his busy hands and mouth. A renewed blast of annoyance and anger had Zoë tightening her lips. *Why the fuck did I ever agree to this?*

"On foot? On horse?"

"Look, Quent, if you can't keep up with me—"

"Right, then, we'll go my way." His lips were pressed as flat as hers. "It's a damned rough way to go, but we can cover ground and travel at night if need be."

She glared up at him, ready to blast him back, but his

expression stopped her words dead. It didn't make her any less furious, but she decided for prudence. His eyes were so angry, so cold.

He walked up to the huge metal door on one side of the old house and, as Zoë watched, he lifted it from near the ground, jimmying it up with his foot, then using his arm to raise it the rest of the way. To her surprise, it bent as it scrolled up into the top of the building. But when she saw what was inside, and realized Quent's intent, she began to back up.

"No damned way."

Inside sat one of those big black vehicles that Raul Marck and the Strangers used to get around in. It gleamed maliciously as she watched Quent walk up to it. He hesitated for a moment, then opened one of the doors as her mind jumped to the past and the night she'd first seen one. The cutting lights in the dark, the low creepy rumble of its motor, the crunching of its tires on the ground as it drove away from the destruction its occupants had wrought.

That same growl of a motor erupted now, in the daylight, and she heard the change in its noise as the vehicle began to move out of the house—the thrust of power and then the squeak as it stopped with a subtle jerk.

Quent opened the truck's door, got out, and closed the scrolling door of the house. "Let's go, Zoë," he said. "Climb in."

Zoë realized her hands were ice cold. Her pulse stampeded through her body. How could she even sit in something that big and black, something that rumbled and roared and grumbled? She'd be trapped. Inside.

He walked up to her and she stiffened, keeping her face blank.

"What's wrong?" His voice was marginally softer, his eyes the faintest bit questioning. But he still held himself stiffly, and she knew his anger was merely banked and not departed.

"I don't like those. I'd rather walk."

"We'll find Raul Marck faster. It's the most efficient way to go—that's why the Elite still use them, even though the roads are completely buggered up."

Zoë looked at the evil black thing, drew in a deep breath, and walked over to its other side. It took her longer than it should have to figure out how to open the door, and then she realized it was so tall she'd have to climb onto a step to get in . . . but she held her breath and forced herself to do it.

Her belly squished with nausea as she settled in the chair of worn and split leather, sliding her quiver and pack onto the floor. The interior smelled like . . . something. She didn't know what. But it was unfamiliar. After a moment, she realized she had to reach to pull the door closed. All the while, Quent said nothing. He didn't even seem to be watching her.

He must be pretty damned pissed.

Well, so the fuck was she.

Zoë swallowed hard when he reached in front of her to grab something—a strap—from behind her right side.

"Buckle up," he ordered, then proceeded to fit the strap's metal link into a holder with a sharp clip. All without even brushing against her.

Zoë realized she was high off the ground, and that she could see much farther than when on foot. She gripped the edge of the seat as the vehicle started off with an unfriendly lurch, then proceeded to jounce and jolt along.

A wave of panic rushed through her and she drew in a deep breath. Quent might be blind with fury and wordless with anger. He might never touch her again—which was fine—and he might even leave her somewhere. But she didn't *fear* him.

He might look like he was ready to kill her, but he wouldn't. She just knew it.

So Zoë settled in her seat and gave him directions to the place she'd found Remy. Since that was the last place she'd seen Raul Marck, they'd start there.

And, she had to admit grudgingly, they'd arrive much sooner in this black behemoth than if they'd gone on foot. Or even on horseback.

God, it just fucking figured that, on top of everything else about him, he had to be right about this too.

For the remainder of the day, Quent could hardly allow himself to look at Zoë although he was fully aware of every damn breath she took, every time she moved. But the ice inside him, the emptiness in the pit of his belly, kept him distant.

Burned, his eyes now fully opened, he retreated.

They'd driven—if one could call the rough, bumpy motion driving—to what had been a small downtown area in a sort of Main Street USA, where Zoë had seen Raul Marck and rescued the woman who turned out to be Remington Truth. Arriving there just around noon, they had full daylight to search for and locate tire tracks, which they'd followed east as far as they could before the trail of matted-down grass and broken branches disappeared. It had been excruciating, getting out of the vehicle every few yards to see which direction the ambiguous trail went, but Zoë did it and she was damn good at it.

And Quent had the added pleasure of being able to eye her perfect arse in those low-slung pants she liked to wear when she bent to examine the trail.

Once they'd lost the path, their only plan was to keep traveling in a circuitous route from where the trail ended and try to pick it up, or, when night fell, see if they could locate the headlights of a vehicle that might be—or lead them to—the Marcks. Now, it was near twilight and they'd settled in a middle-class suburban neighborhood for the evening to wait, and hunt.

He glanced over to where Zoë stirred a pot of some sort of stew made from two small fowl, which reminded him of quail, and greens with wild carrots. He'd been impressed when she pulled a little drawstring bag from her pack and added dried herbs, salt, and even pepper-corns to the dish. It smelled damned good and he was hungry; perhaps that explained why she always smelled a little like cinnamon.

"My *naanaa* always said if you're going to cook, you'd best do it the right way," she'd explained when he commented about the sack of spices. "Even in the most primitive conditions."

She'd built a small fire in what had been a bathtub and cooked over it, using a pot that had clearly been utilized since the Change. In fact, she seemed to know her way around in this old house so well that he realized she'd been here before.

"So is this a regular stopover place for you?" he asked, settling back against the wall in the hall beyond the bathroom. This was after he'd investigated the possibility of sitting on an old armchair that sat in the corner, and rejected the idea when he discovered what lived inside. He didn't mind mice, but he didn't need to get up close and personal with them.

"Yes," she replied. She crouched next to the bathtub and those low-riding pants dipped away from the smooth curve of her back. Quent looked away and made his gaze follow the smoke as it trailed out through a crack in the nearby window.

They had no reason to hide their presence by obscuring the fire's smoke, but he had taken the time to drive the humvee into an old garage and close the door. A few weeks ago, Elliott and Jade had coopted the vehicle after fighting off its Elite driver, and since then they'd parked it secretly in that old garage outside of Envy, making it available to any of the Resistance members.

At first, they'd worried about using it and running out of gas, but Wyatt and Fence had dug around under the hood and discovered some wicked-looking batteries that powered the engine, recharging as the motor ran. Quent hid the humvee tonight because no one wanted the Elite to know that they had acquired a truck. It might make them suspicious about what other information, technology, or abilities the Resistance had obtained.

Part of the strength of the Strangers was in keeping the humans ignorant and simple, and in using their own technology and strength to do so.

Quent looked down at his gloved hands and felt a thrust of distaste. Hated that he had to wear them so often, but when he was in a strange place, he dared not take the chance. Back in Envy, in his room and the other places he frequented, it had become easier to hold back the memories. It was as if his body became used to them when they weren't new or unfamiliar.

He'd taken care with what he touched from the time he opened the old garage to pull out the humvee—when he'd pulled on the gloves—until now. Part of the trick, he was beginning to learn, was how he touched something and what condition his mind was in when he did so. As long as he didn't use the pads of his fingers, he didn't "read" anything. And if he did touch something with his fingertips, and concentrated, and planned, he could slow the tumble into the memories . . . or even, sometimes, keep them at bay.

But he had to be prepared. And that was why when he fell in the alley, he hadn't expected to touch that old car, and that was what had dragged him into the deep, dark pit.

A well-nibbled book lay next to him on the floor, and he reached for it, after stripping off a glove. His mind steady, focused, he picked it up. The memories and images tugged at him, but he held them back, pushing at the colorful splash at the corners of his mind.

Yet one slipped through . . . a laughing girl of maybe ten, her blond hair in pigtails, hands smoothing over the cover of the book, then shoving it into something dark and close—a backpack . . . The memory threatened to drag him with it, but Quent controlled the impulse and made himself look at the cracked wall in front of him. *Reality*. The old electrical outlet, rusted and mildewed. A broken table leg. His scuffed, dirty hiking boots.

And he breathed more steadily when he replaced the book on the floor.

It was getting easier.

If only other things were.

He glanced at Zoë, who was scooping the aromatic meal into two shallow bowls.

Anger still burned in the pit of his belly. Anger, shock, betrayal. Something had gouged deep inside him when he watched her this morning, gathering up her belongings.

He'd expected her to try it, but he had hoped that she wouldn't. He'd hoped so hard that when he saw her actually open the door to leave, without a backward glance, he'd nearly let her go.

But no. She was the first real hope he had to find his father—she obviously knew her way around, and she was looking for Raul Marck. A bounty hunter would have connection with, and a process to contact, the Elite and that was exactly what Quent needed.

An entrée to the Elite. A way to find them, where they lived—and where he could track down Fielding.

But he sure as fuck didn't need anything else from her.

Not anymore.

She'd made her position crystal clear.

Zoë walked toward him now, offering him one of the shallow bowls and a spoon. Then she moved on past, heading out into an old bedroom. Quent gathered up his gloves and pulled to his feet, agreeing with her implied suggestion that they eat in the larger space.

"This is very good," he told her after he'd settled against an old bed and taken his first bite, still bare-fingered, testing himself with the spoon. Focusing on the taste, the smell, the environment around him. The tease of images nibbled at the edge of his mind, but he was able to keep them away, and after a moment, they gave up and allowed him to eat in peace.

A little victory. But, yet, a meaningful one.

By age thirty, Quent had dined in the world's finest restaurants, been cooked for by the most elite of chefs, and had even dabbled a bit in his own kitchen when he'd hooked up for an interesting week with Solange Poutentade, who'd been touted as the next Escoffier but was a hell of a lot prettier. He'd also eaten in the most mean of conditions—in Haiti, in the wilds of Nepal, in the mountains of Peru, and the villages of Cambodia and Zimbabwe. Everything from mopane worms to snake meat to *momos*. And, for the most part, he'd enjoyed them all, especially the Nepalese *momos*.

But perhaps not quite as much as this savory meal, in this decrepit old house with the woman across from him.

Zoë had nodded her thanks for his compliment as she sat cross-legged to his left, where she could look out a filthy window. The sun had nearly set, but a great slice of light filtered over her shiny black hair, full lips, and the gentle curve of her bicep. Quent shifted and looked away.

"So you'd have killed Raul Marck if you had the chance. Just dropped him dead?" he asked. "No questions asked."

"Hell, yeah," she replied. "Without hesitation." Her eyes settled on him, large and brown, shaped like almonds. "Are you saying you wouldn't nail the guy who took everything from you?"

Oh, you have no idea. "Not saying that," he replied. "I'd just want to find out why he did it. As in, why my family, why my village . . . Aren't *you* curious?"

"No. I just want that bastard dead." She settled her empty bowl down with a clatter. "Sun'll be gone soon. *Gangas* will be out. You're going to stay here."

Quent didn't bother to reply. "I need to talk to Raul Marck before you kill him."

Zoë snorted. "You won't have a chance. The minute I see him, he's dead."

He tried to picture her raising her bow from a high-up perch, like a primitive sniper, a ruthless assassin, and knew she was capable of it. But the thought bothered him. "No questions asked? You'd just shoot a man in cold blood?"

"He killed my family in cold blood," she replied, her voice icy. "What, should I get to know him first, give him a damned chance to get away again? I've been looking for him for almost ten years. And the one fucking time I find him, before I can get a good shot off, Remy decides to play hero and blows it. And then I have to rescue her."

Quent set his bowl aside. "Have you ever killed a man?"

"Not yet. But I will."

"Without hesitation. Without giving him a chance to defend himself?" For some reason, his mind would not relinquish the thought. "Where I come from . . ." Then he stopped. *Damn it.*

Where he came from no longer existed. The laws, the jails, the judges and juries. The authority.

What had Lou said? *It's like the Wild West in some ways. A man takes the law into his own hands because there's no other way.*

Hard to believe after fifty years, there wasn't. But then again, it wasn't so difficult. The settlements were small and widespread, like buggering *Little House on the Prairie* . . . and in Envy, Vaughn Rogan had a good handle on things. Kept things settled and everyone safe. And he was going to have Simon help in that vein.

So why did it bother Quent so much?

He fully intended to kill Fielding the moment he laid eyes on him.

But what made this different was that Fielding should have been dead long ago. He was no longer a human being. And he'd caused the Change.

"What if there was a misunderstanding? What if

Raul didn't know what he was doing? What if he was ordered to do it?"

"Why in the *hell* are you making excuses for him?" Zoë demanded, her eyes flashing in the low light. "He killed my family. In cold blood. Burned them out of their fucking houses. Watched the *gangas* tear them into pieces and *feast* on their flesh!" Her voice choked and now he saw the glitter of tears in her eyes. "I'm not going to listen to you defend the man who took everything from me. *Everything.* Do you have any idea what that feels like?"

Quent swallowed. *Yeah.* He started to reach for her, but she leapt to her feet. That was probably a good thing, he told himself. A quick dash of the back of a hand over her eyes and she was stalking away, snatching up her quiver and bow.

"I'm going hunting. Stay here, Quent. I mean it. I'm not in the mood to be saving anyone's ass tonight, especially yours."

He watched her go, took a few minutes to gather up their bowls and sloshed a bit of water to clean them. Then he went to his pack, digging through for what he needed.

When Zoë found him last night, he could have convinced her to depart Envy with him then, but Quent knew he didn't want to be on a hunt for Fielding without being prepared. And prepared he was.

Just as he heard the low rumbling *Ruu-uthhh . . .* from below, he pulled out the makings of his own weapon. Skirting a hunk of drywall and an old rusted-out computer, Quent moved to the window to look down.

Maybe ten zombies down there, staggering along in an irregular cluster. He wondered where they'd come

from, how they'd come to be here. Did they sleep somewhere nearby during the day, and come out when the
sun went down? And why would they be here, in an
abandoned neighborhood if they sought human flesh?

*They're brainless. Haven't a thought to spare among
the lot of them.*

As he watched, something glinted as it whizzed
through the air, and one of the monsters stumbled,
then crashed to the ground. Though he was one floor
up, Quent fancied he could feel the vibration when the
heavy creature landed. And he was pretty sure he saw
the straight black bolt sticking up from the monster's
skull.

Nice aim, luv.

He looked, trying to figure out where she was. As
high as he was, it seemed. But maybe in the next house
over.

Quent opened the plastic bottle he'd taken from his
pack and poured pungent alcohol into a glass wine
bottle he'd found earlier today. He had another one in
his pack, but better to take advantage of this new one.
Eyeing the *gangas* below, and measuring the weight of
the wine bottle, he deemed he had enough in there to
do what needed to be done.

After stuffing the strip of an old T-shirt that had belonged to Elliott down inside the neck of the bottle,
Quent moved to the window, rubbing out a circle in the
dirt with his elbow.

The *gangas* were below, but they'd moved on down
the street. And he didn't want to break the window in
order to get to them—too loud, for one thing. They
seemed to be wandering through the streets, looking
cursorily around. Even from above, he could hear the
shuffle of their feet and the lost-sounding groans.

Did they scent him or Zoë? Were they just marching through, looking for any human flesh to eat? What would happen if he and Zoë followed them instead of killing them?

Another *ganga* dropped like a stone and Quent smiled in spite of himself.

Very elegant and precise. But watch this.

Moving through the house to the next bedroom, he found a nearly glassless window, and that just beyond was the roof of a garage. The *gangas* trundled along below. Still smiling to himself, Quent carefully crawled through the window. The glass scratched against the side of his jeans, and his boot heel knocked a piece aside, but it didn't cut through, and he stepped onto the garage roof.

Silent, his feet straddling the peak of the roof, he walked along the top, hoping the roof wouldn't give in and he'd go tumbling through . . . but the rest of the structure seemed sound. And he was at the strongest part, at the peak of the trusses. He'd learned all about trusses in Haiti. Quickly, carefully, pulse working harder, adrenaline rushing through him, he got to the end ahead of the zombies.

He lit the edge of the T-shirt that trailed from the neck of the bottle and counted—*one, two, three*—then tossed the little bomb down smack onto the cluster of *gangas*.

Boom!

The explosion lit the area with a flash of yellow light. Definitely enough alcohol to get the job done. *Score.* Quent stood there on the roof, looking down as the smoke cleared. Nothing moved.

Gangas: wasted.

Not elegant or precise, but very, very effective.

And then he heard her. Lord, that woman had a rubbish mouth.

Next thing he knew, she was standing in the street below, amid the zombie remains, hands planted on her hips and glaring up at him.

"What the *fuck* are you doing?" she yelled up.

"Killing *gangas*," he replied, trying not to smile. "A little more efficiently than you."

"You damned idiot! Where's your bandanna? There you are, with the moonlight shining on your golden hair for anyone to see."

"You're just pissed that I took them all out at one time."

"Fuck you."

He shook his head, still grinning. *If you insist.* Then the smile faded as he remembered. He was yanked at her.

No, indeed, that wouldn't be happening any time soon. He might want to put his hands all over her, but he wasn't about to do it. The desire had gone, that deep tug that made him ravenous for her. Oh, yeah, he still admired her sleek body, those full lips, those long legs, but it was different.

He knew every part of her, what she smelled like, tasted like, how smooth her skin was, the two little marks on her belly, the scar on her hip. That she liked his mouth on her neck, and the way to bring her to the edge by kissing her breasts just the right way. He'd heard her moan his name as if she were dying, felt her nails down his skin and held her while she slept. He knew how she looked when she let it go and gave herself up into orgasm . . . that most intimate, most vulnerable of moments. Heartbreakingly beautiful.

But he didn't *know* her.

He thought he'd begun to know her, to understand her . . . and then she'd left him this morning. And somehow, that doused the fire that had burned between them. *In* him, whenever he thought of her.

He wanted her, but he no longer *wanted* her. Needed her.

Craved her.

He looked away, out over the dark night. From here on the roof, he could see for miles over the trees and shadowy humps of ravaged twenty-first-century America.

And then he saw something else . . . lights. Moving. Two of them, in the distance.

Headlights.

CHAPTER 7

"Where do they come from?" Quent asked.

"The *gangas*?" Zoë grabbed onto the handle of the truck door and tried to calm her pounding heart.

She wasn't certain if her pulse was going crazy because of this harrowing ride—fast, in the dark, with their headlights half covered so as not to draw attention to their approach—or because she might actually find Raul Marck again. Kill the damn bastard at last.

Quent had seen a pair of headlights moving slowly about five miles away, and they'd wasted no time in packing up and going after them. If it wasn't Marck, it was someone just as dangerous.

"Yeah. Where do they go during the day? If they sleep in dark places to stay away from the sunlight, why don't you just attack them then, during the day? Why put yourself in danger by stalking them at night?"

Zoë gasped and squeezed her eyes closed as a large object suddenly appeared in front of them. Quent swerved the truck and she slammed into the door, then back toward the center of the seat as he straightened out, the tires making weird noises on the dirt.

If I make it out of this fucking truck alive, I'm going to kiss the damned ground. I'm going to fucking make out with the dirt and roll in the grass and wrap myself in leaves and wildflowers.

Driving at night, much faster than they should, the only illumination being a half moon and the obscured headlights . . . *He's omigod crazy. He's going to kill both of us.*

She opened her eyes and saw a row of buildings ahead of them, and the hint of orange zombie eyes in the distance, but, fortunately, no large obstacles in their path.

Then she recalled his question. "Lots of times, they come from the water. The *gangas*. When the sun starts to come up, they head for the nearest body of water and just fucking walk into it—all the way in, till they disappear. Then when the sun sets, they come back out. Water, swampland, even caves or something. Dark buildings. But mostly water. They always head west when the sun starts to go down—toward the ocean."

"You never follow them? Try to catch them?"

She shrugged and braved a look back out the front window. "A few times, I found some in a building and got off some shots. When I come across *gangas*, there are no survivors when I'm done. If I find them, they're wasted." She stifled a shriek. "Watch *out,* you damned idiot!"

But he seemed nonplussed as he turned to avoid a deep dark shadow, which appeared to be a pit of sorts. A *pit*. That he nearly drove them into. *Crazy-ass idiot.*

"This is not nearly as bad as driving in Peru. At least the truck has doors."

"Where? No damn *doors*?" Zoë shook the handle to make sure the door was still attached.

"Peru." He looked at her, as if waiting for some sort of reaction. "Near Machu Picchu. Ever heard of it?"

"Watch where you're going!" she shouted. "Don't fucking look at *me*!"

"But you're such a pleasure to look at," he said, with that note in his voice that made her go soft inside. It had been missing for a while—that smooth, silky way he looked at or spoke to her.

But there it was . . , for a minute at least. And then she saw his mouth settle and his full lips tighten as he focused his attention on the terrain in front of them.

"Won't they hear us coming?" she asked.

He nodded. "They definitely might. I'll have to slow down a little when we get close, but at some point, we take the chance of being seen, or we have to get out and try and follow on foot."

On foot sounds like a plan.

"In fact, I'm going to stop up here and climb that tree, see if I can still see them. We've got to be closer, we were going pretty fast."

No fucking shit.

Before Zoë could respond, he slammed his foot down and the truck jerked and swerved, skidding over the bumpy ground until it stopped. By the time she'd removed her heart from her throat, the idiot had gotten out and was climbing the tree.

Damn. He was almost as fast as she was, and smooth, too, and before she knew it, he was out of sight among the leafy branches. They shivered and shone in the moonlight, and then Quent's silhouette erupted from near the top, his head forming an awkward hump in nature's handiwork.

Nature's handiwork? Fuck, that sounds like something Naanaa would say. What the hell is wrong with me, thinking ass-crap shit like that?

Rolling her eyes to herself, Zoë opened the truck door and grabbed her bow. Those *ganga* eyes had been about a mile away . . . she itched to run over and take a few out. But first, she'd better get an update from Tarzan.

"What do you see?" she called up.

"Nothing. Bloody nothing." His annoyance was evident. The tree branches began to shake as he clambered back down.

"Dammit! Are you fucking *sure*?" Zoë felt her hope drain away. "I thought you knew where they were. You said you saw the landmarks! Where the hell did they go?"

"Yeah, I did. We're almost to where I saw them—see that spire over there? That skinny thing, looks like it was from a church? They were just to the left—east—of that when I saw the lights. Now I don't see anything. Anywhere."

"They're gone, dammit." She kicked a stone and it flew through the air, clanging into the side of the truck. She hoped it made a big dent in the stupid vehicle.

Quent dropped from the tree, and landed lightly on the ground next to her. His blond hair—uncovered, of course—shone in the moonlight, thick and unruly. She couldn't help admire his form for just a moment: those broad, square shoulders, covered by a light shirt that buttoned down the front but still revealed a bit of golden-brown hair springing from the vee. The shirt was tucked into belted, loose pants with many pockets, and some of them seemed to sag with a variety of contents. Who knew what he had in there?

"We're going to drive to where I saw the headlights, and spend the night there. In the morning, we'll look for tracks again," he said, walking past her to climb back into the vehicle. "You coming?" That soft note that had been in his voice was gone, and it was back to cool, emotionless tones, shaking her from the moment of admiration.

Who the hell put you in charge? she wanted to say.

But she couldn't argue with his logic. *Damn it.*

Zoë climbed in, despite the fact she hadn't kissed or otherwise made out with the ground, and she was damned overdue to nail some *gangas.* "Drive that way so I can take out a few of those zombs," she said, pointing to where she'd seen the orange glows.

"Maybe I should walk over there and let them take me . . . maybe they know where the truck went," Quent said. In the mean time, wonder of wonders, he'd done as she'd ordered and turned in the direction she indicated.

"As tempting as the idea of you as zombie bait might be," she said, "I'd just as soon have you drive up after them and let me shoot. I could get off quite a few the way you fucking drive."

"I thought I drove too erratically," he said, and beneath the steering wheel, his leg moved sharply. The truck surged forward and Zoë found herself grabbing on to the seat again.

Damn him. "You do, and you also drive too fast. It's the speed that would give me a chance to nail a bunch of them before they got away, not the damn swerving and jerking."

"Hold on," he said grimly.

"I already am damned holding on," she managed to retort, somewhat steadily as he swerved yet again. This time, the truck actually fucking *tipped* to the side, on two wheels, and she gave a little squeaky cry and squeezed her eyes shut. *"Stop that!"*

She swore she heard an evil little laugh, but when

she managed to open her eyes and glance at his profile, he seemed as sober and annoyed as he'd been a minute ago.

"So why'd you do it?" he asked, glancing at her, and she saw that his face had definitely set again.

"Do what?"

"Sneak out of bed and out of my room."

Zoë didn't answer right away. "Because I didn't want a liability slowing me down."

"Bugger that. You know I'm not a fucking liability."

"Oh, yeah? How do I know that? All I know of you is how goddamned hot you are in the sack," she flared back. Then snapped her mouth shut.

This, *this*, was what happened when you spent most of your damned life alone. When you meet someone you can talk to, you fucking *talk too much*.

"So I'm hot in the sack?"

She cast him a withering look that she knew he couldn't see. "Don't be an idiot."

"Then why, Zoë? You could at least tell me why. The truth. Why did you leave, again, after we agreed that I'd go with you?"

"We didn't agree, Quent. *You* insisted, and blackmailed me into it, threatening me and making up asscrap reasons why you should come." *Reasons that I fell for too damn easily.*

"So you'd really rather be alone." His voice sounded flat and cold over the rumble of the engine.

Her palms had gone damp, making it harder to hold on to her bow and the door handle. *Why are you asking me these damned questions? I don't want to talk about this.*

Then she saw the orange eyes. *Saved.* "Right there,

Quent!" She pointed, and began to roll down her window—a practice she'd learned during the hot afternoon. "Get closer."

He did as she asked, and she whipped an arrow out of the quiver that she held between her knees. The truck jounced and bounced, making it more difficult for her to lodge the arrow into place . . . but she had a close view.

"Stop for a sec," she said, and hardly noticed when he slammed the vehicle to a halt. They were only yards away from the *gangas*, who had turned to look toward them when the truck rolled up. Probably thought she was Raul Marck or another bounty hunter. *Boulderheads*.

She aimed at the nearest *ganga*, sitting on the edge of the open window, and for a moment realized how damned handy having a vehicle was. Then she drew back the bowstring and let the arrow go.

The sound of its flight, the smooth *twang* and ensuing *swish* comforted her—but when the point slammed into the forehead of the nearest *ganga*, that was when Zoë felt the real rush. Accomplishment.

One less zombie to tear into a human.

She hadn't noticed Quent moving around next to her, but just as she nocked her next arrow in place, easing herself out of the window even more fully, he ordered, "Get in!"

She ducked back into the truck, whirling in her seat, just as the vehicle lurched into action. "What the hell?" she shouted, angry that he'd interrupted her aim.

Then she saw that, as he drove, he was half standing, head partly out of the vehicle. His left hand whipped up and out of the window next to him, and flung something over the top of the truck toward the *gangas*.

Boom!

The explosion shook the ground, sending zombies sprawling and debris flying.

And off they barreled, much too fast, jouncing almost out of control. Zoë bit back a scream as the truck went into a terrifying skid, missing a tree by a whisker, then swerving narrowly past a large rusted-out metal thing.

"There," he said, glancing at her now that he was settled back on his ass. He had a bit of a smile on his face, *damn him*, and seemed as unruffled as a sleeping hen. "That's the lot of them. Where to now?"

Zoë pushed back into her seat, grinding her teeth. *Fucking show-off.* Sure, she could have picked off the monsters one by one, used five or six arrows that she'd have to try and retrieve, and taken ten minutes to do so . . . or she could let him use his fancy ass-crap explosives and do it all at once.

He looked at her again. "When we need it done stealthily or precisely, your way is the way. But you have to admit, mine is more efficient."

"Bite me."

That was his cue to dip his voice lower and say, *Just tell me where, luv.*

But he didn't. Instead, he looked at her again and said, "I'm thinking we should head to where I saw the headlights. We can stay there and check things out in the morning, or drive on tonight and look for more *gangas.*"

She glared into the darkness. Part of her absolutely had to know how he made those bombs because, *damn him,* he was right. Again.

The other part of her was pissed off because she knew he was annoying her on purpose. And another part of her was . . . well, hurt.

Deep inside. She felt oddly empty and lost. Simply because he wasn't flirting with her? Because he'd chilled?

And suddenly, she was *tired*. Sleep would be good—they'd been going since dawn and it was well past midnight. Her skin prickled when she thought of settling down to sleep. With Quent. Her belly tingled and shifted and her heart picked up speed. With Quent . . . warm and familiar. And *safe*.

She rerouted her thoughts. "They could have turned off their truck lights. Stopped for the night. They might still be there."

Quent nodded. "Right. So we'll want to approach on foot. Park some distance away."

They drove on in silence, with Zoë only closing her eyes about a third of the time, instead of half the time. And her fingers actually loosened their grip on occasion. Progress.

"I'm parking here," Quent said as they approached a row of dilapidated houses.

Zoë agreed with his choice: it was dark and shadowy, and when he pulled the vehicle in between two close buildings, lining it up near one of them and behind a thick bush, she agreed that no one would see it.

But when she reached to open her door, he moved, leaning over to stop her with a hand on the handle. "Wait."

She turned and he was close. Very close. His arm, bare where the sleeve was rolled up to hug his substantial bicep, brushed her belly. Her pulse stuttered for some ridiculous reason, and it occurred to her, suddenly, absurdly, that this was the longest time they'd spent together *not* rolling around in bed, or slamming against the wall or sliding skin to skin in the shower.

And now, here he was. So close she could feel the gentle warmth of his breath and see the faintest outline of his cheek, tufts of tousled hair. But she couldn't make out his expression at all. He removed his arm and settled back in his seat.

"Be careful, Zoë," he said. "Just . . . take care."

Then he turned away. She released her breath and swallowed her heart back into place.

By the time she did that, he'd already slipped out of the truck and closed his door quietly. She followed suit, bow in hand, pack and quiver over her shoulders, and noted that he also had his pack, and that he carried something else. The moonlight gleamed on it and she saw that it was as long as one of her legs, and slender, metallic. An iron or metal pipe of some sort.

She nodded to herself. Guy wasn't as good with a bow as she was, he had to have something to smash *ganga* brains. *Hot damn. Wouldn't mind seeing him in action with that, muscles bulging and shifting, all sleek and sweaty.*

Definitely not a liability, despite what she'd said earlier. Not the man who listened to her telling the horror of her family's massacre and seemed to care, nor the one who ate her stew and enjoyed it, nor the one who had just as many—well, almost as many—right ideas about how to do this as she did. And that didn't include what he could do with his hands and mouth and that hot-damn-and-holy-shit fine body.

They walked about two miles, sticking close to shadows and listening for the sounds of *ganga* moans, voices, or even the spine-chilling rumble of a vehicle.

But the night was silent other than nature's noise: the distant baying of wolves, the scuffle of nocturnal animals, the low hoot of an owl. The occasional bat dipped and dove soundlessly above them.

Zoë smelled them before she heard them. *Gangas*.

Quent held out an arm to stop her at the same moment, and she looked up at him. Their eyes met and he nodded. Zoë gestured to the right, where the shadows spread long and dark, and he nodded again.

As she slipped toward them, she realized how easy that had been. How . . . natural. Exchanging wordless glances, intent. Communicating with a partner.

And then she shoved it away, for the *gangas* were there, suddenly, spilling out of a building in front of them. As if they'd been in wait. The creatures smelled, and their graying flesh sagged from the burning orange eyes and open, groaning mouths.

But they weren't saying *ruu-uuthhhh* as they had for as long as she remembered. They were sighing and moaning something like *duu-aaane . . . duuu-vaane . . . leee . . . vaaane . . .*

Ten of the creatures, staggering toward them with surprising speed. And even a bit of agility. Without a glance at Quent, Zoë fit an arrow and shot.

Right between the eyes. The *ganga* stumbled, knocking into a companion, and they both fell over in a pile of awkward legs and flailing arms. A cool smile tugged at her lips as she whipped another arrow from her quiver and let it fly.

By this time, the zombies had advanced rather quickly, again, surprising her, and Zoë realized with a start that she needed to move . . . back. Normally, she was up and out of sight of the monsters—she'd learned the importance of that early on—but this time, they'd taken her by surprise. Meeting them on their level wasn't quite as simple as shooting from a tree branch or rooftop.

Next to her, Quent swung the metal pipe at one of the creatures—who towered over him by several feet—and managed to smash the *ganga* in the side of the head. Its constant *duuu-vaaane* choked off, then continued as the monster lunged at its attacker. Ducking beneath the creature's groping hand, Zoë's blond genius slipped around and behind the staggering *ganga* and brought the pipe down again, on the top of his head.

The zombie dropped like a stone, and Quent jumped out of its way, winging his pipe with a powerful stroke at another monster that surged forward on uncoordinated legs. The weapon struck its arm, and the limb went flying through the air, yet that didn't slow its owner. But Quent was more agile and dodged out of the way, jumping over a fallen tree trunk. The creature followed, stumbled into the tree and lost his balance. Quent brought his weapon down on top of the creature's head with an audible crack.

Zoë reached for a third arrow, and realized she was too close to get a good aim. *Holy shit, are these zombies on some sort of drug?* Moving faster, groaning differently . . . She ran back a few steps as she fit it into place, and yelled, "Where the hell are your fancy bombs now?"

"Need a minute to dig one out," he shouted back, whaling on a duo of advancing zombies. "Can you hold them off?" *Damn.* He seemed much too fucking cool and calm.

But then, he was in good hands and he knew it.

"No sweat," she said, sending her arrow flying.

She saw Quent streak to the side of an oncoming *ganga*, then slip around a rusted out car next to a nearby building. The vehicle would provide no protection other than a momentary shield, but hopefully it would be enough time for him to dig out his explosives.

Her pulse pounded and adrenaline rushed through her as Zoë shot an arrow into the back of the zombie that had gone after Quent. The arrow lodged in his skull and he staggered, then fell. *Four for four. Hot damn.*

There were three or four *gangas* left, and Zoë spun, ready to skewer a fifth and saw that the leader had tripped over one of its fallen comrades, slowing them down for a moment. She was just about to shout at Quent not to waste an explosive, that she could finish the last three off, when she saw something in the dark.

Silhouettes . . . two, no, three . . . inside the window beyond where he crouched. Inside was dimly lit, as if a low light burned to illuminate the interior for humans.

She nocked yet another arrow, splitting her attention between the sparser group of *gangas* and the tableau inside as she ducked behind a big metal thing called a Dumpster. Whatever the hell it was, it gave her a moment to hide from the boulderheads . . . and to get a better look inside that window.

People hiding in the building? Or more *gangas*? Quent was busy, and far enough away from whatever it was. She didn't want to distract him . . . or draw attention to where he stooped next to the car.

She looked again, peering around the corner of the rusted metal thing. Inside the window—they were definitely humans, too short to be zombies. No burning orange eyes. Two taller ones, a shorter one.

She looked back at the *gangas* and let her arrow fly at the nearest one, which happened to be much too near for comfort. The metal bolt slammed right into its decaying nose. *Score!*

Zoë reached back into her quiver and realized she was low on arrows—only another four left, she guessed, in that brief moment. *Crap.* As she pulled one out, she looked again toward the window. *Holy shit!* The figures inside were shifting around and she saw a small, moving crystal that glowed. Right on the front of one of the people.

A Stranger! She peered at the dark, excitement and dread rushing through her. Possibly with Raul Marck? Could she be that damned lucky? Her mind divided as she considered the situation and settled an arrow once more. Then she looked up.

Shit! The *ganga* was right there, right in front of the Dumpster. *Fuck.*

"Quent!" she shouted, and realized suddenly that another zombie had come around the other way. Then, as Quent rose from his hunkered position, she saw the bottle in his hand. "Wait!" she shouted, suddenly envisioning the bomb landing in front of her—

She tripped as she moved back, *dammit*, tumbling back onto the ground, still clutching the bow. Son of a bitch, her breath was knocked out and the next thing she knew one of those massive gray hands was reaching for her, swiping at her. Strong, reeking fingers closed over her shoulder, but she stabbed up with the arrow in her hand, shoving it right into the orange eye.

Something plopped down on her, something putrid and sticky and wet and she rolled away just as the monster shuddered, then started its slow fall. Zoë scrambled to her feet just in time to see Quent as he ran up behind the last of the *gangas*.

It was a breathtaking moment, watching his gloved

hands slam the metal pipe into the back of the zombie, then shifting and dodging, fleet of foot, around and behind, battering the confused monster. Perhaps he was showing off a bit, taking his time finishing off the creature, but Zoë didn't care. He was fast and powerful, and watching him made her all weak-kneed. It was only a moment before the last of their attackers slumped to the ground, his brains spilling onto the dirt.

"You okay?" Quent asked, coming over to her. "What's that on your face?"

"Zombie brain," she said, using the hem of her tank top to wipe at a last dot of the glistening junk on her cheek. Then she pulled at his shirt, tugging him down behind the Dumpster and pointed. "In that building. I saw three people—one of them is a Stranger. I saw the crystal glowing."

"Raul Marck too?"

"I sure as hell hope," she said. "They must know we're here. That we've beaten off the *gangas*."

"Bet they heard us coming and set them out after us. They're probably long gone."

Zoë nodded. She'd come to the same conclusion. She opened her mouth to speak, then realized he was looking at her. In the low light, in this proximity, she could make out the heat in his eyes—the same avidity that always made her belly drop to her knees, and her female parts tingle. Her breath caught and she knew her voice came out husky. "What?"

"Watching you—how fast, and smooth and cool and damn *good* you are—makes me forget how yanked I am at you for sneaking off this morning. I want to tear off your clothes and shag the hell out of you, luv. Right here."

Shag? Whatever that was, it sounded good to her.

She smiled, unable to keep back the rush of pleasure and lust from his words. "Anytime, blondie."

His sexy lips twitched and gave her the urge to taste them. "I'd be tempted to kiss you if you didn't have zombie brains on your face."

"Comes with the job," she said. And she stood, pulling him up to peer out from behind the Dumpster. "Do you see them?" Through the window, she saw the same faint cast of light, but no longer any moving silhouettes.

"Nothing. Let's go check it out." He led the way, and she allowed him, slipping from the shadow of the hulking metal thing to the car near which he'd stooped. She noticed that, while he no longer had the metal pipe in his gloved hand, he had something better. A gun.

"Where'd you get that?" she whispered. "Does it work?" Working firearms were as rare as running vehicles, and mostly found in the possession of Strangers. Zoë had found a few rusted-out guns over the years, but only one that worked—and by the time she figured out how to use it, she'd wasted all the bullets. And couldn't find anymore.

"My bag. Of course it works."

"Then why the hell didn't you use it on the *gangas*?"

"I liked watching you in action. Besides," he added, very close to her ear, "it's better for other types of threats."

Right.

They'd sneaked across the way, Zoë casting a look at the array of dead *gangas* still sporting her arrows. She didn't have time to grab them back now, but there were only three left in her quiver. That was a lot of work sitting out there, encrusted with zombie brains.

She and Quent approached the broken window. The world was silent, but the hair on Zoë's neck prickled and she sensed . . . something. They were around somewhere . . . the Stranger. Raul Marck. It had to be him. She hoped it was him.

Quent tensed next to her, and she knew he felt it too. Warm and sturdy, his arm shifted as he turned to look behind them.

Nothing. Neither of them saw anything. No unusual sounds. And even the sense that someone watched and waited eased.

"I'm going in," Quent said, gesturing to the window. "Coming? Or want to stand guard?"

Zoë, surprised that he'd even thought to ask her opinion—she wouldn't have—considered. Separating was a good and bad idea—she could watch from here, and if they were separated, they couldn't be trapped together. She could see what he was doing inside while keeping a watch out here . . . "Go." And maybe she'd have a chance to dash over and pull a few arrows from scrambled brains.

She watched Quent climb through the window, the gun gleaming briefly in his hand before he slipped into shadow. Standing near the building, she looked around and listened, and sniffed for *gangas*. Nothing.

"Nothing," Quent called softly from the other side of the wall.

Zoë nodded and, still holding her bow with an arrow in place, moved toward the zombie carnage a few yards away. She glanced back toward the window, saw Quent moving around, and bent to pluck up an arrow.

When she pulled it free and flung the last bit of glop aside, she happened to look past another old car down to her right . . . and saw him. Standing no more than a long arrow flight away. His moonbeam hair, brushed back from the gaunt face that haunted her dreams, his slender, skeletal body.

He didn't notice her at first; she was hidden by the rusted-out vehicle. He faced another person—smaller, slighter, and with a crystal glow in his chest. Now Zoë heard the soft sounds of flesh and bone against flesh and bone accompanied by quiet grunts of exertion as the two men fought.

Heart pounding, Zoë looked toward the window where Quent was still moving around inside, and tried to catch his attention. She could shoot her arrow in there, but that would be a waste. Instead, she scooped up a rock and tossed it toward the open window, then turned her attention back. The smaller man—the Elite—seemed to be struggling with Raul Marck.

Where's the third guy?

But their battle or argument seemed a good enough reason to move in. To fix her aim on the man who'd taken her life. She duck-walked closer, staying low and quiet, and watching as the Elite swung out with something gleaming, slicing at Zoë's own damn target.

No you don't! He's fucking mine!

She nocked the bow . . . he was a little too far away. This shot had to count.

The Elite's arm had moved sharply and Zoë saw Raul stumble back a little, but then lunge for his opponent again.

Something moved behind her, a shadow slinked in her peripheral vision, and she nearly fainted before she saw the hint of blond hair and realized it was Quent. He must have interpreted her signal and come out to join her.

Still a few yards away, he settled into the shadows too. Zoë ignored him. She had to. *You'd just shoot him in cold blood?*

Fuck yeah.

She inched closer, settled the arrow in place, holding her breath hoping that Raul was too distracted with his own battle to notice that she was sneaking up on him. The arrow fit nicely.

She was close enough . . . she could see blood streaming from Raul's arm, and just as she lifted the bow, drew in a deep breath, the smaller man sliced again at Raul. Stumbling back, Zoë's nemesis gave a loud cry as the smaller man took off into the dark.

Zoë looked in Quent's direction, but he'd sunk deeper into the shadow and she could no longer see him. She looked back at her target, who'd moved closer. Now he was near enough that she could see the collar of his shirt, the flipped-up cuffs of his sleeves, and the dark stain spreading over his shirt.

Close enough that her shot would count.

She drew back on the bowstring, bringing it past her ear, steady . . . eyes clear and cold.

Don't you want to know why?

It doesn't matter. He took everything from me.

And she released the arrow.

It was a beautiful day today, and the first one in months that I have truly felt lucky to be alive.

The seeds I managed to save and to find, and the cuttings salvaged from my garden and other places have found their homes at last. If all goes well, we will have a large garden of vegetables and fruits, herbs and even some spices.

Devi watched me dig in the soil with that affectionate, bemused smile on his face, and I was happy to feel its warmth once again. He has not smiled in many months. Nor have I.

But the sun was alive and steady today, and we have had much more rain than the desert has in the past. Greenery has begun to sprout everywhere, and even a limited array of flowers are budding.

Perhaps I should note that six weeks ago, Devi, James, and I packed everything we could into three large vehicles (again, I cannot quite call them stolen, for the Babishes and the Ytrezes and the Gladwins no longer have need of anything) and drove to the southeast, hoping to find other survivors.

Drive is not the most accurate of terms for the sort of all-terrain traveling we did, for the quakes and storms wreaked havoc on the roads and signs and bridges.

After two days of driving a total of fifty miles, stopping often to look for signs of life, we did find a group of five living in a restaurant and we were invited to stay with them. Devi and I found a small house that had sustained little damage and we have taken it as our own.

The high school's football field has become our farmland.

—from the diary of Mangala Kapoor

CHAPTER 8

Still inside the building, Quent watched from the shadows as Zoë raised her bow. She'd hardly taken her eyes from the slight, white-haired man struggling with another slender figure, about thirty meters away. An arrow fit into place, and he could barely make out the determined expression on her face.

She's going to do it.

For a moment, he thought about stopping her—about stepping out from the shadows and drawing attention to himself, exposing their presence. To keep her from that burden of taking a man's life, and to have his own chance to pummel the information he wanted to get from Marck. How to find Fielding. Where to go.

From what Quent had heard about Raul Marck—not only from Zoë, but also from Jade, who'd known the bounty hunter during her captivity by the Strangers—it would be no loss to this world for such a mercenary, ruthless man to be killed. No worse than snipers taking out terrorists before they blew up another car or nightclub.

No worse than destroying the man who'd help annihilate the human race.

But . . . Zoë. Despite her acerbic manner and strength, she had a fragility about her that he'd only recently begun to recognize. Something under the surface, something that lurked deep in her eyes.

Something he'd noticed when he'd looked at her when they weren't dusting up the sheets together.

At that moment, Quent saw a shadow move, slinking from beyond where Zoë crouched, creeping up to the tree just behind her. A cold chill washed over him before he submerged the rush of fear, then he steadied when he saw that the newcomer's hands were empty. Tightening his fingers around the handle of his own gun, feeling the comfort of its trigger, he eased himself closer.

Zoë pulled back on the bowstring, steady and intent as, meters away, Raul Marck cried out from what looked like the stab of a knife, somewhere vital. His opponent took the opportunity to stagger into the darkness, but not before Quent saw the hint of a faint glow near his shoulder. An Elite, fighting with Raul Marck?

A soft *thwang* broke the night and the sleek arrow shot through the air.

And just as it left her bow, the shadow behind her moved. A split second too late, coming out of the darkness more quickly than Quent anticipated.

She whirled at the sound, hand going automatically to the quiver over her shoulder and whipping out a new bolt. But she wasn't fast enough, and the imposing man stood barely a yard away. Pointing a gun at her that he hadn't had in his hand a moment earlier.

Aw, hell.

Quent edged along the darkness, moving closer so he could get a good aim, as the newcomer spoke. "You again. Hunting for my father."

Even in the dark, Quent could see the cold look she aimed at him. "A little damned late, weren't you, Ian?" She lowered her bow a trifle. "Or was that the way you planned it?"

Quent glanced along the street and saw the dark shadow of Raul Marck on the ground. Unmoving. Even from his distance, he could see a glistening pool on the man's skin and ground. If not dead, then very close.

Ian Marck laughed. "Ah, Zoë. You're about the coldest bitch I've ever met."

She laughed back. Just as meanly. "Worse than Remy? She lured you in, then took you down. I saw it. *She's* a cold bitch. At least I never fuck and run."

Oh, really? I must have imagined your streaking out of my bed so fast the sheets fluttered. The anger that had slipped into admiration and lust when he saw her fighting off the *gangas* now came back in full force.

Ian seemed surprised at her comment, but he also appeared to know what she was talking about. "So that *was* you, two nights ago." Whatever had happened, the reference pissed him off. He stepped closer, gun gleaming in the moonlight as he gestured to her bow. "Put that down."

"And you'll want to do the same," Quent said, stepping into view, the barrel of his gun aimed at Ian.

The man didn't move, barely leveled a glance in his direction as his lips formed a silent, but very obvious, *fuck*. "What happened to traveling alone?" This comment was still directed at Zoë.

"More the fool if you believe everything that comes out of a woman's mouth," Quent said icily. *At least I never fuck and run.* Right, that was going to need some pointed discussion later. "You going to put that down, or am I going to have to get serious?" He could mention the fact that he'd been a champ sharpshooter at the Guesting Country Club, but it wouldn't mean dick to this guy.

"What are you going to do? Shoot me?"

"Not a bad idea."

Ian didn't waver, still pointing his gun at Zoë. "Well, I'm not going to shoot her."

"Pardon me if I express my disbelief," Quent said, tightening his fingers on the grip. He'd never shot, let alone aimed, a firearm at another person . . . but he knew that if he had to, he could squeeze one off without remorse.

"I've had ample opportunity to shoot if I wanted to," Ian replied. "I just want her to put the damned bow down."

"You're more worried about the bow than the bullet I'm threatening to put into your head?"

Ian sent him a quick, humorless smile. "Yeah, because she's such—"

"Oh, for fuck's sake," Zoë said. And she lowered her bow, dropping the arrow over her shoulder, back into the quiver. "Put the damned thing away, Ian. Your father's dead, and you didn't have to do it yourself. You should be kissing my ass instead of pointing a fucking gun at me."

"Not as if you haven't tried to get me there, Zoë darling," Ian replied dryly. But then he lowered his weapon as Zoë gave a disgusted snort. "Perhaps I do owe you a bit of gratitude." He looked at Zoë, continuing to ignore Quent. "He's really gone."

"And so's your bounty," Zoë said. Quent noticed that her eyes seemed wide. Was she in shock that Raul was dead? If she was, nevertheless she still copped an attitude. "Bounty stabbed him and ran off into the night."

Ian shrugged.

"You're not going after the bounty?"

He gave a derisive snort. "That's not my game."

"All right, then. I promise not to shoot you when you walk away. This time."

Ian nodded and a flicker of a smile pulled his lips. "Same here." And without a glance at Quent, who still, by the way, had a gun pointed at the man, he turned and melted into the shadows.

Quent eyed him as he disappeared. "You trust him not to come back and blow us away?"

"Ian? He's pretty fucked-up about now. His father's dead, after all. He just wished he had the balls to do it himself."

Some of us wouldn't have any regrets about destroying our fathers. Yet, Quent had had more than one chance in the past . . . and he'd never taken it. Maybe he and Ian had more in common than one would expect.

"He doesn't have any reason to hurt me—or you—anyway. Now that Raul's dead."

When she started off, he put a hand out to stop her. "What about that other person—the Stranger. The bounty?"

"Not coming back. Trust me. You get away from the Marcks, you don't fucking test your luck and come back." She'd already started to walk toward the unmoving body of Raul Marck, and tossed these last words over her shoulder as if they were gospel.

Not quite as trusting, Quent kept his gun out and his eyes open as he followed her.

But by the time he reached where she crouched next to Raul, he felt a bit more relaxed. Just as he approached, she pulled the arrow from the man's chest with an efficient little twist. It struck him as a bit callous, but then again, he supposed leaving it there was just as bad.

Having no desire to dig through the man's belongings or get close and personal with the dead body, Quent watched as she set the arrow aside and then began to feel through the man's pockets. "Looking for something?" he asked, still scanning the shadows for any orange eyes or any other newcomers.

"He had this purple glowy thing that seemed to control the *gangas*," she said, settling back on her haunches. "Thought I'd try and find it. Or anything else valuable. A gun."

Just then, they heard the low rumble of a vehicle— not from the direction they'd left theirs, but closer. As one, Zoë and Quent ducked into the shadows, shoulders bumping. But as they waited, flat against the cool brick wall of a house, the rumble became fainter . . . as if being driven off into the distance. Quent thought he saw the faintest glimmer of light bouncing beyond the buildings around them.

"Damn," Zoë said. "That was Ian. I was hoping we'd get a chance to search Raul's truck too, but now he's gone."

"Obviously."

She stood and looked down at Raul Marck. "I suppose we shouldn't just leave the body here." *So she did have a heart.* "Although it might be sort of fitting if he ended up being zombie food. After all the other people he's fed to the *gangas*."

She stood for a moment, looking down at the gaunt face and skeletal limbs. "Hard to believe it's finally over. He's finally gone," she whispered. She scrubbed both hands through her hair, making it even more spiky and disheveled, then let them drop heavily to her sides. "I can't believe it." She closed her eyes and her lips moved silently. When she opened her lids again, Quent saw that her eyes glistened a bit.

He helped her move the body, and in the end, they decided to put it in the Dumpster.

"Now what?" he asked, realizing that he wouldn't be adverse to some zees. It had been a long day, and an even longer—and more active—night before.

"Marck's dead. Ian's gone. *Gangas* are nuked. I don't know about you, but since we can't have a pizza, I'm all for a bit of sleep." She turned and started away, leaving Quent to wonder if she meant to disappear again. Or try to.

He wouldn't put it past her to melt into the night once more.

But if that was her eventual plan, at least she wasn't ready to implement it yet. Instead, he saw her stoop to pluck an arrow from the mess of *ganga* remains, and then another and another. Even from a distance, and in the half-light, he saw irregular clumps of zombie brains clinging to the tips.

Zoë flung them away as she gathered up her arrows, and as he approached, he saw her swish the arrow ends in water that had gathered in the veed-in roof of a car. "All right," she said, turning to look at him. "Let's find a place to camp for the night."

"Right," he replied, letting his voice mellow. Totally forgetting—*allowing* himself to forget—his bereft anger at her for trying to trick him early this morning.

After a brief discussion, they decided to drive their humvee somewhere else nearby in case Ian Marck doubled back to find them. "I know a place," Zoë told him, and directed him about five miles east to an old church with broken stained glass windows.

The choir loft would give them a place to settle out of reach of the *gangas*, and he had found a hiding place for the humvee among a cluster of thick lilac bushes. Inside, the space echoed with their voices and the scuffle of footsteps, the skitter of tiny claws. Even faint slithering among the leaves. A few bats darted about, entering and exiting through the bell tower. Stained glass windows lined the sides of the small church, dirty and occasionally intact, allowing blue, red, green, and yellow light to spill inside.

The steps to the choir loft had been destroyed, either by nature or by design, but Zoë had a rope ladder and soon they were both in the dusty, empty loft.

A large circular stained glass window looked down on them from the back wall of the balcony. Light filtered through an image of Jesus tending his flock of sheep. Somehow the idea of being in a church—no matter how old it was, and in what condition—and thinking the thoughts he couldn't help but think as a shadowy Zoë stripped off her tank top and shucked her trousers, made him feel a bit awkward. Especially with the faint outline of Jesus's kind eyes gazing down at him.

Quent wished for a basin of water to dunk his hands, face, and, hell, all of him into. Between the heat of the day and the dust and grime of climbing through old buildings, he felt a little rough. As if reading his mind, Zoë walked over, dressed only in a long (fresh) tank top, and offered him a skin of water. "It's no hot shower, but it's wet," she told him.

By the time he finished his limited ablutions and stripped down to a pair of shorts, Quent noticed that she'd walked over to the edge of the choir loft. She stood at the railing, looking down into the semi-darkness where sagging and splintered rows of pews made irregular shapes.

He wanted to warn her away from the waist-high wall, for fear that she might tumble through a weak spot, but he didn't. If there was one thing he'd come to accept about Zoë, it was that she could take care of herself. She needed no one. She allowed herself to rely on no one.

And she was a stubborn prat.

Oddly enough, he could understand that, because in all the years he lived under his father's roof, he'd learned the same.

"You okay?" he asked, walking up next to her.

She turned to look up at him, her high cheekbones and tousled hair gilded with moonlight, her eyes sober. "I can't believe he's dead. *He's really dead*," she added in a whisper.

Quent nodded, knowing it wasn't the time to speak.

"Now what?" she said, staring back out into the darkness. "Now what the hell do I do?" She tipped her head back a bit, exposing her long, graceful neck as she squeezed her eyes shut. "I've been looking for the bastard for so long . . . and now he's gone. Finally." She swiped roughly at her eyes with a forearm. "I can't believe I did it."

Quent wanted to ask if she regretted her decision, but again he held his tongue. Instead, he reached over and closed his large hand over her smaller one where it rested on the rough railing. So delicate and slender, her fingers. Yet, they were rough and capable.

"Maybe I should have waited. Asked him why," she said bitterly. "Why the hell he chose my family. Why he chose to do it all. But what if I never had another damned chance? And every day that went by meant that more people died because of him. Every day."

She drew in an unsteady breath and he knew she was off on a bloody roll now. He'd just let her go, let her work through it. And listen.

How often did she have someone to listen?

"I can keep hunting *gangas*, of course I can keep hunting them," she continued in a voice that had become rougher, lower. "That's what I'll do. Every night. Even though that fucker's gone, they aren't. There are still so many of them. Damn, I wanted that purple glowing thing." She drew in another breath, then sank into silence.

Quent stood next to her for a long moment, his hand covering hers, waiting. But she seemed to be finished. "Want to get some sleep?" he asked, trying to make the suggestion sound as innocent as he meant it. Which was to say, very innocent.

Because he was a bit shaken inside. *She's lost.*
Just like me.

The second thought, his mental response, stopped him cold. *Lost* didn't begin to describe the way he felt, knowing that he was the progeny of a man who'd helped destroy the world . . . an ugly, frightening world in which Quent was unable to find a foothold. A place to be.

A way to belong.

"I am tired," she said, turning at last from her contemplation of the dark church.

Their eyes met and something shifted deep inside him, like the inner gears of an old watch. Clicked, clunked, settled.

Mouth dry, heart beating radically, Quent reached, sliding his hand along her jaw to curl around the back of her head. Then he eased closer and gathered her mouth gently under his. Her lips, soft and parted, tasted like

Zoë. Just like Zoë, like spice and sweetness, comfort and passion and reality. He closed his eyes, savored her taste and warmth, the tender sensation of an unhurried moment. Their lips melded gently, shifted, then again, as if relearning the mouth of the other. Then he pulled away, gently, from the kiss that simply said *I'm here. I care.*

She had placed her hands flat on his bare chest during the kiss, and now she removed them as she stepped away and turned to where they'd left their packs on the dusty floor. He watched her straighten and recognized the way she pulled back inside her crusty shell, behind the rough shield.

He wondered how long it would be before he could coax her out again. And if she would be different now—more brittle. Or would she be softer?

Try as he might, he couldn't imagine a kinder, gentler Zoë.

And, a short time later as Quent lay next to her on a slender, thin pallet, he looked up at the rafters as they became more distinct with the sunrise, and realized he and Zoë had been together for more than twenty-four hours with nothing more happening between them than a kiss.

Zoë shifted next to him, her breathing steady and deep. Clearly sleeping, somehow able to put aside all that had happened and slip into restfulness while he could not. But despite the low throb of desire he felt, lying next to her slender curves and feeling the brush of her hair, Quent realized he was . . . content.

Yes, that was the word. Content. Settled.

As if the gears that had shifted inside him now worked properly.

CHAPTER 9

Zoë opened her eyes to find yellow and blue light filtering into the room. Quent slept close behind her, so near that she could feel the faint brush of the hair from his legs and the warmth of his torso.

She sat up, her tank clinging and sticky from the heat. If it was this warm, it must be getting close to noon. Hard to tell for sure through the grimy stained glass windows. She sat up, and realized that Raul Marck was dead.

He was *dead*. It was over.

She'd really done it.

The rush of relief, followed by the strangeness of knowing she no longer had to crave revenge on the bastard . . . and that she'd actually killed a man . . . made her feel ass-crap backwards. Weirdly empty. It was a hell of a lot different than scrambling the brains of a boulderheaded monster.

It really was.

She bit her lip, felt a trickle of cold prickle over her. She'd had to do it. One life in exchange for the safety of many. No one else was going to do it; and it wasn't like in the books, where there was a legal system with judge, jury, and prison waiting for someone like Raul Marck.

But now what? The thought made her feel even more ass-crap.

She crawled from beneath the thin blanket, climbing off the flimsy pallet that she kept squashed up into a miniscule size, and stretched. Behind her, Quent breathed slowly and steadily, and she wondered if he was truly sleeping, or if he was waiting for her to make a break for it.

The thought did cross her mind, but one look at him gave her pause, because, *holy crap,* he *was* one gorgeous son-of-a-bitch. His whole golden, honeyish self, tinted a bit of bronze where his skin had been touched by the sun. Those shoulders too—they made her mouth go dry, just looking at the one jutting up from where he slept on his side. Wide and square, with the shadowy dip of his collarbone and a healthy dusting of hair below it. And the smooth bulge of a very capable bicep rising from beneath the blanket.

A shoulder. She was lusting after a freaking *shoulder.*

But that was because she knew exactly what went along with it.

Zoë was even warmer now. Time to find somewhere to wash up. In fact, she was fairly sure a creek ran nearby. She'd stayed in this church once about three years ago, and remembered the area.

A glance at Quent indicated that he was still sleeping, and not for the first time she wondered at how he slept so heavily. She woke at the slightest shift of the wind or sound of a *ganga* groan, but how many times had she risen, dressed, and left without him noticing?

Taking care not to disturb him, but leaving her belongings so that he knew she wasn't leaving again—not that she cared what he thought, but she didn't want the genius to hurt himself trying to chase after her down the rope ladder—Zoë pulled on shorts, grabbed her little

pot of soap, and left the church. Her path led through
a cemetery studded with overgrown gravestones and a
rusted iron fence.

The creek was just where she'd remembered it.
Whether it had been here when the church had a following and the homes nearby were occupied by humans,
she didn't know.

Cool and clear, the water felt like paradise. She
stripped and used the soap to wash her clothes, then
laid them over a bush to dry. Then she waded into the
water, which, upon reflection, she decided was more
of a small river than a creek. Though the current was
gentle, the depth in the center reached to the underside
of her breasts.

She dove under and allowed the flow to shuttle her
along. Allowed the purity of the water to wash away
her weariness and the lingering feeling of emptiness.
When she opened her eyes, she was downstream from
her clothing, and amid the tops of the trees she saw the
bell tower of the church where she and Quent had slept.
And in the other direction, even farther away, she identified just the tip of the other church's spire, near which
Quent had seen the truck headlights last night.

Zoë flipped onto her belly and swam easily upstream,
enjoying the feel of her long muscles stretching against
the gentle pull of the water. She passed the bush where
her clothes rested and her heart skipped a little beat
when she saw that Quent had arrived and was prepar-
ing to join her.

Smiling to herself, she pretended to ignore him and
arced under. Swimming even farther upstream beneath
the water, she imagined the feel of two slippery bodies
twining sleekly under the warm sun. Not a bad way to
start the first day of the rest of her life.

Not a bad way at all.

She emerged from the water and looked back in time to see the smooth arc as Quent dove shallowly into the river, his pale ass gleaming briefly in the sunlight. Zoë smiled to herself and went under again. He'd catch up with her. And that would be half the fun.

She swam with long, strong strokes, playing hard-to-get and keep-away, making progress against the current . . . knowing that the float back would be sweet and relaxing. And as she turned to take an easy breath, she saw it—*them.*

Holy crap. White fingers, half curled and palm up, protruding from the tall grass onshore.

Zoë gasped and nearly choked on a mouthful of water, then struck out toward the hand.

From her very first impression, she knew it didn't belong to someone who was simply taking a nap in the sun. Splashing onto shore, disregarding her nakedness, Zoë hesitated, then walked toward the . . . body.

Yes, indeed, and holy-mother-lode-of-shit, it was a body. Fully clothed, lying half on her side, arms and legs akimbo as if she'd collapsed, or been dropped. Dark hair cascaded over her face, and for a moment, Zoë was afraid it was that Remy woman. Again.

But when she knelt and rolled the woman onto her back, feeling the warmth of her body and the shudder of a breath, the hair fell from her face. Not Remy. The woman's eyelids flickered and her mouth moved as if she meant to speak. Then she half groaned and tried to push Zoë away.

But the woman was weak and could do little but brush against her arm. Her white shirt and pale green trousers were stained with brown splotches—dirt for certain, and, she was all too certain, blood.

"Hello," Zoë demanded, lightly slapping the woman's cheek like they did in movies. "Wake up. Wake the hell up!"

For fuck's sake. Who the hell decided that she was going to be the finder of people in trouble lately? First Quent, then Remy. Now this *not*-dead person.

The woman's shirt buttoned down the front, and Zoë figured she might as well see if any of those blood-stains were from injuries that needed to be staunched. Just as she began to pull the fastenings apart, she saw Quent swimming up from the corner of her eye.

"Hey!" she shouted, waving to him from the shore.

He stopped and turned toward her, and she had a moment—just a moment—to admire the sparkling droplets of water on those big-ass shoulders before she turned back to the injured woman, who had begun to shift beneath her ministrations. She rolled her head around as if in some sort of terrifying nightmare. "No, no . . . I don't *want*—"

Her hair clung to her grimy, sweaty face, and her breathing grew faster, but she didn't attempt to keep Zoë from looking beneath her shirt. Zoë pulled the fabric away and sucked in her breath, lurching back on her bare haunches in the cool grass.

Holy fucking shit. A Stranger.

The crystal, just barely bigger than Zoë's thumbnail, nestled in the soft flesh just below the woman's collarbone. Its edges flush with her skin, the ice blue stone rose in a smooth, shallow dome. Despite the fact that she lay in the shade, the sunlight was too bright for Zoë to tell if the crystal glowed with life or not.

She'd never been this close to an Elite. Her heart began to pound. This must be the bounty that had escaped from the Marcks last night. It had to be.

But she didn't appear to be injured anywhere . . . there were no marks on her skin. What was wrong with her?

"What th— Bloody *hell*!" Quent said when he saw the woman. He squatted next to her and looked at the crystal. "Is she dead?"

"No," Zoë said, and at that moment, the woman shifted again and groaned out something that sounded like "Father." She rolled her head and the obscuring hair fell away, exposing her face.

Quent did stumble back onto his ass. "Oh my God. Bloody *mother-fucking shit*. No fucking way." He scrambled onto his knees, leaning toward her now. "Marley?" He took her by the shoulders and gave the woman a little shake as Zoë began to ease back. "Marley!"

He *knew* her? What the hell kind of name was Marley?

The woman groaned and shifted, and somehow she ended up in Quent's arms. He stood, gathering her up as if she were a rag doll, and the woman was easily as tall as Zoë, but rounder in the ass, and thighs too. Oh, and the boobs. Zoë resisted the urge to frown.

Standing there in the tall grass with his bundle of woman, Quent looked like some feral warrior, all naked and glistening from shoulder down to the flat muscles of his belly, and that wicked cock of his, at the moment fully at ease. His blond hair, dark with water, was slicked back from his face, which still bore the tension of an ass-crap amount of shock and disbelief. And, now, cold anger.

"Let's get her out of here," he said, already starting toward the river. "At least get her somewhere where we can see to her."

"Who is this woman?" Zoë asked as he stepped into the shallow edge of the current. "How the hell do you know a Stranger?"

"Her name's Marley Huvane. *Goddammit*, I should have *known*. I should have fucking *known*." He started walking downstream, avoiding the overgrowth along the edges. "It's a long story," Quent told her, his face tight and angry. And he kept walking.

Now Zoë did frown, despite the fact that she had a perfect view of his tight ass as he manipulated his way in knee-high water, over and between slippery rocks as gracefully as a cat.

The woman began to move in his arms, her legs and arms beginning to struggle. "Water," she murmured, flailing so that her dangling toes skimmed the river. That was what she'd said earlier, not "Father." "Water. Need . . ."

"You want something to drink?" Quent asked, holding his burden with one arm as he scooped up a palmful of water and tried to dribble it into her mouth.

She didn't seem to care, instead she twisted her face away and repeated, "Water."

He just gave you water, dumb-ass.

By now they'd reached the bushes where their clothes lay, and Marley of the assy name and big boobs seemed to have settled down a bit. Quent stepped onto the shore and let her slide to the ground in a gentle heap. No sooner had she been released than Marley began to look toward the rushing river and, determination marking her face, reached for it.

Meanwhile, Zoë snatched up her black tank top and pulled it on. She had no desire to be butt-naked when the wench became aware of her surroundings. Apparently, Quent had the same idea, yanking on a pair of shorts with a variety of pockets as he watched the woman struggle toward the river as if her life depended on it.

"Do you want a drink?" Quent asked again, walking toward her, his T-shirt in his hand.

Marley shook her head. "No . . . water."

Zoë shook her head. *What-the-fuck-ever.* She was ready to ditch them both and get on her way.

There were always *gangas* to be shot. Or, if she got Quent to teach her how to make his fancy-shit bombs, she could blow them all up at one time without any interference from him. Zoë pulled on her panties and cargo pants with stiff fingers.

Marley had reached the river and now simply trailed her fingers in the water. Her eyes closed as she sagged onto the ground, but her movement was one of relief, not exhaustion.

Quent, still shirtless, crouched next to her. "Marley," he said in a voice that was more commanding than coaxing.

The woman opened her eyes, and recoiled, obviously seeing him for the first time. Her eyes bulged and her mouth dropped open. Not a particularly welcoming response, Zoë noted snidely. Especially for the guy who carried you to safety.

"Quent!" she half gasped, half whispered. Marley seemed paralyzed, unable to move except for her chest, which was heaving in shock beneath her open shirt. "Oh my God. My *God*, he told me you were *dead*. All these years . . . he told me you were *dead*!"

To Zoë's surprise, Quent rose to stand over the Elite. His dark expression had not eased and he put his hands on his hips as he looked down at her. "He assumed I was. He certainly didn't attempt to offer me the same arrangement they obviously gave you." His tone slapped flat with revulsion and loathing.

He watched impassively as Marley pulled herself into a more upright position, but even Zoë could see that she was too weak to stand. She kept her hand in the water and Zoë realized it must have something to do with her recovering her strength. She needed to touch water, not drink it?

"Which, by the way," Quent added coldly, "I would have told him to go fuck himself if he did. Then I would have goddamn *killed* him before I let him do what he did." He stepped closer to Marley and pulled her firmly to her feet.

Zoë, who faced down *gangas* single-handedly, nearly recoiled herself when she saw the burning hatred in his eyes.

"My God, Marley. I can barely stand to look at you." His voice shook.

This was a different man. There was nothing about him—his expression, his stance, his voice and attitude—that even hinted at the tenderness she'd seen last night, when he'd covered her hand on the choir loft rail. Nothing that indicated he was the same man who'd kissed her gently, or the man who'd made bawdy jokes to coax her to bed, or the man who'd eye-fucked her at the bar in Envy.

This man was vibrating with restrained power and anger, and at this moment, he alarmed her more than Raul Marck, Ian Marck, or even any of the Strangers she'd ever seen.

Silence stretched for a moment, broken only by what should have been the soothing rush of water and a birdcall.

Then, "Well, screw you, Quent Fielding," Marley spat, shifting away to look up at him. "You don't know a damn thing about what happened and how I came to be here."

Fielding? Zoë's brows knit together.

"Right. I sure as hell would like to hear your story," he said. His voice rang cold. "I'd love to hear your excuse for how you became one of *them*."

Marley swayed a bit and though Quent held on to her, his face showed no sign of sympathy for her weakness. He suddenly turned to look at Zoë, fastening those angry blue-brown eyes on her as if she were on his shit list too.

Well, screw him. She straightened, lifting her chin.

"I need to go somewhere . . . safe. Your hideaway. Wherever the hell you go—"

Zoë was already shaking her head. No fucking way was she bringing this Stranger to her home. "Forget it."

Quent shook his head. "Zoë," he said, his voice marginally—*marginally*—softer. "This is important."

"You said it was a long story," she bristled, throwing his words back in his face. "Too long and complicated for me to understand, I'm certain." Her hands had found their way to her hips and she glared up at him.

"Goddamn it, Zoë. I need to be somewhere hidden for a while." His eyes focused on hers and behind the anger and revulsion, she caught a hint of the man she knew. And with that, a flash of desperation. "This is my—my Raul."

Fuck. Zoë pressed her lips together and ground her teeth. She crossed her arms, glared at Marley, who was staring at Quent's fingers around her arm as if they were a coiled snake, and finally said, "All right. But *she's* blindfolded. You would be too if I knew how to drive one of those things."

"I'm not going anywhere with you," Marley told them. She looked up at Zoë, who recognized not only weariness but a shitload of stubbornness in her eyes.

"I need information, and you're going to give it to me," Quent told her in a matter-of-fact tone. "Figure it's part of your penance for what happened."

Fascinated in spite of herself with their conversation, annoyed as shit that she'd agreed to take Quent to her place, and realizing she was hungry, Zoë turned sharply and started back toward the church. "You two figure it out. I'm leaving."

Quent was relieved when Marley got into the back of the humvee with a minimum of fuss, despite her earlier protestations. He didn't like to think about the fact that he would have had to force her if she hadn't. Didn't particularly care for the thought of restraining a woman . . . except under more pleasurable circumstances.

They had a history together, he and Marley. If he'd ever considered a woman to be a friend as well as a lover—occasional as any of their interactions had been—it would have been Marley Huvane. Yet, that wouldn't have stopped him from doing what he had to do to get her in the vehicle and somewhere where no one would find them—*gangas*, bounty hunters, Strangers—until he got the information he needed.

Like, everything she could tell him about the Elite and the Cult of Atlantis. And most of all, his father.

And Marley, who looked exactly the same as she had fifty years ago, actually seemed ready to recline on the backseat of the truck. Whatever had happened to her, she was weak and exhausted, and, according to Zoë, hungry.

"We're almost there," Zoë said, breaking into his thoughts. They'd been driving for about two hours, perhaps fifteen miles or so.

Quent turned to look at her, realizing that, despite her reluctance to take him to her hideaway, she had agreed to do so—and without understanding why. Without him telling her the story.

Did that mean she was beginning to trust him? Or did she have some other trick up her sleeve?

"Do you want to blindfold me and drive the rest of the way?" he asked. Marley was asleep in the back; he could hear her exhausted little snores. "It's not hard."

Zoë looked at him suspiciously as they bumped along, and he could see the calculation in her eyes. At last, she shook her head. "No, but you're going to teach me how to drive one of these things, and how to make those fancy bombs. I've got work to do."

The implication being that she'd be on her own doing her work.

Quent adjusted his grip on the steering wheel and turned to avoid a tree. Zoë made an annoyed little noise, but at least she wasn't clinging to the handgrip anymore.

"I'll tell you my story," he offered. "If you want to hear."

She inclined her head regally, as if she were doing him a favor by allowing him to tell the tale. For a moment, Quent nearly smiled. What a hell of a woman she was. Then he remembered. He had work to do too.

"It's hard to know where to start, but I'll begin with the basic. Have you heard of Fielding? One of the leaders of the Strangers?"

"Yes. What—are you related? Is he your father?"

Quent nodded. Quick study, she was. "Yes, but here's the hard to believe part. I was born in 1980. Before the Change."

"Before . . . " she began. Her voice trailed off as she seemed to consider. "You're not crystaled. And you sure as fuck don't look eighty years old." Her eyes narrowed and he saw her reach reflexively for her bow. "What, are you a vampire or something?"

Despite his dark thoughts, Quent couldn't hold back a twitch of his lips. "If I were, wouldn't I have tried to drink your blood and turn you into one?"

"Maybe you were just trying to lull me into trusting you before you did," Zoë replied, giving him a sidewise look.

He laughed a little, in spite of himself. "Right. I've certainly been attempting to lull you into something." Then he sobered. "I'm not a vampire, but I don't really have any explanation for why I'm . . . like this."

"Like what? Immortal?"

Quent shook his head. "I'm not immortal."

"How do you know?"

He opened his mouth to answer, then snapped it closed. *Damn good question.* How did one know if they suddenly became immortal? "I'm quite certain I'm not immortal because one of my companions, one of the other men who was in the cave with me, died after we came out." He drew in a breath, knowing that he was approaching the story backwards. But she didn't interrupt, obviously trusting that he would fill in the blanks.

"Fifty years ago, some friends of mine and I went into some caves in an area called Sedona. There was an earthquake or something and we blacked out. When we woke up, it was five decades later and the world had changed."

"So you're really from that time, before the Change?" Zoë's voice was rife with skepticism. "That's how you know her?" She thumb-pointed toward the backseat.

"Yes." He looked over at Zoë again. "But there's more."

"I'm listening."

"Since I've come out of the cave, I've discovered that I have a special power." Quent gave her the details about his psychometric capability. "Which is what had happened when you found me in the alley in Envy that night."

Zoë didn't respond after this speech, and he presumed she was digesting the information. Perhaps for someone who'd grown up with Strangers and *gangas*, having a paranormal ability wasn't so unbelievable.

When she spoke again, it was to give him directions. "Over there, behind that big building with the Star-M on it."

He drove past an old Wal-Mart, the Star-M, as she'd called it, for that was all that remained of the letters on the building.

"You do realize that Marley was the bounty that the Marcks were taking back," she said at last. The words came out reluctantly, as if she were admitting some great fault. "Did you notice that the *gangas* were moaning differently last night? They were saying 'Marley Huvane' not 'Remington Truth.' "

"And why would an Elite be a bounty? Don't they control the bounty hunters and the *gangas*?"

"Not if they're running away from the Strangers. Then they're a bounty," came a rusty voice from the back of the truck.

He looked into the rearview mirror and saw that Marley had sat up. Her thick brown hair, streaked with highlights, was tousled around a face that was still dirty and a bit bruised. How much of their conversation had she heard? Over the rumble of the truck, and with him and Zoë in the front, she probably hadn't heard much.

"Hey," Zoë said, turning around to face her. "Lay down or put a blindfold on." Then, to his surprise, she added, "Don't worry. There's a big stream nearby."

Marley almost smiled, but then she looked back at Quent and her face tightened. "We have a lot to talk about, Quent Fielding. Like how *you* managed to still be alive. Who the hell did you sell *your* soul to?"

Not waiting for him to answer, she lay back down, and there she remained for the next fifteen minutes of navigation beyond the old Wal-Mart and through an old schoolyard to what looked like a ghost town of Main Street USA. Every structure that lined the little street had had a brick façade. Many of them appeared to have been built well before the twenty-first century, perhaps even in the early twentieth. They would have been quaint little shops in their day; he recognized the town for the upscale clientele that it must have attracted, filled with overpriced knickknacks and high-priced martini bars and cafes.

"I don't know where the hell you're going to park this thing," Zoë said. "Stop here."

They were in front of a caved-in storefront. The roof had collapsed in the front, and its neighboring structure—with which it shared a wall—sagged on top of it.

Quent looked around and found a narrow space between buildings that wasn't too overgrown due to low sunlight, and pulled the humvee into it.

"Watch out for Fang," Zoë said as she climbed from the truck. "He's not fond of strangers."

Fang? That sounded ominous.

Quent pocketed the keys and opened the door for Marley, who murmured, "Not exactly the Chateau Marmont, hmm?"

"This way," Zoë said, reappearing from where she'd disappeared behind the collapsed building. Impatience colored her voice and she disappeared again.

As Quent followed, he came around the corner and met Fang. At least, he assumed the mangy-looking wolf with iron gray fur and angry blue eyes was Fang.

The canine growled low in his throat, and although he wasn't blocking the way, he was standing off to the side with his paws planted wide and his ears tipped forward menacingly. A very big deterrent to passing by.

"Quent, what the—oh, there are you are, Fang," Zoë said, reappearing once more. Her voice softened as soon as she noticed the wolf-dog.

Fang glanced at Zoë, but then back at Quent and Marley, as if determining it was more important to detain them than to be petted. But he did give a little flick of the tail when Zoë spoke to him.

"Fang, chill," she said, and walked over to pat him on the head, murmuring softly. But Quent heard her say, "They're not going to bother us for long. I'll make sure of that."

Right, then. He guessed he knew where he stood.

Our little community has become as comfortable and settled as it can. We've established permanent electrical generators by using wind and solar power, which has allowed us to live in a fashion similar to our previous lives with lights and refrigerators and other electronics.

Of course, the power is limited—but we find it easy to live more simply. We are much busier outside, too, growing our food, rebuilding what makes sense to re-build, and searching for any useful items we can find within a few mile radius of the community.

The change in climate is a great blessing, for if it had remained desertlike or become colder and more wintry, many varieties of plants may have been lost to this earth forever. As it is, I continue to seek out new ways to prop-agate everything from nuts to berries to herbs, spices, and vegetables.

Three nights ago, we were awakened by an odd sound. A low, anguished moaning that was almost human. We've become accustomed to the surge in wild animals—everything from wolves and mustangs to es-capees from petting zoos, farms, and even circuses—and so we take care at night.

Devi insisted the sound we heard was not an animal, and he feared someone was injured. But he took a rifle with him and we went outside to look. We saw glow-ing orange eyes that belonged to some tall, bulky crea-ture that was much too large to be a human. And it was sighing or groaning something like *"Ruu-uuth"* over and over again.

I confess, neither of us wished to investigate further. We went back into our house and closed and locked the door.

And even as I write this, I hear the same mournful *"Ruu-uthh"* sound again. I suspect I know what it is, but find it impossible to believe.

—from the diary of Mangala Kapoor

_____

CHAPTER 10

Zoë's hideaway turned out to be inside the collapsed building, with the entrance through a rear courtyard, well tended and flush with herbs and vegetables. Quent walked in and was immediately struck by the amount of light that made its way through the four large windows that Zoë was in the process of uncovering from heavy tarps and simple shutters. Because of the way the little building and its neat garden was situated, hemmed in on all sides by other structures, and its roof buckling, no one would suspect that anyone lived here.

Inside, the asymmetrical space was clean and smelled of cinnamon, of course, and other spices. Bright fabrics draped like canopies from the uneven ceiling and hung on irregular walls—orange and crimson and rust, along with indigo and violet. Large round cushions surprised him, for they mounded in the corner and were so feminine and tidy-looking that he could hardly assimilate this luxurious, cozy place with his hard-assed Zoë. The floor was covered with a variety of braided rugs and what could only be a bed was piled with fur pelts, including that of a white tiger that he knew wasn't faux. In the corner by the cushions sat a low square table and rows of books on neat shelves.

Beads and shells, irregular and random, hung in long tails over an entrance to some other dark space beyond. A bathroom? A kitchen?

"That's my forge," she said, seeing him glance at it. There was an element of pride in her voice. "Where I make my arrows. I cook in there too. Don't need a fire in more than one place."

She walked over and turned on a small light. *Electricity too?*

"You live here alone?" Marley asked, looking around with wide eyes. She was the dingiest, most disheveled part of the room, an anomaly for a woman who had once worn only designer clothes and had a weekly spa appointment.

"Fang and I." Zoë pointed to a corner with one flat cushion and two bowls. More books lined the walls behind it. "He comes and goes, but that's his place."

"This is beautiful. I haven't seen anything this warm and inviting for . . . oh, God, for decades." Marley's voice broke and without being asked, she sank down onto a low, square ottomanlike chair.

"My grandmother was a mechanical engineer," Zoë said, that pride still coloring her voice. "She and her husband survived the Change and they built their own place to live and farm afterward until he died two years later. She taught me how to do everything."

Then she seemed to snap into attention, to realize that she had softened, and her demeanor became more abrupt. "I'm going to get something to eat. Stay here."

Zoë breezed out, but Fang remained, as if to keep an eye on them. Quent, intrigued and more than a little turned on, wandered over to the bookshelves. What would a crusty woman like Zoë read when she came back from her hunting trips? Before he got here, he would have guessed her passion to be . . . well, not books. And if books, then they'd be nonfiction, about wars and weapons and hunting. What was that magazine? *Field & River*?

But after seeing her cozy abode, Quent thought maybe she'd lean toward lusty romance novels. With harems and sheikhs.

He was wrong. Zoë's library consisted mostly of murder mysteries. Many of the books were hardcover, with the dust jackets either missing, or with plastic protectors that identified them as library books. Some were familiar to him, others weren't: Christie, Anne Perry, Kellerman, Cornwell, Robb, even Hammett.

Right. He could definitely see her reading Sam Spade.

Quent noticed multiple copies of many books, and saw that, as was to be expected, they were in a variety of conditions. Water stained, mildewed, warped, missing or obliterated pages. Burned or scorched.

"Some of those were my *naanaa*'s," said Zoë, emerging with a few empty dishes from between the clicking beads. The waft of something that smelled delicious followed her. "Others I found over the years. I was damned pissed when I got to what I thought was the end of one and the last few chapters were unreadable. It took me three fucking months to find another copy, so now I don't start a book until I have more than one of them."

She put the dishes on the low table and Quent had the presence of mind to ask, "Do you want me to help you with anything?"

Zoë looked at him as if contemplating his ability in the kitchen—which, truth be told, was rubbish—and shook her head. "I don't need anyone in my way." And disappeared into the back with a swish of beads.

Surreal. The whole thing was beyond surreal.

Here, in this oasis of warmth and comfort with the brittle, foul-mouthed woman who was literally cooking dinner in the back room as if it were a dinner party. And Marley Huvane, sitting here with a goddamn crystal in her skin.

The reminder brought all of Quent's anger and disappointment rushing back to the front of his mind and he turned to Marley.

"She's a real piece of work," she said with a breath of admiration. "To have put this all together herself. For God's sake, I didn't last two weeks in this wilderness."

Whether or not she meant that as an entrée into the subject that had plagued Quent since he recognized her, he decided to take it as one. "You were running from the Strangers for two weeks?" He tried to keep the snideness from his voice, but wasn't certain he succeeded.

As inconceivable as it had been to know that his father, that hated, narcissistic man, had been a member of the Cult of Atlantis, it was beyond comprehension that Marley had also been one of them.

But she reached for him, her fingers closing over his arm. "Quent, I don't know how you came to be here, what you did to live through it all, but you have to understand. *I didn't want this.* My father didn't tell me what was going to happen. He just told me we were going into hiding because there was a nuclear war." Her voice stretched and thinned and she looked up at him, eyes burning with anger. "When I figured out what happened—that's why I ran away."

He gave a sharp, hard laugh and pulled from her grip. "Fifty years later, you took a stand and ran away?

It took you half a bloody century to realize that your cult destroyed the entire human race so they could live forever? Fifty years to realize that was a mistake?"

"It's not my cult!" she cried. "Dammit, Quent." She lowered her voice, but it still shook with emotion. "How do you think I felt when I finally figured it out? Yes, it took me a long time—almost thirty years before I realized it was all a lie. Everything was a lie. And it took many years for me to confirm my suspicions, and to figure out how to escape."

"Escape?" Quent said, forcing skepticism to flavor his voice. But it was becoming harder to do so. He believed her. He knew Marley, and in spite of his need to lash out, he believed her.

"Yes. Did you think they were just going to let me walk away and tell everyone what I knew? Not that it's that much." She laughed bitterly. "And even then when I got out, I didn't get very far." Her voice turned grim and she looked down at her filthy shirt.

"And the worst thing is . . . " Her voice fell to a pained whisper. "God, Quent . . . I have this damned crystal. This horrible, *horrible* crystal *inside me*. I can't take it out, or I'll die. And if I don't . . . I'll live *forever.*" Tears filled her wide, anguished eyes. "I didn't ask for it, I didn't want it. I simply woke up one day with it in my body."

"That's how they did it?" he asked, horror filtering over him. Horror and renewed revulsion.

She nodded, composing herself as she tucked a lock of hair behind her ear. "I didn't have any idea what was going on. They—my father, and . . ." She stopped and looked up at him as her voice trailed off.

"Mine."

Marley nodded. "Fielding was one of the spearheads,

Quent. He and a small group of others were the ones who managed it all. Oh, my father reaped the benefits, just like the rest of them. But he wasn't part of the inner circle."

"They just needed his money. And, yes, I know about Fielding," Quent said. "And that's what I need you for." He gave her a pointed look. "Whether you want to or not, you're going to help me."

"What are you going to do?"

"What do you think I'm going to do, play the prodigal son and ask for my own crystal? I'm going to fucking kill the bastard."

"There's no way," Marley said, shaking her head. She crossed her legs and managed, somehow, to look elegant in her pose, despite her dirty shirt, tear-streaked face, and wrinkled trousers.

Zoë walked in at that moment, carrying a covered dish and a flat package of fabric. Absolutely delicious smells wafted with her to the low table.

"My God, she can cook too?" Marley muttered as Zoë disappeared back into the other room.

"Whatever it is, it smells unbelievable." Quent realized how hungry he was. The last time he'd eaten had been late yesterday afternoon, when they'd stopped for the night to hunt. "And, I'm going to find a way, and you're going to help me."

"Even if you could get to him, how would you even do it? He's not going to let you cut the crystal out of his skin. And that's the only way. Believe me, I know." She looked away. "I've thought of it myself."

"There's got to be a way. I'll do it or I'll die trying."

Although Zoë must have heard his last statement, she gave no indication. "Eat before this shit gets cold," she said, gracious as only she could be.

The meal consisted of flat brown bread called *naan*, as well as fresh tomatoes, carrots, and avocados sprinkled with cilantro and salt. She'd also pan-cooked some sort of poultry and seasoned it with lemon and cumin. The pot contained a mahogany-hued tea that was still warm.

"That's tea made from *canela*," she told him when he asked about it. "My grandmother had a cinnamon tree from . . . Mexico?" Quent nodded in affirmation, and she continued, "growing in her garden before the Change. She saved it and managed to keep one growing in every place she lived. *Canela* is just the bark." .

Then, as if she wanted to forestall any further conversation with Quent, Zoë looked at Marley. "After we're finished, he can take you to the stream. It's there." She pointed off in a vague direction. "I've got things to do."

Marley looked at Quent, then back at Zoë. "I could use a washing up. I . . . uh . . . don't have any other clothes."

Zoë looked pointedly at Marley's generous rack. "I don't have much that would fit you." Then she seemed to recall her hostess duties, as grudging as they might be. "But I'll look."

Quent was managing to use the unfamiliar utensils and cup without allowing the memories of the objects to submerge his mind. Although they teased there at the periphery, like some low buzz of white noise, he was able to keep them there. *Progress. Definitely making progress.*

"Tell me about the compound where Fielding lives," he said to Marley. The sooner he could start making plans, the better.

"It's in the ocean," she said. "An island, a floating community about five miles from the shore. They fucking named it Mecca—of all the insulting things they could have done, calling a symbol of destruction after a holy place." She shook her head, bitterness evident in the action. "There's a long bridge that leads to it and the only way onto the bridge is through a gate that's guarded by crystaled mortals. CMs."

"You mean Elite?"

She shook her head. "When we say Elite, we—they—mean only the people who were alive before the Evolution. The Change."

"Members of the Cult of Atlantis."

Marley nodded. "Yes, or people like me who were family members or friends brought along and given the immortal crystals."

"How many are there?"

"Maybe three hundred Elite."

"That's *it?*" Fuck. Three hundred people had brought about the mass destruction of the human race and caused the whole planet to change. The seasons, the environment, even, according to Lou and Theo, the axis of the earth itself had shifted.

"We can't procreate. Well, the women can't. The men are able to, but they have to impregnate normal mortals. That was how I started to figure out that what happened was not as I had been told. All these young, nubile girls started showing up. It was like something out of *The Handmaid's Tale.*"

Nausea rose in the back of his throat. "And CMs? What exactly are they?"

"They're immortal too, but they weren't original members of the Cult. They're people who have been given crystals and immortality, but over the last fifty years. Some of the women had their boy-toys crystaled, or even their damned pets." She glanced at him from beneath lowered lashes. "I didn't, but that's only because David Beckham didn't make the Elite's cut."

"Did they actually *find* Atlantis?" Quent asked. "Is this what was all about?"

Marley's lips pursed in thought. "They found something. I suspect it, but I don't really know, Quent. They kept things pretty tight and close, and once I started asking questions, even more so. But, I mean, these immortal crystals have to come from somewhere. Maybe the bottom of the ocean, maybe Atlantis, maybe not. I know the Inner Circle of the Elite—the ICE—leave the compound regularly. No one knows where they go, but they could be mining more crystals, or going somewhere else. To Atlantis."

"Some friends of ours, a set of twins from before the Change, hacked into satellites about a year after all the events. They found a new landmass in the Pacific Ocean, which now covers all of California to Vegas. Is that the compound you're talking about?"

"What?" Marley said. Her eyes had grown wide and he saw her face drain of color. "I had no idea." She shook her head, looking about as nauseated as he felt. "In Mecca, you're completely cut off from whatever is left of the world. Until I got out of the compound, I had no idea what the rest of the earth looked like. In fact, I expected a wasteland. Like in . . . um, that old Mel Gibson movie . . . *Mad Max*? I mean, what about all the nuclear power plants? What happened to them and their waste? It's got to be Radioactivity City around them for miles."

"Or at least, it was. Even Chernobyl is—was—coming back green ten years after the accident." He turned the subject back. "So if the compound is only five miles from shore, it couldn't be the separate landmass they saw."

"God, maybe they did find Atlantis," Marley whispered.

"But how? Did it rise from the bottom of the ocean? Impossible. And I've studied the legends. Atlantis was either an island in the Mediterranean, likely off Greece, or it was in the Atlantic. No one's ever suspected it was in the Pacific."

"Someone must have been wrong. Or it's not Atlantis. It's something else."

"Well, for now, I just want to get to Fielding. Where is Mecca?"

Marley looked at him a little helplessly. "Quent, you have to understand. I was running for my life in a terrain completely unfamiliar to me, and then the Marcks caught me. I'm not sure I can help you find it."

"Can't or won't?"

She drew in a long breath, then let it out. And looked away. "It's too dangerous."

"That's not your damned decision, Marley."

Before Marley could reply, Zoë stood abruptly and began to gather up the dishes. Quent began to help her, but she gave him a look and said, "Take her to the river. I've got an ass-load of things to do here and I don't want to be bothered." And she turned and walked back through the beaded doorway.

"Guess you'd better listen to her," Marley said with a glimmer of her old sense of humor.

And that was when Quent realized what Zoë was doing. Severing their connection. Sending him on his way—in more ways than one.

He looked at Marley, who, despite her flash of irony, still had a deep weariness in her eyes and a pale pallor to her skin. But she was familiar. And she understood him. She'd known him and his silver-spoon world in ways that Wyatt and Elliott hadn't comprehended.

"Right," he said.

Just then, Zoë stalked back into the room, pushing the beads rather more roughly aside than she needed to, and strode over to a trunk shoved up against the wall. She dug around in it and yanked out several articles of clothing, rejected some and bundled up the others, and thrust the wad at Marley.

"Water's nice for a swim. Here's some soap if you want to wash up. Sun'll be setting in about two hours, so you have time to enjoy."

Run along with you, kiddies, Quent could almost hear her say. *Have fun.*

Fine. He straightened his shoulders and replied, "We'll be back."

The last thing he heard as he followed Marley out of the room was the clanging of dishes, and the low, threatening growl from Fang.

As if he were saying *good fucking riddance.*

A rubbish-mouthed dog, just like his mistress. If he weren't feeling so dejected, Quent might have smiled at the thought.

Zoë didn't relax until she heard Fang walk over and lay down on his bed. He'd remained on guard through the whole meal, glaring at their visitors in a way she wished she'd been able to do.

Well, at least at Marley Huvane. Who hadn't bothered to button up her shirt, and had been flaunting her substantial cleavage in some light blue bra since they arrived.

She washed the dishes as quickly as possible, then set them aside to dry. After she fed Fang some left-overs, which he wholly appreciated, Zoë drew in a deep breath.

What now?

She felt odd. Off balance, which never happened. Maybe she'd eaten something that didn't agree with her.

The sun would be setting soon. She should hunt, but that would take her out of her home and leave Quent and Marley here. She could be gone for days tracking *gangas* if she went too far to make it back in one night. That would mean they would be here, in her house.

Not a damned chance she was going to let that happen.

She could make more arrows. She *should* make more. She'd almost run out last night, and if that had happened or if she'd been alone . . . bad fucking news.

She didn't feel like doing that either.

If she wanted to take a night off from hunting, as she did occasionally, she would normally curl up with a book and read. With Fang nearby and a cup of tea.

But Quent and Marley would be back. Wet and slippery and—

Ah, for fuck's sake. That was *not* something she wanted to think about.

So why the hell was it niggling at her? She had no claim on him.

Zoë slammed down a cup that, fortunately, was made from tin, and poured more *canela*. He could do whatever the hell he wanted to.

Just like Zoë would. She nodded to Fang and slogged back a huge drink of tea. It scalded the shit out of her mouth and she blinked back tears of pain, swearing silently. *Dammit.*

What the hell was she doing, wasting time anyway? She had too much to do, and now that Marley was here, she didn't have to worry about Quent the blond genius anymore. Marley could take care of him.

Good riddance.

Yes. Marley with the big boobs and the lush curves and the eyes for Quent. They had a history. Oh, Zoë had recognized it right away. Fuck-buddies, maybe even real lovers. The pain and betrayal in his eyes, the shock, pleasure—then hurt—in hers.

Whatever had happened between them, they'd work it out. Down by the river.

Good for them.

And then they could get the fuck out of her place and she could get back to her life.

Quent heard the splash behind him and only then did he turn to look toward Marley, in the river. She rose from the gentle rush, her hair slicked back from her face. Even though the lowering sun was behind her, blinding his vision, he could sense her pleasure.

"You need the water?" he said, coming to sit on a huge fallen tree near the shore. There was no beach to speak of, just a well-worn track through the grass and overgrowth that led from the remnants of the town's old road here.

He'd noticed other indicators of Zoë's homesteading presence—three solar panels affixed to the eastern side of a building and a crude waterwheel tucked beneath an old bridge. Subtle signs that would easily be missed unless someone was looking for them.

Like him.

"Yes. Can't live without it. And the water's beautiful," Marley said, treading in the middle. "You look miserable. Come on in. I'll tell you about it."

For the first time since Zoë'd discovered her, she looked like the Marley he'd known. Her face was clean, her hair sleek, and her eyes sparkled. And on the right side of her chest, just below the collarbone, he saw the small crystal. It was still too light for the glow to be noticeable, so now it simply looked like half of an ice blue marble stuck to her skin.

He glanced at the array of clothes strewn over a bush, noting her white shirt, taupe trousers, and the blue bra and matching panties she'd discarded. He figured he knew what would happen if he joined her—it always did with him and Marley.

They'd known each other since they were teens, since he was living with the bastard that was his father. Brandon Huvane, founder of a successful biochemical firm, and Fielding had been close associates, and the families often vacationed together.

And throughout the rest of his life, the Huvanes and Fieldings continued to run in the same circles. More often than not, if Marley and Quent were at the same function—fundraisers, premiers, parties—they'd find a chance to ditch their dates and sneak off for a bit. Sometimes they'd snog or shag, sometimes they'd simply gossip about the other attendees.

Quent pulled off his shirt and began to unfasten his shorts. The river did look inviting, dark blue sparkling with red and orange as the sun settled onto the horizon.

Another hour of daylight, and then they'd have to go inside or chance running into *gangas*.

His thoughts flickered to Zoë as he peeled down his briefs and started toward the water. Unease that might be defined as guilt sneaked up in the back of his mind, but he ignored it. She'd sent him away. With Marley.

Her intention had been clear.

And aside of that, she'd already tried to ditch him more than once.

And she was probably right: he and Marley fit together much better. They had so much in common. They understood each other. They'd come from the same world.

They'd both been betrayed by their fathers.

He walked into the water, quickly wading up to his hips. The coolness felt damn good, and he dove under, coming up some distance from Marley.

It struck him that he'd been in the same position only a few hours earlier with another woman, and at that time, he'd expected a totally different outcome. The visions of warm, sleek limbs sliding together, hard and hungry mouths clashing had stoked him this afternoon as he swam after Zoë. He'd enjoyed that moment of the hunt, the thrill of anticipation.

"Right, then," he said, pulling himself back to his current companion. Treading water so that the current wouldn't carry him downstream, he asked her, "You need the water for healing?"

"For energy," she told him. They were far enough away that their submerged frog-kicking legs wouldn't nudge against the other, but close enough that they could talk in normal voices. "I was away from running water for too long. That's how the Marcks caught me.

Otherwise," she added grimly, "I'd like to think I could have kept ahead of them longer. I, at least, have the advantage of understanding what hiding places might have been in a building—back stairwells, fire escapes, you know. And also what sort of objects I might find in one. I managed to get into a hardware store and found a saw on the tool aisle that was a very effective weapon."

"I saw you fighting with Raul Marck. You put that saw to bloody good use. You nearly killed him."

"Good riddance."

"Tell me about the crystals."

She nodded, ducked under, then emerged with her hair replastered over her head. "The crystals are living entities. They can't survive without the energy from running water. As long as we're near it, we're all right. And I could even be away for a couple days, but not much longer. As I learned."

"You really didn't want the crystal?" he asked, his eyes trailing over to it.

Marley looked at him for a moment, a range of emotions crossing her face. "I seriously can't believe you'd even ask. Immortality is one thing, I suppose, and yeah, there are times when I don't want to die. Like last night, I was pretty sure it was over, until I managed a last slice at Raul Marck and got myself away from him. But to have it forced on me? And for the price paid? God, Quent. I thought you knew me better than that."

She dove under the water, treating him to a glimpse of her sleek arse, no doubt purposely. When she broke the surface again, she was a bit farther away. "So tell me about Zoë. She's a piece of work. A post-apocalyptic Martha Stewart. And I mean that mostly in a good way."

"She's also a hell of a zombie hunter."

"The attraction surprises me," Marley said with a knowing smile. "You generally tend toward more sophisticated types."

"There aren't too many movie stars or socialites around anymore," he said. "Makes it a bit hard to find someone who can tell the difference between beluga and osetra." He laughed, but even to his ears, it sounded forced.

"You know," Marley said, treading closer to him. Her foot brushed against his leg and he could see the three little beauty marks on her right cheekbone, along with the tops of her breasts floating in the water. And, now that the sun had lowered behind some trees, he made out a hint of the crystal's glow. "I always figured that when you stopped running around adding notches to your bedpost, avoiding anything that hinted of real intimacy—and I figured out what I wanted to be when I grew up—we'd end up together."

She cocked her head and looked at him with a faint smile, and for a moment, he tumbled back in time, remembering their easy camaraderie. His eyes fastened on her mouth, the wide, full lips that she hated because she said they looked like horse lips. He told her they reminded him of Julia Roberts. She told him he looked like Robert Redford on a good day.

Then, Marley surprised him and swished away on her back, like a skittish mermaid. Her breasts flashed fully for a moment, then were modestly covered by the darkening water.

Before he could think of what to say—for he, too, had often had similar thoughts, deep in his mind when he was being honest with himself—Marley swore. "Damn. I left the soap over there."

She swam back to shore and, seemingly uncaring of her nakedness, picked up the little pot of soap. She scooped out a hunk and waded back in to her hips and began to lather up.

Quent swam back and stepped out of the water, his back to her so that she might have some privacy, and pulled on his shorts. Thinking.

He *knew* her. He wouldn't have to worry about Marley sneaking out on him, taking off into the dark after toe-curling sex. Disappearing for days.

She was funny and smart and hot. She was a poor little rich girl to his poor little rich boy. And both of them had been transplanted into this new world where they had nothing.

"So," she said, "are you going to tell me what happened to bring you here?"

"I wish I knew," he told her, and explained about the cave.

When he finished, which was about the time she splashed onto shore behind him, Marley said, "You don't really know if you're immortal like me, or if you just time-traveled, or if something else happened."

"I've used the term cryogenically frozen, but I suppose time travel is possible. I have no explanation for it other than the fact that Sedona was known for being the center of such strong energy sources, like ley lines, and if some great upheaval happened that caused them to overload or to somehow connect, a massive energy surge could explain it."

"You've always been so fascinated by those sorts of things—explanations for how the pyramids were built and lined up a certain way with . . . what was it? Easter Island? Or Machu Picchu? Halfway around the world from them."

"Easter Island. And some nodules on the bottom of the ocean." He gave a little chuckle. "So you were listening to me all those times I droned on about those things."

"And about the lost treasures you wanted to find, and Atlantis."

The mention of Atlantis stopped him. "You must know they—our fathers, and the others—were all members of the Cult of Atlantis before this happened," he said.

"Yes . . . but, God, Quent, how did you ever find out about that? It took me years, and I was living with them."

Shrugging, he decided not to tell her about the Resistance quite yet. "Putting the pieces together."

He could hear her getting dressed behind him and steered the subject back to his experience. "As I was saying, one of the guys in the cave with us died after we came out, so it's pretty clear we're not immortal. And although I haven't had to shave but once in the last six months, some of the other guys have noticed their beards and nails growing again too." He shrugged. "Maybe whatever it was simply stopped us from aging or changing for a while, and it takes some time for our bodies to get back to normal."

"I'm done," said Marley, walking around so that he could see her. "And it's getting dark. My little friend is glowing." Though she gave a short little laugh, he heard the bitterness in her voice.

She was wearing one of Zoë's tank tops, which stretched much too tightly over her breasts and fully exposed the crystal. He could see that she'd been unable to snap the cargo pants, though they were fully zipped.

"You can't imagine how glad I am to find you, Quent. I've missed you." She looked up at him and he saw sadness and hope in her eyes. "It was like finding a friend after fifty years of being alone. Fifty years of looking in the mirror and seeing the exact same person, *every day*. Do you know," she said, her voice taut, "that I've had a broken nail for fifty years that's never grown back? And I've never had to have my eyebrows or legs waxed, or my hair cut—thank God I was having a good hair day when they put that damned crystal in my body. I haven't changed a bit. For *fifty years*." Tears gathered in her eyes, ready to spill over.

"I can't imagine," he replied. "You must hate them." A renewed wave of fury reminded him how much he hated his father. And how he had his own work to do, his own vengeance to take.

"I do," Marley said, her voice breaking with anger and frustration. "And I've been alone for so long. Without a friend, or anyone to talk to." The next thing he knew, she was in his arms, and he was folding her close, feeling her shoulders shake and the damp tears wetting his neck. "Dammit," she sniffled. "I swore I wasn't going to cry. But I'm so *angry*, and so glad to have found you, Quent."

He made soothing noises, rubbing her back with his large hands and feeling the water drip from the ends of her hair down over them. Being a man, he was also fully aware of the swell of breasts pushing against him, and being a man, he had a little bit of shifting down in the nether zone as a result—but that was purely nature.

"They're going to come after me," she said, her words muffled by his skin and her tears. "Will you help me find somewhere to hide?"

"Of course. I have to have your help. I'm going to need to know everything you can tell me about them."

"You'll never get to him, Quent," she said, stepping away to look up. "He lives in a compound with other Elite, including my father, and there's no way to get in or out without being seen. Let alone get close to him."

"I'll find a way. And you're going to help me."

"Aren't you listening? There's *no way*, Quent. I'm telling you. I lived there. You'll be killed before you get close enough to do any damage. And you can't kill him anyway."

"I can if I cut the mother-fucker's crystal out of his goddamn skin."

"Quent, please . . . can't we find another way for revenge?"

"It's the only thing I can do, Marley. I've got nothing else. I've got no money, no influence, no skills. For God's sake, I was an Indiana Jones-wanna-be, going on adventures that meant nothing, spending money and trying to get myself killed so I'd have great stories to tell Bonia Telluscrede or Lissa Mackley so I could get them into bed. And now that it's all gone, I've got rot but the drive and the purpose of killing my father. If I die in the accomplishment, or even trying, I'll have done the best I can do. There's no other place for me."

Marley was shaking her head. "You're selling yourself short, Quent. You forget, I've known you for . . . well, too long. More than sixty years, though a woman should never admit to knowing anyone that long. And yeah, you're all those things. But you changed so much after that trip to Haiti. That was when you began to grow up."

He snorted. "Yeah, the trip that I signed up for purely

to spite my father. The minute I got off the damn plane, I wanted to turn around and get the hell back to my luxury condo in Naples. It was bloody hell."

"But you didn't. And you stayed and tore your hands up, working on that hospital. And you met Wyatt and Elliott. And when you came back, you'd changed. You didn't want to show it, but you did. And don't think I don't know about the contributions—the hundreds of thousands you donated afterward. And the other humanitarian thing you went on to Malawi."

"That was just so I could try to meet Madonna on one of her adoption trips, and shag her," he quipped.

"Quent." Her voice was steel and something inside him started to unravel.

"It's all true. But I don't have any of those resources anymore, Marley. I'm no bloody good to anyone here except to get close enough to kill Parris Fielding. Oh, he'll want to see me. He's egotistical enough that I'll be able to get to him. And then . . . well, we'll see what happens."

"You might not have the money anymore, Quent, but you're still the same person. Inside. And . . . I just don't want anything to happen to you, now that I've found you again," she said, stepping into him again. She pulled his face down for a kiss.

Marley, Marley . . . was all he thought.

He kissed her back, their lips cool from the water, bodies warm, mouths familiar and knowing. Sleek and deep and everything comfortable.

They both pulled away at the same time and he saw that she was smiling crookedly at him. "Well," Marley said, giving him an affectionate pat on the cheek, "if that wasn't the most distracted, obligatory kiss I've ever had."

Quent blinked and opened his mouth to deny it, but she was already shaking her head. "When you're ready to move on from Zoë, which I know you will, I'll be waiting. But I'm not going to be your consolation prize anymore." She wrinkled her nose. "I've grown up over the last fifty years," she added with a little laugh. "And while I would always wait for you, Quent, I'm not going to play the games we used to play."

"Fair enough," he said, still wondering what had been wrong with his kiss. Then, since they were on the subject, and he was, after all, a man, he asked, "Right, then. Uh . . . what are you doing for birth control nowadays?"

Marley burst out laughing and gave him a little shove as she turned away. "Don't tell me you've been abstaining and that's why the air's so tight between the two of you."

"Not exactly," he said, thinking about the two . . . or three . . . times he'd not managed to make the withdrawal soon enough.

Bugger it. Zoë could be pregnant with his child. Right now. A flush of heat and emptiness flooded him. What would she do if she found out she was pregnant?

"Can't help you there," Marley said, and he heard the deadness in her voice again. "I haven't had a period in fifty years. No need for me to have birth control. In fact, I spent the first five years screwing any guy I could just so I could forget about what happened." She looked at him, and the humor was gone from her face. "You know, the fucking nuclear war that destroyed the whole earth. Including you."

"Right," he said. What else could he say? His mind was already edging back to the cozy sanctuary where Zoë was hanging out with Fang.

Or . . . his heart stopped. She might have gone. Out, hunting. Putting herself in danger.

Or out . . . just out. Just . . . gone.

"Let's get back," he said, trying to get his lungs to work again.

CHAPTER 11

Fang bared his teeth, showing off a broken eyetooth that nevertheless looked wicked enough to do a good bit of damage.

Quent looked at him and said firmly, "Fang, chill," and walked through the courtyard, toward the entrance to Zoë's hideaway. Despite his cool actions, the hair at the back of his neck prickled as he strode confidently past the annoyed wolfhound, who sat right inside the doorway.

But other than a low, warning growl, the creature remained still and Quent considered himself successful when he got into the little flat unscathed.

He looked around, but his first instinct was right: Zoë wasn't there.

Marley had followed him, of course, and when she came in behind, Quent stepped aside and gestured. "Make yourself comfortable. I'm going to see if I can find Zoë. I may be gone awhile."

Ignoring Marley's amused grin, he walked across the room toward the hanging beads. A low glow came from beyond, and he gathered up the clinking strings and walked through. He found himself in a short little passageway, and then came upon a pair of swinging doors like one might find in a restaurant. The glow was stronger, and he felt a wave of heat emanating from beyond.

When he pushed through the metal doors, which were warm to the touch, Quent was blasted by a wall of heat. Immediately, he felt the weight of the heat in his nose and lungs, and the sweat springing along his lower spine.

Kitchen and forge, indeed. The only light came from the red-orange glow of coals spilling from inside an arched brick opening in the center of the room. Heat waves radiated from the oven that had originally baked bread or pizza, shoved in on long wooden paddles. Zoë stood to the side, and as he watched, she used a long pincerlike tool to fish a slender metal rod from deep in the fire pit.

The tip of the rod glowed yellow-white, and she applied a different tool to pinch and flatten the molten metal. Without acknowledging his presence, Zoë rested the metal rod safely on one of the small industrial kitchen's steel countertops, lining it up with several others. Then she turned back to the forge and reached her tool in for something else.

Her bare arms bulged and gleamed with sweat, and she'd donned a white tank top that appeared to have been trimmed to just below her breasts. Its frayed hem curled up in the back, exposing the long flare of her waist, and a hint of the dimples just above her arse rising from low drawstring trousers. A heavy apron covered the front of her body, strings crisscrossing into a low tie at the back. Zoë's messy dark hair shone, winging about in every direction except where it was flattened by the ski goggles she wore for eye protection. Gloves covered her hands, but the rest of her mahogany skin glistened and her lean muscles shifted and slid as she used two clamping tools on what looked like the tine-end of a fork.

Quent realized he was having trouble breathing, and it wasn't just because of the heat in the air. She looked like some sort of exotic, science-fictiony blacksmith, slaving in the throes of hell.

As he watched, fascinated and quite as hard as a rock, she bent the outside tines in toward each other in a half circle, and he realized she was making one of her arrows. The fork tines, their normal curve now exaggerated, were the starburst parts that were ejected from the tip of the arrow when it hit its mark. That brain-scrambling aspect was what made the weapons so effective in fighting zombies.

At last she acknowledged him with a curt look from behind ski goggles framed in neon orange. "Back so soon?" she said, digging through a bucket of metal objects with loud clangs and clinks.

"It didn't take Marley long to wash up."

"Not when she had a bit of help," Zoë replied, her mouth quirking beneath the goggles.

Quent stepped from the wall, which, away from the direct line of the oven, seemed to be the least sweltering area of the room. He came toward her, feeling as if he were wading through the heat. God, it was stifling. Steamy and heavy . . . and all he wanted to do was get his hands on her hot, slick body.

"Not from me," he told Zoë firmly.

That caught her by surprise, for he saw her biceps flex and glisten, her elegant throat convulse, then relax. "I find that hard to believe, genius."

"Why don't you put that down and I'll show you how easy it is to believe." He'd moved up closer behind her now, feeling the unbearable blast of heat from the forge that somehow made the moment even more charged.

"I'm in the middle of something," she told him, turning to dip a pinched object into the tub of water in front of Quent. A loud hiss of steam rose between them, but their eyes met through the smoke, through her lenses. Even in the dimness, he felt a renewed blast of heat that had nothing to do with the forge.

"Put it away, Zoë," he told her. "I'm not feeling very patient right now."

"You're going to get burned if you aren't careful."

"I've no doubt of that. *Put it away.*"

"If I don't finish it now—"

"Zoë." Quent couldn't keep his hands still, couldn't stop himself from moving toward her. His shirt stuck to his back, a trickle of sweat slid down his temple and another down his spine. Even his feet felt a little slippery in their sandals, and he could hardly breathe the sultry air—but he had to have his hands on her.

He fitted his fingers around the warm, damp curve of her waist, beneath the apron, and bent to kiss the bare side of her neck. Salty, moist, cinnamony and hot.

God. He closed his eyes, slid his hands up under the apron, lifting the frayed edges of her tank to cover her neat, high breasts. She arched back a little into his chest and he heard the dull clang as the tools clunked clumsily together, but Zoë, his Zoë, his obstinate Zoë, wouldn't put them down. Not yet.

That would be admitting defeat.

"Quent, for fuck's sake, I have to fin—"

"Don't let me stop you," he murmured into her ear.

Her nipples thrust hard beneath his finger pads, and he stroked leisurely over them, one after the other, delicately and diligently. She bent her head to see to her task, but he felt the rough hitch of her breath against his chest. The back of her neck had bared when she looked down, and he found the little hollow there where nape met shoulder, kissing and nibbling on her damp skin.

Her arms moved above his and he felt the jolting rhythm as she hammered on a piece of metal. *Clang, clang . . .* in the same rhythm of the need pounding inside his body, in the pulsing of the massive erection straining his zipper.

"Quent, I'm not . . . fucking . . . kid—" she said, and then gave a little gasp. He heard a metallic clunk as she stopped hammering, then silence. A breath later, she arched and shuddered beneath the rhythmic fingers on her nipples.

He smiled into her hair. *There we go, luv.* "That was a nice surprise," he murmured, sliding his apparently very talented fingers down beneath the loose drawstring of her pants. "And here I thought you'd just be making jokes about turning up the heat."

"All right," she said, obviously trying to keep her voice hard, but failing miserably, "now let me get the fuck back to work." She tried to sidle away from his grip, but between the hot-and-heavy pokerlike object she held, and the way the workspace was set up, Zoë had nowhere to go.

Quent smiled.

"I don't think so," he said, discovering the slick warmth of her sex down beneath those loose pants. "Definitely not." *Oh, yes.* She was full and wet and he found the hard little knot buried in the heat of her panties. "Ah, Zoë," he half sighed, half groaned into her ear when she shivered at his touch.

There was another dull clang as she dropped the metal tools. "Watch out," she muttered sharply, and he heard something roll and then clatter to the floor near his foot. "Serve your . . . ass . . . right if it . . . landed on . . . you," she managed.

"I'm overwhelmed by concern," he murmured, shifting his feet around in front of hers so that their legs were twined, and her feet tucked backward so she relied on him for balance. He felt her weight shift forward and tightened one arm around her damp belly to keep her steady. Somehow she pulled off her gloves and the next thing he knew, her hands had come to settle around behind her head, onto the back of his, elbows wide and akimbo. The heat clustered in his nose and mouth, settled heavily on his skin, burned from her, but he wasn't going to let her go.

"I've never seen anything so sexy," Quent told her, sifting, sliding, swirling his fingers in long, sleek strokes, "as you playing blacksmith."

She tightened against and beneath him, and he felt her gathering up again. Her breath roughened and her muscles trembled, and he buried his face in her shoulder, smelling and tasting the familiarity, coaxing her to the finish once again. Zoë made the little surprised gasp she always did and shuddered from deep inside, her fingers tightening in his hair.

Then he spun her around and tore the goggles away, diving down for a deep, hot kiss, crushing her mouth and shoving her against the wall. Her hands settled on his shoulders, curling there as if they belonged, and she met him, arching against his body as he pressed her into the bricks.

She murmured his name, low and desperate, and the frantic sound sent a surge of need rushing through him. She needed him. And, oh God, he needed her. He suddenly couldn't imagine life without her.

I love you.

The words popped into his head, clear and solid in the midst of the hot, close desire, and he almost stopped breathing. He'd never said those words . . . to anyone. Never. *I love you, Zoë.*

Then something moved; he saw it out of the corner of his eye. Quent dragged his mouth away as Marley came into view. *What the—*

But then he stopped when he saw her face. Frantic. "I'm sorry, really sorry," she said, holding up a hand as if to hide her face from what was going on. "I called, but . . . uh, no one heard me," she added, still looking away.

Zoë pushed Quent away and straightened her tank top, giving him and then Marley an evil glare. "You can put your damn hand down," she said, picking up one of her forgotten tools. "There's nothing to see."

But Marley had continued. "There's something wrong with Fang. He's growling and pacing and he looks really upset. I'm afraid there's something out there." She looked at Quent, her face shadowy in the low light, but her crystal blazing soft and white-blue on her golden skin. "I'm afraid they're out there. Looking for me."

Zoë dropped her tool with a clatter at the first mention of Fang and started out of the forge without hesitation. Quent looked after her, then back at Marley.

"I'm a little more subtle than that," she told him with a roll of her eyes. "If I wanted to interrupt you, I'd have found a much less obvious way. I don't give a shit if you're balling her, even in a sweaty, stinky place like this. I told you, I'll be there when you're tired of it."

He raised his brows. "The thing is, I'm not so sure I'm going to get tired of it. So don't hold your breath."

Frustrated, still pounding with desire—not to mention terrified at his realization—he started off after Zoë. But when he got to the curtain of beads, he stopped and turned back to Marley. "Stay here, just in case."

She met his eyes, her face taut with worry, her salon-streaked hair tumbling around her shoulders. "I will."

He started across the room once more, stopping only to rifle through his pack for the limited weaponry he had, and turned back to her again. "If we're not back in thirty minutes, you're on your own. Take this." He handed her a knife and the gun that had belonged to Raul Marck—which left him a gun, a bottle bomb, and a much smaller knife. "And find a way to get to the city of Envy—you saw where the humvee's hidden. Wyatt and Elliott are there. In Envy. Go north and you'll find it."

Zoë burst back in at that moment, Fang on her heels. "Son of a bitch," she said, rushing over to the windows and pulling the tarps back into place. Quent rushed to help her, closing shutters. "There's a—a what the fuck do you call it, a truck, out there. Heading this way. Ass-wipe bounty hunter, probably. Might not be looking for you, but you never know."

Marley's lips tightened, but she didn't run screaming off to hide. "What do we do?"

"Stay here. You too, genius," she said flatly. "There's a secret exit through the forge. You'll find it. I'll see if I can distract them, and you can take her to safety."

"Zoë," he began, starting toward her. At her glare, he stopped and changed tactic. "You mean you trust me not to get my arse in trouble without you around?"

"What the hell is an arse?" But a flicker of humor crossed her face, then was gone. "We don't have any other choice, do we, if she doesn't want to get her *arse* dragged back to the Elite. I'm giving you the chance to get away. Do it."

He gritted his teeth. "I'll take her back to Envy," he said. And she was gone. Quent flexed his hand, then curled his fingers tightly. Waiting.

"Thank you," Marley said.

"I'm not fucking staying here while she's out there," he told her, and started for the exit. "I'm going to cover her. I'll be back only if the worst happens."

"Quent," she said, stopping him once again. "What I said earlier, about you getting tired of her? I don't think that's going to happen. But," she said, her eyes serious, "when she's the one who walks away . . . I'll be waiting."

And with those happy, gut-truth sentiments ringing in his ears, Quent stalked out after Zoë. And came up short.

Fang sat there, barring the way. And he didn't look as if he were going to let anyone pass.

From her perch high in a tree, Zoë watched the humvee drive away. Her bow slung over her shoulder, its quiver full, she stared until the shadowy box of a truck rolled off into the darkness.

Why the hell was her chest feeling so damned tight? She'd given him no choice but to leave. Of course he would choose to keep the Elite woman safe.

She clamped her lips together and looked back west, in the direction she'd seen the other vehicle. The one that had set Fang off by coming too close to her hideaway. But it hadn't stopped, and had continued on its journey to wherever. Whether they were bounty hunters or Strangers looking for the escaped Elite, or simply hunting humans for the *gangas*, they were long gone.

Envy was to the east, the opposite direction, so she had no fear that Quent and Marley would inadvertently be discovered. They were safe. He was safe.

So she didn't need to be having any damned trouble breathing.

After a while, when she was certain he was really gone, Zoë climbed down from the tree. She was itching, just itching to come across a band of zombies about now. She had a whole bunch of pent-up something that needed to come out. Violently.

But there was not an orange eye glowing anywhere to be seen. Where the hell were the bastards when she needed them?

On the ground, she walked back toward her hideaway. She heard the quiet rustle of Fang, now released from his guard of the house, moving in and out of the bushes and tall grass. He took off suddenly, barreling into the darkness. At least he had something to hunt.

The soft rush of the stream in the distance reminded her of Quent swimming with Marley, how he'd come back with his hair all damp, and smelling of fresh river, when he found her in the forge.

Great. Now she wouldn't be able to do any damned work without thinking about the way he'd come in there, invading her sanctuary, emblazoning his presence, stamping his touch on the space. *Dammit.*

Her belly pitched and she felt that familiar little tingle, deep in her core. He sure as hell knew how to push her buttons. And, yeah, surprisingly enough, when to listen, and when to talk.

Last night, in the church. *Ugh*. She'd fucking babbled on and on . . . Zoë rolled her eyes in memory. He must have been cringing inside. Yet, he'd listened. Simply touched her hand instead of trying to distract her by getting her naked. As if he'd cared.

It had been a long time since someone cared about her. Or since she'd cared about someone else.

She knew he didn't understand why she'd had to kill Raul. But he hadn't said a word of condemnation about it. He just listened. And part of her wanted to tell him how it hadn't been quite as easy as she'd made it out to be.

But she couldn't. She wanted to put it behind her.

And Quent didn't try to impose his opinions on her. He didn't treat her as if she didn't have a brain, making all the decisions and giving orders like the men did to the women in adventure movies. That had always pissed her the hell off.

And this morning, when she went swimming, he came after her on his own time, in his own way. He didn't demand to know why she'd gone without him, where she'd been. He seemed to understand that she needed privacy. Room to breathe.

She was so used to living alone.

So damn lonely.

Zoë actually gasped aloud at the thought, and looked around as if to make sure no one had heard it. As if there was anyone around. Fucking crazy, she was.

But the thoughts wouldn't leave her.

Lonely. Had she ever thought of herself as lonely? After the tragedy of losing her family, damn straight. She'd had an ass-load of loneliness, all wrapped up in meta-grief. For a while. But then she'd become caught up in her revenge mission, and her hunting. And she'd built her own life.

One she liked. Solitary. Simple. So fucking dutiful, she was certain to go to heaven.

Like those homicide detectives in all the books she read, she burned with the need to set things right. To find the truth, to rectify damage done. The same burden and desire drove her.

The only difference was, she had to carry out the revenge on her own. With her own hands. Because there was no one else.

Did they have it any easier—Charlotte and Tom Pitt, or Sam Spade, or any of them—being able to simply find the truth, identify the villain . . . and then leave it up to someone else to ensure that justice was served? They never stepped over the line and took matters into their own hands.

Like she had. And now she'd begun to understand the gravity of that decision. The ripples it effected through her. The knowledge that she'd ended a life—a miserable one, a violent and ugly one . . . but without giving him a chance. A weighty knowledge.

Yet one that she didn't regret. She'd taken a life to save many. She accepted it.

Something prickled down her spine, and she spun around just in time to see a large shadow detach itself from a deeper, stationary one. Zoë had an arrow in her hand before she took another step.

"You can put that away," said Ian, stepping fully into the wisp of moon- and starlight.

"I told you I wouldn't shoot you last night, but that doesn't mean I won't now," Zoë told him. Her heart pounded in her chest.

"Same here," he said, and she saw that he held a gun. "All bets are off at this late date."

"You doubled back." She realized what had happened. Damn her for an idiot. "Without lights on." Thank God she'd forced Quent to leave.

She'd done something right.

"Where are they?" he asked, as if reading her mind.

"Who?" She glanced over toward the horizon. If she could get Fang back from his hunt, it would be all over. Son of a bastard bounty hunter.

Ian's handsome features hardened, half shadowed into an unpleasant mask. "Don't play games with me. The man. Quent. That's his name, isn't it?"

Zoë's belly dropped. What the fuck did he want with Quent? "I thought you weren't after the bounty," she said coolly. All she needed was to whistle for Fang, but— *Shit.* Ian could shoot the poor beast. Although, Fang was pretty damn fast.

"I don't owe you any explanations, Zoë. And I don't plan to hurt you—after all, I do have to give you credit for getting rid of my father. I was about ready to do it myself if you hadn't."

"Why would you grow those balls after all these years?"

"It was the right time." He leveled the gun. "Are you going to tell me what I want to know?"

He could damn well shoot her if he wanted to, but she didn't think he would. He wanted information. He'd be more likely to use some of his father's methods and torture it out of her rather than simply putting her out of her misery and killing her. She thought fast and settled on diversion. "Maybe. But I'm surprised you're wasting your time chasing Quent—or Marley Huvane—when you let Remington Truth slip through your fingers."

That blithe statement had the desired effect. The gun lowered a bit. "What are you talking about?"

"Remy, the brunette you had up against the tree. *Remington Truth.* Obviously, you were so blind with lust that you didn't make the connection. Ian, I'm surprised at you." She gave him a mocking smile.

"Just because I was never blinded with lust in your presence," he shot back.

"Oh, damn. You just ruined my day." He had to keep bringing that up, that one time she'd thought about seducing him so she could get information about his father. *Thought* being the operative word.

His eyes narrowed. "What the hell kind of bullshit are you trying to hand me?"

"Remington Truth—the old man—is dead. The woman you had in your hands, whose throat you were jamming your tongue down, is his granddaughter. And she's the only connection, the only damn link to him."

She waited, watching as he seemed to assimilate the information.

Then his face settled into comprehension. "You could be telling me the truth. It's possible. Remington Truth is dead. And his granddaughter is alive." He smiled. "And no one knows that but you . . . and Quent Fielding."

Zoë's stomach flipped violently. *Fuck.* He was going to kill her *and* he knew Quent's *name. Holy shit. Holy fucking crapload of shit.* Whatever that meant, it wasn't good. Without another thought, she raised her fingers and gave a sharp, short whistle. A bit more desperate.

Ian turned, his gun wavering, just as the bundle of fur blasted out of the darkness, leaping on him before he even saw it.

The gun flew from his hand as Ian fell to the ground. Zoë scrambled to pick it up and said, "Fang. Done." She snapped her fingers sharply, and the wolf, dejected at having his sport interrupted, looked at her from where he had his paws planted on Ian's chest.

"Now, Fang." The wolf came to stand next to her, still watching Ian with a menacing curl of his lip. She had the gun pointed at him and her finger tightened on the trigger. She could finish it now, and Quent would be safe.

Ian looked up at her, his eyes cold and flat. Challenging. *Do it.*

She couldn't. The handle felt slippery in her hand. The gun heavy. Much too heavy.

Holding her with his gaze, Ian stood smoothly and dusted off his jeans as if he hadn't nearly just been mauled. She guessed someone who was not only blond but worked in close proximity with *gangas* had come close to that sort of situation more than once. "And as soon as I walk away, you'll put a bullet in my head." He said it almost as if it were a challenge. Or a request.

"Is that what you want?" Zoë remembered feeling that way. And that sometimes the feeling crept back in, deep in the night when she had nothing with her but her thoughts as she waited for the *gangas* to appear. Lonely, lonely days and nights.

He straightened, and for a moment, she thought she saw bleakness in his chiseled features. Or maybe it was merely acceptance. But the world was dark and lit only by celestial bodies, and she couldn't be certain of either.

"You've got the gun. I can't stop you." Ian turned and started off into the night, insolently presenting her with his back as he strode away.

She watched him go, the gun hanging unused in her hand. Then, taking the opportunity while his back was turned, she eased into the shadows so he wouldn't see where she was going. Her home was well hidden, but Ian was smart enough to find it if he followed her.

And she had the sudden urge to get back into the forge. She had work to do. And things to forget.

6 January 2011
9:00 P.M.

A new year has come, and I believe it is fair to say we've adapted as well as we can to this world and its dangers.

The creatures have ceased to come every night now. But we've learned to stay inside with the doors bolted when we hear their distant moaning.

I suppose it is foolish for me not to give them a name, for we all know what they are, though no one has spoken it.

Zombies. The living dead. There is no doubt in my mind that somehow when the world changed, these organic monsters were created from all the casualties of the events. All of those bodies littering the streets and buildings were suddenly gone. And although Devi disagrees, I believe they've been brought back to—what would one call it? Non-life.

Garth Macomb, one of our neighbors, was attacked by the creatures not long after they began to appear, before we knew what dangers they held. We could do nothing as they picked him up and threw him over the shoulder of one of them, carrying him off.

Devi and James meant to go after the zombies, but I stopped them. Bullets seem to make no difference, nor do arrows. Fire frightens them, but doesn't kill.

I am not certain whether I should be horrified at the thought of bringing our child into this new world, but I will. I estimate that he or she will arrive in early May; I confess, I've lost a bit track of time during these last few months.

Devi is as delighted as I am, but there is still that underlying worry in his eyes. Yet, a baby will be yet another sign that life does go on.

—from the diary of Mangala Kapoor

CHAPTER 12

Zoë can take care of herself.

Quent had to remind himself over and over during the rest of the night. He and Marley had escaped through the hidden exit out of the forge as Zoë directed, and drove off as quietly as possible in the dark humvee.

She's been doing it for years.

Yet, driving away, leaving her behind in order to save Marley—and his chance to find Fielding—was the hardest thing he'd ever done. He never would have anyway if Fang hadn't been standing guard at the exit.

The wolf-dog had had no intention of allowing Quent past. He tried the "chill" command, but as soon as he took a step forward, the bared teeth came out and the creature moved to stand in his path. With the hair rising in antagonized spikes around his ruff, and his ears perked forward, Fang made it clear that he wasn't going to back down.

Rot. She'd made certain he wouldn't follow her.

Now the sun rose in the east. He'd been driving without headlights, slowly and cautiously, hiding behind buildings whenever possible, speeding up when there seemed to be nothing but trees and a few little hillocks in the way. Once they'd come upon a group of *gangas* moaning "*uuu-vaaaaane*" and "*truuuu-uuuuth*," and Quent had bulldozed the monsters down with the truck. Knowing that Zoë would grudgingly approve of his blasting through the gray-skinned, rotting-faced creatures had made him feel marginally better.

Now that it was morning, and the danger from the orange-eyed zombies was over, Quent wanted to turn around and go back to check whether Zoë had returned to her little home. But that would do nothing to keep Marley safe and get her to Envy. If the others were waiting back there, somehow having learned where their prey had gone, he and Marley would be buggered.

Zoë knows what she's doing. She'll be safe.

And if he didn't go to Envy, she'd never be able to find him. He'd told her where to meet him. She'd come. If for no other reason than to learn how to make bottle bombs.

So he drove on, reluctant, but convinced it was the best decision. They'd left without food or water, except what little was in his pack. He guessed at the rate they were traveling, it would take much of the rest of the day to get to the walled city unless they needed to stop to forage for sustenance. But Marley wanted him to keep going.

"I feel exposed," she said, looking around, then down at her very tight tank top. "Especially looking like this."

He raised his brows, leering appreciatively. "I'm not complaining."

"Another obligatory response," Marley said, settling back in her seat. She looked out the windshield. "You're really into her, aren't you?"

He nodded briefly, his attention focused on the terrain ahead. Marley opened her mouth to speak again, likely to belabor the subject, and he swerved rather harder than he needed to in order to avoid a large metal lump that might once have been a wagon. She squealed in surprise and shot him a dark look, but seemed to accept that the topic was closed to discussion.

An hour later, he pointed to the ragged skyline of Envy. "There it is. All that's left of Vegas."

He hid the humvee back in the old garage and took Marley in through the hidden passage marked by an old Wendy's sign. Crawling through an old boxcar and up through rusted cars and other junk, he led the way, one hand safely ensconced in a glove, and the other free to touch. Another of his experiments, testing the boundaries of his control and the strength of the memories.

Quent found himself gritting his teeth when the flush of a dark image threatened to bulldoze him, but by focusing his mind, he kept it at bay. *Yes.* He might be able to beat this curse after all.

The first thing he did once they got into Envy was to bring Marley to his room. The second thing was to find Lou and get him up there to meet her.

"The first Stranger I've ever met," Lou said. He adjusted his glasses as he looked at her, his eyes lingering perhaps a bit longer than necessary on her very tight tank top.

"They generally use the term Elite," Marley told him. "Just FYI."

"You look familiar," Lou replied, dragging his gaze up to look at her. "Sorry." He smiled a little abashedly. "It's been a while since I've—er—"

"I think the first order of business is to get me some clothes that fit," Marley told him.

"Oh, I was staring at the crystal, not your very— er—"

She laughed and sank onto the bed. "You were saying I look familiar? I'm the daughter of Brandon Huvane. If you ever happened to read the gossip columns or Page Six, you probably saw at least one photo opp."

"There was that time they caught you topless in Costa Rica," Quent offered. "Everyone saw that one. Right after you got that tattoo on your left—"

"Okay," Marley interrupted. "How about we talk about something other than my breasts, hey? I know they're nice and perky for being eighty years old, but still."

"Sorry," Lou said again. "So you're going to help Quent get into Mecca to find his father?"

She curled her lips into themselves. "If he really wants to risk his life, I'll tell him what I know. But I don't think it's a good idea. You can't kill Fielding." This last was directed at Quent. "It's nearly impossible to kill an Elite, let alone get close enough to try. Aren't there other ways to get your revenge?"

"It's not impossible to kill an Elite. Simon killed one, and so did Lou's friend Jade. Get me in there, get me close enough, and I'll take care of Fielding. I'll have the element of surprise on my side. Okay?"

"They killed two Elites?" Marley seemed suitably shocked. "How?"

"Hacked out their crystals. There's probably a prettier way to do it, but I haven't found it." It wasn't lost on Quent that she had curled her fingers around her own crystal. "Good idea to find you some clothes that will hide that too."

"What happened when the crystal was cut out?" she asked in a low voice.

Quent realized what he was saying and softened it a bit. "They did a Dorian Gray—just kind of shriveled up."

"And died."

He nodded. Then added, "You'll be safe with us here, Marley. Elliott's not going anywhere, and neither is Lou."

"I'm looking forward to the chance to talk with you, too, Marley," Lou interrupted. "I'm sure you have information that will help us in our efforts."

Just then there was a knock on the door. Quent opened it to admit Fence, Elliott, and Theo. They were, understandably, intrigued by the presence of a nonthreatening Stranger who could be questioned, not to mention appreciative of the package she came in. Fence's enthusiastic grin said it all.

Quent chafed and finally had the opportunity to turn Marley over to Fence, with Elliott acting as chaperone and promising to get her to Jade for some appropriate clothing. He wanted everyone the hell out of his room in case Zoë showed up.

And if she didn't, he was leaving at the first light of dawn to go back and check on her.

He rested poorly that night, despite the fact that he'd not slept since yesterday morning in the church with Zoë. Dreams wound through his mind, of crystals and flames, of Fielding and the riding crop, of Zoë and the burning forge.

And when he woke, and it was morning, he found himself alone, tangled in the sheets and the remnants of his nocturnal thoughts.

A short time later, he and Jade left the walls of Envy. The sun was still near the horizon, just about half of its sphere had risen.

"Thank you for your help," he told Jade as she whistled for one of the wild mustangs. She had a way with horses, and Quent had gone to her for help getting a mount, and to ask if she'd take care of his friend while he was gone. "Marley's all right?"

"She's got new clothes and slept in a comfortable bed at Flo's last night. We left the water running a bit in the bathroom so that she could continue to build up her strength," Jade replied. She smiled as a buff-colored mustang with a black mane and tail cantered up. "You okay with bareback?"

"I'm going to have to be," Quent said. He'd played polo growing up in England—another convenient excuse for cuts and bruises, so it had been encouraged by his father—and of course had ridden through jungles and up mountains in his other travels, but that was with saddles and bridles. "I'll make better time than by truck."

She nodded. "That you will. And you're going where again? Elliott's going to ask."

Dred had been called to the infirmary, so he wasn't there when Quent knocked on their door and awakened Jade. "I'm going back to where Marley and I were yesterday."

"With Zoë?"

He clamped his lips. Marley, the rotter, couldn't keep her bloody mouth shut. "I want to make sure she's all right."

"I don't think you should go alone, Quent. With your . . . ability. What happens if you touch something and get lost?" Jade's dark red hair glistened brighter than usual in the new day's sun. "We'll never find you."

What, did every fucking woman think he was incompetent? First Zoë, then Marley, and now Jade? This never would have happened back when he was known as Quentin Brummell Fielding, III—this second-guessing, this mothering. Of course, all they wanted from him then were expensive gifts and prestige.

He gritted his teeth. "I've got these." He pulled the gloves out of his pocket. "I won't take them off." He yanked them on a bit more roughly than he needed to.

"Wyatt would go with you, or Fence."

"I'll be fine. I'll be back by tomorrow night, latest. And by then, I hope Marley's been able to work with Lou and Theo to figure out where Mecca is." He'd been patting the horse, and after offering him an apple and a handful of carrots, he gathered up a fistful of mane. "Thank you for your help, Jade."

"Be safe, Quent." She looked up at him with worried green eyes. "Elliott's not going to be happy that I let you go alone."

He smiled down at her. "I'm sure you'll find a way to make it up to him." And he kicked the horse into a light canter, kicking up a little tuft of grass as they started off.

Thirty hours later, Quent slid off the same mustang in the same place he'd first mounted him. Exhausted, heartsick, tight with anger that battled with fear to be the most consuming of his emotions.

He gave his horse the last bit of carrots—harvested from Zoë's little garden—and swatted him gently on the flank. As the mustang cantered off to join his pack, Quent turned and walked back to Envy.

Reentering through the city gates, he went immediately to his room. Heart pounding with the last remnant of hope, he opened the door and walked in. Held his breath.

And felt nothing but solitude.

The room was empty.

He slung the pack from his shoulders and switched on the lamp, then stripped off his gloves.

And then he saw it. On the bed.

Skin prickling, he walked over. It wasn't an arrow, as he'd first thought. It was longer, and thicker. Perhaps ten meters long, the metal rod was about as thick as an old man's cane, maybe a bit more. But the end was . . . different.

Curious, hopeful, he picked it up. And immediately, he felt Zoë.

The sensation blasted over him, the familiarity swamped his mind and he felt himself sink onto the bed. But he didn't give himself over. Much as he wanted to sink in, he tested himself, forced his mind away.

If he could control it here, where he really wanted to go . . . he believed he could do it anywhere. He struggled for a moment, the desire was so deep. Zoë sifted around the edges of his consciousness, her hands, her strong arms. Her mouth, pinched in concentration. Heat. And when he was confident he could manage it, Quent lifted his hand from the weapon. His mind cleared. Then, once more, he gathered up the weapon and looked at it.

Without allowing himself to tumble in—he'd save that for when he was finished with the examination, figured out how it worked—he scrutinized the metal object. One end had clawlike petals and there were two smaller rods smaller than a woman's little finger that extended along the large one. Quent looked at it, moved it around, all the while conscious of the tickling at the periphery of his mind—and then he figured it out.

He'd seen a device like this before, years and years ago. When he was young, living on the Brummell estate. One of the gardeners had had a tool like this.

He stabbed it into the ground, pulled on a lever, and the claws closed around a weed and its roots, allowing it to be plucked quickly and efficiently from the earth. Dandelions. Crabgrass or chicory.

Or a crystal.

Quent hefted the weapon in his hand. Solid, but not too heavy. Holding it like a spear, he thrust it experimentally into a pillow. The force of the movement caused the claws to close with a metal snap, and he pulled it back. A jagged circle of cushion came with it, neat and tidy.

Oh, Zoë.

He settled back onto the bed, holding the weapon, smiling. Knowing she was safe. Knowing she'd been thinking of him. And he allowed himself to sink into the place he wanted to be . . . into the deftness of her hands, the orange heat of the forge, the knowledge that, though she might deny it, she cared.

For it emanated from the cold metal, mixed with the blast of the forge, the pinch of the pliers: affection, desire, love. Loneliness and fear.

With the iron bolt in his hands, he slept. Still smiling.

Ian raised his finger in a gesture the bartender recognized quite readily. Moments later, another small glass of whiskey appeared in front of him on the scarred counter, and the empty one was whisked away. Ian placed a ten-dollar chip labeled with an ornate *B* on the counter.

He didn't particularly care for the scruffy, grimy joint called Madonna's, but when a guy needed a pick-me-up—or a wind me down, or simply needed to blow everything out of his mind temporarily—convenience mattered. Since there weren't many options outside of Envy, a place he refused to set foot in unless he had to, Ian had to settle. Besides, he figured the alcohol would kill any germs that might linger. And he certainly wasn't hungry.

The bar's patrons consisted of transients like himself: bounty hunters, traveling scavengers, and an occasional farmer or rancher who dared stop into the dark, dank place. Settled in the middle of nowhere, the former boxcar, still situated on a rusted track, was well known to those who ventured beyond the safe walls of the small, scattered settlements. It was also a place used by the Elite to meet up with their bounty hunters, and Ian suspected that was why the establishment was still in business.

At least they didn't have to worry about deadly germs in their drinks, he thought sourly. Nothing that simple would kill those bastards.

The lone female in the place was always behind the counter. It was she for whom Ian had originally assumed the place was named—although, with the prickling bitch hairs on her chin and the faded red turban, she looked as far from a Madonna as a bulldog. Today, she wore a strapless leather thing, laced up on the sides and back, and jeans. Whoever had done the lacing had had their work cut out for them, for massive amounts of white flesh bulged through the diamond-shaped openings.

As it turned out, the bar was not named for its proprietress, but after the singer, and it had taken him a few visits to realize that all of those pictures on the wall were of the same person, and that all the music played there was by the same artist.

The whiskey tasted just as good the second time around, and Ian closed his eyes, savoring the warmth as it rolled down into his belly. He was just beginning to relax when the door opened and his day hit a shithole.

There was no sense in trying to melt into the shadows, though Ian figured if he was going to remain unnoticed, he was sitting in the right place, here at the darkest end of the bar. But, no.

Her eyes found him immediately and she sauntered over, taking her time so that every man in the place could admire the tall, slender figure she cut on skinny heels. Jeans sat so low they exposed her hipbones and the slight curve of her belly, sagging a bit in the back where her gun rested, its barrel purposely positioned down along her ass crack. At least on Lacey, the laced-up, strapless top looked like it belonged there. It also clearly displayed the small, glowing crystal set into her skin. Lacey's white-blond hair was twisted into a number of bumps all over her head, with spiky strands fanning out from each one.

"Ian," she said, sitting on the stool next to him, bringing a waft of musk. "Where the hell have you been?"

He took another sip of his whiskey, savoring the taste before he swallowed. He responded with a curl of his lip.

"Where the hell is Marley Huvane?" Lacey demanded. "Raul messaged that you had her, and then I hear nothing. Fielding's going to send that bastard Seattle out after her when he gets back—he's after that damn *ganga* hunter, with the weird arrows—so if you don't get Marley by then, we're out of the running. And that's a cock-honking big bounty."

"I don't have her."

"What about Raul?" Lacey leaned closer, bumping her leg into his. Purposely. "Does he still have her? She's worth—"

"Raul's dead," he drawled.

Lacey jolted a bit in surprise, but it wasn't her way to give up any weakness, so it was quickly masked. "Dead. How?" He could fairly hear her mind calculating, working, conniving.

Ian shrugged, gestured for another whiskey. And lied. "I killed him." *Now go the fuck away.*

"You're openly admitting that?" Lacey said, her voice dropping for the first time. "What the cock is wrong with you? Fielding's just waiting for a chance to—"

"Fielding isn't going to care because I've discovered something much more valuable to him." The whiskey arrived and he finished off the second one with a gulp, noting that, so far, it had done nothing to dull his senses. Especially now that Lacey had arrived. Now she'd planted her hand on his thigh, like she owned him.

Unfortunately, she practically did. Thanks to Raul.

"What?"

"His son."

Lacey's face displayed absolute shock. Then she broke into a greedy smile, which didn't do much to soften her foxlike features. "Well, son of a bastard, Ian. You're smart *and* pretty. I love that you always seem to have a surprise up your sleeve." She squeezed him through his jeans. "I never believed it possible. You're certain it's him?"

He concentrated on the whiskey and its trickle of warmth as he sipped from the third. That was the bad part about Raul being dead. There was no buffer between him and Lacey. "I've seen his damn photo often enough," Ian replied. "Right on Fielding's desk."

"Where is he?" she prodded.

"I'm tracking him. It won't be long. And since no one else knows about him, I don't expect any problems."

Lacey smiled, her lips wide and red. Men found her attractive until they got to know what was beneath the surface, hidden inside along with the crystal's tentacles. Ian had made that mistake. Once.

"I'll pass the news along. Fielding wouldn't be any happier if you'd said you found Remington Truth. This's about the only thing that would save your ass from his wrath for killing Raul."

"I was certain he'd feel that way." Ian bared his teeth in a humorless smile and took another sip of the drink. Fielding had no idea what kind of compensation he was going to demand.

"Whatever you do, keep ahead of Seattle," she ordered. "You get Fielding before that cock-sucker even figures out he's alive."

Meaning, Ian knew, that she didn't want the bounty hunter getting powerful enough to convince Fielding to have him crystaled. That would mean she and Seattle would be on equal footing, and it would make her fucking crazy.

Just then, the door opened.

At first he didn't recognize her. But the simple fact that it was a woman who stood in the entrance caught his—and everyone else's—attention, and then when he got a closer look, he felt his world tip. He was pretty damn sure it wasn't because of the whiskey.

Impossible.

Ian checked again as she stood in the sunny doorway. *Tall, curvy. Yes. Long, dark hair. Pulled back and up, but yes. Startling blue eyes. Mmmhmm. The haughty face of a princess—the type that got caught in a guy's dreams. Yep.*

"Who the hell is that?" Lacey said, her voice pitching high and tight.

"That," said Ian, standing and slipping smoothly from her grip, "is my new partner."

CHAPTER 13

Remy knew the minute she opened the door she'd made a mistake.

But she was too slow, sluggish from lack of food and sleep, to react. *Ian Marck*. At first she couldn't believe her eyes that it was him—had seen her. Their eyes met across the dark space and he was on his feet in an instant.

How could this happen? What were the chances?

Before she could fully assimilate the situation and back out, Ian was there, grabbing the door she would have closed. Behind him, Remy saw the woman he'd left, sitting at the bar, staring after him with a pissed-off expression. And then she noticed the glow of the woman's crystal, proud and bright.

Unbelievable. Into the fricking fire.

"Don't say anything," Ian ordered in a low voice, standing in the doorway between her and the rest of the occupants. "Just play along with me or you're toast."

"You've got to be kidding me," she said, her heart thumping, her palms slick. As if she'd trust Ian Marck to have her interests at heart. "I'm leaving." Dantès sat beneath a tree, where she'd ordered him, and she glanced over at the dog, whose ears perked up.

"If you leave, you'll be followed." His stormy blue eyes held that same cold look they always did. Except that time he'd kissed her. Then they'd been flat and furious when he pulled away.

Remy felt the weight of too much attention from too many eyes. "I'm not worried about that. Dantès will take care of them," she replied.

Ian shook his head. "He can't compete with a bullet."

"Just leave me alone." Remy turned and would have walked away if he hadn't reached for her arm.

He didn't hurt her, but his grip was firm. "I can protect you better if you come in and act as if nothing is wrong."

She would have laughed in his face if she hadn't been so exhausted and hungry. Instead, she asked, "And who's going to protect me from you?"

His mouth thinned. "You've done a fine job of that yourself in the recent past."

Which made her frown, because she hadn't hurt him badly enough that night she escaped. She knew she hadn't disarmed him with that single elbow thrust and instep-stomp, but he'd fallen to the ground as if in pain. Allowed her to get away.

That knowledge made her uneasy. Ian Marck had secrets, and he was even more ruthless than his father.

Ian glanced behind him and then turned back to her. "The opportunity is going to pass by in about ten seconds. Either come in and play along with me or you're going to be in over your damned head."

"Is the food any good here?" she asked, caving in to basic needs.

"No, but it'll do, and she pours a good whiskey."

She had to eat, at least, or she was going to be a worthless puddle anyway. No one knew her secret. She had nothing to fear.

Except from Ian Marck.

Who was now volunteering to be her protector.

What the hell did he want in return?

Quent expected Zoë to make an appearance within the next day after leaving the weapon, but after three nights of no sign of her, he began to wonder.

He debated riding back to her hideaway, but what if he missed her again? Without any form of communication, they could do that for weeks. And when he'd visited her home last, he'd left no sign of his presence, which, in retrospect, had been foolish.

She wouldn't even know he'd been there.

Nevertheless, despite the nights of half-sleep as he waited for his nocturnal visitor, Quent's days were busy. Filled with plotting and planning, practicing with his Elite-Killer, or the Eeker, as Fence had dubbed it one night after several too many pints, Quent grew more and more determined to walk away from Fielding alive, and carrying the man's crystal.

Theo, Lou, and Jade had worked with Marley to help determine where Mecca was, using landmarks and Quent's assistance in regard to where he'd driven. He wished for Zoë at that time as well, for she was as well traveled as any of them.

At last, they felt confident the proper location was determined, and with Marley's description of the compound, its guards, and her own strategy for escape, Quent had his plan in place.

"I've never been to Fielding's private quarters," Marley warned. "Only to his public parlor and dining room. I have no idea how it's set up, or what you'll find."

Quent shrugged off her worry. "He thinks I've been dead for fifty years. I've already got the advantage.

And why would I want to harm him?" *Let me count the goddamn ways.*

He could already feel the thrust of the Eeker into flesh, the satisfaction of the twisting of it into his body and watching the man's face curdle in agony as he yanked it free. Quent closed his fingers and imagined . . . freedom.

Freedom from regret. From hatred. From guilt.

From wondering about him, thinking about him. How the man he so hated haunted his thoughts, drove his actions.

"It's the escape afterward that worries me the most," Marley said. "As if they're just going to let you walk away after cutting out Fielding's crystal."

"Who the fuck knows? They might be celebrating," Quent replied flippantly. He didn't care. He just wanted it over with, one way or another. He'd die happy if he knew his father was on his way to hell.

But what about Zoë?

Beneath the moon, Quent walked his regular path between the hulking buildings and remnants of them, hoping that she'd find him this last night before they left. Where was she? Why didn't she come?

But she didn't.

Fence and Theo were on board to accompany him, and at last, they were ready to embark. Armed with homemade Taser guns made by Lou and Fence from old electric razors, along with a variety of other equipment, they opted to ride horses instead of taking the humvee.

"We'll camp tonight," said Fence, who'd been their guide in the Sedona cave all those years ago. "And tomorrow we should arrive with plenty of daylight to spare."

Although Quent chafed at waiting yet another day before coming face-to-face with Fielding, he'd been on enough excursions to know that pacing was important. That was why he'd given Fence the charge of planning the trip, certain that he'd put good sense aside in his zealousness to get there and get the confrontation over with.

"Marley and me were getting a little cozy last night," Theo commented as they rode along in a southwestern direction. "That bother you, Quent?"

"Marley and me? Wasn't that a movie?" Fence said. The sun would have been shining on his dark bald head if he hadn't tied a handkerchief on it. "Wasn't Marley the dog?" He laughed, a big rolling sound.

"Doesn't bother me," Quent told Theo. "But Marley's a bit of a free spirit." He knew that the other guy was still nursing a broken heart over Sage and Simon hooking up, and he figured Theo didn't need any more heartache when he'd been carrying a torch for Sage for years. That was part of the reason he had insisted on going on this mission. The computer room had become a hell of a lot smaller in the last few weeks.

"Marley's got a thing for you," Theo said. "But that gives us a lot to talk about."

"You got a thing for Quent too?" Fence replied. "Damn, am I going to have to find another place to sleep tonight, bro?"

Theo grinned in spite of himself. "As long as we get the extra blanket."

"Fuck that," Fence responded. "You'll have each other to keep warm. And what do you mean, you have a lot to *talk* about with her? What the hell are you doing, *talking*? That woman is one hot piece of ass. You oughta be getting some of that instead of talking."

"If we see any *gangas* tonight," Quent said, imagining what Marley's reaction to being called "a hot piece of ass" would be, "I want to try and catch one of them alive. In fact, I want to make a point of it."

"Dude, what the hell is wrong with you? Those mothers smell like . . . hell, I can't even describe it. Death. Rot. A fucking outhouse. And if you get too close, you get all weak and shit from the odor."

"Why do you want to catch one?" asked Theo, still smiling at Fence's theatrics.

"I want to practice with my Eeker." The truth was, Quent could hardly say the name of the weapon without laughing, it sounded so bloody ridiculous. But it was better than saying the long metal weapon, or the crystal grabber. "On a living thing."

"Don't you mean a *non*-living thing?" Fence replied. "Or is it unliving? Undead?" He looked at Theo, the resident pop culture geek. "What's the PC term?"

"I believe they prefer the term unliving."

"So, what are you going to do, tie it up and keep stabbing at it? Fuck, that'll be a mess with all that stinky, rotting flesh lumping all the hell over the place. You're gonna keep yanking out pieces of it? My man, that's called torture in my book. For both the thing and me. It's gonna stink to high heaven."

"Since their skin's always dropping off in clumps anyway, I don't think it would care," Quent replied blandly.

But Fence was shaking his head. "I don't know. You better be careful, or you're going to have PETZ on your pretty British ass."

"Pets?" Theo asked, obviously waiting for the punchline. He knew Fence, and therefore knew it was coming. "Like, dogs or cats?"

"You never heard of PETZ? P-E-T-Z. People for the Ethical Treatment of Zombies," the big guy replied with a grin. "They'll be picketing and demonstrating all around Envy if Quent ain't careful."

They all laughed, even Quent.

And so the day went, peppered with Fence's absurd comments as they rode quickly along the route he'd plotted out. Quent didn't mind the distraction his friend provided, and he suspected Theo felt the same way.

As planned, they found a safe place to camp that night, on the second floor of a large house. The ceilings were high, making the second floor safe from *ganga* reach once they hacked away the bottom half of the sweeping staircase. Having done this many times in the past seven months when they were traveling around trying to find Envy, the three of them made short work of the lower ten steps and used a rope ladder to climb up.

"And here we have the spacious loft," Fence said with a sweep of his muscular arm. "Complete with broken skylights, filthy windows—some of them even intact—and the hospitality of a variety of rodents. The three sofas, inhabited by any number of creatures, need a little work, but with a bit of paint and trim, this loft could be cozy as a little bungalow." He grinned. "My mama was in real estate."

Quent offered to take the first watch, but after some discussion, they agreed that there was no need for a guard. The *gangas* couldn't sneak up on them, for even if they managed to find their hiding place, the moans would betray their presence soon enough. An arsenal of bottle bombs would chase them away should they come close enough, and predatory animals couldn't make it through the closed front door or intact windows on the ground floor.

Nevertheless, Quent settled himself near one of the floor-length windows where he could keep watch as he lay on his pallet. Despite his plan to stay awake, or at least alert, he must have dozed off because something caused him to waken.

Not the sudden jolting of coming to consciousness, but a gentle, slow awareness. A spiderweb brushed his face or some insect, and he pushed it away. And connected with solid warmth.

He reached for the Taser beneath his pillow and his eyes sprang open, just as he inhaled a breath of cinnamon. And he caught himself, his heart suddenly slamming.

"Am I dreaming?" he murmured, reaching for her, closing his eyes again. "If I am, don't wake me."

She eased on top of him, her body aligning with his. One leg slid between his, caressing the inside of his thigh as she held his face in her palms, arching her body over him. Her hair brushed his face, her weight settled low on his belly. Their mouths met, hot and fierce at first, then eased into a long, languorous kiss.

Desire rolled through him like a barrel downhill, fast and crazy. His breath stole away, lost in the rush of soft lips and the slick, deep tangle of tongues, the gentle click of teeth and the welcome feel of her warm curves against his.

His eyes closed and he concentrated on her taste, the length of her waist and hip, the curve of her arse as he rode his hand up over her trousers and settled her against his cock, straining beneath the thin blanket. And then he suddenly remembered where he was.

And that only a few meters away, Fence and Theo slept in the darkness.

Quent froze, his eyes springing open, and he pulled his mouth away from Zoë's delicious one. "Hold on," he managed to breathe into her ear, even as he sampled the warm skin beneath her lobe. But she wriggled her crotch more heavily against his, and he had to draw in a deep gust of air as his own body responded with a great big *Who the fuck cares?*

Her hands had moved beneath the shirt he still wore, slender, calloused and confident, and her mouth nibbled at the edge of his jaw and down to his neck. He couldn't find it in himself to release her hips and shift her *off* him, where she belonged . . . the pressure, the grinding pressure, felt too damn good.

Instead, he concentrated on remaining silent, on holding back the rough breathing, the gut-deep groan when she reached between them and tugged his shorts halfway down his thighs. His cock shifted free and ready, and the next thing he knew, she was shimmying out of her own trousers.

Oh, luv. He had the presence of mind to glance over at the two lumps that were Theo and Fence, presumably sleeping. He hoped they were sleeping.

But for the life of him, he didn't care at this point, especially when he felt Zoë lift up, and her sleek, hot channel slide down over him. *Yes.* Quent closed his eyes and gritted his teeth, and just managed not to let go right then, even when she plastered herself torso to torso with him and began to shift her hips. Slowly. Cockteasing in a most delightful way.

Fogged with lust, he grabbed blindly for the blanket she'd discarded and managed to tug it over the top of them, just in case someone got curious about the rustling noises.

And then he dragged her against him for a deep, serious kiss. She moved her hips slowly, and he felt her smiling against his mouth when he tried to speed things up. Zoë shook her head against his, murmuring into his ear, "not so fast, genius," and settled back down against him, holding steady while he tried to collect the pieces of his brain. But they were scattered and all he knew was the warmth of her skin against his, damp and hot, and the smooth rise and slide of her hips above him.

She held him off, keeping the rhythm slow and long, with great pauses in between whenever he felt like he might start to rise close enough, and then a sudden fast stroke, down and hard, taking him by surprise and nearly forcing a groan of desperation. He saw the curve of her cheek—the woman was smiling as she fought him silently, sending his eyeballs rolling back as he tried to keep quiet and at the same time, let loose . . . and just when he thought he'd give it all up and slam her onto her back, sleeping companions or no, she gave in. The long easy strokes became faster and more serious, and he was able to rise and meet hers the way he needed to . . . on and on until he lost track of where he was.

Zoë gave a soft gasp in his ear, deep and husky, and as she pulsed against him, that was the last barrier. Quent's restraint shattered and he slammed up inside her one last time, holding her hips in place, his body taut with relief.

She sagged down on top of him, their bodies half clothed, moist and warm, tangled together. Panting,

Zoë smiled into his throat, smoothing her hand over his chest and trembling belly as though she owned him.

She did. Oh, she did.

"What the hell took you so long to leave?" she demanded softly in his ear.

"Leave?" Quent gathered his wispy thoughts together, one arm curled around Zoë, the other splayed lifelessly above his head. *Bugger it.* His toes still curled, his vision blurred, his body lay empty and loose. "What?"

"Leave Envy," she said, her lips brushing against the shell of his ear. "I've been watching for a damned week. Waiting for you to get your ass going."

"Why?" he murmured back, smoothing his hand up along her spine to the curve of her shoulders, then down over that very fine arse.

She shrugged against him. "I thought you'd be sharing your room with Marley."

He stiffened, and not in a good way. "I'm not screwing Marley."

"No shit," she snapped tightly. "But you'd be hiding her in your room. You promised to keep her safe, didn't you? I didn't want a damned audience."

Quent closed his eyes. "But I wasn't. So you tortured me for a week by staying away because you thought she was in my room?"

"Torture?"

Damn her, she sounded much too pleased with herself. "No, you're right," he said, kissing the soft skin in front of her ear. "That wasn't torture. Tonight . . . that was torture. With a fine ending." Except that . . . *hell.* He'd neglected even the most rudimentary of protection again. *Fuck.*

He glanced over at the human lumps outlined by the faint moonlight. They were either still sleeping, or being very polite. Since one of them was Fence, who didn't have a prudent bone in his body, Quent assumed the former.

He returned his focused to Zoë. "You could be pregnant."

"I'm not," she said. She pulled away and straightened her tank top, pulling it down to obscure those tight, perky breasts. And then she began to fasten up her cargo pants.

"After tonight, you could be. What would you do?"

She looked at him. "I'd tell you."

Despite the fact that she was dressing, pulling away from him, her words were a balm. He believed her. "I'd want to know."

"I know that." She held his eyes for a moment, there in the dim light, and he believed her. *A baby? With rubbish-mouthed Zoë?* His mouth ticked into a little smile.

"Thank you for the weapon," Quent said, sitting up. The blanket fell away from his chest, and he noticed that her attention seemed to snag on his bare shoulders. "It's bloody brilliant."

He could make out the curve of her smile in the dark. "Damn right."

He reached to touch her arm, and when his fingers brushed it, she winced. And he felt something rough and sticky. "What's that?" he said, barely remembering to remain low-voiced. "Are you hurt?" Without waiting for an answer, he tugged her toward him, where a pool of moonlight glowed on the floor.

Though it was dim, he could clearly see a wide,

dark patch on her bicep. "What happened?" The blood was dry, but still crusty and the way she caught her breath when he gently probed told him it was fairly fresh.

"Had a little tangle with a bounty hunter," she said. "It's fine."

"What happened in this little tangle, exactly?"

"Be quiet, you'll wake them," she whispered.

"Fuck that. What bounty hunter? Marck?" He hadn't let go of her arm, though she tugged at it.

"A guy named Seattle. He thought he was going to catch me, but I gave him the slip."

"There's a bounty hunter after you?" Quent's heart thudded. As far as he knew, the Marcks hadn't ever been tracking Zoë. *As far as he knew.* Of course, he didn't know bloody much about her, did he? "How long has he been after you?"

"I don't fucking know. I didn't ask," she said, clearly finished with the topic. But that didn't mean he was.

"You're staying with me," he told her. White fear shuttled through him. *Gangas* were one thing, but being tracked by smart, gun-toting, daylight traveling bounty hunters was another. "It's too dangerous."

Zoë made an annoyed sound and pulled back. But he didn't release her. "Let go." She sounded wary, and her voice was too loud.

"You're staying with me."

"What the fuck? Do you think you're my father?"

"No, I'm your *lover*. Or hadn't you noticed?" He spoke from between gritted teeth. Someone shifted across the room, but he didn't care. Didn't she fucking understand? It was dangerous. This world was goddamned dangerous, and at any moment, she could be trapped or captured or torn apart.

Of course she didn't understand. She'd made him a fucking special weapon to use when he went in after his father—a bon voyage gift for a mission that would most likely result in his own demise. *Good luck, genius. Have fun storming the castle!*

The sweep of a chill washed over him. Didn't she worry about him? Didn't she care? Why wasn't she begging him not to go?

Or was this all really just a lot of great sex? Spiced with a bit of intrigue, her sneaky comings and goings? Was that the attraction? The danger?

"Zoë," he began, knowing at that moment, the whole situation blinding in its clarity, that if he never saw her again, he'd be lost. "I don't want anything—"

"If you don't fucking let me go right now, I'm going to scream."

What the hell was the point? He let go, and had a malicious little twinge that she had to catch herself because she'd been tugging so hard.

"Nice way to blow a perfectly good afterglow," she said, crossing her arms over her middle, unobtrusively rubbing the one he'd gripped.

Quent didn't trust himself to say anything, for he knew it would come out . . . unpleasantly. To say the goddamn least. "So where are you off to now?" he managed from between numb lips.

She seemed to catch herself, then replied, "Wherever."

Where the fuck ever.

He felt the weight of her eyes settle on him, then whisk away. He fought for something to say, something that would come out right—not too pathetic, not too overbearing. But for once, words, tact, diplomacy failed him.

It was as if she'd sneaked out of his room all over again—that same hollow feeling. The feeling grew deeper, gouging his innards, as she pulled to her feet.

"Good luck, Quent."

She might as well have been saying good-bye. He fought the urge to drag her back down next to him. He refused to debase himself any further. And why pursue something that could be moot anyway?

He figured there was an eighty percent chance he'd never make it back out of Mecca. So he said, "Be safe, Zoë. Stay away from those bounty hunters. They're not as friendly as I am." He forced a little laugh and watched as she straightened and walked away, melting into the shadows.

Just as she disappeared, he glanced out the window and saw that the sun had started to light the sky.

And so began his day of reckoning.

That went well, Zoë thought to herself as she climbed silently down the rope ladder. Her lips, which only a short time ago had been swollen from kisses, now felt tight and hard. Her belly churned and she tried to dismiss her memory of Quent's expression.

He'd thank her in the end.

She wasn't playing a damned melodramatic martyr. That wasn't what this was about, leaving Quent for his own good, that sort of thing. Zoë'd read two books where the man did that, and she'd ended up throwing them against the wall—and then giving them to Fang to chew on.

It wasn't like that.

She wasn't *leaving* Quent anymore than she'd done in the past. She'd never been with him, and maybe if things had been different they might have been able to build a home like the one she'd grown up in. A twinge in her middle turned into a sharp pain.

But what she could do was give him the gift of freedom. And life.

That was what she intended to do. Hers was already destroyed. His didn't need to be as well.

Her horse was where she'd left him, a nameless black-splotched mustang who flew like the wind over the terrain. Fast and sure-footed, he'd get her to the meeting place in plenty of time.

And then she could put her plan into action.

3 May 2011
7:00 P.M.

I suspect that the baby will come tonight or tomorrow. I haven't said much to Devi for I don't wish to worry him after what happened with Marie, but I'm certain I'm having contractions. They seem to be fairly regular and growing more painful as the hours go by.

There was another one. A bit stronger this time. Perhaps I had best put this journal away and tell my beloved doctor to prepare to bring his child into the world.

There are no zombies out tonight. It would be a good night to be born.

—from the diary of Mangala Kapoor

CHAPTER 14

Quent's first sight of Mecca came filtered from between thick trees and the rise of low hills. His first impression of the place was that, from a distance, everything was white. Clean and pure.

An irony for sure.

The compound sat, just as Marley had described, out in the ocean. She'd guessed five miles from shore, but upon seeing it, Fence and Quent agreed it was no more than three. White walls rose around it like a medieval castle and its bailey, and the irregular rooftops and a few angular towers jutted up from behind. There was no keep sitting on a hill, surrounded by the smaller buildings belonging to underlings, although there was a slight rise in the center.

The five hundred acre floating community housed fifty to seventy of the most powerful Elite, including the Inner Circle. They lived there with their servants, which numbered in the hundreds, and, from what Quent knew, a good portion if not all of them were humans lured, kidnapped, or bred into slavery by the bounty hunters and other crystaled mortals.

The Elite rarely if ever left the compound, preferring, as Marley put it, to keep themselves safely out of sight and uncontaminated by non-Evolved humans. While most of their food was grown elsewhere and shipped in through bounty hunters, CMs, and some humans, certain luxuries—cocoa and coffee beans for example, along with silkworm farms—were propagated only on the island itself.

A long walkway or bridge connected the compound to land. At the shoreline, which was devoid of buildings or growth, sat a gatehouse. There'd been more security at the cinema back when there were cinemas, Quent thought. Here there was a single gatehouse and a long, floating walkway. It seemed oddly open and unprotected. But Marley had assured him that no one passed to the compound without clearance. Aside of that, according to her, sharks lived in the waters surrounding the floating community. They were kept in the area by some sort of sonar device beneath the surface. The ferocious sharks were taught to attack anything in or on the water, so the boats that brought approved shipments to the island were outfitted with special crystals that sent signals through the water that kept the sharks at bay. Any other vessel—or person—would attract the beasts and be torn apart.

As they rode closer, Quent noticed that Fence seemed to become quieter. Fewer jokes and comments, and a bit of a sheen appeared over his bald head.

"You okay?" Quent asked, realizing his own pulse rate had begun to rise. This was it.

"That bridge looks damned unstable," replied the black guy, "floating on the water like that."

"Marley said it's the only way on or off the compound without a protected boat."

"The walls aren't very high," Fence continued. "Could fall right off, into the water, the way it's moving with the waves."

"It doesn't seem very secure," Theo agreed. "But

there's a couple horses coming across on it now and it seems all right."

Fence snorted, subsiding into silence as they approached a thick cluster of trees. The sight of Mecca was now completely obscured by the edge of the forest, and an old gas station.

"Here's a good place to stop," said Quent, pulling back on his mount's mane. "I've got a bit of a change of plans."

"Fuck that," Theo said. "We have it all worked out and you're not going to screw it up."

Quent shook his head. "Sorry. Unexpected circumstances." Except he wasn't sorry at all. He saw no reason for Theo and Fence to get their arses fried on his death mission. And aside of that, Fence was looking more than a little unwell.

"This is how it's going down. I'm going in there—I have the best chance because Fielding is going to be shocked at my unexpected appearance. Why would he not think I died fifty years ago with everyone else? But after I do what I have to do, it's bloody sure I'm not getting out. It's not like they're going to let me just walk away after he's dead."

"Yes, we've been over this," Theo said tightly. "But—"

"Circumstances have changed," Quent said, overriding him.

"Since when?"

"Since this morning. I had a visitor." He leveled a serious look at them. "Just hear me out. I'm not expecting to make it back, and there's someone who needs to be taken care of should my early demise occur."

"Zoë?"

Quent didn't ask how Theo knew about her. Elliott, he supposed. "In the event that she's pregnant—which is a possibility—someone's got to take care of her. She's got fucking bounty hunters after her. She lives alone. She rides out and hunts zombies every night."

"Man, you don't have to go over there. Maybe we could find a way to draw Fielding out? If he knew you were here, he'd come."

Shaking his head, Quent interrupted Fence, "No, he'd just send his men after me and I might not make it alive to see him. Who knows if he'd want me dead or not. And besides, that would take away the element of surprise if I just show up." He adjusted his seat on the antsy horse. "And I *do* have to do this. I should have done it sixty years ago, then maybe none of this would have happened."

Theo snorted. "Sorry to say, Spidey, but your father wasn't the only guy with his hands in this mess. His untimely demise wouldn't have made a difference."

"It would have to *me*." Quent rubbed his hand over his face. "Fence, I need you to stay here. Promise me that you'll find Zoë if I don't come back out of there, and take care of her. Even if she's not pregnant, I need to know that someone will keep an eye on her. All right?"

"So you're going to walk in knowing that you might be leaving a kid behind?"

"I'm not walking in there with a bloody death wish. I sure as hell would like to come out on the other side. I know it's a distinct chance I won't, but this has to be done. And I'm the one to do it. But I'll be better able to do it, knowing she'll be safe. All right?" And without waiting for a response, he gave Fence directions to Zoë's hideaway. "She uses it as her home base.

She'll be there eventually." *If she doesn't get caught by a bounty hunter.*

Quent closed his eyes against the thought and then reopened them. "Can I count on you, Fence? Or whatever your real name is."

"Bruno. But, yeah, brother. You got it." Fence extended his massive hand and Quent shook it. At least he had one less thing to worry about.

"That was my one other regret before I died," Quent joked with a wry smile. "Afraid I wouldn't learn your real name. That, and how you got a ridiculous moniker like Fence." He looked at him. "Thanks."

"Nothing," Fence replied with a wave of his hand. "And I'll tell you the story on the other side."

Quent slid off the back of his horse and adjusted his pack. "I want you to leave now, so that if anything happens, you're well away. I don't know what kind of reception we're going to get."

Fence looked at him for a long moment, then nodded. "All right. I'm gone." He turned his attention to Theo. "Take care, brother." And he was gone.

Theo nodded, and looked at Quent. "So you're letting me go in with you?"

"No." Quent held up his hand to ward off any arguments. "Lou needs you, and so does the Resistance. But I want you to be my backup for escape. Stay back here, and if I succeed, I'll shoot this flare into the air. Then you can be—"

Quent never finished his words, for all of a sudden four people emerged from the trees, surrounding them. Before he could react, Quent saw Fence, on foot and a gun held to his head, prodded from the bushes by a fifth man, who was nearly as bulky as his prisoner.

"What the hell is going on?" Quent said, looking

around the circle. They'd done nothing suspicious, hadn't even gotten within view of the gatehouse. "Are we on private property or something?" he asked, realizing how odd that sounded.

A man with long blond dreadlocks and darkly tanned skin smiled, his teeth white and crooked. He held a shotgun cradled unthreateningly against his leather vest. "No, you aren't. But you've just made me a very happy man."

A strange little prickle started down Quent's spine. "What do you mean?" He glanced at Theo, who was inching his hand toward the Taser in his pocket. Wouldn't help much from this distance, but at least it was something. His own gun was in the back of his jeans and he placed his hand slowly on his hip. The closer the better.

"I didn't believe it was possible," the dreadlocked man said. As he stepped closer, Quent saw the scar on his left cheek, curling around at the chin. "But here you are, in the flesh. Quent Fielding."

How the bloody hell did the guy know his name? That strange prickle down his spine turned into a heavy ball in his belly. "Right, then, you have the advantage of me," he replied calmly, though his mind was racing.

"So sorry. Uh, *not*," the man replied. Then he adjusted the gun in his arms. "But what the hell? It's no secret. Name's Seattle."

Quent felt as though he'd been punched in the stomach. Seattle. It could be no coincidence that the bounty hunter Zoë had "tangled with" had shown up here, as if expecting him. Knowing his name.

His mouth tasted like sawdust. "Where is she?" he said, moving toward the bounty hunter. "What did you do to her?"

Seattle raised his gun and pointed it at Theo. Not at Quent, which was telling. "Don't move or I'll blast his head off. He's not worth anything."

Apparently, Quent was, however. How the hell had this guy figured out who he was? "What did you do to her?" he asked again, his heart pounding so hard his fingers shook. He should never have let her go. He should have made her stay.

Seattle smiled, showing teeth that looked as if they'd been punched inward on top. "I didn't do anything. She walked away on her own two feet after she got what she wanted. My opinion, she got the cocked-up end of the deal, but who am I to judge?" He gestured, and two of the men started toward Quent. "She doesn't come back, I have you. She comes back, I have you and her other offerings."

So shocked was he by the bounty hunter's words that it took Quent too long to react. He reached for his gun, but didn't quite grasp it before a whip snaked out and curled around his legs. The next thing he knew, he was on the ground, the gun fumbled away. But he recovered, rolling quickly onto his back, swinging his legs up in a bent-knee position. As one of his attackers lunged, he kicked out, tossing him through the air as if he were a doll.

As Quent scrambled to his feet, shrugging off the second assailant, there was a shout, followed by a gunshot. Quent froze, locking eyes with Seattle, who gave a sharp nod as he looked behind him. "See what you made me do."

Quent spun. Theo was on the ground. Unmoving. And as he started toward him, Quent saw the pool of red spreading over his friend's shirt. But before he could get there, the sound of a gun cocking stopped him.

Heart sinking, Quent looked over at Fence, who was still upright and under the control of the bulky man with the gun that had just been cocked, right next to his eye. Their gazes met and Fence shook his head slowly.

Fury chilled him and Quent turned back to Seattle. "I'll come with you if you let them go."

The bounty hunter sneered. He reminded Quent of a prep school kid he once knew—tall and skinny, filled with his own importance, and stupid. If Franklin Dover had grown dreadlocks and gotten his pale ass tanned, he'd look a lot like this bounty hunter.

Quent shrugged. "You shoot him"—he gestured to Fence—"and you've got no more leverage with me. I don't fucking care if I die. And I'm worth nothing to you dead." Ignoring everyone, he walked over to Theo and knelt next to him.

Hell. He was in bad shape. Quent hid his horror and tried to find a way to stanch the blood flowing from the hole in his chest. In a lung, likely. Too high to be the heart. He hoped. As he knelt, tearing off his shirt to use as a bandage, Quent slipped his hand in Theo's pocket and sneaked the Taser out and inside his boot.

"I'll cooperate if you let them go. He needs medical help, and trust me, if he dies," Quent told Seattle, "you'll be hunted down."

"Do I look like I care?" Seattle replied. "They can hunt me all they want, whoever they are, but it won't do them any good." Quent could almost hear the *nyah-nyah-nyah* along with Seattle's taunt.

The Taser comfortably in next to his ankle, Quent stood. "Let them go and I'll play nice. If not, I'll fight my way out of here and you'll have nothing left to bargain with."

Seattle's face hardened, lengthening the scar along his cheek, but he must have realized he had no choice. Quent's superior strength and leverage gave him the upper hand. For the moment.

The bounty hunter gave a short, sharp nod to the bulky guy who had Fence under his control, and the gun fell away. Fence gave Quent a meaningful look—*wanna fuck 'em up?*—but Quent shook his head briefly.

Theo needed help, and there was no time to waste. The chances of him getting back to Envy in time were in the pit, but at least Fence could try. And at least Lou would be able to see Theo again.

Besides, if Seattle was going to trade Quent for a bounty—presumably to Fielding—that would serve his purpose: getting him inside Mecca. He could take it from there.

"I want them all kept here," Quent said, gesturing to Seattle's men. "While my companions leave."

"Who's calling the shots here?" said the bounty hunter in a voice with a distinct whine.

"I am," Quent told him with a humorless smile. *Just wait till they're safely gone. Then you'll really see who's in charge. Stupid wank.*

Fence didn't wait any longer. He hurried over, easily lifting Theo in his massive arms, and started off into the woods where, presumably, he had left his horse. His last glance back at Quent offered luck and determination.

"All right, then," Quent said a few moments later. "Now what?"

"Come with me," Seattle said with noticeably less bravado than before. Noting this, one of his henchmen didn't move quickly enough, apparently, because the bounty hunter raised his rifle and pulled the trigger. No hesitation whatsoever.

Quent turned just in time to see the man fall to the ground. Another perfect shot, this one just as deadly as the one in Theo's chest.

"Not a great way to keep the help," Quent commented dryly.

Having reestablished the size of his dick, Seattle snapped an order. "Tie him." This time, his cohorts moved without hesitation. Two of them rushed to lash Quent's wrists behind his back, and he allowed it because he knew the final result would be exactly what he wanted. They patted him down, checking his multiple pockets but not, stupidly, his boots.

The next thing he knew, something dark and muffling was yanked over his head, and he was off to the bloody races.

What an ass-crap fucked up place Mecca was.

Zoë felt smothered and stifled just standing there in the narrow space between two buildings. And the sense had nothing to do with the fact that she'd been stuffed inside a container of wool for the rocking trip from shore to shore.

Damn good thing she didn't have a weak stomach, or she'd have puked and ruined the scratchy, stinking shit for sure. She hoped they washed the stuff before they made it into clothing or no one was going to want to wear it. And she was going to smell like sheep for a week.

The two buildings rose on either side of her, blinding in their whiteness. Everything looked the same— smooth, white, and angular. Except near the ground, where the white had become dingy and stained.

From a distance, the city looked like a pearly, beautiful place. But up close, the grime and shit showed through. Just like everything else.

Water rushed through in channels along the walkways, and tumbled in slides or in free-fall from upper levels. She understood why, having met Marley Huvane. Like pictures of the Lost Gardens of Babylon, ivy trailed from each level of many of the buildings. Red, pink, and yellow flowers sprung from occasional balconies or alongside the channels, but other than that, there was little natural growth. Just white, smooth, flat. Creepy as all hell.

Picking yet another clump of the damned wool from her shirt, Zoë walked quickly away from the loading dock on the north side of the city, out of sight of the shore. No one seemed to pay her any mind, for the dock was just as busy as the ones she'd seen in movies—lots of activity, people moving crates off boats, shouting and calling out orders.

Her bow slung over her shoulder, her quiver still on her back, she knew she had only a short time to get away before someone did notice her. Keeping her eyes averted from passersby, she hurried along, gripping her arrow.

She wasn't worried about Quent. He couldn't be any safer than with Seattle, who'd protect the valuable bounty with his life—until Quent escaped, which was inevitable. Seattle was no match for Quent's intellect, calmness, and strength. Which was why she'd chosen Seattle instead of Ian Marck.

And if Quent didn't happen to escape, she had a backup plan that would make Seattle just as happy. All she'd had to do was mention Remington Truth, and he'd been slathering all over her deal—so anything else she told him later would only sweeten the deal and ensure Quent's release.

But for now, all Zoë needed was a bit of time, a delay. That would give her the chance to do what she needed to do.

Looking for the large building with the red squares on it, she shielded her eyes from the blazing sun. She'd done the right thing. Of course she'd done the right thing.

Quent would be safe, and he wouldn't have to take the risk.

He wouldn't have to live with the decision.

She found the building with the red squares that edged the roof and walked toward it, up a narrow street and down another one. The thoroughfares were quiet, with an occasional passerby now that she was away from the dock. Zoë passed a glassed-in building that looked like it housed plants. Along another street was a garden where three young people hoed and weeded beneath the sun. The city was eerily silent, and seemed almost as if it was asleep. Nothing like Envy, where people walked around in the habitable areas all the time, and the sounds of voices and children playing always filled the streets.

When she found the walkway to Fielding's red-tiled house, she paused and looked up. Her palms felt a little damp and she tightened the grip on her bow. The structure resembled a squared-off pyramid, with four stories. A bit of greenery, neat and cropped short, made two small squares in front of the entrance, which was behind a high gate.

She approached the pair of guards boldly. "Tell Fielding that Raul Marck's killer is here to speak with him. Make it fast."

One of them gaped, while the other reached for a device that looked like an old telephone. Zoë had fit an arrow into place and she held her bow ready, but pointed to the ground. She waited as the guard spoke in a low voice into the speaker.

At last, the guard hung up the phone and said, "He'll see you."

To her surprise, they didn't require her to leave her weapons behind—but, of course, what damage could a bow and arrow do to an Elite?

The guard sent her up a walkway to where tall, double doors opened at her approach. They were made of massive glass wedges set in silver hardware, and beyond she could see a gleaming marble floor and a large vestibule.

"Follow me," said a man dressed in white, with colorless hair and pale blue-gray irises. "Mr. Fielding is waiting."

Moments later, Zoë found herself alone in a large room. White, of course. *Good fucking grief, do the Strangers have a problem with pigment? Or are they simply trying to convince themselves of their purity and innocence?* The sound of rushing water was really beginning to get on her nerves.

Unsettled, she walked around the space, brushing her hand over a shiny glass table that was inset with seashells, examining the crystal pitcher of water and matching glasses that sat on a clear tray.

"So you claim to have killed Raul Marck. I heard it was his son who did the deed."

The voice surprised her. Its familiar accent, a bit more clipped and formal than Quent's, caused her heart to bump a bit. And when she turned and saw Parris Fielding, Zoë's stomach did a quick flip.

At first glance, he looked too much like Quent. Tall, but not as broad and muscular. More elegant, precisely groomed, and older by perhaps two decades. Very handsome, dressed in a slate gray jacket and matching trousers. A black shirt, unbuttoned at the neck. Gleaming black shoes. A knobbed cane in his hand that he didn't seem to need.

He wasn't alone. Three beautiful women, all dressed in floor-length silver gowns that seemed to be painted onto their bodies, came into the room with him. A dark-skinned, dark-haired one on his arm, and a dark blonde and a platinum blonde floating in their wake. Behind them trailed a very handsome young man with curling bronze-colored hair. He wore a shiny white shirt, half buttoned, and dark trousers. He had bare feet. The glow of a crystal shone faintly through his light shirt on the right side.

Zoë focused her attention on Fielding. "Ian claimed to have killed Marck? What makes you think he'd finally grown the balls to do that? It was me."

"You've come to brag about it? I wonder why." Fielding strolled farther into the room. The woman on his arm looked up adoringly at him but he ignored her. "You've come to beg my forgiveness, perhaps? For eliminating one of my best bounty hunters?"

Zoë met his eyes. They weren't like Quent's, although they were the same brown-blue color. Fielding's were more aloof. Barely lit with curiosity.

Her hand at her side, she felt the heavy metal weapon hanging beneath her loose trousers, from hip to knee. She could pull it from inside her pocket and have it in her hand in a moment. She didn't even care if there were witnesses. Fielding's companions seemed oddly vacant in the expression. And aside of that, she had her bow and arrow as well.

But which side was the man's crystal on? Damn it to hell. The young man's crystal was on his right side. And Zoë remembered Marley's being on her left. Was it a gender thing? Or random? *Crap*. She couldn't do a thing until she knew for sure.

"Please, sit," Fielding offered, gesturing to a long white sofa. The two floater-women took his suggestion and settled on the furniture. "It's been a terribly exhausting day, and I have no desire to be on my feet any longer."

For some reason, the platinum blonde found that an amusing remark and she giggled. Fielding patted her on the head as he walked around behind the sofa. "Yes, indeed, Lila, you were very helpful, chasing my golf balls. I'd be even more exhausted if I hadn't had you running around on your hands and knees."

Zoë watched in fascination as Fielding walked over to the handsome young man and adjusted the collar of his shirt, then patted him intimately on the chest. "Much better. If you'd had it pressed like I told you, you wouldn't have offended me."

"It won't happen again," the man replied.

Then he looked at Zoë, spreading his hands in dismay. "If they didn't have me to help them, they'd be a bloody mess." Smoothing his hands over his trousers, he settled them on his hips, pulling back the suit jacket he wore. "Now, what's the purpose of your visit? You're interrupting my afternoon massage."

"And your manicure," added the young man.

"And your meeting with Liam," said the dark-skinned woman. She still clung to Fielding as he moved about the room as if unaware she was attached to his arm.

"Oh, damn Liam. The man can't make a decision to save his life," Fielding said. "If I weren't here, I can't imagine what this place would be like. Dirty, falling apart, disorganized." He shook his head woefully, and Zoë realized with a start that he wasn't jesting. "I always have the plan, I always execute the plan. Everyone else just waits for me to tell them what to do."

"What a burden that must be," Zoë said, trying desperately to keep the sarcasm from her voice. She wasn't certain she succeeded when Fielding looked at her sharply.

His eyes had turned cold. "You're wasting my time. What do you want?"

"I want to talk to you alone," she told him.

He lifted an eyebrow. "Is that so? What makes you think I'd acquiesce to such a demand?"

"Because," she said, "you're obviously the most intelligent man in Mecca and I know I could help you. You don't want everyone to know about your secret weapon."

He pursed his lips. "I don't need anyone's help."

Zoë simply raised her eyebrows. "If the rest of your people are as incompetent as this Liam person, and Raul Marck, of course you need my help."

Fielding looked at her for a long moment, then gave a sharp jerk of his chin. Without another word, the three women and the young man got up and left the room.

"Well, that was a pretty good trick," Zoë said. Her heart started beating faster. If she could figure out where his crystal was, this was her chance.

"You're wasting my time," he said flatly. "You have

two minutes, you ill-bred bitch. The only reason I haven't thrown you out to the sharks is because you claim to have killed Raul Marck. I've been wanting him dead for five years, so I can only assume you've got something worthwhile. But don't waste my fucking time. Get to the bloody point."

"Raul Marck was a careless ass-wipe. I took him off your hands. I'm a perfect shot with a bow and arrow."

"And how might your perfect shot with a bow and arrow serve me?" He walked over to a waist-high channel of water and trailed his fingers into it. "And why would you wish to?"

"A man like you must have need of a secret assassin."

If he took off his jacket, she might be able to see which side the crystal glowed on. How the hell was she going to get him to do that? *Damn*. She hadn't planned for this sort of cat-and-mouse dancing around shit. She wasn't good at it. Nor was she any good at groveling.

"I'll need to see proof of your skills before we have any further discussion."

Zoë nodded. "Whatever."

Fielding looked at her for a long moment, and she felt as though a hundred spiders crawled up her spine. Not a hint of weakness anywhere. Nor a hint of softness. Nothing but cold.

In the books, and the *Law & Order* episodes, the cops always managed to find the soft underbelly, the—what was it called? the Achilles' heel?—of the perp. They figured out what would mess him up, and manipulated the conversation that way.

But that wasn't her thing. Her thing was the metal bolt in her hand and measured boldness. Female *cajones*.

Fielding seemed to have made his decision, for he walked over to the glass table and began to arrange the crystal glasses in a wide pyramid. "Shoot the top one."

But Zoë wasn't satisfied. "I could do that with my eyes closed."

She went to the table and rearranged the glasses so that they were much closer together, still in a pyramidal shape. The gaps between them were smaller and she took the orchids, separating the blossoms and stuck each one into a glass, for a total of five. She settled the flowers so that each one hung over a gap between the glasses. Just big enough for her arrow to fit through.

"Three blossoms. Three shots. I won't knock over the glasses," she said.

Ah. At last a reaction. His brow twitched, and there was a flare of interest.

She stood as far away as the long room would allow, nocked her arrow, and let the first one fly. The faintest tinkle of a glass clinked, then the *thwang* as the point struck the wall, impaling the orchid.

She settled a second arrow and repeated the process flawlessly. She looked at Fielding, raised a bold eyebrow, and said, "Seen enough?"

"That's quite brilliant." The admiration on his face was genuine, and the smile transformed it to an engaging one. "I do believe I could use a woman of your ability. Has anyone else here seen your skill?"

She shook her head. "No one but you and Raul Marck. But he doesn't care anymore."

Fielding speared her with sharp eyes once again. "Tell no one about it."

She nodded. "Duh."

"What did you say your name was?"

"Zoë." Her heart pounded radically. *Holy crap, he looks like Quent even more with that grin.* For a moment, she was frozen, realizing she'd likely never see him again.

"Zoë. A lovely name." He scanned her, his attention more than the cursory, derogatory skim he'd given her earlier. Now he seemed more interested in the details. "Perhaps a bit of work on your wardrobe might be in order." His lip curled a bit.

"The fucking victim doesn't care what his assassin is wearing," she retorted. Suddenly nervous with his regard, she wandered nonchalantly back to the pyramid and replaced the glasses on the tray.

Fielding gave a little laugh. "I suppose that might be the case, but your boss cares." There was a hint of that steel in his voice. "And we haven't discussed compensation. That could be a deal-breaker."

Shit. She hadn't thought about that. Zoë took her time arranging the glasses, thinking. She had to say the right thing. "I want what everyone wants," she said, turning to look at him. "I want to live forever."

CHAPTER 15

Quent limped along the floating walkway, the Taser safely back in his boot, his Eeker in hand masquerading as a cane, and his eyes fixed on his target. Mecca rose in a low smattering of angular buildings, shining in the sun like an angular, flat Taj Mahal, or a pure white Paris.

He knew from Marley that the streets circled the oblong islandlike compound, angling around and around and up the small incline in the middle. Two main thoroughfares cut the island into quarters, ending in a large circle encompassing City Center, which was where Fielding's quarters were. The closer to the center of the city, the larger and more powerful were the residents who lived in the cookie-cutter buildings with Babylonian vines hanging from them.

Quent gave little thought to Seattle and his comrades, who were likely still recovering from the one-two-punch-and-slash tase he'd given them when they'd been foolish enough to acquiesce to his request for food, water, and a chance to wash up. He'd garnered no more respect for the hotheaded bounty hunter who'd left the work to his less-than-competent men while he relaxed.

If he'd acquired a bounty that would "set him for life," Quent would have taken much better care of it.

At any rate, they were behind him now and he was

on his way to find Fielding. The only hiccup was that he'd lost his gloves in the tussle with Seattle and his cohorts, but Quent had become more confident in his ability to keep the pounding images of his psychometry under control. He'd never been more focused in his life, and he intended to stay that way.

The guards at the gatehouse on shore had been reluctant to allow him access until they were tased into two crumbled heaps on the ground. Quent had to admit, the reformulated electric razor was one hell of a handy weapon, especially when one pretended to stumble into one's opponent with one in hand.

As he limped along, he passed several other people moving in both directions along the walkway. None of them gave him a second glance, nor did he recognize any of them. And as he drew closer to the island, he located the building with the red tiling. His heart picked up its pace and he felt the familiar cold, dead sentiment weight his belly.

The same feeling he always had when he knew he'd be around his father.

More than fifty years had passed since he'd seen Fielding, and the man still had the ability to affect him. To drive his actions. To give him sleepless nights, and to put his belly in knots.

To destroy his life.

Fathers, good or bad, had untold influence on their sons' lives. Quent wondered, as he had more than once, what sort of influence it would have been if he'd had parents who actually *cared*. Just one.

One thing he tried not to think about on the seemingly endless walk was Zoë. Seattle's taunt still hung in the back of his mind. He didn't want to believe the implications that she'd bargained for her freedom with

Quent, giving the bounty hunter information about him in exchange for . . . whatever.

The possibility left him cold, and threatened to paralyze his thoughts—which was a distraction he didn't need right now, especially being gloveless. So he thrust it away. If he made it out of Mecca, he'd hunt her down and find the answer. If he didn't, it wouldn't matter.

That was what he told himself. Over and over. Step by limping step.

Once he alighted from the walkway onto the actual ground of the compound, he realized it was soil. Solid ground—dirt, clay, and stone made up the surface. He wasn't certain how deep it went; was it possible this was simply part of Nevada or California and hadn't been completely buried by the change in the Pacific's shoreline? Or had Fielding and his Elite accomplices somehow built a floating piece of land?

As he walked alongside the ever-present aqueducts of flowing water toward City Center, he passed residents of the community. Most of them wore loose, simple clothing in what appeared to be undyed linen. They kept their eyes averted and seemed to be out on some mission, for they walked quickly and purposefully without interacting with others. Rickshaws spun by, pulled by brawny young men, and, occasionally, a brawny young woman. Most of them were empty, but occasionally a well-dressed man or woman in white was seated inside, watching languidly from their perch.

Quent felt as though he'd slipped back in time to some exotic nineteenth-century resort, and a strange unpleasant taste settled in the back of his mouth. Did his father reign supreme over this medieval Shangrila? Was this how Fielding and the members of his cult pictured their utopia?

White and pure and unemotional.

The only significant patch of green was a golf course, empty of players at the moment. Rolling hills and sand traps splayed beyond tall walls making up no more than nine holes. And as he walked by, Quent noticed that it was *moving*. The ground undulated slowly, buckling, flattening, tilting as if it were a thick green blanket and a sleeping giant beneath it shifted in its sleep.

He stopped and watched for a moment while ten acres of ground rolled and flattened, rising and peaking. When it stopped moving, he realized it had changed the terrain of the course. So that the Elite would never play the same nine holes twice, as though they needed to never leave their island.

Bloody clever. And yet, eerie.

Another half mile later, he came to stand in front of the large building that reminded him of a Meso-american pyramid. Red tiles alternated with white ones around the highest level, and blooming bougain-villea vines hung from the corners. Windows glazed the walls at all four levels, making glass stripes around the structure.

"Step away," said a guard, materializing from a small gatehouse. He wore white, which implied that he was crystaled—though Quent couldn't see a glow through his crisp shirt.

Even in the midst of this compound, Fielding had security. *Bloody interesting.* Whom did he need protection from?

He'd decided on boldness and honesty as the most efficient way to get him to his father's presence, so he said, "Inform Fielding that Quent is here to see him."

The guard seemed to hesitate, but Quent spoke again. "He'll want to see me. And I guarantee if you turn me away and he finds out . . . well, I'm certain you know how thorough Fielding can be."

The man grumbled and shook his head, clearly annoyed. But he picked up a wired phone. He spoke for a few moments in a low voice, and his eyes were wide when he looked up. "I'll escort you in."

"Not necessary. Just tell me where to go." He limped heavily over to the gate, which opened silently.

Inside, Quent bypassed the butler, who nevertheless insisted on directing him. He noticed the white marble floor, devoid of black or red veining but cut through around the edges for the ever-present water channels. He took note of smooth white walls, rounded white ceilings, and sparse furnishings. Because of the many windows lining each wall, there was little room for other adornment, although he saw occasional white sconced lighting.

At last he reached the room to which he'd been directed. The translucent glass doors were open and Quent paused. His mouth had gone dry and that awful weight sagged in his middle.

He limped into the room.

Fielding was standing there, waiting, watching the door.

They stared at each other for a moment and Quent shut the door behind him without using his fingertips. The only sound was the rush of water, gurgling and splashing along the edge of the room.

Fielding spoke at last. "It is you. I refused to believe it until I saw for certain."

Quent didn't trust himself to speak. Loathing and revulsion swarmed him, battering him from the inside. He took care not to meet his father's eyes for fear he'd read the hatred there.

"Come in, son," Fielding said, and made a sweeping gesture. "Sit. We have much to catch up on."

Quent's fingers curled more tightly around his weapon-cane. He fought with himself to keep from lunging toward the man across the room. Not yet. "I should say," was all he managed. "What have you been doing with yourself for the last fifty years?"

Fielding smiled and walked over to a glass table with a vase of orchids. "I must confess, not very much at all. I live quite the life of leisure. Although there are times when even I must attend to things. It's necessary when one is surrounded by incompetents."

"You don't have to do much to keep yourself safe? To run your new . . . what is this? A country? A kingdom?"

"I sense a note of disapproval in your voice, Quent," Fielding said, pouring a glass of something golden amber. "I can't imagine why you should since, by all rights, you would be the heir to what I've built. As my only son."

He wore a suit that looked like Armani, but was probably a post-apocalyptic knockoff. Slate gray, with a black shirt, gleaming shoes. "Scotch?" he asked, glancing over at Quent. Without waiting for his reply, Fielding poured a second glass. "I'm sorry I don't have Dalmore. We are a bit limited nowadays."

"Limited?" Quent managed to reply. "What a shame. You can live forever, but you can't have it all."

Fielding's face darkened for a moment, then he smiled. The smile that wooed the world, charmed his competitors, beguiled his colleagues. "But look at what I do have, Quent. And what could be yours as well. I have everything I could ever want. Forever." He took a large swig of his Scotch, and for a moment Quent thought he looked unsettled.

"Where's Starla?"

"I'm sorry to say, but your mother didn't make it through the Evolution. It was tragic, really. She was on location in—oh, somewhere. I don't even recall where." His smile didn't waver as he brought the glass over and set it on a table next to Quent. "She didn't deserve to come along."

"Obviously you felt the same about me."

Fielding tilted his head. "Is that what you think? Unfortunately, no one—including you—has ever been able to anticipate my plans. In fact, I made arrangements for you. After all, you are my only son. My progeny. Who else could even try to fill my shoes?" He sipped again, a more controlled taste this time. "I'd actually given up on your appearance—it's been fifty years."

"Arrangement? What the hell are you talking about? You have nothing to do with me being here." Quent drew in a deep breath, and reminded himself to remain unruffled. Fielding thrived on oversetting his opponents.

"Is that what you believe?" Fielding looked down at him, despite the fact that Quent was taller. It was an affect he'd perfected. "In fact, it's only because of me that you're here." Setting his glass down, he pulled off his jacket and hung it over the back of a chair, just as he had done many times in the past. Usually, that sort of action was a precursor to getting out a riding crop or some other form of entertainment.

This time, Quent would be ready for him. "I know you believe in your power absolute, but that's impossible. Father." He forced out the word he'd refused to use since he was twelve.

"But you're wrong, my son," Fielding said in a dulcet

voice. "I had it all under control. You were in Sedona when the Evolution happened, weren't you?"

Quent nodded. "Far away from you and your Cult of Atlantis."

Fielding's eyes danced. "Ah, so you've put at least that together. I hoped you'd be clever enough to do so, but I wasn't certain. I meant for you to join, you know, when the time was right. But things moved along too quickly for me to have you initiated. The opportunity arose and I had to take it. So I decided to wait until after the Evolution. I didn't dream it would take fifty years for you to find me, but I suppose I shouldn't be surprised."

Quent kept his mouth closed. Too soon to give way to his anger. He didn't know where Fielding wore his crystal; although that wouldn't stop him. He could easily subdue the man and find out. The one benefit of walking out of that Sedona cave was the superhuman strength that came along with his psychometric ability.

"I knew you were going to be in Sedona. I planned it that way," Fielding said.

Quent looked at him, allowing the disbelief to show in his eyes. "*You* planned it." It took effort to keep from laughing at the absurdity. His father had no influence on his life, let alone access to his calendar.

Fielding nodded and sipped again. "I knew we'd been . . . estranged . . . for some time, but I knew that after the Evolution, you'd want to join my ranks. Stand by my side. I wanted you to."

Quent picked up the Scotch and took a sip. It was the only way he could keep from going off on the man before him. Not yet. Not—

Zoë.

He shook his head to clear it. He looked at the crystal glass in his hand, where the images and memories threatened to seep into his mind. *Zoë*. Impossible. But he felt her. Sensed her.

Quent focused on the white wall across from him, battling the impossibility, the slur of images, trying to keep his face blank, to hide the internal battle from his too-perceptive father.

"Son?" Fielding said, breaking into his thoughts. Just the sound of that name coming from Fielding's mouth made Quent want to puke, and it had the additional effect of helping him to gather control. "What is it? Do you at last see what I've done for you?"

Quent pressed his lips together, squeezed his eyes tightly, and gave himself the moment to feel, to test the images. Controlled. *By God, it* was *Zoë*—she'd been *here*. Recently. Willingly.

He gulped the rest of the glass's contents back. The searing warmth blazed through him and filled his uneasy stomach. But it didn't take the edge from his realization.

"I'm flattered. Overcome," Quent managed to say. He focused on the calming sound of flowing water and gathered himself together. Then he looked up at Fielding, praying that the shock and confusion wasn't in his eyes, and that his father saw what he wanted—expected—to see. Reverence. Or at least gratitude. "You did this for me?"

"Not merely for you," his father replied. "But for both of us. Me, leading the way, and you following in my footsteps. Standing by my side."

"And you believe you arranged for me to be in Sedona." Quent grappled himself back into the conversation.

"You don't think it was an accident that you heard about the lost Anasazi treasure, do you? I arranged for you to hear about it, and for you to acquire the documentation that you believed would lead you to its location."

"You set me up?"

"With the help of your assistant . . . what was his name? Trevor? Tracy?" Fielding waved an elegant hand, an emerald ring glinting in the light. "I could never remember his name. But he kept me apprised of your calendar. And other relevant information."

"Why did you want me in Sedona?"

"It's a mecca of energy, of course, Quentin. Even you know that. And that fusion of energy was going to be harnessed and exacerbated with the earth's physical change during the Evolution. All those ley lines and power centers intersecting and fighting with each other. I knew something was going to happen. And now I see the results."

"I was an experiment."

"One that turned out better than even I could have anticipated. After all, you haven't changed a bit. Are you immortal?" he asked curiously.

Quent didn't bother to answer. He didn't know whether to believe Fielding, although knowing the man as he did, he suspected it could be true. In fact, if he didn't need to know what Zoë had been doing there, he'd put an end to this abhorrent discussion right now.

"But it doesn't matter," Fielding continued. "I'll have you crystaled."

"What do you do to fill your long, immortal days?" Quent asked. "Fifty years is a long time. You have everything."

"Nearly everything." For the first time, Fielding's pleasure seemed forced. "The women, the food, the entertainment. Not having to go to the office or attend strategy meetings, answer to board members. Everything I wanted, all mine, forever."

"I did see the golf course," Quent said. "How often does it change?"

Fielding smiled. "One of my brainchildren. I have it change every fourteen days or so." He smoothed his shirt and Quent looked for the glow of a crystal to shine through. "I can eat whatever I want, as much as I want, whenever I want. I can have sex as many times a day as I desire, with as many different woman as I want. Life is more luxurious than you can imagine."

"The same thing, day after day. No challenges, no changes." Quent shook his head. "It's not as if you can jet off to Paris or Tokyo or Tahiti any longer. They're fucking gone. What's the attraction?"

"Power." Fielding's smile seemed tight. "There's nothing more worthy, Quentin."

"Over what? There's nothing to control anymore. A few thousand people and an annihilated world?" Quent scoffed openly. "What accomplishment is there in that? You fucking blew it up. There's nothing left."

"I beg to differ. Mecca, as we call this place, has everything I could want. Everything I would have experienced in Paris or Moorea or Rome. All here, brought to me, recreated for me."

Quent rose and began to wander around the room, hoping to discover more about Zoë's visit. From which of the three doors had she entered, exited; had she sat, stood . . . what could he glean? He remembered to limp, using his weapon as a cane so that he always had it near him.

Part of him was ready to use it at any moment. Another part wanted to encourage Fielding to talk further, to see what he could learn.

"Did you find Atlantis?" Quent asked, touching the table. Zoë's essence filtered through to him immediately. "Is that how you got the crystals?"

"Yes, indeed, the crystals come from Atlantis."

That calm pronouncement caught his attention, and Quent paused. In spite of himself, and the revulsion he felt for Fielding, a thrill rushed through him. "You found Atlantis?" he said, turning to give his father his full attention. His pulse spiked and his curiosity was aroused.

The same excitement he felt showed in the other man's face. "I didn't say we found Atlantis, but it does indeed exist. It's more accurate to say that the Atlanteans found us."

For the moment, Quent's hatred for his father filtered away completely. "It really existed? Atlantis? What happened to it? Have you been there?"

Fielding seemed to find his son's fascination compelling. "I knew you of anyone would share my excitement and enthusiasm. If only we hadn't been estranged for so many years, I would have allowed you to share in the glory with me and the other members of the Inner Circle."

"We were estranged, as you put it, because you beat the bloody rot out of me," Quent reminded him. "And I don't believe for one moment that you would have shared your glory with anyone, let alone me."

Fielding shook his head. "But Quent, you're wrong. I had to form and train you to be strong in your youth so that you could withstand life's challenges. My plan succeeded, as you well see, for look at you! And if I were to share my glory with anyone, it would be my own flesh and blood. Not the likes of Remington Truth or Liam Hegelsen. Even Liam doesn't know what I know, doesn't fully understand what Atlantis has to offer."

Quent had to know. "Tell me about them. The Atlanteans. Did Atlantis rise from the bottom of the ocean? There's a new landmass in the Pacific. Is that what caused the Change?"

"You're well informed for not having been among the Elite," Fielding replied, a modicum of surprise on his face. "But then again, you're my son."

He rose and walked toward Quent, coming to stand next to him at the glass table in the closest proximity they'd been for decades. A subtle scent came with him, the essence of wealth and fine clothing, Scotch whiskey . . . and something else that bordered on unpleasant. "I know you have many questions, and I look forward to showing you everything I've accomplished in the last sixty-two years. Oh, yes," he said, "this all began long before the Evolution actually happened."

"How did it begin?"

"I'll show you." Fielding walked to the wall next to one of the water channels. As Quent watched, he flipped open a small panel and seemed to put in a code. Then he closed the little door and a section in the wall slid open.

Quent adjusted the cane-weapon in his hand and bumped his ankle against his other boot, ensuring that the Taser was still in place. A prickling rushed over his shoulders and he started toward Fielding, anticipation sending his pulse spiking. He didn't bloody trust his father at all—this could be some sort of trap; although why he'd need to resort to that was uncertain, since no one knew Quent was here. This was more likely nothing more than what it appeared to be: Fielding's opportunity to boast about his power and secrets.

And Quent's chance to learn more about the people who'd destroyed the earth.

He had to follow him.

4 May 2011
5:30 A.M.

Devi and I welcomed a beautiful little boy this morning. He's healthy, and I'm feeling well.

We've named him David Bakula Kapoor, after both of his grandfathers. Although we don't have a scale, Devi estimates David's weight at eight pounds. He's long and lean, twenty inches.

He's got a full head of dark hair and beautiful cinnamon skin.

I hope he grows up in a better world than the one he was born into.

—from the diary of Mangala Kapoor

CHAPTER 16

Fielding and Quent walked down a windowless corridor that twisted and turned, descending toward the center of the building. The floor here was carpeted in something that looked like bleached sherpa wool, with the effect of smothering the sound of footsteps. And the walls and ceilings, rounded at the corners, were of unrelieved white.

Quent noticed three other doors and wanted to think of an excuse to touch the knobs on each one to see if Zoë had come down this way, but he dared not do anything that might raise Fielding's suspicions.

It wasn't long before they reached the end of the spiraling hall and the door there. As before, Fielding opened a small panel next to it and moved something around before closing the little door once more. The entrance opened and Fielding gestured for Quent to enter.

The octagonal room glowed, undulating with shadows and swaths of light. Its ceiling was glass, and the sunlight beamed down from . . . *above*. It took Quent only a moment to realize that the room was submerged like a large circular aquarium. Dark water surrounded the walls, surging silently against the floor-to-ceiling glass, giving an eerie feel to the space. Lights embedded in the solid floor shone up in soft beams around the edges.

In the center was a pedestal, made of some transparent material, and on the pedestal sat a large pale blue crystal. Of an irregular shape, the stone looked like a piece that had been hacked out of some large stone. About the size of Quent's fist, it had jagged edges along the top, and smooth, striated sides. A faint glow emanated from it, radiating a ring of white light on the surface where it sat.

"What is it?" Quent asked, walking toward it. Fascinated and stunned. It was real. Atlantis was *real.*

Fielding held out his hand to halt him and Quent complied, still staring at the crystal. He sensed the energy in the room as if it vibrated.

"This is how they found me." Fielding moved forward and settled his hand over the top of the stone, caressing it lightly, as if it were too hot to touch directly. "I acquired the crystal, not knowing what it was—"

"Where? How?"

Fielding looked at him with pity in his expression. "I'd been searching for clues to Atlantis for decades. This was the result of years of study and theorization, and millions of pounds of experimentation and research. The crystal was retrieved from the bottom of the ocean in 1998. It took me four years before I realized how to use it."

"For what?"

"To contact the Atlanteans. And the rest, as they say, is history." Fielding smiled and removed his hand from the crystal.

"Do you still use it to contact them? Where are they?" Quent knew he sounded like a query-driven child, but it wasn't every bloody day a guy learned that a mythical civilization had actually existed, let alone still did. "Where is Atlantis?"

"Right now," Fielding said, looking overly complacent, "it's in the Pacific Ocean. A bit north of where Hawaii used to be. And you're looking at the man who put it there."

Quent stared at the crystal. So he and the Waxnickis were right. Somehow, Atlantis had been recovered from the bottom of the ocean. "How?"

But Fielding had tilted his head as if he heard some distant sound, and he stepped away from the crystal. "Ah, I'd lost track of time. Dinner is to be served shortly, and I need to freshen up." He started toward the door and proceeded to input whatever necessary code to open it.

Quent edged toward the crystal, wanting a better look . . . wanting to *touch* the bloody thing. But he knew he dare not. Yet, the mysteries it must hold . . . mysteries that he could read, merely with the touch of a finger. His heart beat faster and he curled his fingers into his palms to keep from reaching for the stone. Even from less than a meter away, he felt the warmth emanating from it. Warmth and energy.

As the door slid open, Fielding said, "I'm not about to deprive them all of my company simply because the prodigal son has returned. You'll join all of us—I'm certain you'll see some familiar faces. There are women aplenty, too, so feel free to partake." He smiled knowingly.

"I'm not particularly hungry," Quent said, dragging his attention away from the crystal. "You needn't prepare the fatted calf on my account."

"But if you want your questions answered, you'll join me. And I see that you have many of them—and I have many for you as well. I'll reintroduce you to the Elite," Fielding said, gesturing for Quent to precede him into the hall. "Yes, that would be best." Then he looked up and frowned. "But I won't have you attend dressed like that."

The door closed behind them and they were once again in the corridor, the crystal safely locked away.

They'd gone only a short distance before Fielding opened one of the doors on the way—not the same one that led to the room with the crystal glasses and table. Inside, he spoke to a young woman. Obviously a servant of some sort, for she was dressed in a loose, off-white dress. She took Fielding's orders to find Quent some clean clothing.

As his father commanded the servant, Quent had a moment to think, and he edged over and touched the doorknob, feeling for Zoë. The images bombarded him because he recklessly opened his mind in a hurry to sift through them and see if she'd been there, and he felt them battle for his consciousness. It was only through a strong force of will that he managed to catch himself and claw back to reality. Progress. But, hell, that had been close.

He blinked and struggled to clear his mind, steady his breathing. Sweat trickled down his spine and he wondered how long he'd been gone. Obviously not too long, for the servant girl was still listening to Fielding.

If she left, Quent would be alone with his father, which was all he would need to subdue the man and crank the Eeker into his crystal.

He could finish it all right now.

But he couldn't deny that the knowledge that Atlantis had actually existed, that Fielding knew about it and could tell him more was titillating. To learn about this mythical world, to find out about one of history's greatest lost civilizations—Quent couldn't ignore the temptation.

And the more patient he was, the closer he could get to his father, the more he could learn about the Elite. And he might be able to find a way to destroy him without getting caught.

But most of all, there was Zoë. If she'd been here so recently, she could still be here—voluntarily or not. Quent wasn't about to leave without finding out.

Playing along with Fielding, stroking his ego and acquiescing to the game for a while was the best plan. If his father continued to take him into his confidence, he'd have ample opportunity to learn about Atlantis, and then to destroy Fielding.

Quent would accept the role of the prodigal son. At least temporarily.

Good fucking grief. What the hell had she ever done to deserve this?

Zoë couldn't decide which was more uncomfortable: the nuked up shoes that lifted her heels four inches off the ground, making her constantly feel like she was going to tip onto her face, or the dress her body'd been forced into by a shy but determined maidservant. A crapping *maidservant*! Zoë could hardly believe some chick she didn't know had seen her naked. And helped her dress. She'd thrown the woman out while she was bathing, but the bashful little thing had found her way back in and then manhandled her into some horribly tight underwear.

And this thing she was wearing, she was afraid if she took a breath, the seams would split and it would all fall away. The dress was so damned tight it showed every single bulge and curve and the neckline was fucking cut down to her belly. She had no damned under-wear on and the stupid zipper dug into her skin. There was no back. And the skirt was so long it practically dragged on the floor, despite her heels. She was going to trip and fall on her ass.

And she didn't have her damned bow over her shoulder, which made her feel even more vulnerable. At least she'd been able to hide it in a corner behind one of the waterfalls, along with her quiver. But the weapon she'd made for digging out crystals was back in the room with her clothing. Hidden of course, but damn if it wasn't a pain in the ass the way things had happened.

I should have just nailed the bastard when I had the chance.

But she hadn't had the chance anyway, because no sooner had she mentioned her compensation than there'd come a knock on the door. Someone had rushed in to tell Fielding something that apparently shocked the hell out of him, for he'd sat unmoving for at least a few minutes. His face had gone white and his hands still, and damn her for not acting in that moment alone, servant or no. And then he'd sent her off with one of the many servants he kept in the red-tiled house, giving clipped orders that brooked no argument.

At least at that time.

Apparently, Fielding wasn't exaggerating when he said she needed to change. He expected his assassins to be as uncomfortably dressed as the hordes of women and men who seemed to fawn all over him. She was going to have to have a word with the ass-wipe and explain that assassins needed to actually be able to *move*—oh, and to breathe—in order to get their job done.

But that wasn't going to happen any time soon, for she'd entered the dining room and had yet to even see Fielding. There were at least fifty people, some with crystals blatantly glowing on their shoulders, milling about, talking, laughing, eating—and that didn't count the people wandering to and fro with trays of food and drink. She'd seen parties like this in movies, where everyone was dressed in fancy clothes, looking like they had sticks up their asses, and they all crowded around and ate and drank and sometimes there was music.

Ass-crap boring. And ridiculous. How the hell did anyone fucking walk in these damn things? Now the toe next to her big one was starting to hurt, along with the back of her heel. She was going to be limping tomorrow. Just damned great for her getaway plan.

She had to give Fielding credit for the food, though. She'd never had such a variety at her meals, nor food that tasted so delicious—even though she didn't know what half of it was. But it was beautiful and elegantly presented, sometimes ridiculously so. Standing straight up, or garnished with bright pink and red flowers. There were odd-colored vegetables like purple cauliflower, and everything seemed to be sprinkled with something, as if it couldn't just be served as it was prepared. If she weren't so hungry, she'd be afraid to eat it.

Zoë found a corner and backed herself against the wall where she could watch and try to figure out how she was going to get the hell out of there. As she nibbled on a little pastry that one of the miserable-looking waiters brought by, claiming it was something called shrimp quiche, Zoë finally spotted her new employer.

At first, her heart skipped a beat, because from behind, the man looked *so* much like Quent. But his hair was lighter, and he wasn't quite as tall, nor nearly as broad in the shoulder. But the movements, the gestures—they were so reminiscent of his son. Her throat tightened and she swallowed hard. *Don't be an idiot. Don't think about him.*

Staying in the shadows, willing herself to remain unseen, Zoë watched as Fielding stepped onto a dais where a long table had been placed. A busty blond woman who looked as if she were no more than twenty-five years old, and a redhead who seemed about the same, had their arms linked through his. Their hands were everywhere—molding over his chest, brushing hair from his face, adjusting his jacket or tie. Three other women of equally large boobs, tall hair, and low-cut dresses clustered around as well. Apparently, he didn't have a preference for immortals over mortals, for Zoë could see that two of the fawning women had crystals, but the others didn't.

Does he screw all of them at once? Or one at a time? It was clear from the way they were touching him he'd done each of them at least a few times. And that each of them thought it was worthwhile enough to want to do it again. At least she was safe from his attentions, for apparently, the man preferred his women to be stacked.

Although if Zoë attempted to seduce him, she'd be able to find out where his crystal was. That certainly bore consideration—because how else was she going to get him to show her?

Not an appetizing thought, but a necessity. Although she didn't see how she'd push her way through the posse of big-breasted women tonight.

Zoë settled back into her corner, wondering how the hell long she had to stay here, wondering why she didn't just leave while Fielding was busy with his harem—it wasn't as if he'd notice—when a man caught her attention. Across the room, standing with his back to her in a group of men and women.

Her stomach plummeted. Broad shoulders. Thick, tawny hair. Smooth, elegant gestures that were much too familiar. Amusing enough to send the entire cluster around him into gales of laughter.

No fucking way.

But even as her heart sank and her palms dampened, Zoë's mouth flattened in pure pissed-offness. That damned idiot Seattle couldn't keep Quent out of the way for a few hours? *A few hours?*

She shook her head. If she got out of here alive, she was going to kill that fool bounty hunter.

And even as she thought about the way she'd like to flay the skin from the tops of his toes, or pluck out Seattle's eyebrows and pubic hair one by one, Zoë edged deeper into the shadows. While she didn't give a shit what Quent thought if he saw her here—she didn't owe him any explanation—she was damned curious about how a man who professed to hate his father and want to kill him had come to be one of his guests.

Zoë's heart sank as she realized what must have happened. He and his father had reconciled. She'd feared that might be the case, for there was nothing her father could have done that would have made her hate him, or justify killing him.

Blood was, after all, thicker than water. Family came first. She'd loved Papi, and Mami (what she remembered of her anyway), and nothing they could have done would have made her feel differently. Even Ian

Marck, who'd seen firsthand what his father had done over the years, still protected him. And had stayed with him for years.

A person might despise their parents' actions, but to actually turn violence on family? Hell, Zoë felt empty enough having taken out the man who'd killed her loved ones. A stranger. If she'd once known or loved Raul Marck, how much worse would the guilt and grief be?

And now she felt empty. Betrayed, even. Why was she so disappointed? Because Quent didn't carry hate in his heart? Look what had happened to her. Carrying the need for revenge around for nearly a decade had made her cold and crusty and unable to settle into life and be happy.

One thing was certain: Quent was having a damned better time than she was. He appeared so at ease, so comfortable here that it made her feel even more awkward and confused. But of course he fit in. This was the world he must have lived in before things changed. A world of tight sparkly dresses and polite chatter and men who looked like they were about to choke because of the ties they wore.

Zoë didn't know if she was staring too hard, and somehow attracted his attention, but it was only a moment before Quent turned. He looked in her direction, his eyes lighting on her, finding her too damn easily. Their gazes collided. Even from across the room his burned, all dark and accusing. All of a sudden, she was nervous and breathless—something very difficult in the damned dress she was wearing.

Screw that.

Zoë gathered every bit of composure she possessed and stared back in defiance, firming her lips. She met his eyes coolly and though every part of her knew she should flee, she remained in place.

He'd come stalking over here and demand to know what the hell was going on, why she was there. And he'd probably shove her up against the wall and kiss the damn breath out of her. An anticipatory tingle shot through her and she breathed deeply, pushing it away.

But he didn't. He finished with his measured look, then deliberately turned. Back to his group of friends, back to the glittering, glitzy ladies, and their equally prissy men.

Well. That was damn well *that*.

Quent could hardly catch his breath, let alone focus on the conversation surrounding him. What the bloody hell had Fielding done to Zoë?

She looked like some exotic goddess, glaring at him from her position in the corner. Her dress dazzled silvery white, showing off much more of her light cinnamon skin than was decent. Her throat and delicate shoulders, her sculpted arms, a deep vee down past her breasts—so much skin for all to see. Her hacked, choppy hair had become sleek and elegant, framing her face like that of some twenties flapper. Jewels, real or fake, sparkled throughout the smooth black tresses, and makeup around her eyes made them appear even larger and more mysterious.

The look she shot him when their eyes locked made his blood run hot, then cold with anger. He had to turn away, to collect his control before he betrayed himself to everyone in the room. What was she doing here?

What the hell game are you playing, Zoë?

As much as he wanted nothing more than to stride over there and demand an explanation—along with other things—Quent forced himself to remain cool. And patient.

Fielding was surely watching him from over on the dais, and there was no need to give the man any ammunition, any insight into Quent's vulnerability. Nor was it necessary for Fielding to introduce him as his son, for there were several Elite members in the room who remembered and recognized him from before, including Liam Hegelsen and Marvina Duprong.

So he laughed at whatever the woman next to him had said, and put on his charming persona. Effortless and easy it was to slip back into the mode he knew so well, conversing, subtly flirtatious, confident. Because here, in Mecca, back with his father, Quent was once again the man he'd been.

Powerful. Influential. Wealthy.

And now the recipient of secrets and knowledge men had sought for centuries.

Yet, as he bided his time, waiting for the chance to corner her, Quent maintained an awareness of Zoë. Where she was (still in the corner) and what she was doing (eating). She spoke to no one, she seemed to know no one. She avoided looking at him, although he occasionally felt the weight of her stare prickling on his shoulder blades.

Chafing to get to her, Quent drank red wine and ate little, limping his way around the vast white room. Ice sculptures in the shape of Chinese words lined the tables, flanked by white flowers of every imaginable variety—roses, orchids, lilies, and many he couldn't name. Some low-key Forties big band music, played by a trio in the corner, filtered through the conversations, and the food was the only relief to a space dedicated to crystal and white.

At last he got close enough to a doorway and seized the opportunity to excuse himself. Quent set his wineglass down and eased through the door, finding himself in a corridor that he realized led to a different entrance, right next to where Zoë stood. Mouth set grimly, he strode down the hall, his "cane" swinging unused in his hand. The space was empty of all but servants, rushing around to do Fielding's bidding, and certainly unwilling to jeopardize their safety or happiness by questioning—or even noticing—the man's son.

He peered around the door next to Zoë and saw that she'd edged out of her little alcove and seemed to be searching the room. His mouth set in a humorless smile, he slipped through the entrance to stand just behind her and said, "Looking for someone?"

She whirled, sort of staggering as if she'd lost her balance, and though she tried to cover it, he saw the flare of shock splash over her face. "Not you," she said, but by then he'd already curved his fingers around her arm and was directing her back into the shadowy corner behind a tall white pillar.

Zoë stumbled and swore, half falling against him in a waft of some unfamiliar, pungent scent. "I can't walk in these stupid things," she said, trying to pull away even as she clutched at him with her other hand, attempting to maintain her balance. "Let go."

Quent felt his lips twist unpleasantly. He turned her to face him, easily able to maneuver her against the wall in a little alcove, handicapped as she was in heels and a long gown. *And damn.* The shoes now made her as tall as he was. "I'm not feeling so inclined to do that, luv."

Up close she was even more striking—a combination of his exotic, earthy Zoë with this polished, glittery being. Tiny, bejeweled clips sparkled in her sleek ink-dark hair and her skin glowed mahogany next to the blinding white gown, with some golden sheen over shoulders and throat that had not come from nature. Her mouth, crumpled up in annoyance, was the same lush pink it had always been, and now, deliciously, level with his. Her eyes had been lined with heavy dark makeup that made them look more intense. She no longer smelled of cinnamon and lemon, but of something more manufactured. Plasticky. Powdery.

Aware that they could still be seen, he resisted the desire to flatten her against the wall and see if she still tasted like herself. Instead, he tried to pull one of the myriad of questions he had from his scattered, lust-filled, *relieved* brain.

She was safe.

But before he could pluck something relevant to say from the whirlwind that was his mind, she squirmed under the firm grip on her bare shoulders and crossed her arms. "How the hell did you get away from Seattle so damned quickly?" she hissed.

Incredulous fury superseded desire and he straightened. "So you admit that you set me up?"

"I didn't want you in the damned way," she replied. "I knew you'd eventually outsmart the nuke-brain, but I didn't expect it to be so quickly. And you're limping."

Quent wasn't certain whether to be insulted or complimented by that. "He's a bloody knobber. I'm surprised he got the best of you before," he added, gesturing to the cut on her arm that was from Seattle.

Zoë glared at him, eye to eye. "So you've made up with your father," she replied, changing the subject. "How damned cozy is that? Speaking of which, you looked like you were enjoying yourself quite a bit."

"Who the hell did you up like this?" he shot back, unable to keep a lift of jealousy from sifting over him. As soon as Fielding or any of the other wanks saw her, they'd be sniffing all around. He sidled over to block her from view of the rest of the room.

"It wasn't my idea, genius. Apparently, this is how the women dress from your world. I don't know how the fuck they walk in these shoes. You seem delighted to be back."

"And what do you mean you didn't want me in the way?" Quent demanded, ignoring her comment. Two could play that game. "What the hell are you up to?"

Zoë swallowed and stilled, her lips curling in. For once, she didn't seem to have anything to say. Her eyes, always large and brown, now seemed even more so. Her lashes spiked long and thick beneath perfectly arched brows. Fielding certainly hadn't wasted any time in remaking her.

Had he slept with her yet? How could he resist?

Even now, Quent was ready to shuck aside his confusion and sink right into that compulsion. He could figure out what she was up to later.

"Seattle wasn't going to hurt you," she told him, the defiance back in her voice and expression. "He was just supposed to keep you from Mecca for a few days. Why are you limping?"

"Your plan didn't work out too well, luv. He may not have hurt me, but he shot Theo." He kept his voice flat.

"No!" Her eyes widened in shock, misery washing over her face. The defiance was gone, and he felt her deflate under his hands. "Is he dead?" She curled her hands over his shoulders.

"He got shot in the chest. Probably a lung, Zoë. It'll

be a miracle if he makes it. Fence is taking him back to Envy. If he gets there in time, Elliott might be able to save him."

"No," she wailed softly. "Quent, I'm . . . I didn't mean for that to happen. You have to believe me. Seattle knew that the deal was off if anything happened to you."

"Obviously he didn't think it extended to my companions." Despite his cool words, he felt her remorse, and reminded himself that she hadn't pulled the trigger that injured Theo. This was a dangerous world with many threats. If anyone was to blame besides the shooter, it was Quent himself, for pushing the envelope with Seattle.

"No," she whispered. She shook her head. "I'm so sorry. Not that it makes a fucking difference, but I am."

"What the hell did you think you were doing bargaining with Seattle anyway? He wants to catch you too."

She was no longer his defiant, fiery Zoë. "Not anymore. I promised him I'd tell him how to find Remington Truth when I got finished in Mecca. That was the deal and you were the—what's the word? My guarantee. But I figured you'd escape from him before I got back anyway. Just not so damn soon."

"Remington Truth. You'd sell her out too?" Quent stared at her. Who was this woman? She'd always been mercenary, but this was different.

"I wasn't going to tell him everything, genius. Just that Remington Truth was dead. And that one of his family members was still alive and that he should be looking for someone other than the old man."

"And Seattle would have just let you walk away after you tricked him like that?"

"He's so fucking greedy, he'd take anything and consider it a head start against everyone else. He'd do anything to get a crystal."

Quent shook his head. "A bloody damn risk you took, Zoë. And look how it's turned out."

She closed her eyes. "I know. I'm sorry." She looked away, and he was entranced by the curve of her jaw, a fringe of dark hair brushing against it, right there, a breath away.

He slowly leaned in, close enough to feel her warmth and to smell the undernote of spice still clinging to her. His mouth brushed over her silky skin, there along her jaw, and she breathed a little raggedly, tilting her head as if to give him better access, Quent closed his eyes and moved in closer, his arms going around her, gathering her close, long and tall and warm.

"Ah, Zoë," he murmured, unable to keep from finding her mouth with his. He shouldn't, he knew he shouldn't, not here, not until he got the whole story . . . but he needed her. She was safe. She was here. He loved her.

Their noses bumped as, unfamiliar with her added height, they slipped into a deep, slick kiss. Gentle, with an underlying urgency, a subtle questioning. His hands molded over her bare back, smoothing along the jut of her shoulder blades and over the bump of her spine as she sighed against him.

She tasted the same. Lovely, sensual Zoë.

Who'd betrayed him for a reason he still didn't understand. Quent pulled away. Reluctant, but determined. "Why did you do it?" he whispered. "I have to understand."

How many times had he asked her a similar question? How many times had she evaded?

Would he ever learn who she really was?

Her eyelashes, crusted with makeup, fluttered down to shutter her expression. She was going to try and wiggle out of it, he knew. Part of him, for a moment, was willing to let her. To just slide back into their pattern of hot, frantic sex. She felt so good, he wanted to bury his face in her neck and kiss her until she cried and sighed beneath him. He wanted her hands on him, comforting and familiar. Something steady in this hated world.

He wanted an excuse to forget about Fielding, forget about the temptation of Atlantis, forget about the ugly things he had to do.

But he was no longer satisfied to just have her body. He wanted all of her.

He realized she hadn't answered, and he was about to demand an answer from her again when she looked up.

"I wanted to kill Fielding. For you."

A rush of confusion and heat swirled through him as he recognized the naked truth in her eyes. "No, you don't," he replied automatically. Then, fear rushed over him as he comprehended what she'd said. "No, you *don't*."

She was tugging away from him, determination and something sad in her face. "I didn't expect you to change your mind, but when I saw you here—"

"Change my *mind*?" Quent held on to her shoulders, barely keeping his voice low. "About Fielding?"

"I understand he's your father, and that things have changed. Blood is thicker than water, and that would just make it more difficult."

He shook his head. "No. Nothing's changed. Nothing he could say or do would change my mind. I know how it looks, but *no*. I hate the bastard." Yet, he felt a little tug of something inside. Fielding had secrets and knowledge. He'd found Atlantis.

Maybe there was another way. Maybe he could get the crystal.

Quent focused back on Zoë, and tightening his fingers, he demanded, "What are you doing here, dressed like this, tonight?"

"I offered my services to him as an assassin, so I could get close to him. He'd be dead by now if I knew which damn side his crystal is, and we wouldn't be having this ass-crap conversation."

"Oh, yes, we bloody well would," he shot back, hissing between clenched teeth as he tried to keep his voice down. "Don't you know what a fucking risk you're taking? You might succeed, but you'd never make it out of here alive."

"Might succeed?" she retorted. "There's no fucking *might* about it."

He was close to her face, so close he could feel her warm breath. "Zoë," he said desperately, trying to pare through her bravado to the reason why she'd be so bloody buggering idiotic.

"Fuck, Quent, I know the damn risks." She drew in a deep breath and straightened so that their eyes were once again level. "I want you to be free. I want to do it for you, so your hands will stay clean."

Quent had no words. He simply stared at her, cold and heat battling for control of his body. "What are you talking about?"

"You'd carry the guilt forever if you killed your father. I want to take it from you."

"But no thought to how I might feel, knowing you thought I was too incompetent, too weak to do it myself? That I'm a bloody pansy?" Annoyance turned into anger. They all thought he was damned worthless. "I'm too damned fragile?"

"Oh, for fuck's sake. If I thought you were incompetent, I wouldn't worry about you carrying the damn burden of killing him, would I?" she snapped. "Genius."

"So I'm such a git that I'd let *you* do it for me?" He felt his eyes bulging with anger at her presumption. He had to remind himself not to squeeze too hard on her shoulders. "Who the hell do you think I am?"

"I don't want anything to happen to you," she ground out from between clenched teeth. "You ass-crap idiot. I've already lived through losing everything. I was protecting myself too."

"Zoë." The blinding fury began to ease.

"I knew you'd be nuked. Why the hell do you think I had Seattle detain you?" Now she looked up at him. The spark was back in her eyes, a little subdued, a little hesitant, but it was there.

"We could have done it together," he said, still trying to feel his way through this web of confusion. What the hell was she trying to say? "But you ran away. Again."

Just then her eyes widened as she looked behind him, and the next thing he knew, she'd yanked him against her.

He reacted instinctively, slamming her into the wall as her hot mouth found his and her arms pulled the back of his head close. Quent's mouth opened automatically over her lips, awareness prickling everywhere over his back and shoulders as he plastered his hands against the wall alongside her shoulders. Images flitted at the corners of his mind, but his focus was on Zoë, and he was easily able to keep them at bay.

"So sorry to interrupt," said a smooth voice. "But I do believe your father is looking for you."

Quent took a solid moment before disengaging himself from heaven and then turned to see Liam Hegelsen. "I was hoping not to be disturbed," he told the man haughtily.

Hegelsen's cool blue eyes lit with amusement, then swept over Zoë. And lingered. "I'll pass that on to Fielding. I'm certain he'll accept your apologies."

Zoë had stepped away from the wall, putting a distance between herself and Quent that he didn't care for. But in the interest of keeping his feelings for Zoë under the radar, he resisted the urge to curve an arm around her waist and pull her close. "Ah, that's not necessary. I can pick up later." His back to Hegelsen, Quent shot her one last *we'll finish this later* look, then pivoted to walk away with the other man.

"Where have you been all these years?" asked Hegelsen. The former Dane had been CEO of the hottest electronics and computer company since Apple and one of Fielding's closest associates. He looked exactly the same as he had in 2010, but the woman Quent had earlier seen on his arm wasn't his wife. Not a surprise. "Fielding never once mentioned that you'd 'Evolved' with us."

Quent shrugged and smiled. "It was a bit of an experiment."

"Obviously one that you came through quite happily," Liam replied with an easy smile. "Your father must be delighted that you've returned."

"He is. And I confess, I'm fascinated by all that you've done since the Evolution," Quent replied.

"It's quite amazing, isn't it?"

"The fact that Atlantis actually exists," Quent agreed. "I am thoroughly fascinated."

"I've been living with that knowledge for years and it still never ceases to amaze me. What we could have done with the energy of those crystals! They would have changed the face of electronics, of the way we produce energy, even manufacture. They could have changed everything."

Quent looked at him, surprised at the man's fervor. "But everything has changed."

"Indeed. But there is yet much that could be done. If—ah, there he is." Liam interrupted himself and beckoned toward Fielding, who'd taken his seat on a dais and appeared to be waiting for their arrival. He glanced back at Quent. "You've seen it then. The original crystal?"

Quent had been under the impression that Fielding's underwater aquarium and its contents were not public knowledge. But Liam was a member of the Inner Circle, so of course he would know. "It's quite magnificent. The energy emanating from it alone fills the room."

"So does that mean you'll be staying with us, here in Mecca? It's a paradise," Liam said as they approached the high table.

Yes, one with snakes in its underbelly. Present company included.

"It certainly looks that way," Quent replied. As he made his way around a cluster of conversing people and onto the dais, he managed to glance covertly back toward Zoë.

She was gone.

CHAPTER 17

Zoë fumed.

She stalked back and forth in the little, windowless room to which she'd been relegated, down some hall in the depths of Fielding's castle. Two white lights burned softly, giving the space a frosted glow. The gown tangled around her feet—she'd kicked off the heels ages ago, whipping them angrily against the wall. Two dark marks marred the pristine white.

All of her other clothes had disappeared since she changed earlier, so she was stuck wearing this crap-ass, Elite dress.

Quent was somewhere, kissing his father's behind. He'd looked pissed off and too damn removed, unapproachable, in that smooth dark suit and slate blue shirt he'd been wearing in the dining room. It was as if he'd turned into someone else with cold eyes—and a stick up his ass.

Except when he'd leaned in to kiss her. Then everything got all soft and mushy. At least, inside Zoë. She swore again. Loudly. She should have known not to get involved with him.

To let him matter. Son of a bitch.

And on top of every damned other thing, the door to this room was fucking locked.

She was a prisoner.

Zoë paced and stalked and kicked at the wall and

door. She still had her bow and arrow, which Fielding had allowed her to keep *after* he informed her who her first assassination assignment was going to be. Her other weapon, which had been hidden beneath her clothing was still under the low bed where she'd kicked it earlier, during her altercation with the maid-servant.

But neither weapon was doing her any good in this damned space, where there was nothing but a low bed, white walls, and a tiny little room with a toilet and sink.

Finally, she lay down. To think, she told herself, even though her knees trembled with fatigue and—ah hell, she might as well admit it—she was a little frightened. Maybe more than a little.

Here she was, in the depths of the Elite lair. Trapped.

Her chest felt tight and she closed her eyes. The last time she'd felt this way had been that horrible night of the zombie attack, when everything was out of control. Since then, she'd managed to stay in control, to make decisions, to decide what was best for her.

Quent's face settled in her mind. His handsome countenance that had somehow become so dear to her; a face that usurped Naanaa's beautiful, calming one in her mind.

Despite the fact that she wasn't sure what to make of his being here, palling around with the man he planned to kill, for some reason, the thought of him did calm her. When had he come to be so important to her, so imperative?

You're staying with me.

When he said that this morning—no, he'd demanded and ordered it, Zoë had been shocked at the rush of desire that shot through her. *Stay with him.* Stay with comfort. Companionship.

And yet, anger and fear overrode that undernote of temptation. No one ordered her about. Even Fielding, the man to whom she'd offered her services.

He'd locked her away, but he couldn't control her. If the worst happened, and she couldn't kill him and escape, well then, she guessed she'd be joining Naanaa and Papi and the others in whatever afterlife there was.

Something that should have happened long ago.

Now that Raul Marck was dead, perhaps that was her fate as well. Perhaps her life was finished, her purpose completed. Perhaps that was why she felt so . . . lost.

These thoughts, meant to be pragmatic, settled over her. But every time she tried to focus on what was right, Quent's face slinked into her mind.

Zoë sighed, shifting, feeling prickly and nervous. She'd eaten. She should try to sleep, for whatever happened in the morning, she'd need a clear mind and strong body. Focusing on the comforting feel of the bow in her hand, she kept her eyes closed and steadied her breathing.

She must have slept because all at once, she was aware of something touching her face, drawing her from the depths of unconsciousness. She opened her eyes to find a shadowy figure bending over her, but before she could speak, he swooped down and captured her mouth with his. Smiling, she opened her mouth, tasted Quent, felt his warmth slide against her.

Her arms moved up around him as, half asleep, she slipped into a world of slick heat, of knowing hands smoothing over her shoulders. Mouths sliding together, tongues fighting and tangling, fierce and knowing . . . the warmth of skin burning against skin, rough with hair and solid with muscle. A long flush of heat rolled through her as she came fully awake, her body tingling and tightening, flushing with desire.

The bed shifted and his welcome weight sank fully against her, pressing her down into the pallet. She curled her legs around him, stretching languorously beneath the fierceness of his kiss. Their mouths molded together, slipping apart and then back again, tasting and nibbling, pulling away to drag in a breath, and then back for more of the other. Her sleep and fear were gone, evaporated beneath the rush of pleasure, the taste of him—still the same Quent, the same delicious softness that tugged deep in her belly.

His hands moved from her shoulders, peeling the dress down as he slid his knee along her legs. She arched into him, pushing up into his thigh where she throbbed and needed, tearing at the belt around his waist as he buried his face in her neck.

Quent shifted, bending to buss his soft lips along her throat. She felt the brush of his lashes against her skin and the moist trail he left behind, the little prickles on her sensitive skin. Impatient hands peeled the dress away, and his mouth, hot and sure closed over a nipple. The jolt of pleasure from the sudden slick warmth traveled down to her core, and she sighed, clutching his shoulders as he grinned against her.

Then, sucking and tugging, his wicked mouth teased and nibbled on that sensitive tip as one of his hands found its way beneath her dress. Zoë twisted toward him, *needing* to get closer, needing the comfort, wanting to have all of him. In the dim light, he looked up at her from where he licked at her breast, his brows dark slashes over eyes that were smoldering and knowing, so deep and sure.

Then his fingers eased into her, slick and smooth and sure, stroking and playing her as she ground her head into the pillow beneath, arching her neck and her back, letting herself feel.

Zoë couldn't hold back a desperate little moan, shoving her hands into his hair, cradling his head as he sucked and swirled his mouth around her as if he had all the time in the world. Pleasure undulated in waves, surging through her and settling into her belly, plunging lower to where he fondled her, sliding in and out and all around—a little teasing, a little coaxing, then a withdrawal when she began to climb the peak. She shifted, opening her legs as he sighed into her skin, whispering her name.

"Quent," she whispered toward the ceiling, tugging once again at the buttons of his trousers. An edge of desperation tinged her voice, and he pulled from her breast to slide down between her legs.

Zoë tried to pull him back, up to kiss him, to fit him where he belonged—between her legs, joining, but with a little laugh, he slipped away. Then he had her bare, there on the bed, gently easing her ankles apart, and bent down to taste her.

She gave a soft cry, a little lift and dug her fingers into the blankets beneath as that wicked tongue danced around, teasing at first . . . and then becoming very intent. She rolled her head against the pillow, wanting to thrash her hips, but he held her steady. Firm and still as he probed and sucked and tweaked until she tightened her legs around his neck and arched up into that hot, soft mouth.

Zoë lost her mind, shooting over the top and down a long, undulating ride, shuddering and trembling long after it was over, as his tongue coaxed her long . . . a little longer, a little longer, until she gasped, "Enough!" and her body collapsed into bonelessness.

Then Quent was up next to her, his mouth on hers, musky and fierce and hot, drawing her toward him, gathering her close. He kissed her long and crazily, and she met him with her own fervor. And then he dragged in a little shuddery breath and slowed, becoming slow and tender. Little kisses, little nibbles, long easy strokes, gentle tangling of their tongues. She reached down between them, slipping her hand toward the band of his pants, but he stopped her with a desperate little sound, pulling his mouth away.

"Mmm, Zoë," he said, trailing kisses toward her ear. "Thank God you're all right."

"After that, I'm more than all right." She smiled against his cheek, rough with stubble. But when she tried to shift her hand farther down, he firmly settled it on his chest, where she could feel his heart ramming beneath her palm. "Quent, I want to touch you," she said, moving her hand through the hair over the slide of his muscles.

"Not now," he murmured, belying his words by nibbling on her ear.

She shivered delicately, running her hand along the smooth swell of his bicep. "How did you find me?" she said, still soft and loose from the orgasm, but her brain was clicking back to life. "How did you get in? The door was locked."

"I sensed you. Found my way by reading the memories on the things you touched," he told her, pulling himself up on an elbow next to her. Darkness glinted in his eyes. "Who locked you in here?"

"Your father." The reality of their situation settled over her, and she felt the last vestiges of pleasure ebb. She couldn't blame him if he'd found forgiveness for Fielding. And she wondered where that left her.

As if he read her thoughts, Quent's face tightened and he said, "I haven't changed my mind about Fielding. He used to beat the rot out of me, Zoë. For pleasure. He's an evil man who caused the destruction of the world. Did you really think that a bit of luxury and some good wine would change how I feel about him?"

Zoë swallowed as his eyes, disappointed and sharp, bored into her. "I didn't know what to think. You seemed easy and comfortable with him," she replied.

His smile was tight. "I'm a good actor. That's the only reason he didn't kill me long ago. I knew how to play the game . . . most of the time."

"Quent," she began, but he stopped her by holding up a hand.

"I have to ask you a question. It would probably be best if I waited, but I'm compelled to ask now. It won't change the fact that I'm going to get you out of here safely."

Zoë felt her eyes widen even as her body tensed. Her heart swelled, filling her throat. Somehow, she knew it wasn't going to be something she wanted to hear. "Quit fucking around and ask."

His mouth quivered briefly, then steadied. "Why did you really come here to kill Fielding?"

Well, hell. That was easy. Sort of. She relaxed a bit. "I told you. I didn't want you to die in the process. Or to have to bear the burden." It was a burden. If she'd known what she knew now, she might have approached Raul Marck differently. She might have listened to Quent.

"You didn't think I could do it. I'm too weak." The steel was back in his voice.

And at last she understood the underlying anger. A rush of what someone else might call compassion flooded her. "*No*, Quent. It wasn't that at all."

She curled her fingers around his arm to get him to look at her, and touched his cheek the way she had the first time they met, when he lay stunned on the ground after being dropped by the *ganga*. Warm, solid. Familiar. Somehow he'd become so familiar. "Of course you'd succeed. I've never seen you fail at anything, including getting me to take you to my hideaway." She gave him a wry smile. "Which I've never done for anyone. I just didn't want you to . . . uh . . ." Her voice trailed off as she struggled for the words. And they came, and she wanted to beat them back.

A frisson of fear tingled her belly at the risk she was about to take, but she opened her mouth and it all came out anyway. One thing she wasn't was a coward. "Maybe it's a little bit fucked up, but it's the only way I could think of to tell you . . . I . . . uh . . . love you. The only way I could think of to show you, by taking that burden. It's not like you need anything else."

"You wanted to show me you love me by killing my father? So that you can get your arse killed too?" He gripped her arms, his blue-brown eyes close and intense. "What the fuck good would that do? It's a hell of a lot easier to just tell me you love me, for chrissake, Zoë!" Then he pulled her close, hard. Burying her face roughly in his shoulder. "Do you really? Love me?" His voice was low and grating.

She tried to yank free, then gave up and sagged against him. Looking away, she bit her lower lip. "Yeah. Okay?"

His hold on her loosened and she pulled away to look up at him, feeling more naked and vulnerable than she'd ever been. But when she saw the expression in his face, the fear fell away. "What is it?"

"Do you know," he said, his voice unsteady, "that I don't remember anyone ever saying that to me. In my whole life."

"Never?" she whispered. "How can that be? Your mother? Your father? Grandparents? Lovers?"

He was shaking his head. "Never. Well," he added, his voice a little more solid, "maybe once—there was this girl in prep school. I think she might have said it, but that was just so she could get in my pants."

Zoë frowned. "Marley Huvane?"

"No, hell, no, not Marley. Trilby Bunker-Thyckett was her name. And she was hoping to get herself knocked up so she'd have a chance at my billions."

"Billions of . . . oh, you mean money?"

He gave a little laugh, his expression easing. "Right, Zoë. You're pretty damned much the first woman I've ever met who didn't want anything from me."

"I wouldn't say that," she said, slipping her hand down between them once again, trying to ignore the fact that he hadn't said *I love you* back.

"Zoë," he said, once again stopping her. "There's nothing more I'd like than that right now, but I think we'd best find our way out of here and do what we came to do. Together."

She tugged him down for another delving kiss, and felt the surge of response down between them as her tongue slicked deep inside his mouth. "Quent," she murmured against his lips. She pressed herself up against him, letting him burn into her. At least she had this. At least she could feel warm and comforted for a bit longer. "Please . . . let me—"

He pulled away and looked down at her. She could tell by the tightness around his mouth that it was difficult for him, and she sensed there was some other reason he was holding her off. Was there someone here from his old time? Had he slept with someone else?

But she didn't ask.

She was, she guessed, too much of a coward after all.

Zoë eased off the bed, her gown sagging around her hips, the halter straps dangling forward almost to the floor. "I don't have anything to wear but this. They took my clothes," she said, pulling the straps up. "I know women run and fight in shit like this in the movies, but that's a bunch of ass-crap bunk. I can't even damn well breathe. Plus the thing's too long and I'm not going to even try to run in those shoes."

Quent's lips twitched, but he came around behind her and took the straps from her hands, fastening it quickly and efficiently. Obviously, he knew his way around women's complicated clothing. "We can cut it shorter," he said. "But I don't know what to do about the shoes."

"Barefoot is better than those damn things," she said, stepping away. Problem was, even that little touch at the back of her neck, that little kindness of helping her, settled over her with warmth. How had it happened that she let him get so close that even the brush of a finger felt *right*?

She looked down at his thick tawny hair, remembering her admonishments to him to wear the covering bandanna as he knelt in front of her to hack at the skirt. "You've got to make it shorter than that. How the hell am I going to run? At my knees."

"You planning on running?" he asked, looking up.

"I have a feeling we aren't going to be walking the hell out of here," she said. "Maybe you could unzip the back a little too, so I can actually take a damn breath. So what's the plan?"

"Right. The plan is," he said, standing in front of her, a wide strip of shimmery white gown in his hand, "we're going to steal the crystal of Atlantis. And then we're going to kill my father."

"Steal the crystal of Atlantis? Must be something very important." Zoë raised her brows, anticipation sending her pulse faster. Sounded like a fun way to go out. "And kill one of the most powerful Elite? Hot damn. Lead the way, genius. I'm right behind you."

19 July 2012
11:00 P.M.

I can barely write this. Forgive me for my long absence.

Devi has finally succumbed to the cancer that has spread through his abdomen these past months. He left me and David shortly after noon this day.

I have nothing left but David. But I am strong. I'll go on.

—from the diary of Mangala Kapoor

CHAPTER 18

Quent had made certain no one followed him to Zoë's room, and it had been well past midnight by the time he'd sneaked out of the chamber Fielding had given him. The sensation of lurking about his father's mansion had been an echo of nights many decades ago, when he did the same in an effort to remain beneath Fielding's notice . . . and away from the fists and riding crops.

He'd been able to retain his pack and clothing by hiding in his room anything that could be considered dangerous, and leaving the pack out so it could be searched. Which he was certain it had been during the interminable time he was at dinner. Now he'd dressed back in his comfortable clothing—nylon cargo pants and T-shirt, with a long-sleeved shirt over it. And his light boots, complete with hidden Taser. He'd also slipped the cane-weapon into the side-back belt loop of his pants where it would be out of the way but easily accessible.

The most difficult part of finding Zoë hadn't been the bloody tracings of her throughout the building—she seemed to touch every damn wall possible, and he'd become much more adept at only reading the memories he wanted to read—but evading the brunette who'd become a stage-one clinger at dinner. The kind of clinger who'd laughed too long and loudly at each of his jokes, even when he wasn't joking. She'd done everything but stick her hand down his pants under the table or bare her generous breasts.

But Quent was no slouch when it came to dislodging unwanted females, and he'd given her the slip, then made his way to the spacious chamber assigned to him. It was on the highest floor of the building, and he waited there until he felt certain everyone was sleeping. The windows overlooked the glittering sea, dark and infinite in every direction. The only illumination came from the partial moon gilding the floating walkway and frosting the roofs of Mecca below. He examined the terrain from the highest part of the island, planning for a variety of escape routes. And when he was certain the household was asleep, he found his way to Zoë.

Now, as they left her room, he peered down the corridor before allowing her to sneak out after him. Everything was deserted, all was silent but for the faint whisper of water, and he moved over so she could ease past. She sparkled and shone in that white gown, despite its ragged hem, looking like Athena with her bow and the quiver slung over her shoulder.

Quent was able to navigate back to the center of the house without using his sensory powers. Before they left her room, he'd filled her in on the plan to use his psychometry to get to the hidden chamber, certain he'd be able to "read" the history of Fielding's numeric codes and manipulations on the secret doors.

"I want that crystal. I want to learn its secrets and see what it can tell us about the Atlanteans," he'd told her.

Zoë had been fascinated as well as enthusiastic. "It would piss Fielding the hell off, and maybe even show us a way to destroy the Elite."

"My thoughts exactly."

"Won't Fielding be there? Kill two birds with one arrow?"

Quent shook his head. "I don't think so. There's nothing in the room but the crystal. No other furnishings, so it's obvious he doesn't sleep there. The room is down instead of up, with only one entrance."

"So we get the crystal then go up to his private room?"

"First we get him. Then the crystal."

Quent led the way to the room in which he and Fielding had originally met. Since he had to "read" the history, he needed to start here to find the way to his father's private chambers.

Inside, moonlight spilled in, silvering the space. The sound of running water, which had faded into the background like the sounds of a busy street to a Londoner, now broke the silence noisily. Everything was as Quent remembered it, and, tugging Zoë with him, he started over toward the waterfall by the hidden panel. The best place to begin tracing his father's route, he thought, certain that Fielding would go to his private chambers through the secret passage.

As he glanced about the room again, noticing the faint wash of light over the crystal glasses and whiskey decanter, he remembered Fielding's assertion that he'd manipulated Quent's trip to Sedona. And as he looked around that sparse room, the truth came to him suddenly, like a splash of cold water. A punch to the gut. The ugly truth.

Was it possible? The sudden weight in his belly indicated that it probably was—that in spite of his loathing for Fielding, Quent's whole life had been influenced by that very man.

Fed by hatred for the physical abuses, an underlying competitiveness and the absurd need to be seen as formidable—worthy—in his father's eyes, Quent had allowed those emotions to drive his actions since he was a teen. Nearly everything he'd done—seduced and bedded beautiful woman after beautiful woman, embarked on daring and dangerous escapades in search of treasure and wealth that hadn't come from his hated father . . . even given publicly of his time and money to charitable causes, to people and places in need—all of it had been a big damned fuck-you to Fielding.

A way to jab his middle finger right in his father's face. A way to have Fielding see him as a equal, as strong and confident in his own right.

Fielding was right. He had controlled Quent's life.

"What's wrong?" Zoë broke the silence, and he realized he'd frozen as the unpleasant realization settled over him. "Quent? Are you in the black pit?"

His mouth flattened. *Right.* This was a pretty dark pit of self-realization. He wasn't too certain he liked himself much right about now. "I'm fine. Just . . . listening. Are you ready?"

"I've been ready," she said, characteristically impatient. "Are *you*?"

Feeling the solidness, the realness, of Zoë's fingers now in his hand, all at once, Quent wondered if he was making a mistake.

They could leave now. Leave and likely escape over the walkway, or even steal a protected boat from the docks. He had his Taser, Zoë had her bow and arrows. Together, they'd be a force to be reckoned with.

Most importantly, he had Zoë.

He could get her out of here, safe and sound, and tell her what he needed to tell her. Find a way to let her know how he felt. And then if she wouldn't stay, if she left him again . . . then he could come back.

But for now, the boiling, driving need to annihilate Fielding had eased to a simmer. Not because he'd forgiven the man, but because he realized what had happened had been a long time ago. Fielding didn't have power over him anymore. He couldn't hurt him any longer.

And if he left now, without ending his life, Quent could relinquish his father's power over himself, no longer letting Fielding drive his actions.

He still loathed the man. Hated him for what he'd done to him, and to the rest of the world. Hitler had nothing on Parris Fielding.

He swallowed and looked down at Zoë. She'd never looked more beautiful than she did now, her hair every which way, smashed flat on one side, the winging curls limned with silvery moonlight, her almond-shaped eyes big and dark, steady. The curve of her cheek, the long sweep of her neck and throat and delicate collarbones, strong arms bare and gleaming with light.

I love you.

The words sat on the tip of his tongue. But he held them back. It wasn't the right time. He wasn't ready. His palms dampened and he thrust his nerves away.

"We could leave now. Forget everything and get out of here. Or we could try to steal the Atlantean crystal. What do you want to do?"

Surprise widened her eyes and she pulled her fingers from his hand, stepping back to look up at him. "And Fielding?"

Quent took a deep breath and shrugged. "Walk away."

"You're asking for me to decide?"

He nodded. *It's the only way I can show you how much I love you. Give you control.*

He opened his mouth to say it, to leap across that abyss, but she spoke first. "The crystal. We have to get the crystal. It's got to be you, Quent. No one else could ever do it. And you'll never have another chance. If you leave Mecca, you'll never get back in." She looked up at him, gripping his arms. "It could make a difference for all of us. It could help us stop the Elite."

All of that without one curse word. He almost smiled. Was his Zoë softening?

"Right," he said, anticipation sparking him. This was it. The biggest treasure he'd ever had the chance to find. "Let's do it."

He touched the hidden panel, grasping Zoë's fingers once again as a way to ground himself. Reading the memories, he concentrated and memorized the code for opening the door.

Moments later, it slid open, just as silently as it had earlier that day. Zoë grinned and slipped through, and Quent followed. The only illumination was an occasional small covered bulb near the floor, spilling a small ellipse of light. He didn't need to employ his ability to navigate back through the corridors, down to the end where the second secret door was, but he did use his fingers to brush along the wall to see if anyone had come by recently. He sensed nothing alarming and they hurried on.

The second secret panel slid open as easily as the first, but this time he had to concentrate harder to "read" the process to open the actual door to the chamber. The images blurred, dark and murky, layered with malignance and cold. Fielding. All Fielding, strong and malevolent.

Zoë's warm hand, slender and steadying, was the only thing that kept him from sliding into that greasy black pit.

And when he at last came out of the trance of images, he realized his breathing had increased. Sweat trickled down his spine. It was too dark to see more than a shadow, but he got the sense she was looking at him with concern.

"That took too damned long, Quent," she said, an edge to her voice. "What the hell's wrong?"

He couldn't put it into words. "Nothing," he said. "I'm fine. It was . . . dark. And there's a lot of evil here. My father."

She squeezed tightly. "Are you all right? We can forget it."

In the dark, he felt the warmth of her curves as she shifted toward him, the tickle of her unruly hair over his jaw, the low bumping sound of her arrows adjusting in her quiver. "It's up to you. I'm fine. I want to do this."

Zoë nodded against him, then pulled his face down. In the dark, he recognized the curve of her smile and he gave her the most tender, the most loving of kisses—short, sweet, with a bit of a tongue-slip. "Let's go, genius," she murmured. "I'm here."

He pushed the buttons on the keypad, fighting this time to hold back the black images that lurked. Tension settled over his shoulders and he hesitated on the last digit. *Nine* or *eight?* He closed his eyes, let them flood him once again, dark and threatening . . . and then, a bit breathless, settled on *nine*.

The white wooden door to the secret chamber slid open. The ice blue glow of the crystal spilled its hue over the octagonal space, reflecting lightly off the glass walls of the aquarium room. Other than that, the place was empty and dark. Even the moonlight didn't shine this far down through the water.

Quent felt Zoë's intake of breath at the sight of the stone and gently eased her into the chamber. The door closed behind them and he felt the surge of excitement. A treasure beyond all imagining. From it, he could learn the history to a lost civilization, the key to understanding the men who'd destroyed the world. And, he was certain, formulate a weapon to stop them.

It was at that moment he realized why he'd been given the cursed psychometric ability. He was the only one in the world who could translate the stone and learn both past and present from it. The only one who could ever have found it, hidden here in his father's private holding room.

What an irony for Parris Fielding, whose experiment in the Sedona cave had backfired and made his son the only person who could destroy him.

Quent pulled the swath of sparkling white material he'd cut from Zoë's dress out of his pack and stepped toward the crystal. There was no bloody way he was touching it directly until he was somewhere safe and secure.

Who knew what kind of dark pit it would drag him into.

Just as he was about to drape the material over the

crystal, he hesitated. With a quick look back at Zoë, who stood near the closed door, he said, "Be ready. I don't know what will happen when take it off the pedestal."

"Nothing," said a voice. "Nothing will happen because no one can access this room except for me. Or so I thought."

Quent froze, then looked over to see one of the glass panels of the octagon swinging inward. Fielding stepped in, and the door, which was a thick glassed-in slab filled with water—a perfectly camouflaged door—closed behind him. He was holding an object that resembled a gun, but it was unlike any firearm Quent had seen. Where the chamber would have been on an old pistol glowed a large yellow crystal. He suspected bullets weren't the ammunition that came out of that piece.

"I'm not certain whether to be disappointed in you or complacent with myself for my correct assessment of your character." He moved into the room, closer to the large crystal on the pedestal, his eyes steady and cold. The weapon was aimed a bit unsteadily at Quent, and he knew without being told that his father would shoot—or whatever—to kill. "Once a disappointment, always a disappointment."

Quent heard Zoë's breathed *fuck* behind him, but he was too pissed off to find it amusing. "So sorry to have not measured up to your standards once again, father."

"You failed the test, but what I cannot understand is how you found your way into this room," Fielding said. His eyes were bright and he moved slowly. "You were not meant to. Only to set off the alarm at your attempt. How did you do it?"

"Your little experiment," Quent told him. "Obviously backfired on you."

"I would have given this to you," Fielding said, reaching to languidly caress the crystal. He seemed to take in its power, giving a little shudder as he did so. When he spoke again, his voice was stronger, the hand holding the gun steadier. "I meant for you to have it. If you'd but waited. I have—had—plans for you, now that you'd returned."

"You can't seriously believe I would have come to join you." Quent edged back toward Zoë. "After what you and your cult did to the world? And the continued suppression. Kidnappings, enslavement, and zombie attacks. How could you imagine I'd ever want to be part of that?" He couldn't keep the loathing from his voice any longer.

Fielding looked aggrieved. "A rare misjudgment on my part. I suppose a father can't help but hope his son will follow in his footsteps."

"Good thing Hitler never had a son."

Fielding's face tightened and the gun lifted. "Hitler had his points. The idea of a master race isn't so farfetched, particularly considering Darwin's theories. Hitler simply went about it in the wrong way."

"Yes. He was overt about it, and thus stoppable. You didn't give the world a chance. How did you do it? How did you annihilate the whole bloody earth? Did you use that?" He gestured to the crystal even as he stepped another bit backward. Zoë's warm hand brushed his from behind, then withdrew. He realized what she was doing—sliding the weapon-cane from where he'd stuck it through the belt loop in the back of his pants.

"No, that crystal wasn't used in the Evolution. I told you—that's my connection to the Atlanteans. They were the ones who designed and implemented the Evolution, with my help of course."

"I'm sure you were instrumental to the whole project," Quent said dryly.

"Of course. They were fortunate that it was I who acquired the crystal. No one else would have managed to learn how to use it to communicate with them."

"So you were able to reach the Atlanteans. Tell me about them." Quent's curiosity warred with his revulsion for the man and his cohorts. And if he kept him talking, Zoë might have the chance to make a move. He knew she wouldn't stay still for long. Yet, they still didn't know which side his crystal was on.

Fielding's breathing rasped in the space as his eyes lit with delight. "You see, the Atlanteans had been banished to the depths of the ocean for millennia. They wanted to return to the earth's exterior, where they'd lived so long ago. They needed the help of mortals on land in order to raise their city back to the surface."

"And in return for your help, they offered you and your cult immortalizing crystals."

"Yes. It was a bargain I couldn't refuse. And without me, they would never have been able to return. They should have been grateful to me forever." His jaw tightened, making his voice tense.

"You and Remington Truth." Zoë spoke, and Fielding seemed to notice her for the first time. He shifted the gun barrel toward her. Quent wished she'd kept her bloody mouth shut, but that was too much to expect from Zoë.

"Truth was a brilliant man, but weak. Guilt-ridden sap. That was Hegelsen's mistake, wanting Truth to be part of the Inner Circle. I knew he was a bad choice, but Liam claimed we needed him with his connections and knowledge of the American military."

"Remington Truth. He disappeared shortly after the Change and you've never been able to find him. What secrets does he hold that you're so desperate to get him back?" Quent asked, turning Fielding's attention from Zoë.

"Too many." Fielding wasn't taking the bait. He looked at Zoë again, the gun shifting toward Quent. "And you. I could have used you, and you would have lived happily and in luxury forever."

"Why did you want me to kill Liam Hegelsen?" Zoë asked. Quent had to resist the urge to spin and look at her in surprise. "And how the hell could I do that if he's crystaled?"

"It's no matter now," Fielding replied. "It'll all be taken care of shortly. If my son wouldn't have disappointed me, I would have employed your talents to rid him of the man who'd rival him. But since he's made the decision to come here, well, I'm simply returning to my original plan."

"Which is what?"

"Well, I'm delighted you've asked," Fielding said. He shifted suddenly, changing the gun's aim. Quent moved, slamming Zoë to the ground as a ricochet of something like lightning sizzled through the room, zapping at the keypad beside the door through which they'd come. As they tumbled to the ground, a yellow-orange light flashed, lighting the dark space, and the smell of burning plastic and something else sharp and pungent filled the air. Quent looked up to see the panel smoking.

"You won't be leaving that way." Fielding smiled, walking toward the solid door to examine his handiwork. "In fact, you won't be leaving at all."

Suddenly, something *shushed* through the air and Fielding cried out in surprise and fury as one of Zoë's arrows pinned him by the arm to the door. She glanced at Quent, smiling with bravado. "Was wondering how I was going to get him over there." She surged to her feet, pulling another arrow from the quiver.

Fielding still had the weapon, and he was trying to pull his arm free, which had been shot through the upper bicep, without dropping the gun. He grunted in pain and frustration as Zoë sent a second arrow. Another quiet *shush*, and his left thigh was pinned. Fielding screamed in pain and dropped the gun, struggling to pull the arrow from his leg.

Zoë looked at Quent, then gestured with her hand as if to say *help yourself.* He walked over to his father and yanked the two arrows free as Zoë swooped to pick up the gun. Fielding staggered away, blood spattering the white tiled floor.

"I didn't know immortals bled," Quent said callously. "Too bad you can't bleed to death."

"Bastard," gasped Fielding, reaching toward the crystal as if he were a junkie grasping for a fix. His hands trembled and as he moved, he staggered.

"What's wrong with you?" Quent had a sudden prickle of unease. Elite couldn't be murdered. Any flesh wounds would heal quickly, according to Marley. Even a bullet to the head or chest would simply heal around the slug if it remained in the flesh . . . so why was Fielding so weakened? "You're injured."

His father, having touched the crystal yet again, seemed to regain some strength. He looked at Quent, a strange light in his eyes. "Not because of you, fool. You couldn't have finished me. Only my own mistake. My own goddamned mistake has brought me to this end."

Those words, so unexpected from a man who accepted nothing but perfection from himself and those around him, caught Quent's full attention. Fielding was drawing on the collar of his button shirt, pulling it away from his throat.

Repulsed and fascinated, Quent realized the man was showing him his crystal. At least now he knew which side it was on. But when Fielding opened his shirt, exposing his entire chest, Quent saw the darkened skin. He looked up at his father for confirmation and read it in his eyes.

Instead of a single crystal, like Marley wore, Fielding had not one, but three glowing stones embedded in his skin. One of them, on the right side, appeared to be identical to the one Marley had. The other two were different—one was lavender and one opalescent.

But on the left side, the skin had turned black around the lavender crystal. Even from where he stood, several feet away, Quent saw that the flesh had hardened and turned shiny, and that the black infection had spread over his shoulders and chest, down to his belly and beyond.

"Three crystals. Instead of one," Quent said. "Why? What more did you seek besides immortality?"

Fielding nodded. His face suddenly looked old and craven. "You are well informed for being an Outsider. One for strength. And one to regain my youth."

Quent made a soft sound of disgust. Which one had brought the malady into Fielding's body? Which one had been his downfall? Greedy bastard. "There's no cure," he said, knowing that was true.

Even Elliott, who could heal anything, had been unable to cure a young Elite woman with a similar ailment. Quent knew from his friend's description of the hard and shiny black flesh that his father suffered from the infection that would very quickly take over the body and kill him.

"If the body rejects the crystal and becomes infected with the Dark Syndrome, there is nothing to be done," Fielding said, nodding in agreement. "So that was why I was doubly grateful that you'd come. You'd have been the one to take over my role, Quent. Live here in luxury and carry on the tradition. Damned Liam Hegelsen would have no choice but to accept it, if you had the crystal."

"How long do you have?" Quent asked.

Fielding shrugged. "Not long at all now. It's progressed quite rapidly this day alone."

"I noticed you seemed shaky at dinner, and a bit weak, but I assumed you were drunk," Quent said. "You were hiding the infection.

"I've told no one of this occurrence, which, as you can imagine, has put a damper on my physical pleasuring of the last weeks. I dare not take off my shirt."

"What a shame," Zoë said. "I don't mean that you haven't been brave enough to fuck the last few weeks, but that we aren't going to have to finish the job. That you've done it all on your own."

Fielding smiled, stroking the crystal. Then he turned and suddenly lifted it from its pedestal and without hesitation, threw it hard.

Quent moved without thinking, intent on stopping the stone before it broke the glass wall and allowed the ocean to burst in. As he caught the crystal, he realized his mistake. A shock flooded him, blue and hot, and before he could react, the rush of images—dark, cold, revolting and malignant—claimed him.

CHAPTER 19

Zoë dove toward Quent as he leapt to catch the crystal, but she was too late.

He tumbled to the ground, his hands curled around it, holding it against his chest. Now, as she knelt next to him, she bit back a curse at his quick reaction. "Come on, genius," she muttered desperately, trying to pry his fingers from the stone. "Wake up."

A glance up at Fielding indicated his mild interest, but he made no move to assist, or to keep her from her task. Instead, he stood at the now-empty pedestal and seemed to be occupied with something on the platform.

Zoë managed to tug Quent's fingers free and the crystal plunked to the floor. At last. "Come *on*, Quent," she said. "Wake the fuck up."

But this time, when he dropped the object that pulled him into the dark pit, he didn't open his eyes. Fear spiked through her as she noticed his breathing was shallow and fast. His eyes moved beneath closed lids and she saw a trickle of sweat roll from beneath his hair as he seemed to struggle against some unseen assault. His legs and arms, fingers and face, convulsed as if he were battling a nightmare.

She shook him, hard, and then slapped his face as she'd done before. "What the *hell*," she moaned in frustration that edged into stark fear. She glanced up at Fielding just as he stepped away from the pedestal.

A smug smile tipped his lips and she braced herself for him to come at her now. She still had his gun, but he was an Elite, and would be much stronger than she.

But he didn't move in her direction. "I had no idea that would happen," he said conversationally. She noticed he staggered a bit. "What's wrong with him?"

"You bastard," Zoë hissed up at him as she knelt there, an increasing fear swarming her. "Quent, what the fuck? Come *on!*"

"It's probably better that way," Fielding said, just as the room gave a great lurch. "Ah. There it is." His smile grew wider and he turned to look around him. "It won't be long now."

"What?" Zoë demanded, her heart sinking. That lurch hadn't been a good sign, and now she felt an underlying vibration beneath her cold bare feet and knees.

"This is my escape plan," Fielding said. She saw that his neck had begun to darken above the collar of his shirt, and the Dark Syndrome had spread beyond the cuffs to his hands. It was moving frighteningly fast. "I always needed a way to leave them behind, but I didn't expect I'd be dying as I did. So I made a bit of an adjustment to my original plan."

"What the fuck are you talking about?" Zoë cried, and then she felt Quent shift beneath her. It was a smooth movement, not the agitated ones from the nightmare. He drew in a deep, shuddering breath, then eased into some calmer rhythm.

"We're in a little pod that's about to be released from its moorings. In perhaps ten minutes, it'll pull free and sink to the depths of the ocean where you and my son and I will remain in this spacious coffin. I didn't expect to have company in my tomb," Fielding said, his voice rasping a bit now. He couldn't get to the crystal for a new surge of energy, for it was next to Zoë. "But in retrospect, I think it's only fitting. Like the pharaohs, I'll have my own companions with me for my travels to the other side."

"I don't think we're going to the same damn place on the other side," Zoë snapped. *Come on, Quent!* She felt him move again, and looked down. His eyelids fluttered, then sank closed. "What the *fuck*," she muttered, growing more desperate and frightened at his lack of responsiveness. "Please!" If he could wake up, he'd be able to figure out how to get out of this place through the glass-paneled door.

"And when the pod sinks," Fielding continued, "did I mention that Mecca will implode as well?"

That caught Zoë's attention. "What?"

"You don't think I'd leave all of my work behind for Hegelsen, do you? He was planning to destroy me anyway, but as always, I'm one step ahead of him."

"You're going to die," Zoë spat. Quent moved, and suddenly she felt his fingers close around her wrist. *Yes.*

"Of course I'm going to die. But so is he," Fielding replied. He staggered more heavily, nearly falling as the pod gave another great lurch. "When we finally dislodge, the water will rush up through this hole in the center of the floating island and it'll collapse, and sink." He frowned as if contemplating some great mystery, but the effect was ruined by his blackened hand

and labored breathing. "I wonder . . . who will . . . reach the bottom . . . first."

Zoë looked down and saw Quent's eyes open. Foggy and lost, they fluttered closed again. She bent toward him. "Wake up," she murmured, kissing his cheek, caressing his face. "Please. Or I'm going to kill you."

He moved suddenly, his hands grasping and suddenly closing around her arm and a hand. He gripped her tightly and she felt him struggling, his breathing sharp and hard, his mouth flattening as if in concentration.

"Zoë," he whispered.

"I'm here, genius," she said. "Get the fuck out of that pit," she added desperately. "I need you." This was one mess she couldn't get out of on her own.

His mouth twitched in a smile and he tightened his fingers. "Trying."

"You don't have any damned time to try," she told him furiously, glancing over at Fielding. He'd sagged against one of the glass walls and slid to the floor. The black had crept up over his jaw and was beginning to color his face. Shiny and solid, his flesh hardened. His breathing rasped like that evil overlord from the *Star Wars* movies, filling the room with an eerie sound beneath the rumbling movements around them.

"We've got less than ten minutes to get the hell out of here and off this island. Or we're going to the bottom of the ocean," she said, looking back down at Quent.

His eyes were open. A rush of relief blasted her and Zoë bent to kiss him. "Thank you," she said to whatever higher power had listened to her pleadings.

Now that he was back, Quent recovered quickly.

He glanced over at Fielding as Zoë helped him to his feet and explained, "Got to find a way out of here. We're going to sink and the whole island is going with us."

His face was set and his eyes clear of cobwebs as he rushed to the glass panel that served as a door. "Be careful," Zoë ordered. "Don't fall back in again."

"Come here," he said, holding out his hand. She rushed to his side as an anchor, even as the pod trembled more violently beneath their feet. "How much more time?" he demanded.

"I don't know," she said. She glanced at Fielding, but his eyes were closed and his face was nearly black. Shiny and stiff, like a mask. He was going to be no help, even if she had a way to force the information from him. "Seven minutes, maybe?"

"Okay," he said. Grasping her fingers tightly he reached for the glass panel. She held on, mentally sending energy to him as his hand convulsed and his breathing twitched and rasped. His elegant fingers, solid and long, textured with tendons and veins, curved warm and strong inside hers. She felt a wave of regret, and one of some earth-shattering emotion. Damn it, she loved the idiot. She not only loved him, but she wanted a life with him. *Hurry up,* she thought, and curled her other hand around his too.

A moment later, he opened his eyes. Clear and beautiful, ready and intense. "Got it. Get the damned crystal."

She dashed over to gather it up, her feet slapping hard on the floor. Wrapping it in the white cloth from her dress, she shoved the crystal in his pack as he moved his hands over the seam of the door. It swung open, revealing a crooked floor—as if an elevator had stopped at an angle halfway between levels.

"Let's go," he said, starting through the entrance. "We have plenty of time to get to the walkway. This hall's a straight fucking shot to the outside of the building. Then run to the bridge."

She was out the door and after him in the narrow corridor, still holding his hand as they ran. The walls trembled and the floor shifted and tilted beneath her feet. And then suddenly he stopped. She nearly ran into him and he caught her with his arms.

"Fuck it, I can't," he said, turning abruptly. He slung off his pack and shoved it at her. "Take this. Go. I'm going back to see if I can stop this whole thing. Innocent people are going to die."

"Quent," she began, her fingers closing automatically around the heavy pack, warm from the crystal inside. "You've got to be fucking kidding me. I'm not going without you." She turned, but he was already starting back to the pod room.

"Get out of here. Get the crystal to safety," he said, pushing firmly at her. "I want you to be safe, Zoë," he shouted over a loud rumble, but she'd moved past him, back toward the pod. The noise of the trembling world was louder now, and in the distance, she could hear shouts and pounding feet above.

"I'm not going any damn where without you, genius," she shouted over her shoulder, running haphazardly as the world shook and tipped. "You've got to be crazy if you think I would. Fucking idiot. And besides, you can't do it without me."

Inside the pod, she saw cracks in the glass that worried the shit out of her for their safety, but she was with

Quent. She was prepared to go to the bottom of the ocean with him. He needed her to ground him . . . and she—she needed him too.

"How'd he do it?" he demanded, looking around. "What did he—"

"The thing there," she said, pointing at the pedestal. For the first time, she saw a flat panel on its surface. A clear pad of buttons and a little screen, set flush into the glass, had been hidden by the crystal on top of it.

He rushed over and she followed him, grabbing his hand as he planted his other one on the clear glass. "Okay," he said. He looked at her, their eyes meeting in the rickety, dim room. "Hold on to me, Zoë. Hold on."

"I'm here, genius. You can do it. See you on the other side." She pressed a kiss to the back of his neck.

At that moment, the whole space jerked, and Zoë felt it drop as if an elevator had been cut loose, then caught. Stifling a little scream, she curled herself into his back, sliding one arm under his shirt to curve around the warm skin of his torso, and with the other, she held his hand. She didn't want to drown. She didn't want to sink into the black depths of the sea.

She pressed her face against his back, burying her eyes in his shirt, and felt him trembling with tension beneath her. "Come on, Quent," she pleaded softly. "You can do it. I'm here. I'm with you. And if you don't, I'm going to fucking kill you," she added in a whisper.

The room lurched again, this time to one side, and she saw Fielding tip to the ground. He was dead, or at least beyond awareness. She waited, chafing, feeling every shift of the room, listening for the ominous crack of glass that would send water cascading in. She braced herself against the constant trembling and tried to block out the loud rumbles. *Hurry, hurry!*

"Got it," Quent said at last in a tight voice, indicating that he had the procedure. "Now . . . " He began to move, tugging his hand free of her grip so he had two to work with to implement whatever he could to stop the disaster.

Zoë stepped to the side, watching his fingers fly over the keypad. Green words and numbers showed on the dark screen, flying past so quickly she had no idea how he could read them. At the sound of a low pop, she glanced up at the ever-lengthening cracks in the glass. From the look of it, Fielding's tomb wouldn't make it to the bottom of the ocean before the damn thing shattered.

She'd heard that drowning was painless. And fairly quick. She hoped to hell that was true.

Come on! She breathed silently, aware of the heavy weight on her back from the pack, and the ever-trembling floor beneath her feet, and Quent typing furiously. His mouth tight, his handsome face set into something dark and intense.

Suddenly, he looked up at her. "That's it," he said, even as the pod jerked violently. "That's it."

"Let's go," she said, grabbing for his arm.

"Zoë," he said, jerking her toward him. She flew into his arms and he wrapped her, held her closely as the place shifted and trembled around them. One of her feet rested on top of his boot. "It's either going to stop, or everything's going to the bottom. See?" He pointed to the top and she saw that a wedge had appeared between the pod and its moorings. The pod had already loosened. "When it cracks, we get out of here and swim up, okay? It's our only chance."

"Okay," she said, trying to keep her voice steady. She could swim. She loved to swim. She just feared the fathomless depths of the dark sea.

"Zoë, I have to tell you something," he began, crushing her harder to his solid chest. "I—"

And then, suddenly, everything stopped.

Silence. Stillness.

"Hot damn!" she crowed. "You fucking genius." She yanked him down for a big, quick kiss, a wave of hopefulness blasting through her.

"Couldn't have done it without you," he told her, holding her tightly, refusing to release her from being plastered against him. "Thank you for grounding me."

"So what were you going to say?" she asked, a blast of warmth and giddiness swarming her. "Don't tell me you were going to tell me you love me."

"Uh." His mouth opened then closed. "What's wrong with that?"

She rolled her eyes. "Isn't that the most clichéd thing in the world? Wait to tell the girl you love her until you're about to die?"

She pulled away and adjusted the pack on her shoulders, avoiding his eyes. "Look, if it's true, I'd rather hear it when you're not about to die. People say a lot of things when they're about to die, and when they're lying in bed after having just had good sex. You know?" she looked up at him, keeping her expression easy and bright. "And besides, we're not exactly safe yet. We still have to get off this damned island. But first, I'm stealing his shoes. My feet are freezing."

Quent realized his mouth was hanging slightly open as she went over to his father and yanked off the man's leather shoes.

Without putting them on, she started off through the open entrance, which was wet and had become smaller and irregular as the pod began to detach. He looked closer as he followed her, and an ugly shiver tremored through his belly. They'd come too damn close to pulling away and sinking into the dark waters. *Too damn close.*

He hurried after Zoë, wanting nothing more than to get his hands on her and kiss the hell out of her. And to really tell her he loved her this time.

The corridor was solid dark. If there had been any lights, the power had been knocked out during the trembling and shaking. This necessitated them going more slowly than he would have liked, although they had a bit of illumination from the crystal on Fielding's gun. It cast a bit of an orange-yellow glow, just enough to keep them from running into a wall. And he wasn't about to pull out the big blue crystal after what had happened last time.

As if reading his mind, she looked back and said, "Don't even think about taking out the other crystal. I'm strongly tempted to chuck the fucking thing into the ocean, where it came from."

Right.

At last, they came abruptly to a halt when they came around a corner and nearly slammed into a wall. He could hear her feeling around for a door, and Quent eased up next to her.

"Be careful," she admonished, holding on to his shoulder in the darkness.

He hadn't said a word since her little speech back in the pod, and that was just as well. He didn't trust himself at that very moment. And she was right—they weren't out of danger yet. Pushing away those thoughts, he shoved the gun into the back of his waistband then closed his eyes and concentrated on the wall in front of him. His fingers splayed wide, their tips centered lightly on the smooth surface. One hand grasping his lifeline, Zoë, Quent allowed himself to ease into the memories. He'd become comfortable filtering through the emotions and other energy, and focusing on the history of the object he held.

It took only a moment for him to discern Fielding's hand movements—slip the fingers behind this little crevice . . . *Yes, there it was. Pull and lever the little switch, and . . .* "Ah." The wall moved.

And they were outside, in the clean, fresh night air. But it was hardly the darkest part of night, for in the distance, a faint glow tinged the sky. The lack of shadows would make it more difficult for them to escape.

The remnants of the earthquake-like tremors had cracked and broken some of the buildings, for bits of rubble scattered the narrow street. A few random shouts and voices filled the air, people calling for each other, confirming safety and assuring each other that it was over.

Without a word, Quent grabbed Zoë's hand once again and began to tow her through the warren of streets. To his mild surprise, she let him lead, pausing only once to stop and adjust something in her pack as she put on Fielding's shoes. He stepped away, peering around the corner of a building as she crouched on the ground. No one down that street.

"How do they fit?" he asked, taking up her hand again.

"They'll do," she said, hurrying along faster now that her feet were protected.

Most of those who'd come from their beds and outside, seeking safety from the vibrating ground, seemed to have found their way back inside, for as they went on, Quent and Zoë met fewer people, and no one who seemed to take notice of them as they slinked through the streets. They stayed to the shortening shadows as much as they could, mindful of the ever-graying sky.

"We're not out of here yet," she said, again reading his mind. "I don't trust any of them."

He agreed, but was too focused, listening, mentally planning their route, to respond. The walkway was just to the right, no more than another block away. Or they could try for the docks and attempt to steal a protected boat, but that was on the other side of the island.

"The bridge is closer," she said.

"But there's nowhere to hide. It's out in the open."

"We can swim. And I have a feeling," she said, leaning close enough for him to smell her hair, "that the damn crystal in my pack might keep the sharks away."

"You want to risk being wrong?" He closed his eyes for a moment, sniffing, resisting the urge to bury his nose in her hair. God, he couldn't wait to get her somewhere alone, when they weren't running for their damn lives.

"It's closer. I want to get the hell out of here. And we haven't seen a soul."

"Right. With you. And we're running the whole damn way."

And then the bridge was there in front of them, spanning and shifting long and white over the dark sea. As they stood in the shadow of two buildings, Quent looked around and listened for any sign of life. A single light flickered on the distant shore, and the world was silent but for the lapping of waves against Mecca's edges. The graying dawn settled over the world, illuminating shapes, but little detail.

Quent's neck prickled at the thought of walking onto that long, exposed bridge and he looked down at Zoë. She met his eyes in the half-light. "Bend over and zigzag side to side as you run," he told her, just as she said, "Don't run straight, genius, or they'll be able to nail your ass.

He caught his short huff of laughter and bent to kiss her, feeling surprisingly light and happy. "See you on the other side." He released her hand and she darted forward, zigzagging like a linebacker past the large stone pillars on the shore and onto the floating walkway.

He pulled the gun from the back of his waistband and slipped out after her, watching for any sign of movement, his back to the bridge, his eyes scanning the shoreline.

A shout from behind grabbed his attention, and he turned. Zoë had stopped a few meters onto the bridge. What was left of her white dress glowed like a ghostly gown, her quiver and the pack odd-shaped lumps on her back. Her feet looked huge in the large black shoes. "Go," he shouted, his throat burning. He brandished the gun to show her he was armed and backed up toward the walkway, still watching the shadows.

"That's all right," said a voice directly in front of him. "We didn't want her anyway."

"Liam," Quent said. His body didn't react to the sight of his father's rival holding a weapon similar to the one he had in his own hand. It was pointed at him, which was also no surprise—for he'd been under no illusions that they'd be able to leave unharmed. *Keep going, Zoë.* "I expected you to be long gone by now. You're not the type to go down with a sinking ship. Or didn't you realize the ship was sinking?" He took a step to the side and backward, toward the bridge.

The flicker of surprise on Liam Hegelsen's face was brief. Apparently, he hadn't realized what was happening. "Where's Fielding?"

"Dead."

"Dead." Again, the surprise was there and then gone in an instant. "What a pleasant surprise. And one less thing that I have to attend to."

"You can thank me later," Quent said, sidling back toward the bridge. "Or maybe not."

"I'm sorry, but I've no intention of letting you leave. You're the only one who knows where the crystal is, and how to use it. As you so readily informed me tonight at dinner." Liam gave a little jerk of his head, and the two men with him each crouched next to the walkway. "You'll need to come back with me or they'll take down the bridge."

Quent turned and saw that Zoë, instead of continuing on her way, had not only stopped but started to come back toward Mecca. "What the hell are you doing?" he shouted at her. "Get out of there!"

She lifted her hand and he saw, clearly outlined in the gray morning, her upright middle finger.

And she started walking toward them, the pack swinging in her hand. Grinding his teeth, Quent turned back to Liam. "I'll take you to the crystal once she's safely on land."

"As if I'd fall for that, Quentin. Where is it? I'll go after it while you stay here with Hugo and Morris. And if I don't return with it in ten minutes, they'll toss her to the sharks." He smoothed his hair, which tufted in the back as if he'd been roused from sleep. Which he probably had. "I've been trying to get to the crystal for years. Trying to get the bastard to show it to me for decades, and he refused. I'd have killed him long ago if I'd known where it was and how to get to it."

"I'm the only one who can do it," Quent told him, glancing at Zoë, who had stopped about twenty-five meters from shore. "I know the codes."

"Tell me," Liam said, and gestured to the two men who appeared to be Morris and Hugo.

They commenced with turning some levers on the edge of the bridge and the whole walkway began to shake on its suspension cables. Quent saw it shift and sag and, in desperation, pointed the crystal gun to his temple. Zoë had to escape with the crystal. "I'll shoot if you don't call them off, then you'll never get it."

But before Liam could respond, one of the men cranking the bridge's suspension said, "Hey! Look!" He stopped cranking and pointed.

Zoë was standing there on the walkway, the water lapping gently over the top where her weight sagged it into the ocean. She was holding the blue-white crystal in her hands, high and proud above her head. "Don't move or it goes in the ocean. Then you'll never have it."

Liam cursed, then he whipped toward Quent. "You lied, you bastard."

Quent didn't bother to respond, and it was just as well, for Zoë wasn't finished. "Let him go, or I'll chuck the damned thing," she called. "You have till the count of three to get away from the bridge, or it's gone."

"Zoë, no!" Quent shouted, but she'd already started to count.

"One," she shouted, lifting up her pack. As they watched she crouched and dumped the crystal inside the bag—a clever move, so that its glow wouldn't be seen in the water if she did indeed chuck it. "Two."

"Wait!" shouted Liam.

Zoë held up the pack by its straps and began to swing it around. "Let him go. Or this goes."

Damn it Zoë. We need that crystal.

As if reading his mind she looked at him, meeting his eyes in the dim light. He felt their gazes connect and a rush of love swamped him. He stepped toward the bridge. The crystal or being with Zoë?

Zoë would win every time.

"Wait," Liam shouted. "How do I know you'll give it to us once he's there?"

Zoë bent to her quiver, which was lying on the bridge in front of her, and pulled an arrow out. She fitted the pack onto the tip of the arrow and jabbed it into the bridge. Then, hooking her foot around the quiver, she began to back up, lodging a different arrow onto her bow. "I'll leave it there and you let him come. If you take one step onto the bridge before he's at the halfway mark, I'll shoot. Once he's with me, you can get the pack."

"And what's to keep him from picking it up on his way?"

"You've got control of the bridge, dickhead. You can

loosen it and dump us into the sharks." She looked at Quent and he knew they were going to have to run like hell if this worked because Liam was going to dump them anyway.

He started toward her, watching as she focused with her arrow on the men behind him. When he got to the arrow holding the pack steady on the bridge, he hesitated. A crystal from Atlantis. His fingers itched to snatch it up and run . . . but he knew they'd never make it.

He'd seen the terror on his brave Zoë's face when they were in the pod. She'd come back with him, she'd come back twice now. He might risk his own life, grab the pack and make a run—and swim—for it. But he wouldn't risk hers again.

So he walked on past.

He saw the relief in her shoulders, watched as she stooped to pick up her quiver, which was empty of arrows, and he realized she had her last one in the bow. *Holy shit.* They were fucked if she had to shoot.

He began to run and Zoë turned to do the same, heading for the shore. The bridge swayed and sagged, and he felt the pounding of feet behind him as Liam and his men ran toward the crystal.

About the time he reached the shore, the gatehouse in sight, he heard a shout of rage from behind him, then the heavier pounding of feet. Quent didn't dare look back, for the guards had come from the gatehouse and blocked Zoë's path. She didn't hesitate, but let her last arrow fly on the run.

It got one of the guards in the shoulder, and he tumbled away. As Quent ran up, he scooped the Taser from his pants pocket and zapped the second guard just as he reached for Zoë.

Then Quent caught her arm and they ran off into the woods, her quiver bouncing heavily against her back.

"They're going to be right behind us," she gasped.

"What'd you do?" he said, holding her up as they jumped over a fallen tree. He was faster than she was, and worlds stronger, so he swooped her up in his arms. The quiver swung around her shoulder and banged against him and that's when he realized what happened. "You kept the crystal?"

She curled her arms around his neck as he bounded through the woods. The shouts behind them were still audible, but didn't seem to be getting any closer. "Of course. We nearly died for the damn thing, and as frightening as it is, I couldn't let them have it."

"How?" he asked, keeping his side of the conversation short so as to conserve on breath. He saw a good climbing tree ahead of him and made a split decision. "We're going up," he said, stumbling to a halt next to it. "Then we can see, and be out of sight. They won't find us up here."

Zoë didn't argue, and when he boosted her to a limb just above his head, she grabbed it and began to hike herself up like an expert. Pausing to take off her shoes and stick them into the crook of a branch, she scrambled up quickly and easily.

He was right behind her, resisting the urge to look up her short dress. There'd be plenty of time for that later. He hoped.

Once they settled on a large branch high among the leaves, he looked toward the skyline of Mecca. The bridge was in clear view, and he saw a large group of people hurrying toward the shore. Liam's search party. He turned back to Zoë. "They're coming, but we've got the advantage. If they come this way, we can move from tree to tree."

"And once the sun's up, we might be able to spot a few mustangs," Zoë said. "I'm not worried. This is a damn sight better than being on that creepy island."

"So how did you fool them? You had me fooled too."

"I swapped a piece of rubble for the crystal. I'd picked one up when I put the shoes on, noticing it was about the size of the crystal. I figured it wouldn't be a bad idea to have a decoy. When I put the crystal in my pack, when you were all watching, I really put it in my quiver. I was holding the bags next to each other and did a sleight of hand."

"Hot damn, Zoë," he said, and moved closer on the branch to brush a piece of bark from her cheek. "You're fucking amazing."

"I know that," she said modestly. "But I had to dump the arrows out so they wouldn't see that I was holding my quiver, so we're shit out of ammunition. And whatever else was in your pack is gone."

"I don't care. I've got all that matters, right here," he said, squeezing her close.

She turned toward him on the branch, straddling it in her ragged gown, and lifted her face for a kiss. "Too bad we had to hide way the fuck up here," she said, pulling away with a soft release of his lips, but steadying her hands on his chest. "It's not the best place for 'thank God we escaped with our lives' sex."

He laughed and lifted her chin to look in her eyes. "Does it count if I tell you I love you now that we *have* escaped with our lives, and I know I'm not going to die?"

"Nope." She settled back away from him, something odd in her gaze. *Sadness? Tenderness?* He couldn't quite read it in the dim light. "And anyway, genius," she said, "we could fall out of the tree having 'thank God we escaped with our lives' sex and break our necks."

He grinned. "Wanna try it?"

She smiled back. "Better fucking believe it."

Oh, what a bittersweet moment to find my old journal, the memories of those horrible days. It must have been placed deep in one of the bags when David and I moved from Blue Vega all those years ago and I'd forgotten about it, putting it on the shelves with all the other books.

We left Devi's resting place perhaps three years after he passed. David was four and grown very big and strong, and I'd become uncomfortable with some of the dealings between the Wetherbys and those odd people who came in humvees.

We settled in another small settlement that must be in southern Nevada and have been very happy here. I've been farming again and selling my herbs and vegetables to tradesmen passing through.

No one has replaced Devi in my heart, although I suspect that will soon happen, for David's wife, Felicia, has been in labor for nearly five hours, and I am very ready to hold a baby in my arms again.

11:30 p.m.

It's a girl! She's the loveliest creature in the world. She has the same black hair as her father, and the smoothest, softest mahogany bottom I've ever seen. And her lungs are quite healthy, as she's already proven. Her legs are strong, nearly kicking her poor father in the belly as he tried to fasten a diaper around her waist. (How I miss disposable diapers! We were at least able to find enough for David over the years, but there are none left now.)

I do believe little Miss Zoë will be quite a handful, and I look forward to spending all my grandmotherly time teaching her everything I know. I just know she's going to be smart and brave and confident.

And I hope and pray that she'll survive in this devastated world, and find a home and family of her own.

—from the diary of Mangala Kapoor

CHAPTER 20

Zoë spotted the herd of mustangs from their perch about an hour after the sun had fully peaked, and once assured that their pursuers were looking in the opposite direction, they clambered down from the tree.

It was short work to capture the tame horses, and they were soon galloping off toward Envy. Of course they wouldn't make it before night fell, and since they were out of ammunition and had few supplies, they didn't want to be caught by the *gangas* so they'd have to camp out somewhere overnight.

By the time the sun was low to the ground, they were settled on the fourth floor of an old apartment building. Zoë managed to scrape together some greens and wild strawberries, along with walnuts and sunflower seeds that she'd collected on the way. They settled in the dusty, dingy room and watched the red ball of sun disappear beyond the dirty window. Quent had used an old scrap of cloth to wipe a peephole in the glass so they could see.

He looked over at her, his gaze dropping to slide over her body, still dressed in the shimmery white gown. Or what was left of it. Zoë felt the answering tingle in her belly, and tried to subdue it. Their in-the-tree sex hadn't worked out very well, for a very large spider climbing down Quent's arm had ruined the mood for both of them.

But she didn't mind. She had some thinking to do. Despite his joking comment about telling her he loved her, she felt an emptiness in the pit of her stomach. He was holding something back, and she'd noticed he wouldn't look her directly in the eye since they'd made it out of Mecca.

But now, Quent's expression softened when he raised his eyes to meet hers again. "I'll bet you're ready to get some different clothes on. But when I saw you across the room last night, it was a shock. You looked like a silver goddess."

Zoë stiffened a little. "All that damned fake shit? Crap on my face, stuff in my hair, being unable to fucking breathe? I'll never look like that again, so if that's what turns you on, maybe you'd better—"

He was laughing suddenly, his eyes lighting and really sparkling for the first time since he'd found her in his shower—how long ago was that? Two weeks? "Ah, Zoë," he said, reaching over to pull her close. "Remember what I told you awhile ago? When you were kicking arse on those *gangas*? How much you turned me on, how badly I wanted to jump you at that time? It just goes to show that no matter how you look, you've got me. Completely."

She couldn't help an undignified snort. "I looked like every other woman in the room, except they all had bigger boobs."

"And most of them were fake," Quent said, smoothing his hands over her bare shoulders. She couldn't help a little shiver of response from his touch.

"Fake?"

"Their breasts. In my time, women could have them augmented—made bigger." Then he slipped his hands down and covered hers gently. "But I love yours and I'm glad you don't have the option of changing them. They're beautiful and high and tight and I dream of them. And the rest of you. All the time."

A delicious shiver fluttered in her belly. He hadn't said he loved *her*, but this was close. Getting closer.

He pulled her close, ignoring the dust that kicked up when she shifted her leg across the gritty floor, stringy with a long-frayed carpet. His lips were warm and tender as they met hers, and she closed her eyes, sliding her fingers up into his hair, sinking into him. But then he pulled away much too quickly and settled back from her.

"It'll be easier to say what I have to say if I don't have you in my arms, or on my lips," he said with a wry smile.

Her belly dropped. Her heart began to pound. "Not again."

"What?"

"You and your 'we need to talk, I need to ask you a serious question' shit again." She knew her words were caustic, but with her belly churning like that, she couldn't help it.

But Quent didn't seem to care. His wry smile turned to a softer one. "That's my Zoë. Always bloody calling it like it is."

"Whatever." She crossed her arms over her belly. Then she crossed her legs. And pulled her knees up close to her. "Well. Spit it out."

"I really want to make love to you," he said.

She rolled her eyes. "So what else is new? What's stopping you? Although it is a bit dirty, and I think that's rat shit over there. Or worse."

"I . . . well, I don't know if you've noticed, but the last few times we've been together, we haven't actually done coitus."

"What the hell?" She frowned and rolled her eyes. Why in the hell did he feel the need to dissect this? "Yes, we have. When I sneaked in on you."

"Right. Well, that's because you took me by surprise."

"Okay, so, yeah, I did notice. I noticed you haven't wanted to fuck since Marley appeared." There. She'd said it. Her deepest, biggest fear.

Besides losing him.

But if her fear was right, she was losing him anyway.

"It has nothing to do with Marley," Quent said sharply. "It's me. I don't want to get you pregnant."

Well, there we have it, all fucking naked and laid out for all to see.

He spoke quickly. "And can we call it making love instead of fucking?" He jammed a hand into his hair, clearly frustrated. "What I mean to say is, there's nothing that would make me happier than to get you pregnant . . . if I knew you'd stay with me. If you didn't run off all the time. Zoë." His voice dropped and he reached for her hands. "Please put me out of my misery. Either stay with me, or . . ."

"Or what?" she asked in a challenging voice, but her heart had begun to lift.

"Or . . . stay with me. I need you."

She looked down at their hands, remembering all the times she'd held his fingers, stabilizing him while he ventured into the dark pit. And knowing that he did the same for her. She opened her mouth to answer, but he spoke again.

"I've never told anyone I loved them. Ever. In my whole life—"

"Not even your mother?" Zoë couldn't imagine it. She'd told her *naanaa* she loved her every single day. And Papi nearly as often.

"No one. Which is why I'm not very good at it. But . . ." His fingers tightened around hers and she looked at him. "I love you. I've never wanted to say it to anyone. But . . . I love you. I don't want to live without you in my life. You make me feel like I can live in this world, like I have a place. A home. But, Zoë, I can't handle you leaving me all the time."

She tightened her grip on his hand. "I love you, too, Quent. And I'll stay with you, if you'll stay with me. At my hideaway. Sometimes."

"Any time you want," he said. "It can be our vacation home." He laughed and she wasn't certain why it was a joke, but she smiled back, warmth and pure delight rushing through her to settle comfortably in that empty spot in her belly.

"It's been a long time since I've had a family. I'd like to have one again. With you," she said. "But . . . I don't think I can give up hunting *gangas*."

"I thought we made a pretty damn good team," he told her. "We can do it together."

At that moment, she realized that her purpose in life hadn't ended, and that there was a reason she'd lived through that horrible night her family died. It hadn't been to avenge her family's death by killing Raul Marck. Her real purpose was to be the lifeline, the partner of this man—this strong, yet vulnerable, damaged and brave man who had a double-edged ability that could save mankind.

There was no one else who could do what he could,

and he needed her to strengthen him. To stand by his side.

Her eyes stung with tears and she felt happier than she could ever remember feeling. And because getting soft like this pissed her off, she pushed the emotion away and took control.

"But I get to be in charge on the hunts," she said. "And you have to teach me how to drive those trucks. And how to make those damn bombs."

"I promise." He leaned forward and tugged her into his lap, his hands already moving over her breasts. "So, now can we have real 'thank God we escaped with our lives' sex?"

"Damn straight," she said. "But let's call it making love."

And, heedless of the rat shit and skittering rodents, she climbed onto his lap and pulled him close for the kiss of a long promise.

Next month, don't miss these exciting new love stories only from Avon Books

In Scandal They Wed by Sophie Jordan
Chased by scandal, Evelyn Cross long ago sacrificed everything for a chance at love. Bound by honor, Spencer Lockhart returns from war to claim his title and marry the woman his cousin once wronged. But as desire flares between them, honor is the last thing on his mind...

The True Love Quilting Club by Lori Wilde
After twelve years of shattered dreams, Trixie Lynn Parks returns home to the ladies of the True Love Quilting Club... and the man she left behind. Sam Cheek is no longer a carefree boy, but as chemistry sizzles, could he be the one to mend her patchwork heart?

A Most Sinful Proposal by Sara Bennett
When the proper Marissa Rotherhild makes him a most improper proposal—to instruct her in the ways of desire—Lord Valentine Kent has never been so tempted. Though he's every bit the gentleman, he knows even the best of intentions is no match for a passion as desperate as theirs.

His Darkest Hunger by Juliana Stone
Jaxon Castille has long hungered for the chance to make his former lover, Libby Jamieson, pay for her deadly betrayal. At last the hunt is over...but the Libby he finds is not who he expected, and the truth is far more shattering than anyone imagined...

Don't miss any of the sensual, sexy, delectable
novels in the world of
New York Times bestselling author

STEPHANIE LAURENS

Devil's Bride
978-0-380-79456-0

A Rake's Vow
978-0-380-79457-7

Scandal's Bride
978-0-380-80568-6

A Rogue's Proposal
978-0-380-80570-9

A Secret Love
978-0-380-80569-3

All About Love
978-0-380-81201-1

All About Passion
978-0-380-81202-8

On a Wild Night
978-0-380-81203-5

On a Wicked Dawn
978-0-06-000205-3

The Promise in a Kiss
978-0-06-103175-5

The Perfect Lover
978-0-06-050572-1

The Ideal Bride
978-0-06-050574-5

LAU3 1109